By LYN GALA

NOVELS
Desert World Allegiances
Desert World Rebirth

Fettered
Gathering Storm
Urban Shaman

NOVELLAS
Lines in the Sand
Long, Lonely Howl
Shepherd, Slave, and Vow

Published by DREAMSPINNER PRESS
http://www.dreamspinnerpress.com

Fettered

LYN GALA

Dreamspinner Press

Published by
Dreamspinner Press
5032 Capital Circle SW
Ste 2, PMB# 279
Tallahassee, FL 32305-7886
USA
http://www.dreamspinnerpress.com/

Fettered
Copyright © 2013 by Lyn Gala

Cover Art by DWS Photography
cerberuspic@gmail.com
Cover Design by Paul Richmond

ISBN: 978-1-62380-361-2
Digital ISBN: 978-1-62380-362-9

Printed in the United States of America
First Edition
February 2013

Chapter 1

IT'D been a long time since Dilly had been in the weeds. That's what they called it at work, in the weeds. It meant they had some new server who had confused tables nine and twenty-three on opposite sides of the restaurant and forgotten table eleven behind the server station half wall. *Off in the weeds*, they'd snicker to each other as exasperated customers flagged down other servers and asked for managers and ended up wandering into the server station to refill their own drinks. Dilly swallowed and realized he was off in the weeds and didn't know what he was doing. But he pushed open the door and stepped into the bar anyway. The beers he'd had at a friend's house probably helped shore up his courage.

Several men, fifteen or twenty, sprawled across bar stools and laughed loudly. Others danced on the center floor, drinks held high to keep from spilling them as they twisted and swayed. Patrons ranged from a young man in a vest that showed a thin hairless chest to a heavyset man in a red shirt, open halfway down so thick, curled white chest hair showed. Dilly recognized the dress code from the Internet. Old Guard. Flagging. Bandanas and black leather jeans or jackets that shimmered in the multicolored lights. Dilly's gaze went to the whip coiled at one man's belt. Another had a black handkerchief hanging from a pocket, and Dilly scrambled to remember what it meant. Black. Did that mean tying someone up or hurting someone? He couldn't remember. He was so far in the weeds he didn't know how to find the damn path again.

But....

But he couldn't leave. Ever since he'd seen the pictures of all his brother's kinky toys laid out on a bed—the black coiled whip, the leather cuffs and shining chains, the clips and gags and straps that Dilly couldn't even understand—he hadn't been able to get them out of his mind.

The news anchor had discussed his brother and the investigation, and Dilly could only stare at a coiled whip on the screen behind the anchor's head. Dilly figured he was wired as wrong as his brother. He had to be. He couldn't stop wondering what his brother had done—what it would sound like for a whip to hit flesh. What it would feel like to have that leather slap his naked ass.

He inched through the doorway. Outside, the city was cooling after the unseasonable heat of the early autumn day, but inside, the heat clung to the walls and the men.

He finally tore his gaze away from the bar area and looked around the tables. He could see bare-chested men, young men with pierced nipples and mesh shirts or vests. He had woefully underdressed in his black T-shirt and tight jeans, but he had a dark-haired boyish cuteness that could compete with any of them with their gelled hair and eyes lined in black.

Dismissing those, he studied the other men, the ones in heavy boots and black T-shirts. A woman stood near the bar, but then Dilly blinked and realized the person who looked like a woman had one hell of a huge Adam's apple to go with the magazine-ready blonde hair piled on top of her head, and heavy makeup. His head? Dilly sent up a prayer that the man/woman wouldn't come talk to him because he could not afford to offend people in this type of bar.

A man with a leather vest and heavy gold rings looked Dilly up and down, and Dilly faded back toward the wall. Rather than take the hint, the man smiled, pushed himself away from his table, and walked toward Dilly with the loose-limbed stroll of a predator. Dilly might have turned and run for the door, but a group of men were coming in, blocking his retreat.

"You're new," Dilly's admirer said when he got close enough, and then he kept getting closer, crowding in until Dilly pressed back against the wall, the little red box for the fire alarm pull digging into his back.

"Um, yeah," Dilly agreed, his eyes scanning the crowd as he searched for some sort of rescue. A couple of people watched, including a man at the bar who had a perfect haircut, the sort Dilly associated with his brother's lawyers, and a white button-up shirt tucked into black leather pants, a whip hanging from his belt. Dilly noted the dark blue bandana on his right side and a black one on his left. One side meant top and one bottom, but Dilly couldn't remember which was which, and he really didn't understand why a man would have a bandana on each side. He was so distracted with his own thoughts that he forgot his admirer until he felt a warm hand stroke up his arm.

"Eyes here, boy."

Sucking in a surprised breath, Dilly focused on the man. He had a carefully trimmed beard and dark eyes. Dilly swallowed nervously. Up until a few weeks ago, most of his fantasies had revolved around the other students at Riverview High School, which made sense since he'd only graduated a year ago. Okay, maybe he'd harbored one or two *Smallville* fantasies he would never, ever tell anyone about. However, this man definitely wanted to have sex with him.

The man pressed closer, his body trapping Dilly against the wall. "What are you looking for tonight?"

"Answers?" Dilly said, his voice rising at the end, making his uncertainty clear.

He didn't say he wanted answers about why his brother might have taken control away from perfect strangers. He didn't say he wanted answers to why he couldn't stop thinking about letting someone else take control of him. He suspected he wouldn't find the answers he wanted in here, but he didn't know where else to look. He definitely didn't have the sort of family where he could go home and ask. Oh, he had something pretty close to *Leave It to Beaver*—closer than any of his friends, but sometimes he thought they kept that happy-happy family by not talking to each other.

The man leaned back and gave Dilly a good, hard look. Then he gave a laugh. "Someone show the virgin to the bar. He needs a little liquid encouragement before he passes out. When you decide what you want, I'll be here."

Technically, Dilly wasn't old enough to drink, and he had already drunk more than he probably should have. But when the guy shoved him in the direction of the bar, he allowed himself to get pushed through the men who had started to crowd uncomfortably close. A number of men laughed, offering him a slap on the ass as he passed, and Dilly could feel himself blush. His cock hardened, but he didn't know whether the forceful hands on his shoulders pushing him through the crowd or random groping without permission caused his reaction.

His escort pushed him right up to the bar before standing behind Dilly with his hands on either side so he completely trapped Dilly.

"Are you old enough to drink?" the guy asked.

"I…. Um…." He so wasn't. But he felt like if he said that, he'd fail some test.

"Get him a whiskey," one of the others yelled at the bartender.

"I shouldn't—" Dilly tried to say.

The new man leaned close, grabbed Dilly's forearm with a tattooed arm, and pinned it to the bar. "You'll only get this attention when you're new enough to still smell like fresh meat. Enjoy it," he whispered into Dilly's ear, laughing as his fingers pressed into Dilly's arm hard enough that the pain made Dilly suck in a breath.

His first admirer faced off against the new guy. "Fuck off, Halverson." Halverson. The tattooed guy was Halverson, and Dilly grasped onto that fact like a lifejacket. The bartender put a whiskey down in front of Dilly, and even though he really hadn't planned to drink, Dilly grabbed the glass and tried to gulp it. Tried. His eyes watered as it burned all the way down. Gasping for air and coughing at the same time led to serious light-headedness as Dilly gripped the edge of the bar.

"Good boy. Drink your whiskey," Halverson said in a rough whisper, and the barely disguised desire made Dilly's cock ache with need.

"Back off or there's going to be trouble," admirer number one warned, and Dilly was uncomfortably aware of how many people watched with amused looks and chins propped on hands like they were the local entertainment.

"What? You're going to sue me?" Halverson asked condescendingly. "Get off it, Guard. You may have first dibs, but the boy isn't yours. No collar, and poaching isn't illegal, not around here."

Dilly wrapped his fingers around the whiskey glass and kept his eyes on it. The burn settled into his stomach, warming him. While getting drunk definitely hadn't been part of his agenda, it sounded better and better with each passing second. Dilly tightened his fingers around the glass and downed the whiskey. He held his breath as it stripped the skin all the way down his throat until it landed in his stomach like a fireball.

"That a'boy," Halverson laughed. "You have some spunk in ya. Come over to my table, and let's see how far that streak of bad goes." The words trapped Dilly between wanting to obey and fear. He'd wondered what it would feel like to have someone forcing him into a corner, controlling him. Right now, he would call it sixty percent hot with thirty percent nerves and ten percent nausea-inducing terror.

"You aren't the only top in this bar," Guard said. "Some of us just don't demand that men break the law to prove a point." Guard reached down and grabbed Dilly around his cock and balls, then squeezed hard enough to make Dilly go up on his toes and hiss. "So back off, Halverson."

"Now boys, don't go scaring all the cute little boys away before they even get their feet under them," a voice warned.

Halverson looked toward the other end of the bar. "I'm just having some fun, and I sure don't see anyone objecting." Dilly might have objected. Maybe. He couldn't quite decide what to think, because at some point his brain and his cock had stopped talking to each other.

"I see someone drinking when my guess is he isn't old enough. I see two someones using the fact they are big, beautiful bruisers to intimidate a boy who needs a little space before he can truly appreciate the glory of a well-timed intimidation. And I see two men who, if they don't stop their little war over the submissives, are going to be finding themselves a new place to hunt their prey."

Halverson gave a grunt, but Dilly noticed the man behind him— Guard—eased off so Dilly could turn. When he did, he found the man/woman he'd seen earlier standing next to them. Despite the piles of blond hair and perfect red fingernails that tapped the bar top, she had a look that made it clear arguing was not an option. She seemed older than Dilly had noticed from a distance, with deep laugh lines around dark eyes.

"You're not his type," Halverson said dismissively.

Guard bristled, but the man/woman put a hand on his arm to stop him. "Are you arguing with me?" the transvestite asked with all the sweetness of a lion getting ready to star in a nature documentary about the cycle of life and death. It was scary.

The blond man/woman ignored both the tops and flashed Dilly a brilliant smile. "He's the type to know that a gentleman always buys a lady a drink, especially when the lady owns the bar and can make his life miserable by banning him from the best source of beautiful man-flesh anywhere in the state," she warned with a stern look Dilly's way. "Don't you?"

"Um, yes?" Dilly guessed, his mouth so dry he couldn't get more words out. The weeds tangled around his feet so badly that he felt like he'd fallen off the face of the known world and landed in some alien dimension.

The cross-dresser smiled at him, her perfect lipstick lined in a darker shade and her dark lashes fluttering. She reached over and then patted Dilly on the arm. "The boys and I are going to have a little discussion." She let her hand linger on Dilly's arm for a moment, and he squirmed. His first reaction was that he preferred men—scary-looking men like Halverson and Guard and the one at the bar with the two bandanas who watched the whole scene with dark eyes, his five o'clock shadow making him look dark and dangerous. However, the cross-dresser's attitude called to Dilly, whispered unspoken promises, and made his cock hard.

"Yes, ma'am," Dilly finally managed.

The cross-dresser reached up and pinched his cheek the way a grandmother might, which dissipated much of the lust Dilly had been feeling. "What a cutie. You wait right here, and I will be back. Get yourself something to drink." She twitched her shoulders before she caught Halverson around the arm the way a teenage girl might cling to her boyfriend. "Coming?" she asked Guard. Surprisingly, Halverson didn't shake her off and Guard followed, and the three of them headed across the crowded bar. Dilly noticed many of the customers were watching as they whispered to each other. On the far side of the room, beside a door marked "Employees Only," they stopped and talked for some time, and Dilly considered running for the door.

The dark man at the far end of the bar watched, not bothering to hide his stare. Several times, the cross-dresser glanced at him even while she talked to the two men, but everyone else had gone back to their business. *Time for an exit, stage left. Or right.*

"Hey, kid, you want a soda?" the bartender asked, interrupting Dilly's escape plans.

"Yeah, please," Dilly said, reaching for his wallet.

The bartender held up his hand. "Don't worry about it. When you get ordered to drink things, the ones who do the ordering do the buying around here." He laughed and shook his head. After grabbing a glass, he dumped ice into it and filled it. "If you're going to put your toe in the water, you might want to avoid jumping in the shark tank before you know how to swim," he suggested, putting a Coke in front of Dilly. "Halverson there is definitely a shark. Oh, he may not eat you alive, but you'll have a few teeth marks before he's done." The bartender looked down the length of the bar. "Of course, he's not the only shark who's smelled blood on these waters. You'd better watch it, or all the subby boys are going to be jealous."

Dilly frowned, not liking how that sounded. Worse, his cock was still interested, and that didn't make much sense to his big head. "Yeah. Thanks," Dilly said. Even though the bartender insisted his drinks had been covered, he pulled five dollars out and slipped it into the tip jar on the counter. The bartender gave him another smile before working his way down the bar to fill other drinks.

When Dilly looked over, he noticed Halverson was back at a table and the cross-dresser was making her way across the room, laughing with a man here and letting her fingers linger on the shoulders of one of the young boys in net shirts. Eventually she made her way back over to the bar and carefully settled herself down on the stool next to Dilly.

First she sighed at him, and then she shook her head fondly. Dilly was definitely getting some mixed signals. "Sweetie, you need to practice the word 'no'," she said firmly. Guard had followed her and kept on heading toward the door, but when he heard that, he made a loud dismissive grunt. She looked over her shoulder at him, harrumphing in his general direction as he left.

Dilly blushed. He did know how to stand up for himself, but he'd been overwhelmed and more than a little complimented that men like that would even notice him. The cross-dresser chuckled and patted his arm. "You're going to get nailed by half this bar if you keep blushing so nicely."

"I'm new," he offered as an excuse.

His savior laughed loudly, and then she reached over to run fingers through his dark hair. "Oh babe, I could tell that. So could the rest of the bar. You're just catnip in a bar full of tigers."

Dilly cleared his throat and tried to look anywhere other than the ample cleavage right in front of his face.

"So, I'm assuming you aren't just new around here, but new to this whole side of the street, yes?" She let her nails scratch over the back of Dilly's neck, and he shivered.

"Um. Yeah. I was… you know…."

"Horny?" she offered.

Dilly could feel his face heat up. At nineteen, he was technically a teenager, but he hadn't blushed like one for a couple of years. "More confused," Dilly confessed.

"Confused is catnip around this place." She turned around and looked out over the barroom. "So, what is this big question that's driven you to wander into the wilds of leather-land?"

Dilly opened his mouth, and then closed it, terrified. *How do you confess to a stranger that you are terrified that you're like your brother, terrified that your fascination with leather and bondage will lead you to hurt others the way he had?* Right now Dilly wondered about how it would feel to have the whip hit his skin, but maybe something would turn some switch and he'd be like his brother— someone who found a sick pleasure in hurting others. Allegedly. Like they said on the news, Gary was only an alleged rapist.

"Spit it out," the woman insisted, poking Dilly with a bright red fingernail.

"Are you a man or a woman?" Dilly blurted. The second it came out, his blush turned into a full-out nuclear meltdown in his face. He half expected her to take offense and kick him out, but instead, she smiled so wide that the sides of her eyes crinkled up more.

"Is that a shy way of asking to see my cock? Because, darling, I've got a big one. Nice and fat." She reached down to fondle her cock through her dress. Dilly had definitely left the land of normal.

Dilly could feel himself blush. "Well, I know, but are you...? Should I...? What should I call you?" He verbally stumbled into silence.

She pursed her lips and looked him up and down. He had the feeling if he fell short in her estimation, manicured nails and all, she was going to kick his ass. "It isn't complicated, babe. I do not want to be a woman." She held her arms out to show off the tight corset with the black stitching over red velvet and the sizable boobs pressed out over it.

"You—you don't?"

"Nope, I love my dick. I am all man. But you do call me 'she', because I am a queen. You may call me Miss Dolphinia." She reached over and tweaked him on the nose with one finger.

"Oh." Dilly didn't have more of an answer than that.

She raised an eyebrow at him. "And you should always offer to buy an old queen a drink."

"Okay, what can I get you to drink, Miss Dolphinia?" Dilly tried very hard to keep the drowning sensation to a minimum, but maybe he'd already gone down for the third time and hadn't realized it. *How*, he wondered, *could someone who embraced manliness, want to be called "Miss" anything?*

Miss Dolphinia's lips twitched, and Dilly suspected a less polite queen would be laughing right now. "You just tell the bartender that you're paying for the old queen's next drink," Miss Dolphinia said in her husky whisky voice. Her strong perfume washed over Dilly as she came in confidingly close. "I'll tell you the truth, babe; I don't drink much alcohol anymore, so I have him keep a special pitcher of lemonade—with just a little gin for flavor. Go on now, make your contribution to my joint. I have to go take care of business, but you just remember that the word to use when drowning is 'no'." With that, she gave him a peck on the cheek while letting her hand trail down over Dilly's chest.

Then she turned and wandered her way through the crowd, seemingly knowing every person in the place. Either that or she liked to feel up perfect strangers. Considering she'd had her hands all over him, that was possible.

It took some time for the bartender to return. He spent quite a bit of time with two-bandana man at the end before he came back and took Dilly's order, this time accepting the money, and the Old Queen's drink set Dilly back a little more than he'd expected. The bartender winked at him. "You want me to have someone send it over to Her Highness?"

"God yeah, could you?" Dilly squeaked. "Will she...." He stopped. He didn't want to offend her, but he didn't want to get too close to her. He had the feeling she was the deep end of the pool with Mr. Shark, and he couldn't swim in water that deep.

"Naw, she won't bug you no more; you paid up," the bartender offered. "If you want a beer, I can get you one if you promise to dump it the second anyone official comes in. The good thing about this place is that cops tend to stand out."

"No thank you. I think I need to stick with a Coke," Dilly said, pulling out more bills to pay for his soda. Hopefully it would quench the heat in his stomach—unlikely given that every time a leather-clad man looked his way, Dilly could feel the heat grow, but he could hope. The bartender poured the drinks and then raised a hand for one of the waiters to come get Miss Dolphinia's drink.

Dilly rubbed the cold moisture off his soda glass and watched the waiter's black-Speedo-clad ass as the guy maneuvered his tray through the room. Miss Dolphinia raised the highball glass toward Dilly—then seemingly drained the whole thing without swallowing, smoothly turned, and fell deep into conversation with two younger men.

Dilly ordered a second soda and watched the room fill up. *Bears, twinks, and Doms—oh my!* Before those were just words—okay, so they were words and very graphic images on a computer screen as he looked up porn. But that had been different. Controlled. Safe. Now they were people. Men. Hot men. The one truth Dilly knew intimately was that people, that men, carried danger around like a little seed ready to sprout. And hot men were about as safe as a nuclear bomb. The smell of leather and musk, the heat, the noise of rough voices rising and falling like a tide all threatened to overwhelm Dilly.

Turning his back on the crowd, he focused on the glass in front of him. He thought about the black gag lying next to the whip on his brother's bed, the thick bulb on the end. He could imagine the men in this bar strapping a gag across his mouth so he couldn't keep saying stupid shit. Many of the boys already had leather around their wrists, and Dilly imagined what it would feel like to have leather around his skin, holding him as firmly as Guard had held him up against the wall.

"Hey, you okay?" a voice asked, rising over the ocean of voices. Dilly looked over to see the dark and handsome two-bandana man sitting next to him.

"Yeah. Fine," Dilly said with a plastic smile.

The man gave him an incredulous look. "Don't go into acting, kid," he suggested after a second, and Dilly could feel himself blush again. He would wear out his face at this rate. Dilly should be offended by this guy who couldn't be more than midtwenties calling him "kid." However, his common sense had clearly gone on strike because there was something hot about it.

The guy slapped him on the shoulder. "Hey, Miss Dolphinia suggested I show you the back and give you a chance to recover some without all the hungry eyes on you. Interested?" The man took a drink from his beer, seemingly not all that interested about Dilly's answer.

Dilly should have said no. After all, he didn't even know the man's name, but his cock voted to follow dark eyes anywhere. Up close, Dilly could see the wide shoulders and muscled arms, and his gaze traveled down to leather pants so tight that Dilly could see every line. The guy was a little older than Dilly, but then most of the men in the bar were. Dilly's cock definitely wanted more.

"Um, sure," Dilly said, swallowing all his nervousness as he tried to put on a flirty grin. That earned him another incredulous look, but the man leaned closer and ran his hand possessively down Dilly's arm.

"Name's Vincenzo. Mostly people call me Vin, but I think you'll call me 'sir', won't you?"

Dilly swallowed. "Yes, sir," he agreed. When his parents raised him with good manners, including calling adults "sir" and "ma'am," he was fairly sure they'd never envisioned this.

Vin slowly smiled before leaning back and looking Dilly up and down. "Well then, let's go in back," he suggested. He put his beer down on the bar and let his large hand rest on Dilly's back, urging him toward a door that said "Employees Only."

Exiling his last qualm, Dilly allowed Vin to escort him, enjoying the firm hand at his back guiding him through the crowded room.

Chapter 2

THE "Employees Only" door hid a world less interesting than Dilly had hoped. Scuffed brown linoleum from the seventies curled up in the corners to create dirty triangles along the edges. One of the light bulbs in the ceiling fixture shone a lot brighter than the other, giving the room a lopsided feel. However, Dilly's eyes spotted a number of fixtures he hadn't expected in a restaurant or bar. Heavy-duty hooks were set into studs, and the tables all had thick legs, a few with ropes lying on lower shelves. Restaurants and bars generally didn't have a lot of use for rope, but these people did. Dilly counted six different small coils left in odd places.

A couch stood against one wall, a double set of hooks above it, and a wooden table with thick legs and rounded edges sat against the other wall. Considering the narrowness of the table, the legs were too thick, giving it an oddly chunky look. In the middle of the room squatted a steel prep table like Dilly saw in most restaurant kitchens, only usually they were near the stoves, and this clearly wasn't a prep area despite a number of chairs stacked up in the corner and a sink with a towel draped over the side. The space could almost pass for a normal storage room, only Vin urged him toward the wood table, and Dilly suspected things happened in this room that never went on at his restaurant.

"So, how new are you?" Vin asked as he opened a drawer on the metal prep table and took out yet another length of rope.

"New?" If this involved talking, Dilly was in trouble because his brain had left him high and dry. Or horny and confused. One or the other.

Vin chuckled, and Dilly liked that sound. "Don't get me wrong. I'm just as happy to indulge you if this is an act to attract a partner for the night. I like my boys blushing whether it's good acting or honest nerves." Vin ran his hands up Dilly's arms, and Dilly got a full-body shiver. Vin's hands were large and warm. When Vin paused and squeezed Dilly's biceps, most of Dilly's remaining blood went straight to his cock. Maybe that explained the painful pounding of his heart.

"Answer, boy," Vin warned in a low voice with just a touch of annoyance to it.

"Um, really new. I don't actually know what I'm even doing sort of new," Dilly admitted. His mouth dried up so that his tongue kept trying to stick to the top of his mouth. Vin pushed him against the wooden table so the edge pressed against his groin. He leaned into Dilly, trapping him and pressing until the pain edged out the desire before he realized what he'd done wrong. "Sir… sir!" Dilly blurted out as the pressure grew. He panted, but then Vin eased off and reached around Dilly so he had Dilly caged in his arms. For a moment they stood pressed against each other, and Dilly could feel the heat of Vin's body soaking into him. Slowly, Vin started working.

Dilly watched, fascinated by the rope that Vin carefully wound around Dilly's wrists. He felt disconnected, as if he was watching one of those porn vids—like nothing was real and he could reach out and hit the power button to stop it all at any time. Not that he wanted to. He might be all sorts of terrified, but not stupid. Nope. He wanted to come more than he wanted to breathe right now.

"What are your limits?" Vin whispered the question against Dilly's neck, his breath stirring the small hairs.

"I… um… sir, I don't know." Dilly scrambled for words as his various brain cells all scattered to the far corners of his brain.

Vin paused. He already had Dilly's wrists tied together, and Dilly strained against the rope. His wrist popped and his skin itched, but the knot held. And now Dilly's cock was so hard that he thought his eyes were going to start watering. He'd seen rope before. He'd once tied up

Bobby Johnson during a particularly nasty game of hide and seek, but after this, he was never going to be able to look at rope again without developing a very embarrassing hard-on. Vin's weight leaned into him.

"Are you saying you don't have limits?" After asking the question, Vin explored the back of Dilly's neck, his mouth warm against the sensitive skin.

"More that I don't know what they are, sir."

Vin sighed. "Why does that old bitch-queen set me up for this shit?" he asked wearily.

Dilly tried to twist around, but Vin tightened his arms and nipped at Dilly's neck. "Oh no. You're mine now." Vin's voice turned silky, the dark and dangerous tone sending shivers down Dilly's spine.

Just a moment earlier, Dilly had been suffering that heavy feeling—the one that said you'd fucked something up without understanding how. Actually, he did know how. He had given the wrong answer. But now Vin started sliding his hand over Dilly's body, and he kneaded Dilly's ass. All was clearly forgiven. Dilly sank back into that fuzzy, warm world where he could feel his body without engaging it somehow. He rode along with his body, watching as Vin manipulated it, and boy did Vin know how to do just that.

Vin barely brushed his fingertips over the skin on the inside of Dilly's right elbow, a feather touch scarcely more than a tickle. His elbow had never been an erogenous zone before, but right now, Dilly suspected he could come just from that fleeting touch. Unfortunately, Vin's touch moved on to tease other spots.

"You came in here looking for someone to take control, didn't you?"

"I think so." Dilly blurted out a quick "sir" when Vin's weight started pressing him into the table. "I might... well... I found this forum discussion online, and it said that this place was...." Dilly fell silent when he realized he sounded like a bigger dork than usual. His brother would be calling him Dill Weed and telling him to shut the fuck up by now.

"Did you want to get fucked? Did you want to taste a whip against your ass? Did you want to get spanked? What exactly are you looking for, boy?" Vin's warm breath skittered over the back of Dilly's neck, stirring the small hairs back there.

"I, uh...." Dilly could feel his face heating up as he remembered the image of that coiled whip on Vin's hip, but he couldn't get the words out of his mouth. The problem was that if he didn't ask for it now, he'd chicken out. Still, the words wouldn't come.

"Oh boy, you are like a seal pup swimming with sharks."

"You mean Halverson and Guard?"

Vin gave a rough laugh. "They're the least of your troubles. You need to seriously figure out what you're doing before someone really dangerous spots you." For a second, Dilly thought Vin planned to turn him down, but then Vin grabbed the trailing end of the rope he'd used to tie Dilly's hands and leaned forward to loop it around a hook set in the wall and pull the rope tight. He forced Dilly to bend over the table before tying it off. Dilly nearly came in his pants. Clearly he wanted this, even if he didn't have the words for it.

"So, how much Internet research have you done?" Vin slipped his fingers under Dilly's waistband and ran along the over-heated skin. Sweat gathered until Vin's fingers slid easily over the skin.

"More than I would want my mom to know about," Dilly confessed. He heard the sharp slap before the pain of Vin's hand connecting with his ass registered. He yelped and pulled against the ropes, but the hook didn't yield.

"I gave you a rule, and you will follow it." Vin had a sharpness in his voice that sent a shock of fear through all the lust, and yet that just made Dilly's cock even harder.

"Yes, sir," he answered, squirming as the heat of that slap slowly spread through his body. It stung. It stung a lot. But the pain felt weird... like when he stretched a muscle cramp and felt his whole body sing with the need to stretch more.

He liked it.

"You want rules, don't you?"

Dilly shifted his weight from foot to foot. "Yes, sir," he admitted.

Vin pulled Dilly's belt free of the buckle. "Sir, couldn't someone walk in here?" Dilly asked, his voice hitting an embarrassingly high note at the end.

"Yep," Vin agreed. "Does that worry you enough to want this to stop?"

Dilly opened his mouth, but he couldn't get any words out. Yep. He kept silent because of a dry mouth. That was his story and he was sticking with it. And if a little part of him wanted this more than oxygen, he didn't have to admit that, not even to himself. He swallowed as Vin unfastened Dilly's pants and reached inside to grab Dilly's hard cock.

"The love tap went over well, so do you think you might want to play with a little more pain?" The question was clearly rhetorical because Vin's hand came down on Dilly's ass again, striking him twice. Dilly sucked air through his teeth and arched away from Vin as the burn intensified. "Oh, you would enjoy it if we took the time to break you in nice. But we don't have time for that, do we?" Vin's voice had that silky danger to it again, and Dilly swallowed down an almost instinctive urge to beg for it… and he wasn't even sure what the "it" was.

Vin shoved Dilly's pants down, and Dilly wrapped his fingers around the rope that tethered him to the wall. He didn't have a choice. He would never volunteer to be naked in a room where anyone could walk in, but he didn't have a choice. That's what made the moment possible, because Dilly knew he was way too much of a coward to do this on his own.

"Spread your legs."

Dilly shifted his feet. The air drifted past his exposed ass before Vin pushed close and the texture of his jeans against Dilly's ass made him hyperaware of his vulnerable position.

"Good boy," Vin praised him before he sucked at Dilly's neck. Once Dilly was completely distracted by the way Vin's teeth felt against his skin, Vin brought down his hand hard on Dilly's ass. Dilly yelped as the sound of the slap startled him before the heat blossomed in his ass. "Are you complaining?"

"No, sir."

"Didn't think so." Vin gave him a second slap on the left side. This time Dilly managed to avoid making some embarrassing sound, but when Vin slipped a slick finger inside, Dilly instinctively tried to stand. The rope around his wrists tightened, and Dilly collapsed back onto the table as his attempt failed.

"You *were* going to ask me to use a condom, right?" Vin asked, but he slipped a second finger inside, and Dilly had trouble focusing on anything other than the stretch in his ass and the odd feeling of utter helplessness. Vin could do most anything, and Dilly really couldn't stop it. Or he could by screaming, but he couldn't physically free himself, and that had turned some switch in Dilly's head. He didn't want to think about anything but the stretch and burn as his body tried to accommodate whatever Vin did. Dilly writhed as the fingers filled him.

"Well?" Vin asked, and he punctuated his question with another hard slap against Dilly's hip.

"What... sir?"

Vin spread his fingers, and Dilly arched his back as his muscles struggled to adjust fast enough. The speed of the whole foreplay excited him, and Dilly desperately wanted his hands free so he could jerk off, but he needed his hands tied so he could let himself experience everything. A hundred needs caught at him all at once, and only the rope kept him from flying apart.

"Someone is tight," Vin commented before his fingers came out. Dilly thought Vin would start fucking him, but instead Vin started spanking him, each slap lighter than the earlier ones, but they came down on Dilly's ass over and over. The heat grew as each slap moved in search of new flesh. Dilly panted and fought the rope with his whole being. Finally the spanking stopped, and the sound of his own panting and the pounding of his heart stuffed his head. Before his brain could catch up with reality, Vin's cock pressed against his hole and forced it open.

Dilly went up onto his toes as Vin pushed in slowly. He hadn't spent as much time prepping Dilly as most of Dilly's previous lovers, and the cock felt enormous as it steadily pushed its way in. Vin's fingers pressed deeply into Dilly's hips, holding him perfectly still. Panting heavily, Dilly let his eyes drift closed and clung to the rope. He was caught. Pinned. Pinned and being skewered. He wanted more, and he squirmed in need, but nothing changed Vin's slow pace.

"Settle, boy."

Dilly forced himself to relax, to focus on the sound of his own labored breathing instead of fighting the strong hands that held him in place. Finally Vin was all the way in, and he leaned over Dilly's back before biting at Dilly's shoulder. "Good boy. You're all mine, aren't you?"

Dilly nodded. He was. With Vin's cock shoved up his ass, he couldn't imagine lying under anyone else. His body sang under Vin's hands. "Yes, sir," Dilly added.

Vin chuckled. "Such a beautiful boy you are. I'm going to fuck you so hard you'll walk bowlegged for a week."

Dilly sucked in a breath, but before he could figure out what he was supposed to say to that, Vin pulled back and then slammed in hard. Dilly cried out and arched his back. "Yes!" he screamed as Vin repeatedly pounded him. The force of each thrust drove Dilly into the edge of the table, and some distant part of his brain registered the pain in his hips where bone and wood met, but he didn't care. He wanted more. As the world faded away and reality focused on Vin and his cock, on the rope that held him captive, on the feel of hot hands forcing him down onto the table—Dilly just wanted more. He wanted everything to vanish so this could be his whole reality.

After an eternity of hard fucking, Vin reached around and grabbed Dilly's cock. Before Dilly could even twitch, he came all over the underside of the table, his body coiling tight and then spasming out of control. Dilly flailed and fought the ropes, but Vin caught him by the elbows and pinned him to the table with such strength that Dilly couldn't do anything as Vin finished, his own thrusts growing erratic until he came.

Too soon Vin pulled out, his hands working efficiently at some task behind Dilly, but Dilly could only lie boneless, every ounce of will drained from him as he felt his body radiate heat. Sweat soaked his shirt, and his muscles trembled with fatigue.

"Such a good boy you are." Vin stroked his bare thigh before pulling up Dilly's pants. "I can't call you 'boy' forever. What is your name?"

Dilly had to try and capture a few circling brain cells before he could answer. "Dilly Carter, sir."

"Dilly?" Vin was tucking Dilly's cock away. "That's a child's name, and I don't fuck children. Try that again."

Dilly frowned, not sure what to say for a moment. His brain was definitely on some sort of vacation without him. "Um, Dylan. Dylan Carter."

"Dylan. That's a good name."

Since Vin didn't seem to need any more information, Dilly closed his eyes and let himself drift on the blissful wave of lethargy that held him down, even as Vin untied his hands. Nothing mattered. Nothing other than the ache in his ass, that is. He could still feel the heat of the spanking and the stretch of the hard fucking, and his body had never felt better.

"Up you go," Vin said, but luckily Dilly didn't have to figure out what he wanted because an arm half lifted him and guided him across the room. Dilly let his body fall onto the couch, not caring where various limbs landed.

The couch tilted, and Dilly let Vin arrange his body as he wished. Dilly ended up in Vin's lap, Vin's fingers combing through Dilly's sweat-soaked hair.

"Oh sweetie, you found a keeper with that one." Miss Dolphinia. Dilly recognized her voice. He also couldn't bring himself to care enough to open his eyes.

"You're assuming a lot."

"I heard him screaming for you, darling. Trust me, that's not assuming. He's going to be back and begging for it; only next time, use a gag. The whole bar heard that, and as much as I do love the sound of a begging, screaming boy, if we'd had a pig in the house, that would have cost me my license."

"You would have had the cop arrest us for indecent exposure and claimed to be the innocent victim." Vin sounded annoyed, and Dilly focused for a moment, recognizing the rough fabric of the couch under his hand and Vin's leg under his cheek and the fact that Vin's annoyance was directed at Miss Dolphinia. That's all Dilly needed to know, and he drifted back into focusing on the delicious feel of his own body.

Miss Dolphinia laughed. "You're right. I would have. You're a big boy, so you can take care of yourself."

"And Dylan?"

"Oh don't worry, I would have bailed him out and taken *good* care of him." Miss Dolphinia laughed again. "Oh, Vinnie, that's your jealous look, isn't it? Now, now, you wouldn't hit an old queen, particularly not when she gave you such a sweet piece of meat tonight. That boy is so far into his own subspace you could do pretty much anything to him, and I can think of more than one delectable thing to try."

"I wouldn't do anything to a man this far into his own head."

"That's your problem, sweetie. Cute little boys like that one want you to play a few games when they're out of it."

"Maybe that's how you see it. I don't."

"A tiger doesn't change its stripes, and a Dom doesn't change his taste in flesh."

"Fuck off before I decide that punching you is more important than taking care of Dylan." The voice was calm and fingers worked their way across Dilly's back, but Dilly distantly noted that the words weren't exactly friendly. However, Miss Dolphinia laughed again.

"Now, now. No need for violence. That's the solution for small minds. Besides, I don't want to break a nail. You had a wonderful night with a beautifully subby little boy. Enjoy the afterglow. That's the problem with the younger generation—you never appreciate what you have. Like that boy in your lap. If he reacted like that to a spanking, imagine how high he'd fly at the taste of your whip."

"He wasn't ready for it."

"I know that. I'm not suggesting that you try to take him out on the racetrack his first time behind a wheel, but how easy would it be to train him to beg for it? How easy would it be to teach him how to writhe and cry as your whip traced lines in that delicious flesh? You know you're not going to be able to stay away from that lovely piece of catnip, not a tiger like you."

"Watch me. And tell whoever wants to play with him next time to use leather cuffs, not rope. He's going to hurt himself fighting that hard against rope."

Miss Dolphinia laughed. "Just you watch. The first man who tries to do anything to that boy, you're going to change your mind about this idiotic rule of yours."

"Don't try to tell me what to do." Vin's voice had a darkness that made Dilly stir. The words were important. He knew that, but he couldn't quite engage the brain enough to care.

"Me? Oh sweetie. I would never tell a Dom what to do. That's a fool's game, and I'm no fool."

"No, you're just manipulative."

More laughter. "Of course I am. I'm a queen. I'm a grand queen. We love drama in all forms. Just don't forget that I've been around enough blocks enough times that I know how to play to win."

"Manipulate me and we'll see how long you survive."

Dilly noted laughter and the swish of fabric skirts rustling before high heels clicked over the linoleum floor.

"Shhh. Just hush, Dylan," Vin whispered, and Dilly listened to the voice, slipping into a half sleep where his fears and his brother and the various bodies moving through the room around them were all water and he, the boat it slid past without soaking in.

Chapter 3

DILLY lay in bed feeling every gloriously sore spot on his body. When Vin had driven him home, Dilly asked to get dropped at the corner just so he could indulge in the feel of each muscle stretching in new ways as he walked the last block. While he wasn't the most experienced gay man on the block, he'd been down enough streets to know he didn't usually get fucked this good.

When he clenched his ass muscles, he could feel the lingering burn, and his legs were so sensitive he felt like the hot water running over the back of his thighs in the shower would be enough to get him off. And now, this morning, all he wanted to do was wiggle his ass this way and then that, feeling the rasp of the sheets across his hot ass.

Of course, eventually he knew he was going to have to deal with the whole weirdness with Miss Dolphinia at the end when she was getting cranky with Vin. And he still didn't have an answer to the question that sent him to the club in the first place. He didn't understand his brother any more today than yesterday. He understood himself better, but that wasn't the same thing.

However, until reality forced him to face the less than perfect facts of his life, he planned to lie in bed and enjoy the morning. Slipping his hand into his pajama pants, he explored the curve of his inner thigh and teased himself as he worked slowly up to his cock. His skin felt hotter than usual, and his ass sent up little flares as his wiggling put pressure on his deliciously bruised butt. If he lived alone, he'd go stand in the bathroom and explore every mark, every bruise, every scratch on his body. However, five people and one bathroom meant that someone would knock and interrupt him at the worst possible time if he tried.

The light leaked in through the edges of his old vinyl window shade, making the dust dance in the air as Dilly ran his hand up and down his stomach as his prick slowly hardened. He had practice doing this silently, turning his back so the curve of his shoulder hid the slight movement of his hand as he ran his thumb over the slick slit of his cock.

Arching his back, Dilly let his eyes drift closed so the plaid bedspread and old oak dresser faded away, replaced by the cracking linoleum of Miss Dolphinia's back room. Vin's large hands were on his hips, holding him down so Dilly didn't have to try and control himself. He could do anything... anything that Vin's hands allowed him. He could feel his balls tighten.

"Hey, move your ass," Carmine's hissed voice cut through the fantasy so sharply that Dilly sucked in a startled breath, ruining any chance of pretending to still be asleep. *Crap.*

"My ass is happy in bed," he complained. Carmine landed on his bed, bouncing hard enough that Dilly had to yank his hand out of his pajamas and grab the edge of the twin before he got bounced right out.

"Mom is doing breakfast."

"I hope breakfast and Mom are very happy together," Dilly muttered, but he didn't do it soft enough.

"Okay... is that a really bad sex joke? Because if you're making corny sex jokes about Mom, I'm going to kill you and worry about hiding the body later." A sharp finger poked him in the kidneys, and Dilly rolled over rather than risk sudden attack without a way to defend himself. His sister was mean enough to attack a man when he was down and helpless. Either Frank had a masochistic streak that Dilly didn't know about, or the man was going to be surprised as hell after the wedding. Dilly almost felt sorry for him. Carmine knelt on his bed, her fiancé's Texas Tech T-shirt tight across her boobs. Dilly considered for one second warning her that Dad would have a hissy fit if he saw her in it, but these days, it was every Carter for himself. If Dad was focused on Carmine's inappropriate shirt, he wasn't focused on Dilly's life.

"This family can only afford one felony defense attorney at a time. I'm safe because Gary has the market cornered right now," Dilly pointed out smugly.

Carmine shoved an unruly black curl behind her ear before "accidentally" kneeing him in the side as she shifted on the bed. "Knock that shit off. If Mom hears that, she's going to give birth to more kittens. She doesn't need any more grief, so shift your sorry ass out of that bed."

Propping himself up on one elbow, he checked his alarm. "God. It's only seven." That meant he'd gotten somewhere between three and four hours. So not enough.

"That's because someone stayed up too late and made all the pipes in the house rattle by taking a fucking shower at three in the fucking morning. Moron. And you're going to be smiling and eating pancakes by seven ten. Seriously, Dill, Mom needs some emotional support here, and you and I are it."

Dilly collapsed back down onto the bed. "Let Dad support her."

"Dad's already at work. Someone has to pay for psycho boy's defense."

For all Carmine's talk about not annoying the parentals, she sure spent enough time using the one name guaranteed to send their father on a screaming binge before storming out of the house to go bang around on someone's car. Either people were getting a lot of extra servicing for their forty-nine ninety-nine tune up, or it was taking their father twice as long to do every job. "Don't say that. Shit, Carmine. Not cool."

"Fuck. Don't start." She flopped around so she could sit on the bed with her back to him. "If you stick up for Gary, I'm going to kill you. He's a psycho."

Dilly was guessing that Carmine had already had it out with someone this morning. Either Gary tried playing innocent, or Mom tried defending him. Yep, the whole family was just all kinds of mentally healthy. "I make a little joke about Gary's defense lawyer and you threaten to kill me, but you get to call him a psycho?" Dilly demanded.

She looked at him over her shoulder. "Because I'm smart enough to avoid saying it in front of Mom, whereas you're a giant goober. If you think something, it pretty much falls out of your head."

Dilly doubted that. "It does not."

"Oh, it so does. You suck at keeping your thoughts to yourself. Mom just needs… she needs a normal morning."

Dilly groaned. People in hell wanted ice water, as his father always said, but sometimes you don't get what you want. "Yeah, and you and Gary are really good at being normal to each other." Dilly poked Carmine in the back.

"He's just a—" Carmine stopped, her voice cut off right in the middle. If he had to guess, she was about to say all sorts of things that if Mom caught her, she'd be crying and muttering in Italian. Three generations in America, and their mother still felt the need to do anything emotional in Italian. He suspected she felt better cursing in a language she'd never taught them. Of course, when they'd gotten old enough to use the Internet, they'd immediately looked up Italian profanity. Their mother was creative in her blasphemy. "Never mind," Carmine said with a sigh. "Look, he's off doing something with his lawyer. I think they're trying to teach him to avoid looking slimy. So, we have a chance to give Mom a nice normal day. So you're going to go down there and stuff your face with pancakes and play nice."

"Great." Dilly lay back and stared up at the stained ceiling.

"Dill." Carmine had an odd tone in her voice.

"What?"

She turned and leaned closer. "Is there something you'd like to share with the class?"

"Um… no?" He pulled his sheet up higher, suddenly uncomfortable because he was getting a very odd look.

Carmine snorted. "Subtle. Yeah, you totally suck at secrets, and from the look of things, someone else sucks too."

Dilly's hands flew up to his neck, and the second he felt the hot bruised skin at the juncture where his neck and shoulder met, he knew exactly what she was looking at. "Eeew. Sex comments from the sister. Not cool. So not cool." Dilly used a foot under the covers to shove her off the bed so he could make a grab for his robe. Who knew how many marks Vin had left on him, and while he didn't regret a single mark, he didn't want Carmine to see any of them. Nope, sisters and love bites were to stay to their own sides of the room at all times—no meeting in the middle.

"I didn't mean it like that," Carmine complained. "Hey, whatever floats your boat. What's he like, other than having a fetish for your neck, I mean."

"I'm not talking about this with you." Dilly tied the robe tightly around his waist.

"Prude."

"Yes. You're my sister."

She gave him an exaggerated sigh. "If I decided to have a big gay romance, I'd tell you all about it."

Dilly eyed her. She might. "I've never prayed for someone's heterosexuality so much in my whole life."

"Dick."

"Nice. Real nice. If you want me to get up and play dutiful son, you should get out so I can get dressed in peace," he warned her.

The second her eyes lit up, he knew he'd made a tactical error. Big sisters were giant pains in the ass, especially when they were physically larger than you. She started advancing on him with that look of gleeful malice she usually got right before stealing his Halloween candy. "Why? Are you hiding some other interesting marks?" She grabbed for his robe, and Dilly spun away, jumping over the startled cat and then stopping when she got between him and the door to the hall. The room definitely wasn't large enough for evasion maneuvers. "Dill? What the hell are you hiding?"

"Nothing!" He pulled the robe closer.

"You're blushing like a twelve-year-old girl."

"Fuck off before I tell Frank all about how you kissed Robbie Robertson on a dare."

"Please. He already knows. So talk."

"Seriously, Car. Fuck. Off." Dilly slapped at the hands reaching for him.

"You should tell Mom." Carmine turned suddenly serious.

Dilly took the break in the physical portion of their fight to tie his robe tighter around his waist. "About my sex life? Okay, that's a worse idea than talking to you."

"Not the details, moron." She punched him in the arm hard enough to sting. "You should tell her you're gay."

Dilly rolled his eyes. "Oh yeah, like she isn't under enough stress already?"

"Being gay is not the same as being a two-faced, sadistic, raping bastard of a son who drains his parents of every cent and smiles that psychopathic little smile the whole time."

"Your issues are showing," Dilly pointed out dryly.

She rolled her eyes. "Whatever. Look, Mom and Dad need to deal with something normal… something real. This would give them a chance to stop obsessing over Hairy Gary and really look at you."

"I don't want them looking at me."

"That's your problem." Carmine threw her hands up in the air. "You never let people see the real you."

Dilly figured that up until last night he hadn't known the real him, but that was a conversation for later, like when they were both a hundred and twenty and dead. "Actually, my biggest problem is a pain in the ass sister."

She gave him a sly wink. "I think someone else was a pain in your ass last night, and you don't seem to have minded."

"Out! Get out. Out!" He picked up a shoe and flung it at her, but she had too much practice ducking flying objects. Laughing, she darted out of the room.

"Carmine Louise Carter! Dylan Lee Carter! Knock it off!" Dylan cringed. Yep—Mom was using-full-names mad this morning. It might be a good day to pretend to take up running. "Pancakes in five!" she yelled. Or not. If his mom made food and anyone didn't eat it, thermonuclear war would follow.

Carmine stuck her hand back around the edge of the door and held up five fingers, wiggling them at Dilly before even her hand vanished.

As he flopped back down onto the bed, Dylan realized that his sister was a lot like a straight woman version of Miss Dolphinia. Hell, Carmine would probably be complimented by the comparison, although Dilly suspected Miss Dolphinia wouldn't exactly appreciate being compared to a mouthy half-Italian with a habit of threatening to kill people. On the other hand, Miss Dolphinia might love Carmine, and the idea of those two meeting was enough to give Dilly nightmares for a month.

His morning-after glow well and truly ruined, Dilly grabbed a clean pair of jeans and pulled them on, groaning when the rough fabric rubbed across his sensitive ass. Dilly might not understand his brother's kinks, but he sure liked his own.

Trotting down the narrow stairs, Dilly ran his fingers through his dark hair, trying to get all the waves going in the same direction at once. By the time his afternoon shift at the restaurant started, he was going to be a wreck. "Morning, Mom." He gave his mom a quick kiss on the cheek before stealing a piece of bacon off the serving plate. She had half her nails painted, so she poked a red nail at him while all the others on that hand were still nude. It wasn't like her to half do something, and the tower of graying hair all carefully sprayed into place on top of her head was a tribute to that. The housewives of New Jersey weren't as careful about stray hairs as his mother. So, whatever happened while he was sleeping, it definitely happened midmanicure.

"Don't steal," his mother admonished him.

"I'm not. I'm just claiming early. As the baby of the family, I know you were planning that piece for me." Dilly smiled as he got his mom to roll her eyes. When he headed for the table, Carmine gave him a thumbs-up.

"You got in late, Dylan," his mom said as she brought the bacon over to the table. Carmine hid a smile behind her orange juice.

"Yeah. I was with some friends." New friends. New sex friends. Dilly could feel his face start to warm up, and Carmine winked at him.

"Your father was worried." She came back to the table with a large pile of pancakes out of the oven, where she'd been keeping them warm. After putting them down, she stood for a second, tapping her half-manicured hand against the scarred wooden tabletop. Carmine didn't waste any time claiming a few of the warm cakes.

Dilly figured his father didn't have time to worry about anything but paying the next lawyer's bill, but he wasn't going to say that out loud. Despite what Carmine thought, he did have at least one or two ounces of common sense. "I picked up some extra hours at work," he lied.

"Put the money in your college account," his mother said, her voice flat. Her eyes drifted around the kitchen as if she couldn't quite figure out what she was looking for. Maybe a sane family.

"Maybe I could help with—"

His mother cut him off. "You save that money for school," she said sharply, but she rested her hand against his shoulder, soothing him. "I'm not taking money from my children. I hate parents who do that. The Lord brought us into this world to take care of our babies—to raise and protect them—and not the other way around."

Dilly sighed. College didn't have a lot of appeal for him, but telling his mother that wouldn't be easy. In his father's day, a good tradesman demanded a lot of respect, but now people always asked about college. *What college does your boy plan to attend*, they'd ask. And his mother, who only wanted the best, wouldn't hear of anything else. Dilly wasn't sure if the "no college" conversation or the "gay" revelation had more potential for disaster. But until Gary's issues got off center stage, he floated in limbo on both. Despite what Carmine said, his parents didn't need any more carnage in the family dreams department.

"You should look into some sort of training, like computers or something," Carmine offered before sticking a forkful of pancake in her mouth. Dilly gave her a dirty look.

"Your sister is right. Waiting tables is fine for a young man, but you're growing up."

"I don't know about the growing up part. He's shorter than me," Carmine said with an overly sweet smile. Their mother gave Carmine "the look" before she sighed and sank into her own chair and started running a finger around the edge of her coffee cup.

"I'm taking some time to think about my options." Dilly's glare hardened as he lasered in on Carmine. If she started pushing the military option again, he was killing her and seeing if Gary's lawyer would give them a family discount.

"Hey, I'm just agreeing with Mom. You should look for something you'll want to work at forever."

Their mother was already nodding. "Exactly. Before too long you're going to be thinking about marrying one of these girls you spend your time with, and then children come, and it's like you're on a path that you never expected, but you can only put one foot in front of the other. My parents were like that. They always told me to have dreams when I was young, but when we're young, it feels like you have more time than you do. And then you're going to have a family and a mortgage, and it's not going to be so easy."

Dilly mentally added the part where you then had a son under investigation for serial rape, reporters who intermittently hounded your doorstep, and a house mortgaged up to the hilt to pay for the lawyers. The worst part was that Gary was guilty. Dilly might not be as loud in his beliefs as Carmine, who had gotten into one too many shouting matches with their father over the whole mess, but he believed it. He didn't understand it, but he believed it.

Gary had always been too smooth, too sure of himself, and too quick to try and talk people into doing things. Dilly remembered Gary's senior year, when he'd talked a whole group of seniors into supergluing all the teachers' doors shut so the school couldn't give finals on the last day.

Dilly had been in eighth grade at the time, but his mother had picked him up after school and made him sit out in the outer office while she tried to talk the principal out of banning Gary from graduation. As Gary sat out there with him, he looked smug. Happy. Their mother pleaded for him, and he just had this stupid smile that Dilly had hated, even back when he was too young to understand Gary's sadistic streak. But Gary had enjoyed the fact that other people got in the trouble with him.

And now… now he'd turned that sort of gleeful smugness into a slick attitude that made stupid women in bars fall all over him. Some days Dilly figured that he was gay because he'd gotten turned off by the number of women who actually thought Gary cute. Their giggling admiration nauseated him. And Gary played them. He played them hard. And if the police had even part of the story right, if he couldn't play them, he just raped them.

"I'm not going to rush into anything," Dilly promised, forcing his thoughts away from Gary. It was ruining his appetite.

"Life rushes us into things, even if we don't mean to," his mother said. "I know you don't want to talk about this with your mother, but if you aren't careful with those girl friends of yours, you could end up with a baby before you mean to, and you know your father and I would not approve of you having an abortion."

Carmine almost choked on her pancakes.

"First," Dilly said as calmly as he could, "I'm not going to get anyone pregnant. Second, if I did, the abortion would be her choice, not mine. Third, you're right, I don't want to talk about this with my mother, and fourth, I'm not going to get anyone pregnant. I say that twice for emphasis."

Carmine gave him a long glare that Dilly ignored. Now was not the time to discuss sexuality. However, he doubted he needed to worry about knocking up some girl. Now, if the tentacle porn online was even a little bit accurate, he might need to worry about getting knocked up, but he was pretty much certain there wasn't a chance of that either.

His mother gave him a look that made it clear that she didn't believe him, but she wasn't going to push the issue now. She'd push later. "You should go with your father, see how you like working on the cars," she suggested, curling her fingers around her coffee.

"Last time I went, I think Dad had to take out a new mortgage to pay for the stuff I broke."

"That was a long time ago," she said dismissively.

"It was last year, Mom. Trust me, I'm not any less clumsy now."

"I'll second that. He really isn't."

"Gee, thanks. I appreciate the support," Dilly said sarcastically as he finally claimed his own pancakes.

"I live to support my baby brother."

Their mother ignored the banter. "You must be better. You carry all those glasses at work."

"Yeah, but then he's cute when he drops them all," Carmine offered with a saccharine smile. She really was a bitch. Most days, Dilly liked that about her. Today—not so much.

"Your father would love to work with one of you boys." Mom's voice had a nostalgic dreaminess to it, but the mention of Gary pretty much chilled the room. The sunlight slid into the kitchen from the window in the kitchen door, but even the yellow sun seemed somehow sickly as it caught every bump and wrinkle in the wallpaper his mom and dad had put up in the kitchen. It was a grape pattern with a white lattice behind tumbling leaves and big bunches of purple grapes. It was ugly.

"Your father always had this dream of you two taking over the shop one day. It would be Ed and Sons." She smiled and her hand drifted up to the edge of her mouth, and Dilly could almost taste the pain in the room. "If that woman hadn't blamed Gary for—"

"Mom, don't start," Carmine warned. Dilly's pancakes turned to rock in his stomach. If he knew how to wave a magic wand and make everything better, he would. But he couldn't. He was stuck watching people he loved come unraveled.

Their mother slapped her hand down on the table. "You should support this family."

"This family? I do support this family. I don't support rapists."

Dilly cringed.

"Carmine Louise Carter! Don't say that."

"We're all thinking it. God, you keep trying to—" Carmine stopped, her mouth twisted into ugly shapes as she visibly fought with herself. The rage and the frustration were palpable. However, Carmine very intentionally settled back in her chair, her fists slowly uncurling. "You're right. I'm sorry. I shouldn't have said it." Carmine brought one hand up in a palm-up gesture. "So, you should ask Dilly about his friends from last night." Carmine looked over at Dilly, and either her skills of manipulation were slipping or she was being more obvious than normal.

His mother ignored the change of topic. "He'll be home. None of this is right. His friends, he always had such bad friends, and one of them is behind this."

"He had bad friends because he's bad, Mom," Carmine said with a sigh.

Their mother pressed her lips together until they made one thin, angry line. "Enough."

Carmine threw her hands up. "Yeah, right. Enough. Always 'enough' when it comes to Gary. Yep, he does no wrong." Some days Dilly wondered if naming Carmine after their great-grandfather had been a mistake, because she could channel the old man's attitude. While Dilly didn't remember much about him, he remembered Great-grandpa Carmine in a bed yelling at the nurses that he didn't need any damn help with his own prick. And oddly, Carmine had inherited the crankiness along with the name.

"Don't talk that way." Their mom got up and poured her coffee in the sink before putting the cup on the counter and heading out of the room. The kitchen door slammed behind her, and a dozen kitchen cabinet doors all bounced and bumped closed again.

Dilly watched as Carmine stood, her whole body tight like a coiled spring. It was just like Carmine to warn him to watch his mouth before she ran her own. She might mean well, but her mouth ran two steps ahead of her brain when she got upset, and it was as if all of them were ants living under some sort of emotional magnifying glass. Some sadistic child was using that glass to focus on the Carter family so the anger and fear all lasered in on them, the temperature rising until their blood boiled. Some days Dilly expected to come home to find out that someone had spontaneously combusted.

"Fuck," she said slowly. "Why can't she see the truth? Why does she have to pretend that...." She stopped and swallowed. Maybe she realized that their mother wasn't pretending. She believed in Gary. Now their father? Dilly figured he was a little smarter than that.

"To be fair, she pretty much believes all of us. I remember when you told her that you were out all night because Tammy Avancelos's car broke down and you couldn't get cell service." Dilly knew the truth because stories of his sister's wild ways floated through the halls of their high school for years. She'd gone to a college party as a sophomore and the rumors had her outdoing some of the college girls.

Of course their mother had totally believed the Avancelos story, and when some girl at the bus stop had called Carmine out, their mother had charged down to the school and threatened to sue everyone from the principal down to the cafeteria workers if the school didn't put an end to the bullying of her helpless, sweet little Carmine. Dilly loved his sister, but sweet would never be an appropriate word to describe her.

"I'm going over to Frank's," Carmine announced, and then she headed out the back door and slammed it so the cupboards rattled again. Yep, ignore the obvious. Dilly understood Carmine's frustration, but their mother truly didn't favor him. Much. Okay, so she favored him, but she was pretty rabid about insisting that all her children walked on water and could turn water into wine on a good day.

Dilly sat alone in the kitchen. "Great. I'll just do the dishes then," he whispered to himself. And here the day had started so good. Maybe he could just find a big rock to stick his head under and hide until the universe turned sane again. After picking up the pancake plate, he headed over to scrape it into the garbage.

Chapter 4

DILLY stuck his head out his bedroom door when the house phone rang for the fifth time. His mom had unplugged the answering machine again, but that wasn't a shock. Usually though, the reporters hung up after the third or fourth ring.

"Mom?" he called. The house was silent. However, she'd taken to using headphones so she wouldn't hear the phone ringing. She'd tried unplugging it, but then Aunt Martha had come charging over, convinced they had all died in a house fire—Aunt Martha tended to see natural disasters behind every door. When the rare hurricane did blow through, everyone appreciated Aunt Martha and her stash of bottled water, canned food, and batteries; however, most of the time, she came off a little odd.

Dilly trotted down the stairs and grabbed the phone off the charger. "Hello?"

"Dylan. Thank God you're home." His father sounded stressed. "I need you to do me a favor."

Dilly cringed. These days, all favors seemed to revolve around Gary, and Dilly didn't want to have to deal with his brother, not now, not when he still hadn't figured out why his brother felt this need to hurt people. "But... um, Dad, I need to go to work soon, and I... I haven't even gotten a shower yet, and—"

His father cut him off. "Come get a car and head over to the lawyers' office to pick up your brother."

"Daaaad."

"Dylan, his next call is going to be to your mother. I don't want her trying to drive down there and run into all the press." His dad sounded pretty frustrated.

Dilly glanced toward the stairs. He suspected his mom wouldn't hear the phone even if Gary called a million times, but if Gary left a message on her cellphone, she would totally run down there to get him. Unfortunately, his mother made a great target for the press. She couldn't stop herself from talking even when she tried, and Gary's lawyers had begged her to try.

Dilly sighed. He could ignore Gary being in trouble, but he had to admit he didn't want his mother in the middle of a feeding frenzy.

"Dill, I've got a Honda you can borrow," his father offered in a weary voice. Part of Dilly wanted to tell his father to go get Gary himself. After all, he'd fathered the bastard. But the fact was his father was working hard just to carry the financial load. He didn't need to deal with the drama too. His father didn't do drama. Mostly when drama happened, he found the nearest engine to stick his head in.

"Fine. I'll be down in a few minutes," Dilly said. *Crap.*

"Dylan...." His father paused. "Thank you," he offered softly.

"Yeah, yeah," Dilly said. He half expected his father to get after him about having a bad attitude, but he didn't.

"I'll see you in a few minutes, then." With that, his father hung up, and Dilly whispered a few choice curses under his breath before heading back up to his room. He'd have to text his manager at the restaurant to warn them he might be late. Sometimes the reporters ignored them, and other times they swarmed like rabid bees. If bees got rabies. Whatever. Even if it wasn't actually possible, rabid bees was a pretty good description of reporters. Fast rabid bees because it wasn't all that easy to outrun them. Hopefully, they wouldn't be there.

Inside five minutes, Dilly was on his bicycle heading for his father's shop. Ed's was a small local garage normally crowded with old cars—either with locals' cars waiting for tune-ups and new engines or with old junkers his father was fixing up to sell. State law allowed someone to sell four or five cars a year... any more than that and the state called you a dealership and tortured you with red tape. It meant that people around here usually went on waiting lists to get one of his father's limited number of project cars.

Coasting around the corner and dodging a long crack in the road with a two-inch ledge, Dilly started down the hill to the garage. The air was starting to get a chill, and his nose was running by the time the road evened out and he started pedaling for the shop. A block away, he could see something was wrong.

Only one of the garage bays was open. The others had their metal shutters down with the painted advertisements for lube, oil, filters, and fifty-point inspections for cars. Two cars sat out front, and on the side, his father's green tow truck sat with two wheels up on the curb that separated the tiny parking lot from the building.

Dilly rode between the cars and the building and stopped right outside the one open garage bay. His father was under a car, his greasy overalls and old hat exactly the same as always. Some days, Dilly figured his father would come through a nuclear war and look the same. His mother showed her age. Oh, she looked damn good, but her hair was streaked with gray, and she wore more and more makeup every year, but his father still looked like he was stuck at about age thirty. He had a thick body and dark curled hair matted down with sweat at the nape of his neck. The only way to tell the difference between him now and pictures of him from twenty years ago was the addition of one or two lines around his mouth. That was it.

"Hey Dad," Dilly called out as he pushed his bike into the corner. Even the music was on soft, and the garage had an eeriness to it that made Dilly think about Aunt Martha. "Where is everyone?"

His father wiped his hands on his overalls and tossed his tool onto a rolling cart. "It's Sunday. People are busy."

Dilly frowned. Okay, that was so not right. "Dad, people are always hanging around here," he pointed out. They were. The shop was the center of Burnt Cedar Road.

His father didn't even bother to look at him. "Dylan, your brother won't wait forever. Go get him. The keys to the blue Toyota are on the hook inside the office."

Walking closer to the car, Dilly ignored the not-so-subtle request that he get out. "Dad, what's going on?"

His father's shoulders drooped. "Dylan...." He stopped. Nothing else, he just stopped. After picking up a rag, he started cleaning his silver tools, ignoring Dilly completely.

"Dad, don't do this. Don't lie to me," Dilly begged.

That made his father look up. "I wasn't planning to." After a second, his father sighed and put down the thingamabob he'd been polishing. "I was trying to avoid saying anything at all," he said with a sort of strained humor.

"What's going on, Dad?"

His father seemed to need a little time to think about that, and Dilly waited with these heavy stones gathering in his stomach. He could almost feel the weight growing heavier with each second. "There are a few people in town who don't want to come around anymore, that's all," his father said slowly. "It's a little harder to keep the shop full."

Dilly looked around at the mostly empty garage. A dozen men would do under the table work for his father—change out a brake thingy here or clean a hose there. However, none of those regular workers stood around the front of the shop hoping for some day work. No one leaned on the chain-link fence, talking politics over the top rail. No one was trying to convince the forty-year-old Coke machine to give up one more can. Dilly had learned every curse word he knew from watching that little ritual. But now... it was empty of both people and cars. Or at least people, and three cars weren't enough to keep even one man busy. "What have you been doing down here?"

"It's not like everyone has abandoned our sinking ship. I have customers. I have loyal customers." His father threw the rag at the rolling cart and started stomping toward the office, his heavy work boots echoing against the concrete and steel bay walls.

"Just not today?" Dilly asked.

"Dylan, enough. This is not your problem," his father said in a voice just loud enough to qualify as a shout.

Dilly snorted. Considering that none of this was his problem, he seemed to spend a lot of time in the middle of it.

His father stopped and poked a thick, oil-stained finger at him. "It isn't. And you shouldn't let it be your problem."

This whole conversation was making those stones in his stomach grow. His father never lost his temper. Well, he did, but he would just grab his keys and walk away. Something was wrong with a capital *W*. "Dad, are you making enough to cover the bills?"

His father's face lost all emotion. "I have taken care of your mother for thirty years. Don't suggest I can't do that now."

Dilly threw his hands up. "I didn't say that, Dad," he almost shouted. "I just want to know what's going on, and if the family's in trouble, I'm making good money with tips, I could—"

"No, you aren't," his father cut him off. With one more step, he moved into Dilly's space and jabbed his finger at Dilly's chest. "You make enough to keep yourself in clothes and concert tickets and trips to New York. When you have a big expense, you come to your mother and me. You don't make a man's wage, so don't suggest that you could do better than I am."

Dilly could feel his heart pound painfully fast, and he backed away from this unfamiliar anger. "I... I'll go get Gary," he offered quickly.

Immediately, his father stepped back and dropped his hand to his side. "Shit." He rubbed a hand over his face, knocking his own cap off. "Dylan, I didn't mean... you are a young man; you're supposed to live that life until you're ready to grow up."

Dilly nodded. "I know."

His father took another step back and sat heavily on a stool and leaned on the workbench. "I used to think your mom and I were pretty good parents, but these days...." His voice cracked.

"You're the best," Dilly rushed to say. His father had done so much for him. He'd taught Dilly how to ride a bike and sat with him while he struggled with cursive in second grade. His father had tried to teach him how to fix a car. He had enough friends with horror stories to know just how good his father was. "You've always been a great dad. You and Mom are both great," Dilly promised.

His father looked up at him. "Are we?" He waved Dilly off without letting him answer. "Your brother is just putting us all on edge."

"It's not your fault Gary's always in trouble."

His father's huff of laughter didn't sound very amused. "If you want to help, I wouldn't mind having a few extra cars to fix up," his father said, "but I can't have more in my name. Maybe we could put a couple in your name."

Dilly nodded. "I have six or seven hundred dollars set aside. Could that buy an old car?"

"Yeah. Yeah, that would help, but if you put in the up-front money, you're getting the profits," his father said firmly. And that wouldn't exactly help the family with money.

"Dad, we both know that your work is worth way more than any junker I buy. I'm not letting you fix up some car without getting paid."

His father pressed his lips together for a second before answering. "I tell you what, you buy the car, and we'll split the profits."

Dilly smiled. "As long as by me buying the car you mean that I give you the money and you don't drag me to the junkyards, I'm good with that," he teased. His father's attempts to interest him in used parts hunting hadn't gone over well.

"You never were into machines. Or dirt. Or fixing anything," his father mused with a shake of his head, and Dilly could feel the tension easing.

"Nope, but I'm a really good waiter."

From the look on his father's face, he wasn't impressed. Of course, as far as he was concerned, a man either built things with his hands or he went to college and learned to think things up with his brains. Dilly wasn't sure his father actually understood anything else.

"I'd better go get Gary," Dilly said, ducking his head as he headed for the office. It was time to get out of Dodge before it turned ugly again.

"I appreciate you doing this," his father called after him.

"No problem," Dilly lied. He was guessing Gary would make it a problem. He usually did. There were only two sets of keys, and the ones to the Toyota would be on the Toyota keychain. Dilly grabbed them and headed back through the garage bay to get the car.

"Try not to work too late tonight. It'd be nice to see you before I go to bed, okay?" his dad asked as he walked through.

"Sure." Dilly nodded. He didn't even point out that his father could do the same. He hadn't been home for dinner in a week now. Well, Dilly assumed that. He would come home from work and find a plastic-wrapped plate of dinner waiting, and his mom had stopped doing that for him when he started working at the restaurant. So, his dad was either skipping meals or eating somewhere else. Dilly really didn't want to think about that though.

The Toyota started after a little cranking, and Dilly headed for the lawyers' place. The traffic was just starting to clear up after the late church services let out, but unless he caught some good green lights, he was definitely going to be late for work. At a red light, Dilly checked his text messages to see if his manager had sent back any particularly vicious or threatening responses to his earlier text. He hadn't responded at all, and now Dilly could feel that sour-stomach feeling return. If his boss didn't see the message and started looking for him to show up at four thirty to do preservice, he was so very dead. At this rate, he was going to get ulcers on his ulcers.

After pulling up in front of the lawyers' building, Dilly dropped a couple of quarters in the meter and started up the wide steps, but he stopped halfway up. Gary stood at the top of the stairs right in front of the large window and chatted with a girl. She was pretty, with light brown hair and a gray business suit-type skirt and jacket with heels, and from the stack of papers she held, Dilly guessed she worked as an assistant. She clearly wasn't smart enough to be a lawyer. If she was, she wouldn't fall for Gary's routine.

He gave her a little-boy smile. No matter how much time he spent at the gym, Gary always had this round face that made him look young. Dilly was the same. However, Dilly didn't mind. When he screwed up an order at work, he could flash someone an apologetic look and get forgiven. However, Gary hated it when people called him cute with his close-cut dark hair and dark eyes and that boyish face.

The fact that he hated it didn't mean he didn't use it well, though. Gary had his head tilted slightly to the side as he leaned close to the woman. She dropped her head down and then gave Gary a coy look. Yeah, Dilly was definitely going to get an ulcer, but not before he threw up all over the steps. Gary moved an inch closer and let his fingertip run over the woman's arm, and she leaned forward. Some days Dilly was really, really happy that women kind of sexually grossed him out because if he had liked women before, watching them fall for Gary would pretty much ruin his libido.

He trotted up the rest of the steps and called out in a cheerful voice. "Hey, Gary, are your lawyers done grilling you to make sure the prosecutor doesn't eat you alive?" Dilly blinked and gave Gary his innocent expression. The girl jerked back guiltily, and Dilly had a second to wonder exactly how far this romance had gotten.

"Dill Weed." Gary narrowed his eyes as he gave Dilly a nasty glare, but then he tucked the hate away behind a mask before smiling at the girl. "Katie, this is my little brother, the one who works at McDonalds."

"I work at Marrakesh," Dilly said in a flat voice. Seriously, Marrakesh was one of the hottest, most expensive, most exclusive restaurants in the damn city. Dilly hated that he couldn't stop being annoyed by Gary's stupid little digs.

Gary shrugged. "You serve food, does it matter?"

Dilly could see the moment when Gary's new little twit finally realized that Gary was an ass. Her eyes sort of glazed over, and she tightened her arms around her files. "I should get going," she said, fluttering a hand in the air.

"Hey, I was actually going to take you up on the offer of a ride." Gary switched back into that oily charm he used on most of the female population, but it was too late. She'd seen inside him. Maybe that's what happened in those other cases. Maybe Gary hurt women who saw beneath his mask. God knows, Gary was an ass to both Carmine and Dilly, and they saw the real him under the mask. Dilly grimaced as that made new connections in his brain that he really didn't like. If Gary wanted to rape everyone who saw the real him, that was a seriously creepy thought. Too creepy. Not even Gary was that slimy.

"You have your ride. It was nice meeting you." Katie gave an insincere smile and then turned to hurry down the steps.

Gary sighed, all the charm dropping off like a cast-off coat as he glared at Dilly. "Classy, Dill Weed. Seriously classy. How the hell are you ever going to fuck anyone if you can't learn how to keep your mouth shut?"

"I'm not looking to fuck anyone," Dilly pointed out.

Gary rolled his eyes. "How did we ever come from the same gene pool?"

Dilly had wondered that more than once, but he didn't need to have a family fight on the steps of the lawyers' office. "Let's just get home. I have work tonight." Dilly started down the steps. The girl had made good time, because she was halfway down the block.

"Yeah, can't be late for McDonalds," Gary pointed out as he followed.

"Stop it," Dilly said wearily. He didn't actually expect Gary to stop, but if he didn't put up some token complaint, Gary just got nastier until he found the right button to push.

"Right," he shot back. "Hey, whose car?" Gary ran a hand over the Toyota's hood and then sneered. He'd sold cars, but he'd sold the expensive new ones. Clearly the Toyota didn't meet his standards, but Dilly didn't actually care.

"It's Dad's."

"Damn. I thought maybe you'd finally found some woman to loan you hers." Gary got in, and Dilly hurried to get behind the wheel before Gary could find another reason to complain. "So, it went really well with the lawyers," Gary announced as Dilly pulled away from the curb.

"Great," Dilly said dryly. The truth was, he didn't want his brother to get off on all the charges. Yeah, he'd like him to maybe avoid the worst of them, but five or ten years in prison might make him a nicer person. Gary's personality might improve if he got taken down a notch or two.

"Yeah, sound a little less excited there, asshole."

"Hey, I got woken up at like six in the morning because Carmine and Mom were on some domestic streak. I'm not in the best mood,"

Dilly defended himself. He didn't need Gary complaining to Mom, because if anyone would believe him, their mother would. And then she'd lecture Dilly about being supportive, and Carmine would use that as an excuse to start another fight about responsibility, and then their father would never come home again. Actually, not going home was sounding better and better all the time.

"You're never in a good mood," Gary pointed out. "I swear, one of these days I'm going to buy you a whore and show you how a real man cheers himself up."

"Don't let Dad catch you talking that way." Their father's Catholic heart would stop right after giving birth to a whole litter of Catholic kittens.

"Please." Gary snorted. "Do you really think that there's a grown man in the universe who hasn't paid for it once or twice?"

Dilly was not going to even think about his father's sex life— there wasn't enough therapy in the world that could fix the damage that would cause. So even though Dilly figured their father hadn't ever paid, he stuck to using himself as an example. "I haven't."

"Because you're a little boy."

"Fuck you," Dilly snapped.

"Awwww." Gary used an exaggerated tone of voice. "It's so cute listening to the little baby boy trying to swear like a real grown-up." The baby voice he used just made it all the more aggravating.

Dilly bit down on a hundred different responses because he knew he couldn't win this fight. The best he could do was distract Gary. "So, what's put you in such a good mood?"

Gary put a foot up on the dash. "The lawyers are going to cream those three bitches. It turns out that none of them went to the cops or anything until they started talking to each other." He laughed and shook his head. "Morons."

Dilly figured they needed each other's moral support before landing themselves in the middle of a rape case. It couldn't be easy to admit that you'd fallen so hard for some cheap asshole that you went home with him and got raped. Gary hadn't been able to stay in his apartment since the police had declared it a crime scene, but it was in one of the hip and trendy neighborhoods. Girls who went there chose to go there because random screaming or the dragging of women caveman style would definitely get noticed.

Dilly thought about the club. If he'd said "no" halfway through what he'd done with Vin… if that had happened, he wasn't sure he could go to someone and admit that he'd chosen to walk in that club and chosen to go in a back room and chosen to let this man touch him before saying "no." Nope, even if Vin had raped him, Dilly wasn't sure he would have the strength to stand up and say so. As far as he was concerned, the women talking to each other and psyching each other up was pretty normal.

"So? Why does that matter?"

Gary gave him an incredulous look. "So?" He shook his head and gave an exasperated huff. "Shit, you really are ten pounds of stupid in a five pound bag. They concocted this whole thing." Gary started talking with his hands, fingers flying as he got excited. "They compared stories with each other before going to the fucking police, you idiot. Hell, they probably only made the story up because they found out that I wasn't exactly faithful. I mean, I may make a few promises to close the deal, but really… any woman who believes that faithful forever shit deserves to end up feeling like an idiot. But these three—they made all of this up, and these lawyers are going to prove it. I'm looking forward to them taking the stand." Gary's smile had a sadistic edge that made Dilly shiver as he thought about those leaked police photos of all Gary's BDSM equipment. Miss Dolphinia or Vin with a whip wasn't actually scary. Shivery, yes, but not scary. Gary with a whip pretty much terrified Dilly.

"You think they just made it all up?" Dilly asked carefully.

"Well fuck. You need to stop listening to Carmine. Yes, they made all this up." Gary slapped the center console of the car so hard that Dilly thought he heard plastic crack. "Do I look like I have to rape women? They beg me for it. I'm the fucking best. I can give a woman a vanilla ride or a hard pounding or anything in-between. I know how to do things with wax and ginger that would make your virgin ears fall off. And if all else fails, I fucking pay for it." Gary hit the console again.

"Hey, I didn't mean it that way."

"Yes, you did," Gary answered. "You listen to Carmine about everything, and she fucking hates me. Part of me thinks that Carmine's in on this. She and I have been fighting for years, and I always thought it was normal sibling shit they talk about on those psychology talk shows on TV. You know, we had some overdeveloped sense of sibling rivalry or something. But maybe my lawyers should look into her." Gary got a thoughtful expression, and Dilly silently cursed the traffic that had him going at ten miles an hour. The longer he was in this car, the less he liked his own gene pool.

"Mom and Dad would not like that," Dilly pointed out as he cut off a truck with dangerously little space to maneuver.

"They aren't running my defense."

"No, but they're paying for it."

Gary shrugged. "I'll pay them back. Do you have any idea how much money I pulled down before all this started? As soon as I win my case, I'm suing all three bitches for every single day of suspension at work, and then I'm suing work for suspending me without even giving me time to go to court and prove my innocence." Gary got an almost dreamy expression.

"But they suspended you with pay," Dilly pointed out. That had seemed like one more bit of unfairness. Gary got to sit home and do nothing, and the dealership dutifully sent him a check every week just to avoid a wrongful termination suit.

"You are just so stupid. A salesman gets paid like nothing by the company. I only made money when I sold cars, and they're stopping me from selling cars." Gary gave another exasperated huff, as if talking to Dilly absolutely wore him out. As far as Dilly was concerned, they could fix that by just not talking to each other. "Next time I go to the lawyers, I'm going to mention that. I need to start thinking about how to put my life back together," Gary said thoughtfully. "I don't know if I want to stay at Oceanside, not after they cut me out of the sales this way, and I was a top performer. I was thinking of heading to New York. You know, 'if you can make it there' and all that."

Dilly figured if that happened, Carmine would lead the cheering section to send him off. Of course, Carmine would rather cheer for Gary's incarceration, but that was out of both their hands.

"Here we are," Dilly said as he pulled up in front of the house.

"I can see that, Dill Weed. Seriously, you are not getting smarter with age." Without another word, Gary got out of the car and headed up the stairs to the front porch. Dilly noticed the weeds pushing up through the cracks in the sidewalk, and part of him wanted to call in sick to work and just sit on the walk and use a knife to pull up every weed, one by fucking one. He was tempted. However, if he called in sick after calling in late, that would look suspicious. Considering that Marrakesh was the best fine-dining place in town, Dilly couldn't afford to lose the job.

Looking at the clock, Dilly saw that he had exactly twelve minutes to get to work. Yeah, he was late. And he hoped his dad wasn't expecting the car back tonight, because Dilly was going to enjoy the rare treat of driving to work today. After his shitty day, he deserved a little treat.

Chapter 5

DILLY eased through the doors to the club, praying that no one would notice him. Well, he hoped one person would notice him, but he hoped everyone else would be busy doing something important. As much as Dilly hadn't worried much the night before, the fact was he'd walked the length of the bar with a post-sex stupid smile on his face after everyone heard him crying out. Yeah, last night that hadn't mattered, but today, Dilly could feel the heat gathering in his skin. He was going to start generating his own little heat wave at this point. However, none of the humiliation could change one thing: he needed this.

The parking lot was almost empty, with a couple of motorcycles parked near the door and a few cars scattered under the parking lights. But then again, last night, the parking lot was only half-full and the bar had been stuffed full of men. Stuffed… good word. Dilly could feel his face reach self-immolation levels of heat.

Despite all his fears, the bar was almost empty, and very few people even glanced at him. A few men played cards at a table in the corner, and a slightly larger group gathered at the bar to laugh. A loud storyteller in a dark blue shirt was either describing a soccer game or making fun of the world's largest dick. He couldn't tell from the hand gestures. Miss Dolphinia sat at a table near the bar, with her long legs crossed and the slit up her red dress leaving very little to the imagination. For a second, Dilly stared at those legs, searching for some sign they were male—knobby knees or hair maybe. All he could see were long, curved calves with impossibly red high heels with a bright red strap around the ankle.

When Dilly looked up at Miss Dolphinia's face, he realized she had caught him. She leaned her chin on her hand and gave him an amused look. Dilly's blush reached all new levels of heat. He was going to break blood vessels at this rate.

Slowly, Miss Dolphinia closed the laptop she'd been using and tapped a fingernail on it several times, studying him before she crooked her finger in his direction, inviting him to join her.

Swallowing, Dilly looked around. There wasn't a reason he shouldn't go over to her, well, other than the obvious answer that she scared the snot out of him. Dilly headed across the floor, weaving between empty tables and scattered chairs.

"Um, hi." Dilly felt uncomfortably like Miss Dolphinia was a boss interviewing him. He hated interviews.

"Well, that's not a proper greeting for a queen. No one teaches manners anymore."

For a half second, Dilly was afraid she expected him to bow or something, but then she held her hand up so the fingers dangled down and she wiggled them. Catching the hint, Dilly took Miss Dolphinia's hand and kissed the back of it, the whole time feeling a little like some extra from a cheesy movie. However, Miss Dolphinia graced him with a huge smile and gestured toward the chair opposite her.

Dilly quickly sat. "Where is everyone?"

Her smile grew. "Pumpkin, it's Sunday."

Looking around, Dilly cringed. It was pretty late, and where he had tomorrow off, most people would have to go to work come Monday morning. That explained the lack of men. "Oh. Guys don't come here on Sundays?"

Miss Dolphinia laughed and flicked her wrist at him. "I think they're all trying to recover from the hypocrisy of going to church on Sunday with the taste of some man's spunk still in their mouth after Saturday night."

"Oh." Dilly just sort of blinked. He wasn't sure what he was supposed to say to that. He'd just wanted to find Vin and maybe have a little sex… or a lot of sex. Either was good with him. But from the looks of things, he was doomed to disappointment.

She sighed and shook her head. "Darling, your expression is sucking the happy out of the room, and as much as I do enjoy good sucking, that does not work for me." She leaned forward and rested her chin on her hand. "Tell old Miss Dolphinia what has your cock in a knot."

"I just... I should come back another night." Dilly stood up to leave, but one word stopped him.

"Sit."

"But—"

"Sit." Miss Dolphinia pointed a red fingernail at the chair, and Dilly dropped back into the seat before his brain could veto his traitorous knees and order them to walk him right on out of the bar. He hated the way she could do that to him. His body parts should listen to him. Only, they didn't. Clearly Miss Dolphinia got to be the boss of his knees, anyway. Even now, they felt shaky.

"So, what brings you back so soon? I assumed you'd take at least a week of living in a rosy little world of denial before your needs would send you back here. So tell old Miss Dolphinia what has brought you running back so quickly."

Dilly looked around, hoping to see a hurricane or machine-gun toting gang to save him from this conversation. Unfortunately, the bar was quiet. "I just... I was hoping to see Vin."

"Vin?" Miss Dolphinia looked confused, which was weird. Dilly was pretty damn sure that she'd walked in on him and Vin, so the fact they were lovers shouldn't come as some big surprise.

"Well, yeah. He was...." Dilly swallowed.

"Blessed with an uncanny ability to fuck his partner into mindless bliss?" Miss Dolphinia finished for him when he faltered.

Dilly blushed. Miss Dolphinia shook her head, but she also had a crooked smile twisting her ruby lips. "You are besotted. And that is not a word I just toss around willy-nilly. However, don't commit yourself to the first man who knows his way around a prick. You are far too young for that. Enjoy life. Fuck the world or let the world fuck you," she said with a wave of her hand. "Either way it's a whole lot of fun."

Dilly could feel his face grow so warm that sweat started to gather at the base of his neck. The hairs back there stuck to the damp skin. He didn't want someone else, and the idea of fucking the world... okay, that was completely hot, but he didn't know how to handle Miss Dolphinia because no one in his life talked this way. Dilly was embarrassed for her, only he didn't think she would appreciate hearing him say that.

"I'll just come back later," Dilly suggested without standing up. He didn't want to get ordered to sit again.

"You can find plenty of other partners. Now Lee. Oh my God. That man has an ass tight enough to make Jesus break his vows of celibacy."

Dilly was pretty sure his eye had started twitching. If the floor were to open up and start swallowing people into hell, Dilly was standing very, very far away from Miss Dolphinia.

"Or Mark. Oh, Sweetie." Miss Dolphinia bridled and gave a flip of her wrist. "If you enjoy the sting of a little pain with your sex, Mark is going to just eat you alive, and I do mean in the very best of ways."

"I really should come back tomorrow." Dilly got up to flee, but Miss Dolphinia could move damn fast for a two-hundred-pound transvestite in high heels.

Putting a hand on Dilly's shoulder, she pushed him back down into his seat. "Darling, if you're blushing that red at the thought of a little wild and free fucking, tomorrow night's crowd would give you an aneurism. You are not ready for the big leagues. Or the wild and kinky leagues, anyway. You sit right down and I'm going to go get myself a drink." She patted his shoulder. "It's not easy looking cool and collected in fifty pounds of chiffon and hairspray. Now, stay."

Dilly opened his mouth, but before he could compose any sort of response, Miss Dolphinia had abandoned him, swishing her way to the bar in a flurry of red fabric. Dilly felt like putting his head down on the table and hiding his face, but he didn't trust what Miss Dolphinia might do while he wasn't looking. On the other hand, her advice had worked out pretty well last time. Dilly chewed on his lip as he watched Miss Dolphinia summon someone over to the bar. It took a second for Dilly to recognize the bearded man as Guard.

Dilly's heart started to pound faster, and he might have called the flutter in his guts a good case of fear, only his cock was already hardening. *Shit.* Clearly he was a big old man-whore, because his cock remembered the way Guard had pressed him against the bar and faced off against the other guy, the one who bought him a whiskey. Before Dilly could decide if that made him a slut or normal, Miss Dolphinia was sashaying her way back to him, Guard in tow.

He looked good. Tonight he had on a black shirt unbuttoned to the middle of his chest, and he had a fair amount of dark, curled hair against his fair skin. The beard was trimmed and was a little too Dr. Who villain for Dilly's taste, but Guard could pull it off. *He looked good.*

"Look who came back," Guard said as he stepped to Dilly's side. This close, he was a huge man, and Dilly scrambled to his feet. Guard's knowing smile made Dilly wonder exactly what Guard knew.

"Someone remembers you, Guard," Miss Dolphinia said as she sat back down, crossed her legs, and arranged her dress to show her legs.

"I like to think I'm memorable." Guard gave Miss Dolphinia a hard look that Dilly didn't understand, but Miss Dolphinia just opened her computer and seemed to lose herself in it.

"You kids have fun, now," she ordered in a clear dismissal. Dilly backed away from her table and tried to figure out what he should do. Leave probably. The problem was Guard looked at him with that bad-boy expression and his beard of evil, which looked cooler with every second.

"Come on, I'll buy you a soda," Guard offered.

Dilly glanced at the door.

"You know you came here looking for something." Guard moved closer, crowding into Dilly's personal space, and Dilly's cock perked right up. Chuckling, Guard herded him toward the bar. Dilly found himself pinned up against the bar with Guard's arm on either side trapping him. This time, though, Dilly suspected that Miss Dolphinia wouldn't rescue him, and Vin wasn't sitting at the end of the bar watching.

"I liked what I heard last night." Guard leaned close and nipped at Dilly's ear before he ordered a whiskey and a soda from the bartender. Dilly's blush deepened as he thought about what Guard might have heard. Dilly had never liked being the center of attention, which was funny because Carmine and Gary adored the spotlight. However, Dilly liked the shadows, and the thought of everyone paying attention to his sex life was not comfortable.

The bartender delivered the drinks, and Dilly grabbed at the whiskey glass, bracing himself before he took the biggest drink he could. Both his eyes started watering.

"Hold on there, boy," Guard said, physically taking the glass out of Dilly's hand. With his other hand, he stroked down Dilly's side and then cupped his crotch. Dilly went up on his toes as Guard squeezed. "You definitely know what you want."

"My cock does, anyway," Dilly agreed. The rest of him wasn't quite as sure.

"That's the only thing that matters." Guard leaned his weight onto Dilly's back, and Dilly squirmed. Right now, he might even agree with Guard. Guard grabbed Dilly's hips and slowly started rocking against him. "So, what are you interested in?" Guard's breath tickled the back of Dilly's neck.

"Um...." Dilly looked around, painfully aware that a number of people in the bar were now watching him.

Guard chuckled. "Am I distracting you too much to think?" he teased before moving his hands up to rest against Dilly's shoulders.

For a second, Dilly was caught between disappointment and relief. Guard definitely had some powers of distraction, but now that he'd stopped, Dilly wasn't quite sure what to say. Desperately in need of some liquid courage, he reached for the whiskey, but Guard slid the glass out of his reach.

"Well, shit. Do you even know what you want?" Guard backed away, and now Dilly had some breathing room.

Acutely aware of all the eyes on him, Dilly took a deep breath. "I was hoping for some sex." Dilly decided to not mention he'd hoped to find Vin. It was stupid of him to assume that Vin would be here or that Vin would want to see him. He tried hard to ignore the slithering discomfort that kept wrapping around his guts at the thought that Vin wouldn't approve of Guard.

"This place is known for the sex," Guard agreed, but he tilted his head to the side and studied Dilly for a second. "Let's find a table and talk," he finally said. He grabbed both his whiskey and Dilly's soda and headed for a table in the far corner under the silent television. Dilly stood at the bar, indecision trapping him as surely as Guard's body had just seconds earlier.

Sucking in a deep breath, Dilly followed Guard and slipped into a chair across from him. Guard was twirling his finger around the edge of his glass, watching the room.

"How long have you been in the scene?"

"The scene?"

"Fuck." Guard dropped his hand to the table. "You really are new, aren't you?"

Dilly cringed. Yeah, he was messing this up. He shouldn't have come at all. He'd gotten sex once already this week, which was about five times better than his usual average for a week, so he needed to learn to not push his luck.

"And here I just thought you had the wide-eyed look down." Guard sounded disgusted, and the unease in Dilly's stomach churned harder.

"I should go home," he said as he tried to slip out of the chair.

"Wait. Stop," Guard said, and Dilly froze, not sure what to do. "Fuck, now I scared you. I thought you were a regular player, one of the boys who likes to play the twink card and convince everyone he's some wide-eyed virgin."

"I'm not a virgin," Dilly said hotly.

"Trust me, I heard."

And that would be humiliation. If Dilly blushed any harder, they were going to be able to see his face from the International Space Station.

"God, kid, you have got to stop blushing, or every asshole in this place is going to want a taste of you. But seriously, you need to speak up and say what your limits are. If someone asks you what you are or aren't looking for and you can't answer, that's an invitation to trouble."

"Why?"

Guard reared back as though shocked. "Because there are way too many assholes who like to take advantage of someone new enough to not know the ropes. For example, are you into ropes, handcuffs, fisting?"

Dilly sucked in a breath on that last one. Sure, he'd seen the Internet porn. What self-respecting gay man hadn't watched at least one fisting scene? But as much as Dilly wanted that, the whole thing terrified him more than he could even say.

"That would be one 'no'," Guard said. "So, blowjobs? Cock and ball play? Whips? Are you looking for a sugar daddy or a bear? Would you try a golden shower or rim someone?"

Dilly was definitely going to break blood vessels in his face at this rate. Watching porn in the safety of his own room was one thing, but discussing specific sex acts with a real man who might actually be willing to try some of those sex acts... that went a little past his comfort zone.

Guard reached across the table and caught Dilly's wrist in a tight grip. "A lot of guys take silence as consent."

"Do you?"

Guard jerked his hand back. "I take consent as consent, and guys that don't... I think they're assholes. If I find them alone in a dark alley, I know how to take care of them. So, let's start over now that I know you aren't playing a scene. What are you looking for tonight?" This time Guard's voice was softer, and Dilly appreciated that the man was trying to respect Dilly's space, but it was hard to let go and just get swept into the moment with someone who wanted you to spell things out.

"Um, I was hoping for sex." Dilly's voice chose that moment to break. Add in some nudity and his sixth grade math class, and this would be fucking perfect.

"I assumed," Guard said dryly. His whole body stiffened, and for a second, Dilly thought he'd managed to piss the guy off. Then Dilly noticed Guard's eyes tracking someone. Dilly turned around, and Vin was crossing the room. He stopped at the bar, his eyes focused straight forward as he bought a drink and then downed it in one swift movement that would have made Dilly choke.

"Fuck. That's a good way to ruin a night."

"What?" Dilly turned back around to face Guard.

"That would be one of those guys who are trouble."

Dilly looked from Vin to Guard and back again. "Trouble?"

Guard drank his whiskey. "Yeah. He's got a bit of a reputation. Luckily he doesn't touch boys after he's played with them once or twice, but when he was younger, he got in some trouble. If you're smart, you'll make sure you keep control when you play with that one."

Dilly's brain spun as he tried to assimilate that information, but Guard's description definitely didn't match Dilly's impression of Vin.

"Well, well, well." Miss Dolphinia strode toward the bar, her dress swirling around her legs as she got in a good hip twist. "Look who showed up. Dilly, Guard, look who we have here."

Vin turned toward them, his expression blank. Dilly's guts twisted as he struggled to understand what that meant. Did Vin feel like he had a claim over Dilly, that Dilly shouldn't be sitting with Guard? Dilly found himself hoping that's what was rattling around behind Vin's blank stare. Wait. Dilly hadn't introduced himself to Miss Dolphinia. Either she'd been listening in during his last visit to the back room or Vin had given her his name. And Dilly had no idea what any of that meant.

"Vincenzo," Guard offered in a cold tone.

"Galvin," Vin returned in an equally cold tone, and Guard stiffened.

"Now, now, boys, play nice," Miss Dolphinia ordered as she leaned backward on the bar, her body centered in one of the brighter lights. It cast strange shadows on her face, and Dilly noticed that Miss Dolphinia was getting old under the heavy makeup and false eyelashes.

"I'm always nice." Guard stood up.

Vin just stared at him, and Dilly was bothered by the fact that Vin wasn't looking at him.

"It's crowded in here. Dilly, if you want, I can get us a cab and we can talk back at my place—set some limits, go over some ground rules, nothing more than you can handle."

Dilly's gaze went to Vin. He expected the man to say something, but Vin just wrapped his hand around the bar rail and stared at Guard.

"I don't...."

"Oh sweetie, go," Miss Dolphinia ordered. Vin's gaze snapped over to her, and if looks could kill, Miss Dolphinia would have been a very shapely blood splatter all over the wall. "Like I said, a young man like you needs to get out there, go fuck some boys and get well and truly fucked by a whole lot of men. Hell, if you were my type and about ten years older, I'd chain you to my bed and keep you there like my own pet, feeding you by hand when you begged prettily." Miss Dolphinia gave Dilly an exaggerated wink, and Dilly's brain browned out for a second. He literally could not remember how to speak.

"I'll get the cab," Guard announced. Vin's gaze returned to them. When Guard passed Dilly, Dilly caught Vin's eye for one long second. Dilly opened his mouth without knowing what he was going to say, but once his mouth was open, he didn't have the right words. He didn't understand what was going on, and Dilly tended to retreat when confused. He definitely felt confused. Then Vin turned his back and stood at the bar with all this stiff body language that Dilly wanted to soothe. He wanted to run his hand over Vin's back and invite all those muscles to unwind. He didn't, though.

Miss Dolphinia sashayed her way toward him. "Don't you worry. Every young man has to get out there and explore."

Dilly didn't protest as Miss Dolphinia caught him by the arm and pulled him toward the exit.

"Now remember what I said. There are more men in heaven and hell than are dreamt of in your philosophy, so don't settle for the first man who knows his way around a prick." She dragged him with one hand and patted him with the other, and before Dilly could get his bearings, she had shoved him out the door. Dilly stood on the sidewalk with the humid air pressing down on him as he tried to get his bearings. Guard stood at the curb talking to a cab driver, and he turned around with a smile on his face. The expression faded.

"Hey, are you okay?" He came over to Dilly.

"Um, yeah. I'm just...." Dilly stopped because he didn't know how to finish that sentence. He'd come here because he wanted to forget awkward relationships and uncomfortable conversations, and he wasn't sure how he felt about landing right back in the middle of both. If he wanted to feel this out of place, he could go home and wallow in the misery and mutual glaring.

Guard glanced at the doors of the Stonewall. "Yeah, that place is full of men who can make you feel that way. If you want, I can drop you off at home."

Dilly felt like a fish thrown up onto the dock. He couldn't quite figure out this new world, and he definitely felt like he couldn't breathe.

"Or," Guard said, stepping closer and letting his hand wrap around Dilly's waist, "we could still go back to my place. I'm not going to push you into anything you don't want." Guard's body heat soaked into him, and Dilly could feel his body react to the strong arm around him and the male scent. Dilly knew one thing—he understood Guard. And right now, he needed to understand someone or something. This feeling of knowing exactly what Guard wanted from him—that was the sexiest feeling in the world.

"Your place would be nice," Dilly whispered.

Guard smiled. "My place it is." With his arm still around Dilly, he ushered him into the cab and gave an address a couple of miles up the road.

Dilly shivered as the sky spit rain and Guard tightened his grip around Dilly's wrist. When Guard pressed closer, Dilly's cock hardened even more. They stopped at a red light, and now Guard was so close that their thighs pressed together, and Dilly had to grit his teeth to keep from either squirming closer or pushing Guard away. Being this close and not being allowed to touch was killing him.

By the time the cab pulled up in front of an upscale condo building converted from an old warehouse, Dilly could feel a stillness start to settle over his limbs. Guard still had Dilly's one hand pinned, and when he let that go to pay the driver, Dilly missed the feeling of something holding him down when he felt like he might float away. Maybe Guard recognized that because as soon as he'd gotten his change, he captured Dilly's wrist again, pulling him out of the cab and onto the quiet street. This late at night, only a few night owls were still out. An old man sitting on a brick half wall turned to watch them, and Dilly turned away. He hated catching glimpses of people's disgust, so he tried to either avoid being publicly gay or avoid looking at other people.

"Nice place," he said as he looked up at the old brick and enormous windows.

"I worked hard to get it. You'll like it." Guard led the way into the condo. "I hope you'll like it anyway," he amended himself. "I went back to the Stonewall tonight because I hoped I'd run into you. I'm glad I didn't know you were new to the scene. If I had, I would have assumed you might take a few nights or a few months to get up the nerve to come back."

Dilly realized that was pretty much exactly what Miss Dolphinia had said. "Really? Why?"

Guard stopped in front of an elevator and hit the button before he turned to Dilly to answer. "It's not easy to do something new, to admit that what you like may not be what someone else likes. Hell, there are a lot of people who eat vanilla when they hate that shit. Exploring other flavors feels too dangerous to them."

"Yeah, I guess so." Part of Dilly understood perfectly. Going into the bar when he knew what he'd find… that was hard. He doubted he would have gotten through the doors the first day, only this whole thing with Gary had him so angry and lost that he'd do anything to find some answers. But staying away didn't seem like an option either. He'd opened Pandora's box, and now all his needs didn't fit back into the box. He'd poured water on those little toy fish made of sponge that expanded, and he wasn't ever shrinking them back down again. He couldn't have avoided the bar if someone paid him.

"I have to tell you, I would love to see those lips of yours around my cock if you're into blowjobs," Guard said as if it were the most casual comment in the world. The elevator doors opened, and Dilly's brain had taken another little vacation, so Guard had to nudge him to get him inside. Guard laughed. "You blush beautifully. Usually the blonds are the only ones who can pull off that particular shade of red."

"It's a talent," Dilly muttered.

"It's more of a talent than you know. You look fucking adorable when you do that. I really hope you're into the oral because right now I am having a wicked good fantasy of you on your knees and me tugging your hair as you suck my dick." Guard leaned closer. "I can almost hear you moaning now. How does that sound?"

"Like I'm going to come in my pants."

Guard laughed. "I take it I have a green light on oral sex."

Dilly nodded. He'd been trading blowjobs with guys since he was sixteen and one particular sleepover had gotten way out of hand. "I like it," Dilly confessed. He'd never actually said that out loud, but the feel of a man's cock filling his mouth and the saltiness of a man's skin… that was about the best feeling in the world. Dilly thought about Vin tying him to the wall and fucking him. Okay, the second best feeling in the world.

"What is one thing you want me to do to this beautiful body?" Guard ran a hand over Dilly's chest, and the pressure sent tingles of pleasure running through Dilly's spine.

Dilly's mind flashed to the image of his hands tied, the rope white against his skin, the feel of his ass stinging, the heat of the spanking soaking into his flesh. He opened his mouth, but nothing came out. Then the elevator dinged, and the doors opened. Dilly stumbled forward as if the sound had knocked him off balance.

"Slow down. We have all night," Guard promised. He pulled his keys out of his pocket and headed down the long hall, and Dilly followed. *All night*. His mind boggled at the number of things they could try if they had all night.

"Home sweet home," Guard announced as he opened the door. The place was nice, with granite and hardwoods and huge-ass windows, but Dilly's brain had caught on the words "all night" and now his thoughts were spinning dangerously fast. "You want something to drink?" Guard asked as he went into the small kitchen and dropped his keys on the counter.

"Water," Dilly said. He could still feel the sting of the whiskey from the bar, and his tongue kept sticking to the roof of his mouth. Guard came out of the kitchen with two glasses. He handed one over before he headed into the living room and dropped onto the gray sofa.

"So, it's just us." Guard's whole body seemed to shake off all stiffness as he sprawled out on the couch, his big biker boots propped up on the ottoman.

"Yeah," Dilly agreed softly. He wasn't sure where to sit—the couch, the chair, the long window seat under the warehouse style window.

"Come on over." Guard patted the sofa cushion next to him, and Dilly was surprised at the sheer power of the relief that came over him at having that one decision made for him. Settling down carefully next to Guard, he swallowed as Guard immediately slipped a hand in the back of Dilly's jeans. "Right, so I'm not some jackass who doesn't ask. I'm going to make a few suggestions, and you tell me green, yellow, or red. If it's red, I'm never going to bring it up again, no questions asked. If something is yellow, we'll save it for another night, okay?" Dilly nodded, his spinning brain now caught on two more words. *Another night*. Guard was planning on another night.

"Bondage?"

Dilly swallowed and nodded.

"Green then?" Guard asked.

Another nod.

"Hey, I need you here, not in your subspace where you'll agree to fuck a duck if someone asks." Guard pulled his hand out of Dilly's pants and angled his body so he was facing Dilly. "Bondage, is that green light go, yellow for slow down and work into it later, or a red full-stop?"

"Green," Dilly said, his voice rasping.

"Good," Guard said with a smile. "I think we can skip asking about humiliation. Your heart couldn't take it. How about spanking?"

"Green." This time Dilly's voice broke.

"Blow jobs?"

"Vivid green."

Guard chuckled. "Okay, how about whips or paddles?"

"Um... yellow?" Dilly guessed. He didn't know, but he was pretty sure he wasn't ready for that.

With a nod, Guard patted his knee. "Good. I'm glad you're really thinking about this stuff. How about rimming?"

Dilly blew out a breath. In porn, every guy liked that, but Dilly wasn't sure what he thought of it. Well, actually, he knew he'd like to have it done to him, but doing it to someone was another of those areas where he just didn't know. This sex was starting to feel like one of those math tests he'd always failed in school. There was a reason he wasn't in college, and this feeling was a big part of it.

"I think we hit orange," Guard laughed. "That's fine. How about bottoming?"

"I thought that was the whole point of subbing."

"Not for everyone. Hell, not even for most, but it's good to know that you feel that way. Actually, I think we have a lot in common in the bedroom," Guard said. "For example, right now I want to go get my wide leather cuffs, tie your hands, and watch you squirm as I suck on your tits and then demand that you suck my cock. What do you think of that?"

Dilly's mouth turned dry enough that he couldn't get words to form, but his cock got so hard that his pants became painfully tight.

"I take it that's green."

"Vivid," Dilly managed to rasp out before he upended his water glass, drinking about half of it in three big gulps.

"Well then, lose the shirt and wait right here," Guard said before he stood up and headed for a heavy door. Oh God, he was doing this. He was really doing this. Shedding his shirt, Dilly wondered when he had become the family slut, but right now, he didn't care. He was going to have hot sex, and for a few glorious hours, nothing else in the world would matter. Hopefully it would last a few hours. Right now, Dilly was so hard that one wrong move and this was going to be over in minutes, and that would be both a waste and an embarrassment.

Chapter 6

GUARD came back with black leather cuffs in hand, and selected portions of Dilly's brain seemed to go offline. He stared at the stitched leather and short silver chain connecting them. His gaze followed the shape of the square buckle and the curve of the leather designed to go around a wrist. He definitely needed more water.

"You are the sexiest thing to walk into the Stonewall in a long time. I don't know how I confused some twink act for the real thing." Guard walked closer, the cuffs dangling from one hand, and Dilly reached out and fisted his own shirt where it lay next to him on the couch. "Hands in front or back?" Guard asked. Dilly just blinked, the meaning of the word "hand" slowly percolating up through a muddy brain. "No one acts that well," Guard muttered before he reached out to run a warm hand over Dilly's shoulder. Dilly leaned into the touch, several more brain cells abandoning their posts as his whole body seemed to overheat.

Tossing the cuffs onto the couch, Guard leaned over Dilly. Imposing. Menacing. His mouth closer until his lips pressed against Dilly's mouth, rough stubble scratching his cheek from the part of Guard's face that Guard did shave and warm hair pressing close from the beard. Dilly gasped, and a warm tongue invaded his mouth— licking, sucking fiercely, bruising. Dilly arched his back and dug his fingers into Guard's wide shoulders. Pulling back a fraction of an inch, Guard sucked a moment at Dilly's lower lip, and the rest of Dilly's brain officially went on strike. Other than the heat that gathered where skin met skin and the hard aching of his own cock, nothing existed for Dilly.

Guard broke contact, and Dilly moaned unhappily. "Fuck, you're pretty," Guard said, ghosting his fingers over Dilly's bare skin, scouting every crease and birthmark. Dilly wanted to grab Guard, to pull him close or wrap his legs around him. He wanted to do something, but he lay on the couch with his mouth open, every nerve focusing on the way his body tingled with every brush of Guard's fingers.

"Do you mind?" Guard asked.

Dilly blinked stupidly.

"Green, yellow, or red?" Guard asked as he slowly let his hands move down to the zipper of Dilly's jeans.

"Huh?" Dilly blinked and tried to restart a few brain cells.

Guard smiled at him and shook his head. "If you can hold on to this innocence, you're going to wrap every Dom in the place around your finger. Everyone is always talking about how the subs outnumber the Doms, but real subs like you, they're a little more rare." Guard ran a hand over Dilly's cheek. "I'd love to see that pretty cock of yours, okay?"

Dilly nodded. "Green," he finally choked out through a dry mouth.

Guard laughed. "You are something." He tugged the button and zipper free, and Dilly swallowed as he felt large hands slip inside. Letting his head fall back onto the couch cushion, Dilly focused on the way his skin warmed and then sent little shivers of chill through him with every brush of skin against skin. Guard's hands urged him to lift his hips, and Dilly felt his jeans being pulled down.

Then Dilly's cock was free. Despite the furnace-hot skin, he felt chilled by the open air, and goose bumps rose all over his legs. Dilly reached out to finger the black leather of one of the dropped cuffs and found the fabric smooth and warm to the touch.

"You only have to ask, babe." Picking up the cuffs, Guard worked the buckles free. "When we have time to work up to it, I really want to take a paddle to your ass. I bet it would look beautiful all red and shiny." He opened the first cuff, and Dilly watched him wrap it around Dilly's left wrist, the leather pressing against him, forcing his flesh to take a real form when he felt like he was going to fly apart in a million directions. Guard locked the matching cuff around Dilly's right wrist, and now Dilly could pull against that chain, feel the leather and metal forcing him into stillness.

Guard caught the center chain, wrapping his fist around it and pulling until Dilly's arms were stretched out in front of him. Dilly looked up, focusing on Guard's face. He smiled. He smiled and the knot of unhappy hiding at the base of Dilly's spine uncurled.

With a mischievous wink, Guard sank to his knees and licked up the length of Dilly's cock. Instinctively, Dilly reached for his own junk, but Guard pulled his hands to the side, and Dilly was forced off-balance, Guard's other hand pressing his hip back into the couch so Dilly was helpless. His cock got harder.

"I love to tease my boys, suck through the fabric of their underwear and tease them all fucking night, but someone went commando."

"No clean stuff," Dilly muttered.

Guard laughed. "Okay. Good to know that you don't recycle the briefs." Leaning in, Guard let his tongue circle the head of Dilly's cock before tracing the line of the slit, and Dilly arched his back and fought as Guard held him captive. "So, how about a spanking? I would only use my hand, but I am having all sorts of fantasies about you squirming over my lap."

Dilly blinked.

"Is that a green or a yellow because your cock is telling me it's definitely not red."

"I… um… green," Dilly finally got out. "Very green. Green like grass."

"Good to know," Guard said. He leaned down and took the tip of Dilly's cock in his mouth and moaned, and the vibration of his mouth around Dilly's cock nearly sent Dilly over the edge. A shiver wracked his whole body, and his skin felt overscrubbed and oversensitive. Dilly opened his mouth, sucking in air as fast as he could, but he still felt like he wasn't breathing. Just as the moment of orgasm approached, Guard pulled back. Dilly dangled over the edge, his whole body drawn tight and trapped in the moment. It was perfect.

"Let's take this to the bedroom." Guard stood up, tugging on Dilly's bound hands, and a hot wave crashed into Dilly, and he came hard, his jizz splattering across Guard's hardwood floors.

"Oh God. I'm sorry."

"Hey," Guard pulled him close, wrapping large arms around him. "It's okay. I'm impressed you can come without anyone touching your dick. It feels like a challenge, you know?"

Dilly didn't know. He was noodle limp and finally free of a million worries that normally crawled all over him. However, he was sorry he'd ruined Guard's fun. The man was still dressed with a huge bulge in his pants. "I'm sorry. I could still give you the blowjob if you want," he offered.

"So, no spanking you?" Guard asked.

Dilly blinked, confused. "Do you still want to?"

Guard laughed. "Babe, you're what? Eighteen? Nineteen? Trust me, that was just the opening act. Consider that taking the edge off because I'm not done with you tonight. Not unless you're worn out and you want to head home."

Dilly shook his head. "I'd like to stay."

"That's good because I'd like you to stay. Now, let's head into the bedroom." Guard put his boot on Dilly's fallen jeans, and Dilly stepped out of them. He was now nude, and Guard hadn't even taken off his watch. Dilly pressed back into the feel of Guard's large body, the buttons of his shirt pressing into Dilly's back before Guard urged him forward into the bedroom.

With muscles too lazy to do more than walk where directed, Dilly allowed himself to be maneuvered through a door and into a large bedroom with more warehouse windows overlooking the city. Guard hit a switch and shades started to rise from the bottom of the windows, covering the glass. When the shades were half raised, he turned on the bedside lights with their yellow glow. The bed was huge, but Dilly couldn't stop staring at the headboard—a series of horizontal pipes that looked solid enough to tie a bull to.

Guard guided him to the bed, and Dilly sat, his legs wobbly enough that he was grateful. This was good sex. If Vin didn't want him, there were definitely options out there. Dilly cringed as his brain drifted to thinking about Vin in the middle of Guard sex. It seemed rude. Guard didn't notice, though. Busy stripping his clothes off, he moved around the room, depositing each item in its place: the watch on his dresser with his cell phone, the leather jacket on the back of a chair, the shoes under the chair. Then he headed for a door. When he opened it, Dilly could see the fancy closet with all the clothes lined up. This guy had money. When Guard came back out, he was naked, and Dilly could see his heavy muscles and the dark hair of his chest tapering down to a thin line that crossed his bellybutton and then touched the thick patch of pubic hair. And his cock. Oh he did have a nice fat cock.

Dilly squirmed, suddenly all too aware of how soft he was compared to Guard. He wasn't flabby, but he didn't have muscle— well, he did, but it was the long, almost impossible to see muscle that came from carrying trays full of glasses and dishes of food. And for someone who had dark hair and eyes, he managed an amazing shade of pasty white.

Guard had a dark tan that made his beard of evil look all the more convincing, and as he stalked toward Dilly, the familiar heat started to return to Dilly's cock. Yeah, he could do round two... as long as Guard was a little patient about how long it took him to get back into the game. Guard kept coming until he stood right in front of Dilly. Resting his hands on Dilly's shoulders, he pressed Dilly back onto the bed. Guard pressed his tongue against Dilly's closed lips until it could get inside and explore. Dilly arched his back, and then Guard was standing up again.

"So, now that your brain is back with us, are you still a green light on that spanking?"

Dilly sucked in a breath. "Yeah, green," he said, his face turning pink at the admission.

Guard smiled and sat on the edge of the bed. Dilly watched him, not sure if he was supposed to be doing something. Reaching out, Guard caught the chain between Dilly's cuffed hands and pulled him closer. "Later we can experiment with so many things. Have you ever been paddled when you had a nice big plug up your ass?"

Dilly swallowed and shook his head.

"One of these days, I'm going to try that. You're going to go off like fireworks, but we should start slow today." Guard pulled and tugged and arranged Dilly over his lap. Dilly's legs were still on the bed, but his front was angled awkwardly off the low bed. Dilly was pretty sure that was intentional because he had to brace his hands on the ground to keep his face off it. It meant he was exposed and couldn't protect any part of himself.

Guard rested his hand across the small of Dilly's back. "Widen your legs," he asked as calmly as if they'd been discussing weather. Dilly spread his legs as much as he could, happy that his face was hidden in this awkward position. Guard tapped his butt so gently that Dilly opened his mouth to protest that he wasn't made of glass before he closed it again. Telling someone how to spank you didn't sound smart, not even to Dilly, and he wasn't the brightest man in all creation. The taps continued, slowly building until Dilly could feel the heat gather in his backside and his cock start to harden. "You are beautiful with glowing pink skin, either from blushing or spanking," Guard commented, and Dilly could feel the heat move to his cheeks.

The taps grew harder, and now each slap came with the sharp crack of flesh against flesh and a more intense heat that made Dilly wiggle. He gasped, and the slaps came faster. Dilly's cock was hardening, and he instinctively thrust down into Guard's lap, rubbing his cock against Guard's bare thigh. A particularly sharp hit made Dilly cry out, and the hand paused and smoothed the hot skin, sending little tingles through the abused flesh.

"Are you ready to suck me off?" Guard asked. Dilly moaned. His cock ached from getting hard again so soon, his butt felt like he'd sat on one of those metal benches that'd been under the full sun all day, and his body was limp. But he nodded.

Guard guided him down to the floor so he was kneeling between Guard's knees. Dilly was on eye level with Guard's very nice, very fat, and so very hard cock now. Leaning forward, he licked the line of juice that had gathered along the tip, enjoying the salt.

"Whoa, wait a second, Dilly. I'm getting the condom." Guard used his knee to block Dilly as he ripped open a rubber and started rolling it over the head of his erection. Dilly preferred the salt of skin, the musk of male, and the nicely sour taste of come. And he didn't have any sores in his mouth, so he was totally willing to take the risk, but he watched as Guard slipped the rubber over himself. Dilly watched until Guard finally opened his legs again, giving Dilly access. He wrapped his lips around the end and sucked before slowly sliding down, allowing his saliva to slick the way.

The cock slid against his tongue and fit perfectly inside his mouth, forcing his jaws wider until Dilly could feel the ache in his face, but he sank down until the head of the cock pushed against the back of his throat. Only then did Dilly pull back.

Dilly started working the cock in his mouth with every trick, sliding up and down on the shaft, running his tongue around the head, using his shackled hands to stroke the inner thighs, and Guard twined his fingers in Dilly's hair, fisting it without impairing his movement.

"Fuck, I'm close," Guard gasped. He tightened his fingers in Dilly's hair, stilling him, and Dilly looked up with Guard's cock still in his mouth. Slowly, Guard eased him back until Dilly had to give up his prize. "If you keep going, we're going to finish here, and I don't think I could go for a second round. Do you want to finish this now or let me come as I pound into your ass?"

Dilly licked his dry lips, the taste of rubber making his nose feel stuffy. He didn't know what he wanted. Sometimes the words and the feelings all got tangled up inside until he couldn't decide what he wanted... well, other than to have someone who didn't ask him what he wanted. He wanted that. "Whatever you want," Dilly whispered shyly, and the heat was already climbing up into his face. He hated his ability to blush, but Guard just stroked a thumb over Dilly's cheek.

"Do you want to finish?"

Dilly nodded. After a second, Guard loosened his hand, freeing Dilly, and he returned to his work, sucking and losing himself in the rocking motion of working a cock and the feel of his mouth stuffed full. He felt Guard's legs tighten and then he came, his come caught in the condom. Guard shouted, and Dilly continued to suck only much more carefully as he pumped his own cock. By the time Dilly came, a weak shadow of his first orgasm, Guard was lying on his back on the bed, one hand holding the base of his cock to keep the condom in place as he gasped for air.

Dilly knelt next to the bed, his head ducked as he watched Guard roll to his side and carefully dispose of the condom in a wastebasket. "Shit. That was good." He propped himself up on an elbow and held his hand out. "And now I'm going to make you feel that good."

Dilly's face burned with a blush as he realized that Guard hadn't wanted him to finish. Crap. He messed everything up.

"Babe?" Guard shifted closer. "Come up here."

Dilly cringed.

"Hey. Are you okay?" Guard sat up and reached for him, and Dilly let himself get pulled up by one arm, his cuffed hands fisted helplessly. He couldn't undo his orgasm. "Oh, you finished already."

"I didn't know you wanted to do more," Dilly explained. The words sounded weak, even to his own ears.

"Hey, I consider it a compliment that you would come with my cock in your mouth. Don't apologize." Guard pulled Dilly down beside him and started unbuckling the cuffs. Once they were free, Dilly wiggled his way around so he had his back to Guard.

"You are a very pretty man." Guard let his hand wander over Dilly's shoulder and then down to his waist. Dilly didn't know what to say to that, so he didn't say anything. The girls at school always called him cute, but that wasn't the same thing. Dilly was almost sure they knew he was gay. Hell, they included him on shopping days and they'd run around in their bras as they tried on each other's shirts, and no one ever even considered asking him to leave. Either they knew he was gay, or he had the invisible act down better than he thought.

"Can you stay the night?" Guard's breath was warm against the back of Dilly's neck.

"Yeah," Dilly answered.

"Great." Guard tightened his fingers around Dilly's arm. "I'm going to grab a quick shower before bed. Make yourself at home." With that Guard rolled away and got out on the other side of the bed, his bare feet slapping against the hardwood floor.

Dilly waited until the bathroom light clicked on and then dimmed behind a closed door before he turned to look at it. The sex was good. Great. But he could feel the discomfort rising like a cold fog. Maybe he shouldn't have agreed to stay, but he didn't want to go home. Guard was nice. Really nice. And if he went home, he'd have to face Gary, who would definitely have something to say about Dilly coming in this late. He didn't want to face that tonight. Dilly spent so much time worrying about what he should do that he was still staring at the bathroom door when Guard came out, followed by a cloud of steam.

"Hey, you're awake. You were so out of it I wasn't sure you would be. Are you hungry?"

Dilly shook his head.

Guard studied him a moment and then nodded before coming to the side of the bed and pulling the covers back. Dilly scooted up so he wouldn't be sitting on them, and Guard dropped his robe next to his side of the bed before getting in. "You are wonderful. I really hope I'll get another shot at that. You know, next weekend I was going to take my boat out. It's a nice little Alerion Express. You're welcome to come along."

"I have to work."

"Too bad. Well, just keep in mind that that's a standing offer."

Dilly nodded.

Guard pulled the covers up and shifted around until he found a comfortable position, and Dilly realized he was still sitting up against the steel bars of the headboard. Feeling like an idiot, he slipped under the covers and tried to figure out where he should put his hands when he was in another man's bed. Sex with men he knew. Kinky sex—not so much. Sleeping in the same bed after kinky sex—not at all.

Reaching out under the covers, Guard rested his hand against Dilly's bare stomach. "I'm glad you came home with me. The Stonewall is a great place, but it's not always the safest for new players, Dilly. I don't want you to get hurt."

"Not the safest?" Dilly looked at Guard. He looked so different naked in bed with his dark tan against the white sheets.

Guard pursed his lips and seemed to think for a second. "Good old Miss Dolphinia is a good… well, transvestite. And she's lived through a lot of crap. She was around back when they called AIDS gay-related immune deficiency or gay flu or some other shit that no one gave a damn about curing. So yeah, I have a lot of respect for the sort of trouble she's lived through, both because of AIDS and because of the legal crap the government pulled in the seventies. I don't know if she's telling the truth, but she claims she was there for the real Stonewall riots. She survived a day and age when a man putting on a dress could end up dead. But she's also a relic of an age that died. She's into condoms optional, negotiation-free sex where the flag you're wearing is all the information anyone needs."

Dilly thought about that. It actually seemed pretty accurate, but Dilly wouldn't have said any of it in the tone of voice Guard was using. He clearly didn't like Miss Dolphinia, but he was also in her club. Sometimes Dilly had customers like that—they complained about the food, but they kept coming back.

"Hey." Guard brought his hand up and stroked his fingers across the curve where Dilly's neck and shoulder met. "I'm just worried about you. Dolphinia puts up with Vin because she doesn't see how dangerous he is. I was mad about her cockblocking me before, but now that I know you are an honest-to-God newcomer, I could strangle her. Vin is not someone you want paying too much attention to you. So, you need to watch your back."

"Why?" Dilly looked over. Guard didn't look like he was angry, and he didn't have that special sort of glee that people had when they were spreading rumors. He looked honestly worried.

"He had some legal trouble," Guard said slowly. "This is not for public consumption, and I wouldn't tell you except that Vincenzo seems to like you, which worries the shit out of me. He stalked an ex-boyfriend. The man said that Vin held him hostage and refused to cut him loose. The prosecutor on the case wanted to push for a trial, but the victim was a drug user, and about half the time he gave witness statements while under the influence, and he contradicted himself more often than not."

Dilly narrowed his eyes. "You're a lawyer. You're in the prosecutor's office," Dilly said.

Guard gave a little huff. "Close, but no cigar. However, I know most of those guys. I'm in corporate law, though. But some of them talked to me because old Vinnie and I run in similar social circles. I told them what I'm telling you: Any Dom that keeps someone restrained after they've asked to be let loose is a criminal. He should have been charged. If he'd done that to a woman, you can bet your sweet ass that the politicians would have bent over backwards to shove his ass in jail. But because he only assaulted and stalked and kidnapped a gay man, and a kinky gay man at that, no one takes it as seriously. So, do you see why I'm worried about him showing too much interest in you?"

"You think he'd hurt me." Dilly swallowed, and all the messy emotional garbage he carried around from Gary's case seemed to spill over him. By liking Vin, was he setting himself up to get raped the way his brother had raped women? "But he doesn't even like me."

"Kid, grow up. Vin came down because Miss Dolphy called and warned him that you were going home with someone else."

"But she encouraged me to go with you," Dilly pointed out.

"Yeah, and I suspect she's back at the bar working Vin up into a jealous rage." Guard rolled away from Dilly and fumbled in the far bedside table before turning back toward him. "Look, this is my cell number," he said, pressing a card into Dilly's hand. "When you leave, take it. If you run into trouble, you text me or call me because I am not interested in having Vin walk all over some new kid who thinks that being a good sub means that you don't have your own opinions. Trust me, you're a fucking great sub, but that doesn't mean you give up your rights. Got it?"

Dilly looked down at the white card and black lettering. "Got it," he agreed, nodding. He got it better than he wanted to. Right now, all he wanted to do was run away from all this, to run away and never go back home where Gary sat in his room playing on the damn computer or the Stonewall where Vin stood with his dark eyes or even Guard's bedroom, where Guard made him face too many ugly truths at once. He didn't want any of it. He carefully put the card on the bedside table on his side.

"Don't worry. Vin has played nice ever since that problem, so I don't think he'll push things if you put your foot down with him. And try to avoid spreading that bit of information." Guard stretched and settled in, his arm coming around Dilly's waist to pull him close. "The friend who told me about this could get in trouble if his boss found out he talked about it outside the office."

"Secrets. I'm actually pretty good with secrets," Dilly said softly.

"I trust you are," Guard said, his voice starting to sound fuzzy with sleep. He was drifting off, his arm around Dilly's waist slowly going slack. Unfortunately, Dilly was left staring at the ceiling and wondering what the hell was wrong with him, because he always seemed to end up in the middle of something nasty.

Chapter 7

"HEY, you want a ride home?" Guard asked as he used a mirror to put on a tie. He looked so different this morning in his gray suit and white shirt and a pink-and-gray tie with tiny diagonal lines in different shades. Okay, he still had a Dr. Who villain beard, but it was hard to look evil wearing a pink tie.

"No, I can catch a bus."

Guard stopped and looked at him. "You don't need to. I'm the boss. I can show up for work late, no problem."

"I don't have to work today, so I might just wander around the city a bit before I head home."

"Okay." Guard's expression was... well... guarded. Dilly wondered if his lawyer friends really called him Guard, though. Vin had used another name. "Do yourself a favor, Dilly, avoid the club tonight, okay?"

"Why?"

Guard finished tightening his tie and turned around. "Technically the club is closed Monday nights, so the people who do things that skirt the edges of legal, that's when they go."

"The edges of legal?" Dilly couldn't imagine Miss Dolphinia putting up with anything illegal in her club. He had an image of her in five-inch heels chasing down some guy and beating him to death with a handbag. Miss Dolphinia was scary enough to do it too.

Buttoning his jacket, Guard said, "Knife play, blood play, some hard bondage. The stuff that goes on there on Mondays is too rough and tumble for anyone without a decade of experience and about a dozen loose screws."

Dilly figured he had the twelve loose screws, and if he didn't have them now, he was working on them. "That's not really my thing."

Guard chuckled. "Yeah, I noticed." Moving closer, Guard brought up a hand and stroked the side of Dilly's neck. "I prefer your thing to all that other crap."

Dilly felt himself blush madly, and Guard smiled.

"Are you ready?" he asked. Dilly nodded mutely, half afraid his voice would crack out of embarrassment. He wasn't used to people treating him like this, the soft touches and the compliments. Sex usually was a quick romp and then, often as not, playing Call of Duty afterward. Either guys grew up a lot in five or ten years so slightly older lovers were way more with the compliments, or the BDSM crowd had an extra touchy-feely gene. Either that or Dilly's fuck buddies stank. Maybe all three. Dilly didn't have enough experience to judge.

"If you don't stop blushing, I'm going to be late for work for a whole different reason," Guard teased, reaching down to wrap his fingers around Dilly's wrist. The feel of the strong grip holding him firmly was enough to make Dilly start to harden. Guard laughed and then let go. "I would love to teach you just how far you can push this kink of yours."

Dilly's blush grew hotter, and he started shifting his weight. He might like doing a lot of kinky stuff, but talking about it just made him squirm, and not in a good way. Guard chuckled again and headed for the door. "So," he asked as he opened it, waiting for Dilly to go through, "are you going to be a regular at the Stonewall?"

"I hope so. Maybe," Dilly said. He honestly didn't know. He'd gone there for answers, and he seemed to have more questions than anything else. But on the other hand, he couldn't imagine walking away. Literally. The very idea of not going back made his stomach sour. Now Dilly had to wonder if that was how his brother had gotten away with raping women for so long. Had he targeted subs? Had they needed this so much that they'd put up with him just to get it? To hear Gary tell it, they'd all loved it, but Dilly wasn't buying that. Gary also claimed he was just trying to help when he cut all the hair off the neighbor's collie and that it was only a joke when he caused thousands of dollars' worth of damage at the school. Gary's definitions of things like "love" and "joke" and "help" didn't exactly match the rest of the universe.

"Well, if I miss you, just know that you're welcome to call, okay?"

"Sure," Dilly said with a shrug.

"And Dilly?" Guard finished locking the door. "Good for you for not giving me a number or showing me where you live. Trust me, I'm not offended, and any Dom worth his salt will respect that you're taking care of yourself. Got it?"

"Yeah, thanks." Dilly failed to mention he just hadn't thought to give Guard his cell number. But Guard patted him on the shoulder and headed for the elevator. Maybe Call of Duty wasn't the best post-sex activity, but Dilly was starting to think it beat long talks about how he should act. He was starting to feel like he was talking to his father. Well, not his father, really. His father just gave him a look when he screwed up, a look that made it clear he questioned Dilly's sanity or intelligence, and usually that sent Dilly scrambling to change whatever he was doing. But Guard was like an uncle who wanted to give him all this worldly advice. Uncle Nick was like that, always explaining how a real man opened doors and invested in blue chips. Annoying.

One quick elevator ride and they were on the street. This was an upscale part of town, and people in suits and running shoes hurried by, vying for sidewalk space with a dogwalker who had five terriers and havanese on leashes. Dilly wasn't sure how he was supposed to say good-bye, but then a long black car pulled up to the curb.

"Have a good day," Guard offered with a slap on Dilly's ass hard enough to sting a little, and then he got in the car. It took off before traffic could even start to honk.

Dilly looked around for a second, painfully aware that his tight shirt was more evening-out-at-the-club than late-morning-going-to-work appropriate. He pulled out his cell to check the time. Almost ten. Either Guard was late to work, or he really was the boss and could set his own time to show up. Dilly wasn't sure he was buying that, though. Guard was too young to be the boss, even if he was a lawyer. Dilly's phone showed three messages from work, and he scrolled though the text messages before calling work.

"Hey, Larry. You rang?"

"Dylan. Please tell me you're close to the restaurant."

"Um, no. I'm downtown."

"Crap. Well, how fast can you get down here?"

"On the bus? In a few hours." With a car, he could make it in half an hour, assuming the traffic didn't get snarled, but no way could he make it back to the restaurant without at least three bus transfers.

"Get a cab."

"Okay, I know I've mentioned once or twice that I'm both poor and cheap, which is a better combination than poor and extravagant, but as long as poor is in there, I'm not catching a cab."

"I'll pay for it." Dilly blamed the lack of sleep for the fact that only now was he picking up on the strain in Larry's voice.

"What's wrong?"

"I'll comp you a new uniform, and I'll pay for the cab when you get here. But four servers and two cooks have called in sick, so get your ass down here."

"What happened?"

"I don't know, but if I find them on YouTube or Facebook either partying or recovering from a Sunday night party, I'm firing all of them. So get in here."

Dilly waved at a cab. "I'm on my way. The cab should get me there in about a half hour, but I'm not kidding, Larry. I would never show up for work in this outfit, so have something ready for me by the back door."

"Well, shit. Are you in drag or something?"

Dilly cringed. He wasn't, but he was close enough. The Queen T-shirt didn't quite reach his jeans, leaving a nice line of soft stomach showing, and it was tight. Really tight. Nearly as tight as his worn jeans. He definitely looked gay. Well, that was one way of outing himself at work. He'd sneak home and change, only Gary was probably up, which was why Dilly wanted to avoid the house for a few hours, anyway. By noon, Gary would be out trying to scam expensive lunches out of ex-coworkers and friends, and Dilly could get in without setting off his brother's gaydar. Luckily, his mother didn't have one. She still thought Neil Patrick Harris was going through a stage and just playing it gay for the cameras and that Ricky Martin only said he was gay to get back on the charts. Of course, she prefaced every statement with "Not that it matters because there's nothing wrong with being gay," but pretty much in her world, no one was gay.

"I'm in clothes tight enough that Burke would fire me if I showed up for work looking like this." Thank God Guard hadn't been a biter, because one good hickey would finish out the slut look. Sadly, a couple of Vin's more enthusiastic marks were still in evidence, but at least his neck wouldn't look like a freshly chewed dog toy.

"I don't care if you show up naked," Larry pointed out. "At least, as long as you don't get arrested, I won't care. I'll pull the right uniform sizes. Crap. We don't have shoes. Can yours pass?"

"Black sneakers."

"They're better than white ones. We'll survive."

"Okay, I'm on my way. Cab's here." Dilly closed the phone and got into the cab for the ride back out to the restaurant. A quick call to his mom to promise that he was fine and had just fallen asleep on a friend's couch and then a call over to an actual friend he'd agreed to help move some furniture and Dilly reached the restaurant with time to spare. Sending the cabby around to the back alley, he found that not only had Larry held up his end of the bargain, but he was standing in the back alley with black pants, white shirt, and a gray vest.

With the clothes draped over one arm, Larry pulled out his wallet to pay the driver while Dilly got out of the back. Things must be desperate, because Larry tipped before sending the cab on its way.

"Thank God. The rush is just starting. You have stations three through seven."

"I what?" Dilly's voice squeaked as he grabbed the clothes. That was a huge chunk of the dining room.

Larry whistled as Dilly headed through the steel door and went right for the bathrooms. "Okay, now that's an outfit that would catch some attention. I didn't think you were a partier, Dylan."

"I'm not." Dilly went into the bathroom and locked the door behind him, then shed his clothes as fast as he could. His butt still felt tender. As he ran his fingers across it, he could feel the ghost of Guard's slaps against his skin. When his cock started perking up, Dilly quickly pulled his hands away.

"I hope not. Because if you're hung over, too, I'm screwed."

"Too?" Dilly pulled the pants on, ignoring the slide of fabric against his ass. He really shouldn't have gone commando. It wasn't even like these dress pants would hide much if little Dilly wanted to start thinking about last night. Dilly predicted he was about to have a very rough shift.

"I had to send Amanda home. Apparently, she was at the same out-of-control party as the rest of the idiots. She nearly passed out."

Dilly opened the door to the bathroom while still buttoning the vest. He and Larry had pretty much started working at the same time, and Dilly had warned him to avoid the whole management thing. The managers didn't get tips, they didn't get to sweet-talk all their customers, and they always had to deal with every bit of crap that floated down the river at them. No way would Dilly ever apply for management. Hell, he couldn't figure out what Larry would have done if Dilly hadn't answered his phone. Put on a server's uniform himself, maybe. "Great. But the next time I ask for a day off, I hope you remember this."

"I will remember it, I will make sure Terrance remembers it, I will make you a fucking certificate of achievement. Now go take three through seven, and check in with Amy so she knows to start seating."

"Deal," Dilly said, his club clothes still in his hands. He looked around, wondering where to put them.

"Give 'em here. When I'm telling this story to everyone, I'm also pointing out that you have a very cute bellybutton."

"Fuck you."

Larry snorted. Back during the days when they'd both been servers, he definitely would have had more to say, but he just headed for the office, letting that one snort make his opinion clear. Dilly didn't hide he was gay, but he sure didn't flaunt it anywhere outside the gay bars, so he hoped Larry didn't tell that story too far or too wide. Most of his coworkers were cool, but he honestly didn't know how others would react. Dilly liked work. He didn't want a couple of homophobic pricks to ruin that for him. His life already had enough drama for him.

"Hey, Amy," Dilly said as he came through the kitchens and ran into the hostess walking back from a table.

"Thank God. Prepare to be buried," she warned in a serious voice, even as she gave all the customers a plastic smile that looked oh so very real. She tilted her head toward the bar so none of the customers could see her mouth and whispered, "I'm going to find who threw that party and gut every last pathetic one of them."

Dilly laughed. "Can I watch? Hey, we could sell tickets." He peeled off and headed for the station to fill a few pitchers with water and iced tea as Amy headed back to the front. Smiling at the next couple, she guided them over to one of Dilly's tables. The next three were his as well, but she knew her business. She kept them all in a straight line between him and the kitchen, and Dilly turned up the charm.

"Wow. The flu wiped out the staff. I mean, they pulled me out the park and just shoved me in one of these uniforms and told me to start offering all the pretty women water," he offered to a couple of older women, who laughed at his ridiculous flirting. "I am so sorry about the wait. We had a number of staff not show up, and the manager is busy writing termination letters," he offered a table of businessmen, right before getting Larry to comp some appetizers after a nasty wait. "You ladies look like you had an amazing shopping day. Is that a Vera Wang bag?" he asked, gaying it up with a group of young women who then degenerated into excited twitters over their purchases, buying him a few extra minutes to get the food out of the kitchen.

The rush continued until after two, and Dilly felt like he was going to fall over and pass out right on the floor. Unfortunately, one of the other servers had already left to pick up her kid, and Amy was seating a new group in his section since he'd volunteered to stay and handle the stragglers until the next shift showed up. Yeah, he was stupid, but larger than normal tips brought out the stupidity in him. It was funny, but when the kitchen blew it the worst, you either handled it and got the best tips, or the customers ate you alive. A good sixty percent of the time, Dilly managed to end up smelling like a rose on those nights when the kitchen smelled like rotting onion.

Dilly put on his best smile and headed over with the water pitcher and tray of glasses even as Amy seated the group of five. An older couple were chatting away, and three people in their early twenties were definitely grown kids. They had the same nose, only it looked better on the two girls. Dad and the son looked a little pinched.

"Hi, I'm Dylan, and I'll be your server. I brought water for anyone who would like some. Any takers?" Dylan went for casual charm. Families weren't usually big tippers, but they could surprise you. Dylan filled glasses as they chatted about some show they'd seen. It was some sort of outing for one of the girls. It didn't sound birthdayish, but Dylan couldn't quite decide what the occasion was.

He put the glass in front of the youngest girl, meeting her blue gaze for a second, and the glass slipped from between his fingers, falling the last inch to thunk against the table and slop water over the side.

Evie Princeton.

The girl with the narrow nose and small mouth and brilliant blue eyes that matched her blonde hair was Evie Princeton, rape victim. Dilly's heart got caught in his throat, and even without asking for drink orders, he fled from the table. Shit.

Shit, shit, and more shit.

Dilly pushed past a kitchen guy who cursed at him, and into the back hall. The manager's door was closed, but given that the universe was collapsing, Dilly didn't care, he pushed it open.

"Larry, I have a problem," Dilly announced.

Larry waved him away with a hand. "We don't have that seating capacity that night, I'm afraid. If your date is flexible—" He stopped, listening to a customer on the other end.

"Larry," Dilly hissed. He didn't have time for patience.

Covering the mouth of the phone with his hand, Larry fiercely whispered, "Deal with it."

"I really…."

"Here, comp them if you need to." He tossed Dilly the manager's keys to the cash register and then fucking turned his back. "That date might work," he agreed, flipping through a calendar. Dilly could feel his frustration rise up until hot anger chewed at his brain, but getting angry wouldn't fix anything. He would just have to pray that Evie Princeton didn't recognize him.

Fuck. Double fuck with a chocolate fucking cherry on top.

Taking a deep breath, Dilly plastered on a smile and prayed he could get through this without his heart failing. The one thing his brother's lawyers had insisted on was that they all stay far, far away from the victims. The fat lawyer had actually been a little scary when he repeated that order several times. And now... now Dilly was going to go take the Princeton family's drink orders. Great.

Luckily, Dilly had the job down, because he sleepwalked through most of their meal. Ricotta sformato, grilled scallops, two grilled chicken, and veal meatballs later, Dilly nodded dumbly, accepting the credit card without even offering dessert. He'd push them right out the door, only that would look a little suspicious.

"Dylan. Are you okay?" Amy pinned him behind the server counter where he had to run the card.

"Fine."

"You look like you're ready to fall over."

Dilly looked around the room. The Princetons and one other table were still here. Funny, he didn't remember the other table, but they had food, so Dilly was guessing he'd served them.

"Are you okay?" Amy rested her hand against Dilly's arm, and he could feel himself start to shake. "Seriously, talk to me or I'm going to go get Larry and make him finish the damn shift himself."

"No. I'm just...."

"Dilly?"

He sighed. "You know the trouble with my brother?"

From the sudden look of disgust on Amy's face, yes, yes she knew all about Gary.

"That's one of the girls." Dilly looked over at Evie. She wasn't laughing as much as the others, and now that Dilly really paid attention, the family's laughter seemed forced.

"Well crap." Amy pressed her eyes closed. It actually made Dilly feel a little better to see Amy do some freaking. It meant he was normal. Amy had to be near forty, and she could weather the nastiest customer without ever batting an eye, but she looked slightly green over this situation. "Is that their credit card?"

Dilly nodded.

"Give it here. I'll get the signature. Go hide in back."

"Thank you."

Amy rolled her eyes. "I'm walking a credit card slip over, not bearing your children. Now get lost while I make up a lie about where you are."

Dilly smiled at her and ducked into the back while she walked the credit card over for a signature. Hell. He really did have the worst luck in the world. The next time someone called him in to work an extra shift, he was playing dumb. He was going to pretend he never checked his phone. Hell, he might drop his phone in the bay at this rate.

Amy stuck her head in back. "All clear. They even left you a tip." She handed over the credit card slip.

"Yeah, because they didn't know who I was."

"You aren't your brother. They should tip you because you're a good server. You do your own sucking up instead of expecting me to smooth everything over with your customers. And speaking of, you have a second table that's ready to stage a coup if you don't get them more bread like you promised."

"Shit." Dilly cringed and headed for the bread warmers. Well, that was one tip ruined, he considered as he tucked the slip in with his others. What were the odds of one of Gary's victims walking in here, and Dilly needed to figure it out fast because if it happened too much, he was so very screwed. This was the only top-notch restaurant without getting in a car and doing some serious driving, but Gary usually raped women from the beer and pretzels crowd. Dilly's crowd. Hell, when Gary wasn't trying to impress someone with his fancy suits, that was his crowd. Their father had raised them to be good-old blue-collar workers. Yeah, and their father must be disappointed. He got one rapist son and one who was a gay waiter. Not exactly bragging material.

Dilly delivered the bread to his waiting customers and apologized profusely as he made up some lie about waiting for a new batch. Right.

"I'll get the coat for you. Wait right there," Amy said, her voice louder than normal. Dilly looked up to see Evie Princeton standing at the hostess station, purse in hand as she stared at him with those blue, blue eyes. Yeah, she was Gary's type. She took a step into the restaurant.

"Hey, you're Dylan aren't you?"

Dilly's guts knotted. "Yep, that's me, Dylan the waiter." He tried offering the goofy grin. However, she shook her head.

"You're Dylan, Gary's brother."

Dilly could feel his face turn hot. "I have to get some work done." He turned to flee, and Amy was hurrying back with Evie's forgotten coat in hand.

"Here you go. Have a wonderful day, and come back again," she said brightly, and Dilly could see her trying to rush Evie toward the door. Evie accepted the coat, but then she detoured around Amy.

"I knew you in school. You were a freshman when I was a junior," Evie said. Clearly this was going to happen right here, and Dilly didn't want his other customers to see it. He really didn't want the entire kitchen staff hanging out the door to watch the show. He hurried toward the entrance and opened the door to the exit for her.

"I'm afraid I don't remember."

"Do you believe he did it? Do you believe he raped me?" Evie asked, an odd little twitch in her neck making her head bob in a way that made Dilly think she wanted to peck him to death.

Dilly retreated to the entrance, silently begging her to follow. "I shouldn't—"

"He did," she cut him off, but at least she followed him into the entrance with its ornate benches and tiled floor, where the words could bounce around like billiards balls and hit him over and over.

"I didn't say he didn't. I *wouldn't* say he didn't," Dilly promised.

"He raped me. He raped all of us. I thought…." She stopped and swallowed. "I thought it was really awesome that he liked me." When her voice broke, Dilly wanted to reach out and comfort her—hug her. He just didn't think she wanted another Carter man touching her. "And that if he was a little rough, it was worth it, only it wasn't." The grief broke, and Dilly could see the pure fury below.

"I'm sorry." Those were the two most pathetic words in the English language, but they were all Dilly could offer.

A rough bark of laughter slipped out before she looked at the ceiling, and Dilly could almost see her gathering up her shredded emotions, struggling to put them back together. "See, that would mean a lot coming from him, but I don't think he can say it. Do you?"

"His lawyers are pretty clear that I'm not supposed to talk to you." Dilly changed the subject. They both knew Gary wouldn't apologize. Apologizing would require him to admit that what he'd done was wrong, and that wasn't going to happen.

Evie took a step closer, and Dilly could feel his discomfort grow. "You could help."

"Me?"

Nodding, Evie leaned in. "Carmine says that you caught most of Gary's meanness growing up. She said he tortured you," she said in a conspiratorial tone.

Dilly shook his head. "He teased me." Sure, the teasing had gone too far, but Gary had never hurt him. "Wait. Carmine told you this? My Carmine?" Dilly felt off-balance, as if the world had tilted.

"If you testified against him, it could make a difference."

"Carmine sent you here? She told you I would testify?" Dilly's voice cracked on the word testify, but that was fair because his brain felt like it had cracked a little too.

"She said that you're a good man, that you aren't anything like Gary."

Dilly shook his head. "I can't. I just can't."

"Can't? Or won't?" She took a step back, and now Dilly could feel the hatred gathering. "There's a difference you know. Carmine told us how Gary locked you in a closet for so long that you peed your pants."

"And then he helped me clean up," Dilly pointed out. That wasn't evil. That really wasn't raping levels of evil.

"Did that make it all okay? Did that change the fact that you screamed for help and he laughed at you?" Evie's tone grew sharp and mocking, and Dilly wanted to just run away, but he had the feeling if he did, Evie would follow him.

"Don't," he asked her.

"Don't what?" She jerked back. "You could do the right thing here."

"Don't put me in the middle with my parents. They're good people, and my mom...." Dilly swallowed. "She believes him. She believes in him. I can't break her heart."

Silence filled the small room, echoing off the walls the way the hatred echoed. Evie looked him up and down, disgust in her eyes. "You're a spineless worm."

Dilly wasn't going to argue with the rape victim over that. Maybe if he was tougher, he could have found a way to stop Gary. Maybe he could have found a way to get his mother to see the truth. Maybe. "Maybe I am," Dilly admitted. "But my mom has to figure this out for herself. I'm not going to help put Gary away, not when I really don't know anything. He never left a bruise on me. Never."

She gave a dismissive grunt. "Right."

"He didn't," Dilly protested. "Yeah, he got creative. And yeah, I know he's sadistic, but I don't know anything that could help you."

"What a dick. Carmine has two brothers that suck." Evie physically pushed him to the side to reach for the outer doors, and now Dilly could see the rest of her family in the parking lot, gathered around an older green car.

They'd set him up. They'd known the whole time that he was Gary's brother. Actually, Carmine set him up, because she would have told them where to find him. But Dilly could see the hard desperation on her father's face. He fisted the car's door frame, large fingers curling around the formed metal as if he could just bend it if he tried hard enough. But he couldn't. He couldn't bend steel, and none of them could bend reality, and nothing could change the fact that Gary raped this woman. Nothing.

"Wait," Dilly called out as the outer door started drifting shut behind her. Evie turned around and pulled it open, a kernel of hope on her face.

"What?"

Dilly closed his eyes and wished the universe would just tell him what he should do. Everyone wanted something out of him. Everyone. And if his mom found out that Carmine had jumped to the other side… it would kill her. "Gary's lawyers," he whispered.

"What about them?"

Swallowing, Dilly had to force the words up and out his dry throat. "They found out you were all calling each other before you went to the police. They plan to make it look like you all found out about Gary's cheating and then you made up the story."

Evie went stark white.

"He told me about it. The lawyers think this is going to get him off."

"We didn't." Evie's eyes brightened, and Dilly just wanted the ground to open and swallow him. "We didn't make it up." She sounded so desperate, and Dilly hated that his brother had done this. His brother had made her desperate to have a stranger believe her.

"I know," Dilly agreed. "I do. I just don't know what to do about it."

Evie's mouth twisted into something ugly as she fought tears, and Dilly wondered if Gary had watched that very expression. Had he watched the pain shining out through her blue eyes and kept right on going? Dilly's gut churned as he tried to avoid dry heaving right then and there. Time pulled tight, reality stretched until Dilly could swear he felt his heart straining to beat, and then Evie turned and fled.

Slowly, Dilly sank down onto the bench, his own eyes warm, but he wasn't sure who he wanted to cry for—himself, his mom, the victims. Maybe he should cry for Carmine, who was watching this pull their family apart with a thinly disguised desperation that had sent her to the victims. The only person who deserved any of this was Gary, but of all the people in the mud and muck who were trying to flail their way out, Gary was the only one who wasn't suffering. This was one big annoyance to him, and he had already moved on with planning the rest of his life.

Amy opened the inner door. "Hey, are you okay?"

Dilly closed his eyes and tried to find some way to drown out all the emotions that sliced at his soul. "No. I am so not okay that I don't even have words for how not okay I am." Dilly's eyes got warm, and Amy rested her hand on his shoulder, but that small offer of comfort couldn't undo the mountains of pain. The universe wasn't fair, and Dilly didn't have any idea how to handle that.

Chapter 8

"HEY!" Dilly waved at someone passing by, but they kept on passing by, and Dilly lost his balance and fell back onto the dirt of the raised brick planter. Dilly giggled at the pale moon hiding behind translucent sheets of clouds. "Amy pills good," he announced to no one. Maybe he was announcing it to the moon as it slowly drooped closer. "Are you tired of being all the way up there?" Dilly asked. He could understand how tiring that was. The moon didn't answer, but it did keep drifting closer and closer, the pale craters growing until they filled Dilly's entire field of vision. Dilly reached up to touch, but it hovered just past his fingertips. Straining, he lifted his shoulder up off the dirt to try and close that last inch.

"Hey, are you okay?" A voice pulled his arm, and Dilly blinked, looking around until he found the person attached to the voice.

"Hey." Dilly smiled. Leather. Leather was good. Leather meant that maybe this guy had something that could hold Dilly together when he felt like he was cracking apart, pieces of him sliding off. "Can you fix the cracks?"

"How much have you taken?" The guy let go of Dilly's arm, and Dilly felt for one second like he might slip off the ground. His feet would go up and up into the sky until they touched the moon, and then his head would swing like a big pendulum. Dilly could almost see it happening. He grabbed at the guy's arm and tucked his feet close to keep them from getting swept up.

"So, that much." The voice retreated so it came from the other side of the world even though Dilly still held the guy. Or maybe he only had the arm. What proof did he have that the arm was still on the person? Dilly lifted the arm he was holding to see if it was attached.

"Let's get you some coffee."

"Going to Miss Dolphinia," Dilly said. "Before all the cracks get moon in them." The moon pressed close. If it landed on them, all Dilly's cracked pieces were going to be so smashed. Smashed. Dilly started to giggle. He was already smashed. *Amy pills good.*

"You're one of her boys? You look a little young for that old queen."

"She scares me. Too confused to be cracked."

"She scares most people. Come on, up and at 'em. You nearly made it to the Stonewall." Dilly felt himself rising, and he flailed as gravity failed him. With only one foot stuck to the ground, his whole body strained against the need to rise up into the sky and vanish like a balloon some kid let go. He didn't want to be let go.

"I have you. Don't worry."

"Leather smells good," Dilly said wearily. "Black cuffs."

"Miss Dolphinia is going to kill you for getting this smashed if you're one of hers. And if someone else got you smashed, she's going to kill them."

"Beat to death with a five-inch heel," Dilly giggled.

"Yep, you know her."

Dilly squinted and a face sort of came into focus. He was a gray-haired man with lots of hair. Hair everywhere and muscles. Hair and muscles and leather. Dilly reached up to grab at the harness. If he could hold onto that, he wouldn't fly off. The harness jerked, and Dilly almost got sucked up into the sky. The harness man yelped, and then Dilly was moving too fast to stay stuck to earth. His heart pounded painfully fast, and he sucked in a breath, holding it for when he hit outer space. But then he was saved. Hands grabbed his wrists, pressing them together, and Dilly let out an explosive breath when he realized the guy had one hand on Dilly's neck and another holding his wrists.

"That hurts. You don't go pulling at a man's chest hair unless you want to taste a whip," the guy growled, but Dilly giggled. He wasn't going to fly into space. *Good.* "I hope someone slipped you something because if you did this to yourself, Miss D's shoes are going to be planted up your ass, and I'm not so sure that's going to be a metaphor." The hands around Dilly's wrists tightened, and he relaxed into the hold.

"Fuck it all. Look, kid, I can't cuff you in public, so let's just get half a block without you doing anything crazy enough to attract police attention, okay?" he hissed.

"Is he okay?" a new voice asked.

"He's wasted. Don't worry about it." Dilly blinked. Voices were ignoring him. He needed to be the center of harness man's attention or he'd go flying off the planet and no one would notice. Dilly threw himself forward, and harness man grunted as Dilly hit him. Dilly started to giggle. He'd worry that he'd pull harness man off earth with him, but that wasn't the way it worked. Other people pulled him into things. He wasn't big enough to pull other people.

"Do you need help?" A face appeared. Weirdly, it didn't seem to have a body.

"I need a good fucking," Dilly announced. The face went away fast. Maybe that was because without a body it couldn't do much fucking. Dilly moved when the hand on his neck pushed him.

"Well, that's one way to get rid of a stranger." Dilly tried to bring his hands up to balance himself, but the grip around them tightened. "Just keep moving."

"Parts of me cracked right off. Left them somewhere. Work maybe. Carmine shouldn't have done that."

"Carmine. He the one who gave you the drugs?"

Dilly started giggling. Carmine always lectured him on how he wasn't old enough to do shit like drink. But he drank. Not a lot, but he'd drink beers when his friends did. And he'd gotten high before. The moon never tried to fall on him before, though.

Dilly let his eyes drift closed so he could just stumble along where the hands pushed him. The hands knew Miss Dolphinia, so everything was okay. Something hit his ankle, and when the hand let go of his wrists, Dilly flailed with fear, his heart pounding painfully fast, but then the hands caught him again. Dilly didn't even open his eyes, and something cool and smooth wrapped around his wrists and then tightened. As long as he didn't fall off the planet, he was okay.

Now two hands were on his shoulders, leading him into a room. Dilly didn't open his eyes, but he could tell from the way voices bounced off walls. Maybe he was a bat. Dilly might test that theory, only his hands were tied.

"My, oh my. Jason, where did you find the little lamb?" Miss Dolphinia's voice made Dilly open his eyes. There wasn't music playing, but clusters of men filled the half-lit bar.

"You scare me," Dilly announced to Miss Dolphinia. "I bet the moon would never try to squish you."

Miss Dolphinia's eyebrows went up.

"I found him about a half block from here talking to the moon. He said he was trying to get to you."

"He did, did he?" Miss Dolphinia moved closer, her manicured nails coming up to stroke Dilly's cheek—he let his eyes close again—over a shoulder, and down Dilly's arm.

"Every time I try to turn him loose, he seems to panic."

"I think we all know how much our Dylan loves to be tied and helpless. But what were you thinking getting stoned in public, my dear? There's living on the edge and then there's stupid."

"I'm always doing stupid stuff," Dilly said. He swayed as the earth spun too fast for him, but harness guy grabbed one arm and Miss Dolphinia grabbed the other.

"I think some guy called Carmine gave him the stuff."

"Nope," Dilly said. "Amy gave me stuff to make me feel better after all the Carmine stuff. But Amy's stuff is really stufflike."

"That it is." Miss Dolphinia patted him on the arm. "Thank you, Jason. You are the gentleman, always looking out for a lady and her property. Tomorrow night when the bar's open, I'll buy you a drink." She batted her eyes at harness guy, and he gave her a nod, but Dilly kept finding the edges of the world streaking out into the black, so he closed his eyes again.

"Come on, you. Three nights in a row. You are a needy one, aren't you?"

"Yep," Dilly agreed. Miss Dolphinia pulled on him, and he followed her. "Need Gary to go away."

"Oh sweetie. Men never go away. A cute thing like you—they just get obsessed and watch from afar after tasting a real submissive's sweetness."

"He's my brother."

"Oh." For the first time, Miss Dolphinia's voice lost that lilting sing-song that Dilly loved so much. He stopped, just to try and find the lilting tone. Maybe she dropped it on the floor, but she pulled him along with a strong grip that almost pulled him off his feet. If he wasn't on his feet, they'd fly up and over his head, but that was okay because Miss Dolphinia would have him. "Come on, now. Be a good boy." Dilly blinked and then followed as she headed back to a cushioned booth along one wall. The table was gone. Dilly wanted to search for the table, but she hadn't liked it when he'd wanted to look for the lilt, so he didn't try. He did try to sit next to her, but she snapped her fingers and pointed at the floor before she started to arrange her dress.

Dilly tried to sit, but gravity was still unpredictable, and he ended up sort of collapsing on the floor next to Miss Dolphinia. He braced his hands against the hardwood and stared at the black fabric tied around his wrists. *When did that happen?*

"Come here, boy," Miss Dolphinia urged, and Dilly pushed himself up and scooted closer, letting Miss Dolphinia pull at him until he was resting against her leg, his head on her knee as she stroked his hair. Dilly could feel the knots of fear slowly unwinding each time her nails raked over his scalp and sent little tingles down his spine. "Look who that is," she said, using a finger to push on his cheek to make him turn his head. Dilly stared in that direction, images floating in and out of focus until he could finally see faces.

"Vin," he said happily. Vin had a whip in hand, his bandanas hanging from his back pocket, left side black, right side blue. No one was standing near him, and Dilly tried to push himself up, but Miss Dolphinia pushed him back down to the ground.

"He's busy right now, poppet. Just watch."

"He didn't talk to me like my Uncle Nick."

"Considering he was fucking you, I would hope not. One simply does not go around reminding one's lover of family. It's poor manners."

"Guard kept telling me I was a good boy for not giving him my number." Dilly watched as Vin shook out a whip. The long line snapped and doubled and then turned back into one whip as Dilly watched it. He squinted, trying to get his eyes to work right.

"So, did it not go well with you and Guard?" Miss Dolphinia kept stroking him.

"He talks a lot."

Miss Dolphinia laughed. "That he does. He likes to talk about his limits and his rules."

"I don't like to talk."

"That's just fine. Plenty of men don't. Despite what some of these Johnny-come-latelies think, one does not need to pre-negotiate every sexual act. I swear. I have watched gay men fight to throw off rules, and I have watched them invent new ones for themselves. Men are just about the most foolish creatures God ever did make. Now watch here."

Dilly forced his eyes open again, and Vin swung the whip overhead, and it came down with a sharp crack. A man cried out once and then went silent. Dilly's brain was struggling to figure out how all the pieces went together, but when the whip came around again, he followed it to the target. A man stood with his hands tied to the bar rail, his dark back showing pink lines carved into the flesh. Thousands of tiny pink and red lines looked like a thousand needles that had fallen so they lay crisscrossing against the floor, only each needle was a pink line in flesh.

The whip fell again, and a white line appeared in the flesh, longer than the others. The man arched his back, his muscles straining, and Dilly instinctively strained with him, leaning forward into the image, but a hand on his shoulder held him back. Dilly held his breath, waiting for the next hit. When it came, he could see every muscle strain as the man pulled against the restraints, his arm muscles cording and his spine curving so that his ass stuck out. Dilly squirmed as he watched that strong body struggle. Two more strikes, and two more lines of white that slowly faded to red. Finally the man cried out again, and then Vin was there next to him, running his hands over the man's back. Dilly could see Vin pinch the whipped back, and the man mewled. A similar sound slipped out of Dilly.

"Mmmm. Isn't that beautiful?"

Dilly nodded. The movement made all the pretty pictures turn into streaks that left Dilly blinking as he tried to refocus. Maybe Amy pills weren't so good after all, because he wanted to watch. Dilly reached down for his own hardening cock and cupped it.

"No. No touching," Miss Dolphinia said, and Dilly made a little whine of protest, but he rested his tied hands on his knee as he went back to watching Vin and his partner. Someone walked between them, and Dilly's stomach churned as the movement made the whole world wobble so badly that he nearly got seasick. It made him miss the next couple of hits. But his eyes came back into focus in time to watch Vin walk up behind his partner, pull his jeans down, and fuck him hard. Either Dilly could hear every grunt, or he was remembering the way Vin grunted when he'd used Dilly. One or the other. Either way, all Dilly could focus on was the rhythmic sound as Vin pounded into his partner over and over, no preparation, no discussion, just lots and lots of pounding into a man tied to a rail. Dilly whined and curled his fingers around the hem of Miss Dolphinia's dress.

She went back to stroking his hair, her voice a distant light that kept dancing just out of sight. He had the feeling she wasn't talking to him, so he ignored it and watched Vin. Vin finally finished and walked into the corner to throw something away, leaving the other man tied with his pants around his ankles and marked with a hundred lines. Dilly could still see the long marks, the ones that stood out against the mass of other marks. He wondered how long they would last.

Vin came back, and Dilly rested his cheek against Miss Dolphinia's knee and watched him slap the man on the ass before he walked over to a table. The idea that Vin left his partner still tied made Dilly squirm. He wanted that. He didn't want someone who carefully unbuckled the black leather and put it to one side.

"I don't want to hold all the cracks together myself," Dilly complained softly.

"Shhh. You're okay," Miss Dolphinia's voice came very close to his ear, and Dilly breathed in her perfume. It was smoky and smelled of roses and lilacs and reminded him of his grandmother.

Vin came back with a long rod and stood next to his partner for just a second before he brought the rod down hard on his bare ass. This time the man cried out and tried to kick. He nearly lost his balance as his own pants hobbled him, but Vin brought the rod down again, and now Vin moved so Dilly could see two vivid marks. The top one was turning red, and Dilly could see a trickle where a little blood wept from a corner of the hit. The bottom stripe was brilliant white against the man's dark skin, but it was pinking quickly even as Vin added a third hit. This time the man did lose his balance. He went to his knees, his hands still tied to the bar so they were pulled up over his head. Vin stood behind him, a hand on his head, and Dilly found himself panting.

Then Vin was untying him, helping him over to a table, and Dilly expected to see Vin tend the man, touch him softly and stroke his hair, and a cold knot of hatred was already forming in Dilly's throat. Instead, the man held out his hand and Vin took it, shaking hands and slapping his partner on the shoulder. Then the guy pulled up his pants and fastened them. He made some comment, and Vin laughed. He threw back his head and laughed and slapped the guy on the arm again, and yep, that was hate Dilly was feeling.

Vin looked around the room, his eyes settling on Miss Dolphinia before that sharp gaze flicked down toward Dilly. Holding his breath, Dilly waited for Vin to come over, but he turned his back and headed for the opposite side of the room.

"Oh that moron." Miss Dolphinia made an uncomplimentary clicking sound. "I swear. If I wasn't around to keep that man on the unstraight and unnarrow, I don't know what he'd do. Okay, up. Up." Dilly blinked and tried to get his feet under him as Miss Dolphinia stood up and tugged on his arm, but his limbs weren't all moving the same direction. The angle of the floor kept changing.

"Dilly, look at me. Right here. Come on, sweetie, focus for old Miss Dolphinia."

Dilly blinked and finally could focus on the long dark lashes and the blue eye shadow and the light brown eyes of Miss Dolphinia.

"Good boy. Now you liked to be tied up, don't you?"

Dilly smiled and nodded.

"Oh darling, don't smile at me like that, or I will give in to temptation, and you are not ready for the big leagues." Miss Dolphinia patted him on the cheek, but Dilly blinked, not sure what that meant. "Do you want someone to stuff that hole of yours full of nice fat cock?"

Dilly nodded again.

A new voice laughed. "The boy knows his mind." Dilly turned his head and recognized the voice that Miss Dolphinia had been talking to when Dilly had been watching Vin. He was a tall man that reminded Dilly of an old picture book and an illustration of Jack Sprat who could eat no fat, but Jack Sprat didn't have chains hanging from his nipples. Dilly squinted to try and see better and leaned closer.

"Now don't you go falling on your pretty little face." Miss Dolphinia pushed him back. "Bret, find me a couple of handkerchiefs, gray and dark blue."

"Don't you think he's a little stoned to play?"

"The boy knows what he wants."

"It's your hide if he sobers up and changes his mind."

"Bret, you were not in here for the last two nights. This one is going to sober up and ask for twice as much. Besides, unless I miss my guess, he's only going to get one of those two wishes tonight."

Bret looked across the room. "Vin?"

"This pretty little piece of tail is exactly what Vin needs."

"You are playing with fire."

"Now honey, what fun is it if you don't? Now go get me those handkerchiefs."

Bret snorted but got up and headed for the bar. Miss Dolphinia cupped Dilly's face in her hands. "Now, if someone else claims pretty little you, I'll keep an eye out, but don't you worry. That big old moron is going to pull his head out of his ass sooner or later." Dilly blinked, not even understanding a word of that.

"I think I'm getting sick. The floor's moving too much."

"If you get sick on me, you will not like what happens. Close your eyes and don't think about it."

Dilly closed his eyes, but not thinking about it was harder. He shifted his feet and tried to keep up with the dip and sway of the world, but without hands on his shoulders, it was so hard. He could feel little pieces of himself starting to slide off. His left shoulder. He was almost sure his left shoulder was starting to separate from his body, but Miss Dolphinia had told him to close his eyes. Something was pushed into the back pocket of his jeans, and the unexpected touch nearly sent Dilly falling on his face, but hands caught him. Dilly leaned into the touch, leaned into the feel of chains that pressed against his chest. The arms came around his whole body, and Dilly relaxed into the hold, happy that his arm hadn't had a chance to fall off.

"Tell me he isn't perfect for Vin."

"I'm more worried about whether Vin is right for him."

"Sweetie, I am never wrong when I play matchmaker." Dilly let the words wash over him, happy that he didn't have to do anything with them. No one wanted anything from him. Well, hopefully they wanted his ass, but he was pretty happy to give them that.

"Zach and Devon."

"Fine. I'm almost never wrong."

"Sunny and that kid with the blue hair?"

"They would have made a great couple."

"They almost killed each other."

"That is what true love looks like. It's messy. It's all about passions and screaming fights and making up against every vertical surface in the house. Nothing satisfies the urge more than some hard fucking against a wall. Here we go. Lean against this, sweetie." Hands urged Dilly up onto something and then bent him over. A cold bar pressed against his hip bones, and Dilly pulled his hands under his head and rested it. Rope passed right under his ass cheeks and then pulled tight, pressing him up against the bar, and Dilly hummed. His feet couldn't go flying off now.

Relaxing into the feel of rope against his skin, Dilly let his muscles go limp. "Should have taken the pants off," Dilly muttered. He couldn't feel the rope as well as he wanted.

"Subtlety is definitely not your strong suit." Miss Dolphinia patted him on the back, and then in a swish of fabric she was gone, her heels clicking over the floor. Dilly felt a little of his happiness fade at the idea of being alone. He didn't want to be alone. But before he could call out for Miss Dolphinia to come back and get him, hands were running up under his shirt. Warm and calloused hands that held him down nicely. Dilly relaxed as those hands promised to keep him from falling apart.

"Only flagging gray? So, are you new, or did you show up on the wrong night? Tonight's when the real men come out to play, little boy."

"He's new." Dilly opened his eyes at Vin's words. "He's also mine."

"I don't see your name." The man was standing behind Dilly, so Dilly couldn't see him, but Vin looked furious. "You've had your bit of ass tonight. If you want to play with another boy, there are lots of others. This one is taken."

"Vin," Dilly said, his voice sounding blurred, even to his own ears. "I bet the moon wouldn't squish you, either. It keeps trying to fall on all my cracks."

"Fuck."

"Okay," Dilly agreed.

"Back off," Vin said, pointing a finger at the guy behind Dilly. The hands vanished, and Dilly mewled his distress.

"You don't run this place, Hauser. You can go fuck yourself."

"Now, now, boys. The only fucking allowed in here is the fun kind. What trouble are you getting into?"

"Hauser thinks he owns the fucking world."

Vin narrowed his eyes. "I think that Dylan came here for me, and I don't think you have a right to put your hands on him without permission."

"Oh, that's funny coming from you." The new man stepped forward, but all Dilly could see was a black jacket with chains.

"Now boys, one more word, and both of you are out, and I'll confiscate Dylan here for myself." A hand patted Dilly's ass, and he tried to stand up, even if it would be awkward being tied to the bar and all. Vin reached out and pushed him back down. "I don't see a problem," Miss Dolphinia said. "The boy has two holes. Between you, you have two dicks. Unless someone has changed the rules of math, two does seem to equal two. Share and share alike, boys."

"You're the one who put the handkerchiefs in there." Vin's jaw bulged, and Dilly tried to reach up to touch it, but his hands were tied. *When did that happen?*

"He came underdressed. But trust me, that is what he wants, a lot of bondage and fucking. If I were picking for him, I would have slipped him a black flag and chained him to my bed. Isn't that right, Dilly?" She patted him on the back, and Dilly blinked, not understanding the conversation.

"I'm not sharing," Vin said, his voice tight with emotion.

"You are just trying to be difficult," Miss Dolphinia said with a little huff. "Dylan, are you with Vin or Tom or both?" Miss Dolphinia asked.

"Mmmm. Vin," Dilly said. He remembered the slap of flesh against flesh and the hands holding him down, the ropes keeping him from flying apart.

"Well, that's solved." Heels clicked across the floor, leaving them, and then the other man left after a few muttered curses.

Vin leaned close, and Dilly watched him, the edges of the world still streaking out into the black. "I don't like getting manipulated, Dylan. You're going to pay for backing me into a corner."

"Okay," Dilly agreed. People should pay their way. "Gary never pays. It's annoying," he muttered. He didn't want to be like Gary. Sometimes he worried about them sharing the same DNA. What if there was something cruel and monstrous in him? Maybe that's why the moon kept trying to smash him.

Vin sighed. "But first, I think we need to let you sober up. Anything I say right now is going to get lost in this trip you're on. Come on." Vin pulled and the rope holding Dilly to the bar vanished. Dilly threw his hands up to keep himself from hitting the ceiling in case he lost gravity again, but Vin grabbed his wrists and pulled them back down. "You are not a happy pot head."

"Pills. Amy pills," Dilly said.

Vin gave him a strange look before heading for the back door, still holding Dilly's wrists.

"You kids have fun," Miss Dolphinia called after them, laughing with that lilting voice of hers.

"Fuck off," Vin offered, but then they were outside. Dilly figured they were going somewhere.

Chapter 9

DILLY groaned as the light burned his eyes. He tried to roll over, to grab his pillow and stuff it over his face, but the sounds of chains and the feel of something tight against his wrists and ankles made him open his eyes. He was in a strange room, a strange bed. Strange unknown and strange odd. It had metal rails all around, and Dilly carefully tugged only to find that he was chained down hand and foot. Squirming around, Dilly struggled to sit up, and the light blanket that had covered him pooled on his lap.

The room had one window up high and on an angle, so he was on a top floor, an attic space of some sort. There was hardwood floor, and the walls were painted soft beige, so it definitely didn't feel like a dungeon, but there were heavy iron rings set in the walls on either side of a heavy double door, and a speaker set in the wall. And the whole room wasn't much bigger than the narrow twin bed Dilly was currently chained to. *What the hell happened?*

"Hello?" Dilly called out.

"I hear you. I'm in the shower, so just settle back down, and I'll be in to get you in a second," the voice answered. Vin. That was Vin. So he had ended up in Vin's house. Dilly let himself flop back down onto the bed since, with his hands chained, he couldn't do much else. Now that the blanket was around his waist, Dilly regretted sitting up. His chest was chilly. And that would be because he was naked. But his ass didn't feel sore. After the first time with Vin, his ass had definitely been sore.

Dilly sorted through memories. After his shift, Amy had told him he needed a break and pressed a couple of pills into his hand. And he was idiot enough to take them. In his own defense, Carmine's stunt had made it a brilliantly bad day. What the hell was she even thinking? Not only did Dilly not deserve that shit, but Evie Princeton deserved better than having to ask her rapist's brother for a favor. A favor Dilly refused to do. Guilt showed up to gnaw on his guts for a while.

"I need to pee," Dilly called out.

"Hold it or pee on yourself. That's not an emergency," Vin answered through the speaker. Dilly could still hear the sounds of the water running behind him. Sighing, Dilly squirmed so he could use the sheet under him to scratch an itch on his shoulder. So Vin was keeping an ear on him, but he wasn't in any hurry to untie him. Dilly remembered something about the moon trying to fall on him. Whatever the hell was in those pills, he would never take them again. For a forty-year-old lady, Amy knew how to party.

Dilly opened his mouth to call out that he needed to call home, but he closed it again. That definitely wouldn't qualify as an emergency. Instead, he started methodically pulling against the chains that held him. He was trapped. His legs had some play in them, and he tried yanking hard enough to break the bar, but no matter how hard he pulled, the bar held. Dilly could feel his cock start to harden under the blanket, and he couldn't even reach it.

Shifting his ass to the side, he tried angling his body so he could use one hand to grab his cock, but the heavy doors slid open. They were pocket doors that disappeared into the wall so Dilly's little nook now became part of a larger bedroom. Dark burgundy covers lay on a four-poster bed, and Dilly's cock hardened more at the thought of being tied to those heavy posts. Had it happened? Had he forgotten Vin tying him down to that bed? Dilly had a memory of the bedspread's gold thread under his arm, itchy where he'd landed on the covers. But then Vin had pulled him up.

"Stop." Vin was fully dressed in black jeans and a dress shirt, and he crossed his arms as he looked down at Dilly. Dilly rolled onto his back, abandoning his efforts to jack off, even though he was harder than ever. "Good boy." Vin grabbed a chair and set it in the middle of the large opening. Then he sat. Dilly blinked up, not sure what he was supposed to do. Well, actually, given Vin had chained him to a bed, he was guessing he should just lie still.

"What do you remember about last night?"

Dilly frowned. "A friend gave me a couple of pills after the worst day in history, and I remember heading for the Stonewall." Dilly stopped. Had he grabbed some guy on the street? He could feel his face start to warm up.

"What else?"

"Um. Miss Dolphinia was there and you whipped someone." Dilly remembered the lines against the man's back, and the hot jealousy he'd felt at each strike. Had Vin then fucked the guy he'd whipped or had he fucked Dilly? Reality was a little fuzzy.

"Do you remember me warning you that you were going to pay for backing me into a corner?" Vin crossed his arms over his chest, and Dilly felt the first wisps of fear. Maybe he should have felt fear waking up chained to a bed, but he never had been the brightest.

"Backing you into a corner?" Dilly tried to keep his voice even. He had a feeling Vin was not a man he wanted to piss off.

"You came to the Stonewall stoned."

Dilly smiled, verging on pointing out the humor in the whole Stonewall/stoned thing, but the comment died when he looked at Vin's face.

"That bitch would have let any top in that place fuck you. She knew I wouldn't let her get away with that, and you played into her hand."

"Um. I'm sorry?" Dilly shifted uncomfortably, but his usual reaction when uncomfortable was running away, and that wasn't happening here. He curled his fist around the short chain that tethered his wrist to the bed.

"I'm not going to get cornered into a situation I don't understand, Dylan, and I have to say, I don't understand you. You act like you're new to the game, but you come back three nights in a row? You get me to fuck you and then Galvin, and then apparently some Carmine that you said screwed you over. Three guys in two days is not a newbie."

"Carmine is my sister," Dilly said, making a face at the thought of Carmine and sex. Hell, Dilly even felt sorry for Frank because handling his sister was not an easy job.

Vin leaned back. "So, you were going for three guys in three days instead of trying to nail your fourth. I do not like to be manipulated. I do not find men who top from the bottom cute. I am not into mouthy subs. I do not like worn-out old queens trying to decide what I should do with my life, so it's time for some of those consequences I mentioned. You're paying for backing me into a corner, Dylan."

Dilly's heart started pounding faster, and still his stupid cock got harder.

"You're going to tell me everything. You're going to tell me what your relationship is with Dolphinia; you're going to tell me why you came to the Stonewall; you're going to tell me every fact about yourself down to how you like your eggs in the morning."

Dilly swallowed. "Maybe you just want to spank me instead?"

Vin stood up. "If you're honest, you might earn a spanking, but until I get some honesty out of you, I'm going to assume that you're one of Dolphinia's whores, and you can consider yourself on the job. And as a whore, you'll do what you're told."

"Miss Dolphinia has whores?" Dilly squirmed up onto one elbow. "Really?" He had never known anyone who did something like that.

Vin frowned and took a step closer. "That's the rumor. Are you actually this innocent or are you this good of an actor?"

"Innocent. I suck at acting. I once lost a job as a tree because I couldn't do it convincingly. I was eight at the time, but still. It's not like it takes mad skills to be a tree, and I couldn't manage that." Dilly offered a smile, but Vin wasn't melting at all. With a sigh, Dilly gave up on charm and went with honesty. "I really don't actually want to pee myself. Could you let me use the bathroom, please? I promise to be good and let you bring me right back, Scout's honor."

"Of course you were a Scout." Vin turned his back and walked away.

"Well, yeah. Most kids are," Dilly called after him. "Vin?" It was strange being left chained to a bed.

Vin reappeared with a curved plastic bottle in hand. Dilly didn't know what he was doing until he swept back the blanket and put the end of Dilly's cock near the mouth. "Okay, pee."

"Oh boy. This is not helping with the peeing," Dilly pointed out. His cock definitely didn't want to do this.

After a second, Vin stood up. "Let's say I believe you. Let's say that Dolphinia has found a way to manipulate both of us into this."

Dilly nodded. "Okay, I can say that." Dilly didn't mind it as much as Vin did, but he could see where Miss Dolphinia did some manipulating. Dilly tried to bring his leg up to cover his now-exposed cock, but of course he didn't have enough chain to do that. And of course the feel of the leather against his ankle, trapping him, just made his cock harder.

"Then you have two choices. I unlock you, and you go to the bathroom, leave my house, and stay the fuck away from me. You don't give me those tragic eyes in the club, you don't stare at me while I am with other men, and you don't seek me out. Ever."

Dilly swallowed. He didn't like that choice.

"Or you submit. You pee into this bottle because I'm ordering you to. You tell me what you're doing, what you're thinking, and what you're planning. And you stop letting Dolphinia turn you into a fucking guided missile pointed straight at me. Clear?"

Dilly nodded. He strained against the chains as every instinct told him to curl up into a ball and vanish, but the chains kept him visible. They pinned him like a bug where Vin could dissect him, and he couldn't just disappear, so he nodded.

"Are you going to pee into this?" Vin held up the bottle.

Dilly nodded again.

Bending over, Vin held the bottle and Dilly's cock. Muttering the names of all the rivers he could think of, Dilly focused on imagining running water. Eventually it worked, and the smell of urine rose as he peed into a bottle. Vin shook his cock a little and then stood, the dark yellow urine in his plastic bottle. "Good boy. Now, while I dump this, you think about how you're starting this story."

Vin walked away, and Dilly was naked and exposed and chained to a bed, and getting harder with every passing second. Guard would call him an idiot, and oddly, that made him even harder. The leather held him down, made him real in a way he hadn't been for too long. Dilly wanted to grab his cock and jerk off. He had enough slack in the chains that he could probably wiggle sideways and do it, but hiding the evidence posed a problem, and Dilly didn't think Vin would be amused. So instead he stared at Vin's bed and tried hard to not think about how much he wanted sex. He was turning into a slut. Luckily he had tonight off work, because as soon as Vin did let him up, Dilly was either asking to get fucked or jerking off until his cock fell off. Either worked.

Vin came back and settled into the chair. "Okay, talk."

Dilly squirmed around, the chains clinking against the metal rails as he did. "You've done this a lot," Dilly said as he looked around at the room.

"Yep," Vin agreed.

"Guard says you're dangerous." Dilly had no idea why he'd started there, but it had slipped out. Talking about Guard was better than talking about Gary, particularly when chained to a man's bed. Actually, he wasn't chained to Vin's bed. He was chained to a bed in Vin's closet.

Vin made a face. "I say Guard's an idiot."

"He is. Well, he's nice and all, but he talks until the sex isn't quite...." Dilly gestured awkwardly with one hand, the chains clinking again.

Looking almost amused, Vin leaned back in his chair. "I would pay money to see you say that to his face. He's a pompous bastard who thinks that anyone whose kinks offend his sense of righteousness is doing it wrong."

"Oh." Dilly shifted again. He wondered if this was where Vin had held the boy he'd been accused of kidnapping. It was a pretty comfortable place to get held captive. Maybe that was why the police went easy on him. Gary never talked about it, but from the rumors Dilly had heard, the girls hadn't had it so easy. The last girl... supposedly there were pictures and she had all these marks. But the guy in the

Stonewall was marked up. Dilly could feel confusion wrapping around his brain. He didn't want to figure this out.

"Are you going to tell me the story? If you don't, I'm going down to my computer, and I'm digging out every fact I can about your life. Computers are my life, so don't think I can't trace you. There's a lot of information out there for someone who knows where to look."

Dilly didn't want to waste Vin's time, but he didn't know how to talk about any of this. Maybe the computer would be best. Dilly knew exactly how much stuff he'd find. "Gary Carter," Dilly whispered.

"Is that your real name?"

"What, no." Dilly jerked hard enough that the chains all rattled. "No. That's my brother."

"And he's related to all this?"

Dilly sighed. He didn't want to talk about this. "He's why I came to the Stonewall," he admitted.

Vin nodded and stood up. He moved to the side of the bed, and Dilly felt a flash of fear that Vin was going to unlock the chains and throw him out. However, Vin pulled the blanket loose, settled it over Dilly, and smoothed it out. He took particular time smoothing it over Dilly's hard cock, and Dilly moaned with need. He would have agreed to anything, but Vin moved to the skylight and closed some sort of blinds inside the glass so only thin bars of light came through. Then Vin took the chair and moved it back out into the main room before taking something off a table or dresser Dilly couldn't see. "This lets me listen, so if you have something to say or if you need me, I'll be on the other end." He held up a walkie-talkie type thing and then pointed at the speaker.

Dilly nodded. His mouth went dry at the idea that Vin was leaving him, but if Vin stayed, he'd want answers, and Dilly couldn't do that. Looking down at him, Vin waited for long minutes, but Dilly just stared up. Eventually, Vin stepped back and pulled the doors closed. A heavy snick told Dilly that Vin had locked him in. There wasn't any lock on this side, so even if Dilly could get out of the cuffs, he had no chance of getting out of the small room. Since he was truly trapped, Dilly closed his eyes and waited.

People he'd known for years had stopped talking to him after Gary got arrested. His father was pretty much going broke, and they got so much hate mail that his mother refused to open the mailbox. She had finally taken to having Carmine pay the bills online, a process she had always called dangerous because sending money though the computer wires was idiotic. Computer wires. Dilly loved his mother, but he questioned her logic on a regular basis. Then again, maybe he should question his own. Chained to the bed of a man he barely knew, he was still more afraid of his family than the near-stranger who, right now, held all the power over him. Panic started forming a bubble in his chest that grew and rose and pressed against his heart and lungs.

"Vin?" Dilly called.

"Yeah?" The voice sounded tinny coming through the speaker.

The panic bubble popped, and Dilly closed his eyes, weary and confused. He didn't know what to say.

"Do you need to be cut free?"

"No," Dilly admitted slowly. He didn't know what he needed, but getting free wasn't it.

"Then hang in there, Dylan. I'm reading right now."

Dilly closed his eyes. Vin was reading. Great. The room went silent.

Dilly was used to city noises. Sometimes when it was foggy, you could hear the ship horns, the low rumble travelling over the water and up into the city. He could normally hear the traffic and sometimes their neighbors fighting over some bill that had shown up. He would lie in bed and listen to a hundred thousand people, but now the silence pressed close. He had to either be up high enough to be away from the traffic, or the room was soundproofed.

Dilly shifted uncomfortably. It would be so easy for Vin to keep him here. Vin was larger and he obviously knew how to keep someone locked up. And part of Dilly wanted that so much that it scared him. He didn't want to look Carmine in the eye and ask her why she'd set him up. He didn't want to watch his mother's face when she realized Gary was going to prison, or worse, he didn't want to see the cold triumph on Gary's face if the jury found him not guilty. He never wanted to see Evie Princeton's face again, even if none of this was her fault. He didn't want any of it, and this little room felt so safe. It frightened him how safe it felt.

"Did he do it?" Vin asked over the speaker.

Dilly didn't bother pretending he didn't understand the question. "Probably," he admitted, not seeing a good reason to lie. He was too tired to lie.

"Why did you come to the Stonewall, Dylan?"

"Isn't it obvious?" Dilly laughed. Maybe it wasn't. Maybe he was an idiot for thinking he could find answers about a straight rapist in a gay bar.

"Why did you come to the Stonewall, Dylan?" Vin's voice was slower, but the tone didn't allow for another distraction.

Dilly closed his eyes. "I wanted to know why people do it... why they tie each other up. I wanted to know why I felt so obsessed with the news pictures of the bondage tools on the bed. I wanted to feel the leather." Dilly stopped and chewed his lip. It sounded so pathetic when he said it out loud. He tried to pull his legs up and felt the leather grow tight against his ankles, trapping him.

"Did you want to be hurt?"

"Yes," Dilly said, the word escaping in a breathy gasp.

The speaker went silent, and Dilly was left alone in the stillness. He did want to be hurt. He wanted to know what it felt like. It was his brother who had hurt those women. His DNA. Dilly frowned as he suddenly understood his father's expression when he would come home late and find Gary in the living room. His father wanted to be hurt. His father felt guilty. Dilly felt the tingling in his nose that meant tears were going to follow, but he couldn't do anything, not while chained to a bed.

"What did Carmine do yesterday?" Vin's question surprised Dilly, but it shouldn't. Dilly had said something about Carmine—he just couldn't remember what he'd said. His father always said that if you told the truth, you didn't have to keep track of the lies. Dilly was too tired to keep track of anything.

"One of the rape victims came to my restaurant and asked me to testify, to say that Gary had hurt me."

"Did he?"

Dilly thought about the time Gary had locked him in that closet. He'd been scared. He'd put his back to the wall and kicked as hard as he could, but their house was old, and the wood was solid. He couldn't get out. He'd screamed himself hoarse and peed himself before Gary had opened the door. He'd laughed and laughed and laughed.

And Carmine had been there in the doorway to the hall, clutching a doll and watching with big eyes. It'd been the first time Gary had babysat them. Gary had been twelve or thirteen, and Dilly must have been seven, with Carmine right between them in ages. She'd been too old for dolls by then, but Dilly remembered her clutching her favorite.

"He never left a mark, but yeah," Dilly admitted.

"The lawyers wouldn't let that in unless it was the sentencing phase. Why did Carmine send this woman now?"

"I don't know," Dilly admitted.

"You didn't ask her?"

Dilly snorted. "Hell, no."

"And you're not going to ask her." Vin didn't know Dilly, but he sounded sure. Worse, he was right. Dilly wanted to forget that the whole incident ever happened, and thanks to Amy's drugs, it was a little fuzzy around the edges.

"Dylan, I'm going to make a call, and I need you to stay silent and just listen. Can you do that?"

"Yes." Dilly was so tired that talking required more work than staying silent.

"Even if I'm calling your sister?"

"Carmine?" Dilly's voice broke. And that was the panic showing up right on schedule. His heart pounded painfully fast. Vin and Carmine. No, no, that was not happening. Dilly struggled against the restraints, but they held him tight. He simply made the blanket shift around some and the leather pull tight against his skin. He could feel the sweat gather on his wrists and ankles, but he was trapped. Helpless. He couldn't do anything, and Dilly could feel some strange emotion threaten to swallow him, a silence, a stillness that forced him to admit he couldn't do anything, so it was okay to do nothing. His breathing slowed and he sagged back onto the pillow. Only then did Vin speak.

"She's left a lot of text messages here. One of us needs to call her, and after what happened at work, one of us needs to confront her about that." Vin sounded so logical, so sure, but Dilly didn't want Carmine hurt.

"But...."

"Let me make this clear, Dylan. One of us is going to talk to Carmine before I unchain you."

Dilly's racing heart was still slowing from the earlier panic, and Dilly closed his eyes. "Well, then we're definitely talking about you because I'm not talking to my sister while naked and chained to a man's bed."

Again, Vin fell silent for some time before he answered through that speaker. Dilly wondered how far away he was. He felt like it mattered if Vin was in the next room or on the next floor or on the next street. It mattered, but Dilly couldn't do anything because Vin had chained him to a bed. Vin's voice had that slow, calm tone when it came back. "Then you need to stay quiet and let me handle this. Okay?"

Dilly thought about that, but there wasn't much to consider. Part of him desperately didn't want to hurt Carmine, but a larger part felt relieved that someone else would get in there and do the hurting for him, because she'd treated him kinda shitty. "Okay," Dilly agreed softly.

Dilly heard the phone numbers and the distant ringing. His phone didn't have the best speaker, but he could hear what was going on.

"Dilly? Where the hell have you been?" Carmine's voice came through the speaker brassy and loud, and Dilly felt his guts tangle up like a fishing line that someone dumped in the bottom of the box. All his emotions were caught in the threads, and he didn't know how to pull them out.

"Actually, this is Vin, a friend of Dylan's. I didn't want you to worry, so I thought I'd return your call and let you know he's sleeping it off at my place."

"Sleeping it off?" Carmine's voice turned wary. "Sleeping what off?"

"That I don't know. He took some pills that someone offered him, and the moon kept trying to crush him. It wasn't pretty. But after the day he had yesterday, I can't say I blame him for looking for something to take the edge off."

"What? What happened? Is he okay? Did Gary do something, because he's asleep in the next room, and I'm totally okay with strangling him in his sleep."

"It's what you did that hurt him."

"What? Me? Okay, I don't know who the fuck you are, but let me tell you something—"

"Evie Princeton," Vin said loud enough to cut her off. Carmine went silent for a long time.

"What did you say?" She sounded cautious now.

"Evie Princeton. You know, the woman who is under the impression that Dylan will testify for her against his brother. The woman who confronted him at work and made him feel like shit, so much so that he took the first drug that someone offered him just to get away from the pain. That Evie Princeton. I don't suppose you know anything about where she would get the idea that you would testify for her or that Dylan would."

"Oh God." Carmine's voice went flat. "Oh fucking hell."

"I don't think God set that one up. Having her ambush your brother at work, that was a nice touch, lady."

Dilly cringed from the tone. Carmine never would have done it if she'd understood how much it would hurt him. She didn't need to have someone get that sarcastic, but his promise to Vin kept him from saying anything.

"Hey, I told her to let me handle it. I said that when the time was right, I'd talk to Dilly. I'd get him to testify when it got to the sentencing phase. But we aren't even there yet. I mean, what he did to Dilly doesn't prove Gary's a rapist, but when it comes time to decide how long to put him in prison, the fact he's a sadist could make a difference. And you have no idea what sorts of things Gary did to Dilly."

"Dylan."

"What?"

"Your brother's not some little boy. His name is Dylan. And if he wants to testify when it comes time for sentencing, that's his choice. And if he chooses to stay out of it, that's his choice too. You don't go making promises to people about what Dylan will do."

There was an awkward pause, and Dilly could almost imagine Carmine gathering up all her arguments for the counterattack. "Exactly what sort of friend are you, Vin? I have to say, I've never heard your name around the house." Dilly closed his eyes. Yep, Carmine's dirty little brain had jumped right to fuck buddy, and it wasn't all that far off the mark. Dilly foresaw a lot of teasing in his future.

"And I bet you're not going to hear it now, either. But if you pull a stunt like that again, you're not going to like how I react to it."

"Fuck you. Dilly's my brother."

"Exactly. Dylan's your brother, not your toy. You can't go promising him to these women."

"I didn't." Carmine nearly bellowed the words, and Dilly seriously hoped she wasn't in the house, because that would bring their mom running. "I told her that I would get him to testify and to leave it alone."

"So you held out hope to a rape victim, you told her that there would be this man who would believe her and help her, and then you told her she had to wait? That's sweet. Because telling a rape victim they have no power to control things and that you needed to handle everything—that's not cruel and thoughtless at all. I don't know who to feel worse for, this Evie or Dylan. But considering that I had to deal with a stoned Dylan who kept flailing in terror over imagined attacks, I think I'll feel sorry for Dylan."

"Terror? Dilly?"

"You know, I'm liking you less and less by the second. Stop being an idiot before you damage something that can't be fixed." Dilly heard the disconnect tone and then nothing. *Well, crap.* That went...

that went about the way he expected actually, but that didn't mean that Carmine wasn't going to be seriously put out. Carmine in a bad mood was a little like a hurricane having a bad day.

"So," Vin said, "you can either lie to your sister and apologize for me, or you can go with honesty. That's your choice. But if you don't tell people you're hurt, they're not going to stop hurting you."

Dilly snorted. "Yeah, or they're going to hurt you twice as much."

There was silence for some time before Vin answered. "Is Carmine the sort to do that… hurt you more if she knows your vulnerable spots?"

"What?" Dilly snorted. "No. I like Carmine. She's the sane sibling."

"So, then you're talking about Gary."

Dilly started when the door to his little closet-room opened because he hadn't realized Vin was so close.

Vin stood with his hands on either side of the pocket doors and the light behind him so that he became a shadow figure, an outline with wide shoulders and a trim waist. "So, is it Gary that hurts you more when he finds your soft spot?"

Dilly sighed and fingered the cover that Vin had thrown over him. This was weird. Talking about this at all was weird, but talking about it while chained to a guy's bed reached a whole new level of totally fucking off the charts weird that Dilly had never before achieved. "Yeah. That's why I figure he did it. If they looked… you know…."

"Vulnerable," Vin provided.

Dilly nodded. "Yeah. Like if Gary saw me like this"—Dilly pulled at the chains—"there would be pictures and humiliation involved."

Vin nodded and stepped into the small room. Now the light caught the side of his face. He was a handsome man with dark hair and eyes, but he looked tired. Dilly wondered if he had kept Vin up.

"He's not like you," Dilly said, and it was true. Vin might have chained him to a bed, but he hadn't terrorized Dilly. Actually, he'd been nicer than most of Dilly's lovers, with the exception of Guard, who took nice a little too far. Dilly didn't want a lover that nice.

Vin stepped into the room and pushed the blanket back so he could stroke up and down Dilly's arm. "You don't know much about me, Dylan." His voice grew low and soft as he sat on the edge of the bed, his leg hiked up over the metal rail.

"I know you were accused of hurting someone. I know you wouldn't actually do anything you thought was hurting them." Dilly thought about Carmine. "Although sometimes we hurt people because we just don't know any better."

"You're making assumptions," Vin warned, but his voice still had that soft tone, that invitation that Dilly so wanted to take. Vin's warm fingers trailed up Dilly's arm to the elbow, tickling the skin before they moved down to the black cuff buckled around his wrist and the silver chain locked to the bedrails.

"I assume you're a good guy. I assume Gary isn't. I assume from what I heard that Carmine only accidentally emotionally gutted me."

Vin rolled his eyes. "Your sister is an idiot."

"So am I sometimes. It runs in the family." Dilly didn't mention that their mother was the biggest idiot of all.

Vin pulled his hand away and straightened his back. "Do you want to know the truth?"

Dilly nodded.

"Fine. I chained Chase to this bed." Vin gestured at the bed, at the room. "He begged me to let him go, and I told him that until he got clean, he wasn't going anywhere. Twice a day I made him turn over so he wouldn't get sores, but I would force him back down onto the bed as he screamed. I told him to scream. I'm sure you've figured out this place is soundproofed." Vin's eyes narrowed, and Dilly could feel a cold shiver as the hard expression on Vin's face trapped him in that moment far more than the chains on his wrists and ankles.

"Every two or three days, I would get the chains and cuff his hands behind his back and force him into a shower so I could clean him, and he'd fight. But I was bigger than him. Just like I'm bigger than you, Dylan." Vin ran his hand up Dilly's arm and pressed on his shoulder, pinning him down onto the bed. Vin was definitely stronger. "Only one day he fought so hard that he slipped on the wet tile and fell on his knee. He split it open, and he had to go to the emergency room, so I uncuffed him and put him in some sweats and put him in the car as he cried and held a towel over his knee. I warned him not to talk to anyone, but the first person who came in, well, I'm sure you can figure out the rest of the story." Vin turned so Dilly only saw his back.

"He told them."

"Yeah." Vin sounded bitter, but Dilly couldn't blame him. "So within an hour, I was in cuffs and the police were all over this house. They found the chains, this room, the blood. Miss Dolphinia had to bail me out. Do you hear what I'm saying, Dylan?"

"Yeah. I hear."

Vin turned and nailed him with a hard look. "Really? Do you hear what I'm telling you?"

"You were trying to save him from drugs, weren't you?" At least that was what Dilly thought Vin was saying.

From the narrowing of Vin's glare, that was not what he'd been going for. "I held him captive. Hell. I don't know why they didn't charge me. So if you're looking for some sort of answers, I'm not the person to give them. I'm dangerous, Dylan." Vin leaned over Dilly, his large hand in the middle of Dilly's chest holding him down, and Dilly's cock clearly liked Vin's sort of danger. "You're a fool for not seeing that, but it's Miss Dolphinia who's playing with fire because she keeps trying to get me to fall in love again. But I don't do love, Dylan. I do obsession. I get possessive." Vin ran his hand up over Dilly's chest until his fingers rested against Dilly's neck, then encircled it so when Dilly swallowed, he was so very aware of that slight pressure on such a vulnerable spot.

Vin leaned close, his voice a rough whisper. "You don't want to get that close to me, but Miss Dolphinia is going to keep pointing you at me because she thinks I should have another grand romance, another chance to get just as obsessed as I was with Chase." Vin licked up the side of Dilly's neck and then nipped at his ear. Dilly shivered so hard the chains rattled. "But that's like trying to get close enough to touch fire without getting burnt. So now do you understand?"

"Because you did that to Chase, you can't have sex with me?" Dilly guessed, but he really wasn't sure of anything except that his skin was fever hot and his prick ached deliciously.

"No. No, you can't be anywhere near me because I don't want to let you go, Dylan." Vin tightened his fingers just a little. "If I let you out of this room, you're going to have to deal with your idiot sister and your sadistic bastard of a brother. If I let you out of here, you're going to be right back to floundering, and sooner or later you're going to discover that your brother is not the only Dom out there to confuse stretching limits with breaking them."

Vin laughed. "Well, you're going to discover another one, because trust me, I don't always know where that line is myself. Right now, there's nothing I want more than to lock that door and keep you here." As he whispered into Dilly's ear, Vin's breath warmed Dilly's skin. "I have the chains already. I could keep you locked in here, and none of them would ever hurt you again. Of course, I'd be hurting you, but I guess in my head that doesn't count."

Then Vin let go and stood up. "Miss Dolphinia is using you to prick me. But if this goes wrong, you'll be the one in the middle. So you think about that, and I'll be back to let you out of those chains when I feel like it. Maybe you need a little time to think about what it means to attract the attention of someone who is a little too obsessive."

Stepping backward, Vin cleared the closet and pulled the doors closed. The lock thunked particularly loudly, and Dilly was alone. Thinking. Dilly hated thinking. He pulled against the chains and realized he didn't have a whole lot of choice, though, because he wasn't going to be doing anything else until Vin allowed it. And worse, Dilly wanted to have sex with Vin more than ever. *Well, crap.*

Chapter 10

"WELL, well, look who finally slept at home last night," Gary snickered as he looked up from his laptop. He perched on the edge of the kitchen table with a mostly empty plate in front of him.

"Don't tease your brother," their mom said in the same rote tone of voice that Dilly had been hearing his entire life. Don't tease your brother, don't tease your sister, don't be mean to the nice dog. And yesterday, Dilly would have been emotionally right there with his mother saying the same things over and over because what else did you do with people who clearly weren't listening? This morning, as Dilly pulled the milk out of the refrigerator, he wondered how Vin would handle Gary. He doubted Vin would spend twenty-five years saying the same thing over and over and over.

"Dill Weed can handle a little teasing, Mom. Geez. Don't emasculate the guy."

"Mom's not," Dilly said. Okay, that was stupid. Arguing with Gary just made the uncomfortable get more uncomfortablish.

Sure enough, Gary declared in a nasty tone, "You are such a momma's boy."

"Garrett Alan Carter!" Their mother's voice snapped out like a whip that made Dilly flinch, but Gary took it in stride. He even rolled his eyes.

"Hey! I am just speaking the truth. And personally, I'm not teasing him. I'm congratulating him on finally staying out all night and coming home with that stupidly satisfied look on his face. If I was teasing him, I would ask whether this new girl requires her own zip code." Gary leaned back and considered Dilly with this extra serious expression. "I mean seriously, you dated the fattest women in high school."

"Hey!" Dilly slammed the refrigerator door closed a little too hard.

"Jack Sprat could eat no fat, and all his girlfriends...." Gary blew out his cheeks and held his hands out to imitate the world's largest woman.

"Jennifer was a very nice girl," his mom said, angrily. She actually turned her back on breakfast and poked a spatula in Gary's direction.

Gary blew out his breath. "Jennifer is in training to make some man very, very miserable, and I don't want that for our Dilly Billy. Besides, if I had to look at Jennifer DiMagdalino over the Thanksgiving dinner table, I would lose my appetite and miss out on all your very fine cooking." Gary finished by giving their mother one of his charming smiles. At least, Dilly assumed that was supposed to be charming. He found it unctuous. That wasn't normally one of his words, but after Carmine had called Gary unctuous about a hundred times, Dilly had actually looked it up. He had to admit it fit.

"People don't always appreciate that sense of humor," their mom said as she turned back to the eggs. Immediately she pulled the pan off the heat and started muttering in Italian.

Personally, Dilly would say that pretty much no one appreciated Gary's sense of humor. Most days, even their mother only put up with it. And when you had a personality that even a mother could only endure, that was so not a good thing.

"Morning, Mom. Morning, Dylan." Carmine stopped and went up on her toes to brush her dry lips across Dilly's cheek in a sister-kiss. Then she looked right at Gary and refused to say anything. He just went back to his laptop.

Mom just sighed. "Good morning, Carmine. I made eggs," she said when it became painfully clear that Carmine was going to keep ignoring Gary.

"Thanks, Mom. You're the best." Carmine went over to give her a kiss and claim a plate of eggs.

Maybe it was the recent stress, but Dilly's brain finally caught up and registered that Carmine had called him Dylan. Carmine never called him Dylan. The power of Vin was an impressive thing to behold.

"A bunch of the girls are going for a late night study session for next week's tests, so I'll be home late," Carmine announced. She shoved food in her mouth before her butt even hit the chair. The fried eggs looked a little curled around the edges, and it went to show how stressed everyone was that their mom had even let them touch the plate. Alicia Carter did not overcook eggs. Ever.

Mom opened her mouth and then closed it again, and Dilly could almost read her mind. She hadn't said a word about Dilly being out all night, but she was getting more and more twitchy about the amount of time Carmine was spending with Frank. Of course, last time she'd said anything, Carmine had gone into full feminist meltdown and bemoaned everything from equal pay to double standards in sexual freedoms. Personally, Dilly had agreed with every word Carmine said, but their mother had come close to an aneurism. And when Carmine had announced that it was her right as a grown woman to have sex in the Statue of Liberty with the entire high school football team if she wanted, Dilly really did think they were going to be planning Mom's funeral.

"Just be careful," their mom settled for saying.

"Yeah. There are a lot of predators around." Carmine gave Gary a nasty smile.

Gary didn't even look up from his computer. "Give it a rest."

"What? I'm just pointing out that women have to be ready to defend themselves. You know, I was thinking of starting a self-defense class... they promise to teach how to kick predator ass."

Their mother was approaching aneurism levels of frustration again. "Carmine Louise Carter. You stop. I swear... my mother always said that having children too close in age led to bickering, but you two don't have to spend so much time proving her right. Now, Carmine, before you go, could you drop Gary off downtown?"

"What? Me?" Carmine's face started pinking up, but the fact was she had the only car—a solid little thing with torn seats and an engine that almost purred. She'd bought it with her first scholarship check, and their father had replaced almost every part on the engine.

"Yes, you. Your brother needs to collect a loan from a friend, and he needs a ride."

"It's called a bus," Carmine said dryly.

"Young lady." Their mother drew herself up. "Your father and I have inconvenienced ourselves at every turn to make sure that you three have the opportunity to do whatever you would like with your life. We expect the same from you."

"Well, yeah. I'll totally drive you anywhere, Mom, but I'm not going to be late for class so that Hairy Gary can go hang out with friends."

Their mom put her hands on her hips, and Dilly smelled imminent disaster. He was just too tired to deal with this, and Carmine did need to get to school, preferably without having her blood pressure rise to dangerously high levels. Although… if you were going to stroke out, doing it in a nurse college attached to a hospital wasn't a bad place to do it.

"I'll ask Dad for a car," Dilly offered.

"Great." Gary made that sound as sarcastic as possible. "I get driven in some clunker that's not even going to make it across town. I don't know why Dad can't keep a decent car around."

"He has his truck," their mom pointed out, but Dilly knew firsthand that the only thing more embarrassing than the clunker cars was the huge, rusted truck with its salt-rotted underside and enormous tow bed and winch. The thing might run well, but it looked like it was ready for the junkyard. Dilly had seen dozens of yuppies and lawyers and suit-types panic when their father's truck showed up to tow them. It didn't look very reliable, especially since that Fiat had gone skidding across the ice and hit the passenger side. The damage might be cosmetic, but it did add a sort of demolition derby charm to an already frightening monster of a truck.

"If you don't want a ride…." Dilly let his words trail off. He was doing his mom and Carmine a favor. He didn't care if Gary was stuck in the house. He just didn't want to inspire his mother to pull out his full name, and as the only Carter sibling to avoid the dreaded three-name mother curse plus glare of death, he wanted to stay on her good side.

"Yeah, if Dad's cars aren't good enough for you, you can just take the city bus," Carmine added, jumping in now that she smelled blood on the water. And from the look on Gary's face, he knew he was beat. He couldn't insult Dad without getting Mom upset, and he couldn't turn down a ride from Dilly without insulting their father.

"Fine," he said, the grumpy almost leaking out of him.

Dilly smiled. One disaster averted. "I'll go put my shoes on and run down to see what Dad has that's drivable." Dilly turned and headed back upstairs before he realized he'd left the milk on the counter, but his mom would grab it. Hopefully.

He had one shoe on before Carmine showed up and leaned against the doorjamb to his bedroom. "You mad?" she asked softly.

Dilly thought about it for a second. Normally, he'd just say "no" and hope all the ugly emotional stuff would stay under the carpet. But saying "no" would be like saying that Vin had gone overboard when he'd ripped Carmine a new asshole, and Dilly didn't want to even imply that, especially since it wasn't true. "A little," Dilly admitted. Wow. That actually felt good. Freaky good, even.

Carmine came in the room and pushed the door closed behind her. Dilly's room was small enough that she ended up just a couple of inches away, their knees facing off against each other as Dilly sat on the bed. Sighing, she looked around at the angled, low ceiling and the window with the little strip of wood that hid the counterweight that kept falling out. It leaned drunkenly, its hidden pocket and all the cobwebs visible. She took so long that Dilly ended up twisting around to see if she had spotted aliens crawling in the window or something. Nope. Just his crappy broken window. "I had no idea she was going to track you down," Carmine finally said in a tone that sounded almost apologetic. "I mean, if I even thought she was going to do that, I would have called her all sorts of names."

"That's kinda not cool considering she's a rape victim," Dilly pointed out. Sometimes his sister didn't stop to think about how other people might take things. She said them, but she didn't even consider that other people were the ones hearing them.

"She's a rape victim, yes, but she's not some fragile glass statue that everyone has to tiptoe around," Carmine complained as she crossed her arms and shifted from foot to foot. She was putting off some pretty confusing body language. "So, Vin. What's he like?"

A thousand different thoughts raced through Dilly's head, but the one that popped out was, "Scary."

Carmine snorted. "Right. Unless you're Dylan. The way he came to your rescue, riding on his white horse of indignation, I'm guessing this is more than a one-night stand sort of thing. How long have you been seeing him?"

Dilly leaned back on his bed. "Actually, he was a one-night stand. We aren't seeing each other."

That made her narrow her eyes as she studied him. "Seriously? He came that unglued after a one-night stand? Okay, either he's a professional knight on a white horse, or he is seriously into you. Which is it?"

The answer was complicated, but complicated would get into discussions of submitting and dominating and fear of dominating and being kinda new to submitting and ex-lovers and police and all sorts of things that Dilly was so not ready to discuss with his sister. Ever. They could be a hundred and ten, sitting in rockers, and Dilly would still not be ready to discuss these things with his sister. "That is not anything I'm going to talk about with you," Dilly said as firmly as he could.

Carmine's arms dropped to her side. "Seriously? Are you seriously telling me to fuck off?"

"Um, maybe?" Dilly cringed.

She kind of pulled back her head and looked at him with wide brown eyes. "Wow. Maybe you are turning into a Dylan. Damn." Smiling, Carmine shook her head. "Anyway, thank you for taking the hit and driving Gary all over creation."

"Hey, no problem. I don't have work today."

"Yeah, but that means you have to spend time with him. Anyway, thanks." Carmine gave him a smile and then ducked out of the room.

Dilly grabbed his second shoe and pulled it on, not sure how he felt about that. He liked being Dilly. But there was something pretty warm and fuzzy about having Carmine call him a Dylan. Of course, a Dylan would have some idea what to do with his family, and a Dylan was someone who would have a long-term plan that didn't involve being a waiter the rest of his life. Or maybe a Dylan would have a plan to get in at some top-notch restaurant where he could make a killing on tips. And a Dylan would definitely know how to take a couple of pills without ending up so stoned that he got chained to a man's bed. Dilly thought about that. Actually, a Dylan was probably smart enough to not take strange pills and then wander on a public street. Maybe it wouldn't be so bad to be a Dylan.

"Christ almighty. Are you coming sometime today?" Gary yelled up the narrow stairs.

"Garrett Alan Carter, watch your mouth."

"Sorry, Mom."

"Yeah, I'm coming," Dilly yelled as he pulled his shoelaces tight. If he wanted to be nice, he'd get Gary out of the house before Carmine went back downstairs. He trotted down the steps, and sure enough, Gary was standing at the base of them, his bag with his laptop slung over his shoulder.

"Get the lead out, Dill Weed."

"Dylan. My name is Dylan."

"Christ," Gary said with a heavy sigh. "Tell me you aren't listening to Carmine's rants about sticks and stones and the power of fucking words. I thought you grew out of that shit."

"I don't think anyone wants to be called a weed, so knock it off," Dilly said as he headed past his brother and out the door. He'd need to bike over to his father's shop, so Gary was still going to be stuck waiting.

"Geez. It's a name. Refrigerator Perry never got all huffy about getting called a refrigerator."

"And a refrigerator is not a weed. Besides, he kinda looked like a refrigerator." Dilly jumped over the last crumbled concrete step and reached for the bike lock.

"And you kinda look like a weed." Instead of staying in the house, Gary closed the front door and slung an arm over Dilly's shoulders. "Let's walk."

"Together?"

Gary gave him an amused look. "Well, you could trail after me like when you were a kid, but that might be awkward."

"Har, har."

Gary smiled but he started down the street. Dilly had the sudden thought that maybe Gary planned to use him as a human shield if their neighbors decided to stone the local rapist. But strangely, they just strolled down the street, detouring around posts and potholes without Gary moving his arm. Dilly could feel the shifting discomfort in the pit of his stomach, but he couldn't put his finger on anything Gary was doing *wrong*.

"Carmine is such a bitch. Her problem is that she doesn't want to believe that women are anything but perfect. To hear her, the world would be a fucking utopia if all the men just dropped dead," Gary commented casually.

"She likes Frank." Dilly didn't add that Carmine liked him and their father, because that would come a little too close to pointing out that she liked pretty much every male except Gary.

"Yeah, she's fine keeping a man around to fuck, but she has no patience for anyone who suggests women aren't superior. And do not get me started on her opinions on kink. I mean, some women like to be tied up, but in Carmine's world, that makes them sick freaks or something. She thinks every woman has to be some ball-buster, and God forbid one of them enjoy getting tied up and taken advantage of."

Dilly's stomach was souring. "This is coming dangerously close to discussing your case, which we aren't supposed to do... remember?"

Gary rolled his eyes. "I am just a big brother enlightening his baby brother on the realities of human sexuality. Although unless you grow a few inches and start lifting weights, you won't really be attracting many women of that sort."

With a snort, Dilly pointed out, "Honestly, that's not a bad thing."

Gary let his arm drop. "Carmine has really played games with your head, you know. She makes you feel guilty because God gave you a prick and made you want to go out there and take over the world. You don't have to feel guilty about being a man. You have testosterone and that's what has driven generations of men out to explore and conquer. It's nature." Gary sounded so damn sure of himself, even though Dilly didn't see himself in this view of testosterone-driven maleness Gary described.

"And if I don't want to take over the world?" Dilly asked quietly.

For a second they walked in silence, and then Gary gave a pained sigh, exaggerated to the point of sounding almost ridiculous. "I'm buying you the Gor books for Christmas," Gary said in a tone of voice that warned Dilly he would not be showing that present to anyone. "So," Gary said in an entirely too off-the-cuff tone of voice, "has Carmine been saying anything lately?"

"Saying anything? You mean like how much she resents Mom's inability to give her the same sexual freedoms that we have?"

Gary snorted. "I almost feel sorry for Frank, but if he was idiotic enough to propose, that's his problem. No, I meant has she said anything about the case?"

Dilly's guts turned cold. Gary knew something. Dilly just didn't know how many somethings Gary knew or how messy it would get when the many somethings hit the fan. He tried shrugging like the question didn't matter. "Mostly she just hates on you a lot. A whole lot," Dilly said. It wasn't exactly a lie. It was leaving a whole lot of things out, including the fact that Carmine was working with the victims and the prosecutor, but he hadn't lied. Technically.

"She has her head lodged so far up her ass that she thinks her own shit smells good," Gary announced loudly as he started walking faster. Dilly had to work a little harder to keep up. "So, nothing else?"

"Hey, my goal is to stay out of all of this."

Gary frowned. "You want to stay out of it? These people have ruined my life. These jealous, pissy little bitches have gotten me suspended from the best job I ever had. They got my fucking license pulled, and now I'm stuck living with my parents." Gary's hands flew into the air with hard, sharp gestures that made Dilly flinch back.

"I think the speeding and crossing state lines after—"

"It was them," Gary cut him off. "Those whores talked the prosecutor into playing tough. And I don't blame him, you know. This world is all about competition. He's making his career off cases like mine—and you know, that's the way the world works. The big fish eats the little fish. Of course, as soon as I win my case, I plan to sue the shit out of all of them and show them how a real winner takes his revenge...." Gary's voice trailed off, and Dilly could almost see Gary's fantasies around him. Some days Dilly wondered if his brother wasn't delusional... if there wasn't some switch that flipped from reality to fantasy and it had just gotten stuck in Gary's case.

Maybe that was the real difference between Gary and Vin. Dilly never got the feeling that Vin was off in la-la land. Vin had some sharp edges that could definitely shred anyone who annoyed him, but he made every cut intentionally and with careful precision.

"So, is there anything you want to tell me?"

"Me?" Dilly's voice entered dangerously girly tones.

Gary kept walking, but he turned his head to look at Dilly.

"Definitely not," Dilly said firmly. And that was him being honest, because he definitely did not want to have this conversation at all.

"Really?" Gary had that calm tone of voice that sent spiders of fear running up Dilly's back.

"Yes," Dilly said, but this time he was a lot less certain. Right now, the idea of Vin locking him in a closet for the rest of his life was sounding really, really awesome because he was clearly in deep shit, and he didn't even know why.

Gary stepped closer, his arm going over Dilly's shoulders again, and Dilly tried to shy away, but Gary held him tight.

"Stop it," Dilly complained, shoving at Gary's chest.

"We need to talk." Gary pulled him toward a tree-lined alley where the locals usually left cars that didn't run. The houses on either side of the alley had been repossessed by the bank, their windows boarded up and weeds pushing through the sidewalks. Dilly squirmed, but Gary caught him by the back of his shirt and hauled him closer.

"I know what you did, Dill Weed," Gary whispered in Dilly's ear.

"I didn't do anything," Dilly hissed. He considered yelling for help, but this was his brother, and screaming for help from a little brotherly roughhousing seemed pretty stupid. Then Gary shoved him up against a rusted Plymouth, and he reconsidered.

He opened his mouth, but Gary planted a fist deep in Dilly's stomach, and all the air rushed out of him in one painful grunt.

"You're the only one I told about the phone calls. The only one, Dill Weed." Gary caught him by the shirt and slammed him back against the car so the driver's side handle dug into the small of Dilly's back. "So how did they find out about our strategy?"

"What?" Dilly thought Gary had found out about Carmine, so this was so not what he was expecting, and somehow, he couldn't quite get his brain to fully engage with the conversation.

Gary shook him, and Dilly could feel his teeth clack together as he clung to Gary's forearms. "How did they find out?"

"I don't know," Dilly said as soon as Gary stopped shaking him. And he was so very screwed. Gary pressed him back onto the car with an arm across his neck.

"You're it, Dilly. You. I didn't tell anyone but you, and now the prosecutor has pulled their phone records, so is that a coincidence?"

"I don't know." Panic and Gary's forearm against the base of his neck made his voice girlishly high.

"If you're coming after me... if you're siding with Carmine in this war... let me know." Gary leaned close. "I can destroy you."

Something hard rose up in Dilly's chest, and before he'd even thought about it, he brought his knee up between Gary's legs. He hit hard enough that he almost pulled his other foot out from under him, and he stumbled to the side while Gary fell to one knee, clutching his crotch. For one critical second, Dilly froze. He simply froze. With both feet stuck to the ground, he stared at his brother until Gary finally looked up, murder in his eyes.

With his heart pounding rabbit-fast, Dilly scrambled to get away. Too late, he realized he'd picked the wrong direction. Instead of going back toward the main street, he was headed into the back of a long strip mall, and unless someone just happened to be taking out the garbage or hanging out a back door smoking, he was going to be alone with Gary. Panic nearly blinding him, he spotted an old Impala with a crumbled trunk and two flat tires. After yanking open the door, Dilly dove in, pulling the door closed behind him.

He barely slammed his palm down on the lock before Gary was there, pulling at the handle. "Open the fucking door, dick weed."

Dilly scrambled backward, hitting his knee on the steering wheel and getting one hand caught in the seat belt before he actually coordinated all his limbs. Gary clenched his jaw so tight Dilly could see the matching bulges on either side of his face, and then he started around the car. Dilly twisted around and locked the passenger door too.

Gary stopped and leaned on the hood of the car. "Dilly, get your ass out here."

"Um. No."

"Seriously… are you going to hide in there all day?"

"I'm considering it," Dilly agreed.

Gary pressed his lips together into a thin line. "You fucking ass. You told them, didn't you? You're like everyone else. You jealous, small little bastard. How could you?"

"Hey, I am staying out of it. But I'm not going to sit still while you hit me," Dilly said, and technically he'd lied because he had totally told Evie, but Gary looked murderous enough without Dylan poking that sore spot.

"Then get the fuck out here and talk to me like a man," Gary shouted.

Dilly crossed his arms. "That worked when I was sixteen and stupid. I'm not coming out."

"I'm not leaving until you do." Gary stood up straight and crossed his own arms.

Dylan reached into his pocket and pulled out his cell phone. "I'll call the cops," he warned.

"You little prick. No, you won't. First, you'll be the one explaining to the cop why you had to cry for help when you don't have a fucking mark on you, and second, I'll make sure Mom knows you did it just because I teased you too much. You'll end up looking like the pissant you are. Or maybe I'll deny that I was here at all. Maybe I left when you ran into some guy who was upset about you fucking his sister. Maybe I walked away instead of getting in the middle of trouble and losing my bail. Maybe that's it. Maybe you're some stupid little fucking twit who left some girl crying, and her brother came after you. I think he had on an Eastside Chargers shirt. Dark hair. Kinda had a funny mark on his chin."

Fuck. Gary was describing Jennifer's older brother, and the guy had been in way too much trouble for any one person. He was a nice guy, but his deck was missing a few cards, a few important cards. He'd spent most of high school in special classes, and the only reason the school didn't expel him was that the other boys were always the ones who talked Jeff into doing something criminally stupid. If the police even showed up at Jeff's house to question him, his father was going to beat the snot out of him. When Dilly had dated Jennifer, about half their dates had ended with her crying on him because of something their father had done to Jeff. Dilly had learned to appreciate his own father through the horror stories of Mr. DiMagdalino.

"So do it," Gary dared him. "Call the fucking police, dick weed."

Dilly could feel his heart start to pound against his ribs. Gary was right. He couldn't call the police, not without dragging a lot of people into a nasty mess. "Just go away, Gary. I'm not coming out while you're being unreasonable."

Gary's mouth contracted into a little point before his expression smoothed out into something dangerously calm. "Get out here and tell me why you did it."

"I didn't do anything," Dilly said, clutching his phone.

Gary tilted his head to one side, and Dilly's heart sped up. When Gary started looking around the alley, Dilly realized he was in deep trouble. There were a lot of weapons that could break out the Impala's glass, and he had one cellphone and a limited number of options, the worst of which was calling the police. He didn't want to get into anything that messy, but the options were narrowing. Gary walked over to the overgrown weeds and picked up a piece of forgotten rebar. He had to yank it free, and Dilly stopped breathing as Gary turned, rebar in hand to consider the Impala. *Shit, shit, shit.*

Chapter 11

DILLY'S hand sweated as he considered his phone's small list of contacts. Anyone from work was out. Not only did Dilly not want this to end up in the rumor mill, but Gary could probably beat the crap out of most of them. Dilly's eyes landed on Guard's number. He remembered how it felt to have Guard's large body pin him up against the bar. Guard could definitely take care of Gary in more ways than one.

Gary hit the hood of the car with the rebar, and the metal reverberated with the sound. "Get out here, dick weed. If I have to come through that window, it's going to be worse."

"I didn't tell anyone," Dilly called out. Yeah, he sounded like he was lying, even to his own ears.

"Don't fucking lie to me. Now get your ass out here and explain, and if your explanation doesn't include you getting seduced by some bitch pussy, you're going to pay for this. You got it?"

Dilly's guts knotted in fear. He hadn't gotten seduced. He didn't even know why Gary wanted him to say he had been. Knowing Gary, he had some plan in his head. And if Dilly called Guard, the man would call in the police and the lawyers and want to do everything by the book. But this was Dilly's family, not a book.

Dilly scrolled down and found another number.

"If you're calling Dad...." Gary let his words trail off, and only then did Dilly realize he could have called their father. Dad had the power to shut Gary up, largely because he was paying the bills since

Gary's job had put him on leave. However, before Dilly could hang up and redial their father, someone answered the bar's phone.

"This had better be good because I need my beauty sleep."

"Open the fucking door!" Gary screamed, and this time he brought the rebar down on the top of the car. Dilly flinched as the old car rang like a bell.

"Who is this?" Miss Dolphinia called. "If you don't identify yourself, I'm getting the police on the other line."

That was enough to loosen the fear that had unexpectedly captured his tongue. "It's Dilly. My brother...." Dilly stopped, not sure what to say. Gary was getting more and more mad, and eventually he would stop just threatening and try to break out a window. And Dilly wasn't sure what he would do. Gary had never left marks before, but it wasn't like Gary hadn't done some cruel things. Really cruel.

"Where are you?" Miss Dolphinia demanded, and there wasn't a bit of that lilting drawl in her voice, that tone that made Dilly want to just sit and listen to her talk all day long. This tone kind of made Dilly recoil in fear.

"In an old car. Lex and 67th, in an alley between a two-story green house and a boarded-up brick one." Dilly blurted the words out, panic making his throat close up.

Gary brought the rebar down on the roof again. "Who are you calling, little Dilly? Your friends from work? The police? We both know you don't have the balls to do that, so get out here and face the music."

"Dylan, you stay in that car, do you hear me? I'm on my way, but you do not get out of that fucking car." Before Dilly could answer, the phone went dead, and the loss of that connection left Dilly even more frightened. It was like talking to Miss Dolphinia kept the fear at bay, but now, Dilly could feel the terror clogging the bottom of his throat. He wanted to yell at Gary to go away, but he couldn't get the words out. He just pulled his knees up close and kept an arm over the bench seat so he could quickly scoot into the back if Gary followed through with this threat to break the window.

A shadow passed in front of the mouth of the alley, and through the trees Dilly caught a glimpse of a woman herding three or four kids ahead of her.

Gary dropped the rebar and moved to the back of the car, wandering slowly as if just out for a morning constitutional. Only once she'd passed did he come back around to the driver's side.

"Seriously, Dylan. Why would you stab me in the back?" Gary pulled out his reasonable voice, which scared Dilly even more. "I'm the one who took you out practice driving when Dad was too busy. I'm your brother. Now, if you're going to tell me that one of those bitches came to you… maybe they sweet-talked you or seduced you, and things came out in pillow talk, I get that. Cunts have been making men stupid for centuries. Hell, if they didn't make you stupid, I'd worry more, so just explain this. Explain this so I can understand why the one person I trusted would have given the other side information on my defense."

Dilly could see the bright, flashing neon signs around that bit of bribery. If Dilly just lied, then Gary would stop torturing him. But what Dilly couldn't figure out was why Gary thought he would take that deal. Dilly wasn't about to help Gary hurt someone. He never had. Hell, Dilly was usually the one to try and patch up whatever animal Gary had injured. He still remembered the long gashes he earned from the old tomcat he'd tried to save after Gary had thrown a knife at it. The animal's guts had dangled from his body, and Dilly had scrambled to hold him, to save him. Instead, he'd earned a serious shredding and a lecture from his mother about playing with stray animals. But nothing in their childhood would lead Gary to believe that Dilly would help him. Nothing. So Dilly wondered what he was missing.

"A friend of mine is coming. You'd better get out of here," Dilly warned.

Gary sneered. Few people could actually pull off a genuine sneer without looking constipated, but Gary could. "First, I'm not afraid of your friends. Second, we both know you're bluffing. You won't risk putting one of your little friends into the middle, and we both know it."

"I did call someone. He may call the cops even if I don't."

"And you'd have to live with those consequences," Gary warned without being specific. Dilly could guess. Gary would try and put all the blame on Jeff, and even if Jeff could convince the police it wasn't him, his father would beat the crap out of him, and Gary would make it sound like Dilly was trying to protect Jennifer, and their mother would probably get all confused and tell the police that they had been discussing Jennifer and the fact that Dilly hadn't come home last night.

Their mother might love all of them, and she would definitely throw her body between any of her children and the nearest gun-toting madman, but Gary had better skills of manipulation. He always seemed to twist her to his way of thinking, and not just her. He had this weird ability to redefine the reality of anyone who listened to him too long.

"Maybe," Dilly admitted. "But when my friend gets here, it won't be up to me," Dilly pointed out. And right about then, reality poked its ugly little head up. If Dilly was trying to go for subtly gay, Miss Dolphinia was not the best person for subtle. *Shit. Shit and shit.* And he didn't have her cell phone number, not that calling Miss Dolphinia back would prevent her from coming if she wanted to come. He had the feeling that Jesus on a Sherman tank couldn't convince Miss Dolphinia to change course if she had her mind set.

Dilly rubbed a hand over his face and tried to just wish reality away, but it was a tenacious pit bull of a bastard, and it clung to him like cobwebs. Dirty, clumpy cobwebs with desiccated fly bodies and dead beetles in it.

"God you're an idiot. I know you didn't call anyone, and you're not going to call anyone, so get your ass out here, Dill Weed." Gary leaned against the car, both his palms on the hood as he peered in the window. Theatrical, yes, but effective. Dilly could feel his fear ratchet up. "Now, Dill. Get out here now. Either that or I'm going to have to find a more creative way to get you out of there."

Dilly swallowed.

"Well, what do we have here?" A tall man with buzz-cut gray hair and a matching gray T-shirt strolled down the alley.

"Fuck off," Gary suggested without giving the guy another look. Dilly, however, couldn't stop looking. The cadence of his walk, his way of throwing his shoulders back reminded Dilly entirely too much of Miss Dolphinia, but this guy was a man. Well, Miss Dolphinia had man parts, but it wasn't the same. This guy was on the manly side. A five o'clock shadow gave him a slightly rough look and his buzz cut made him look like some retired military officer. Even his arms looked different. They had long, corded muscles that gave him a dangerous edge that definitely made Dilly sit up and take notice, even if older guys weren't normally his thing.

"Now, that's articulate." The words dripped with sarcasm. "Young people do assume the word 'fuck' can work anywhere, but I assure you that those who are educated can find far more creative ways to tell people to fuck off without sounding like a low-class troglodyte with an IQ rivaled only by his inability to fully master the English language." That might be a gray-haired man in old jeans, but *that* was Miss Dolphinia. That was *pure* Miss Dolphinia.

Gary finally turned away from the window to size up the new arrival. "Seriously, buddy, family matter, get lost."

"If this is a family matter, I can see why young Dylan spends so much time avoiding family."

Dilly flinched. Yeah, subtlety and Miss Dolphinia did not go together, even when she wore jeans.

Gary squared off against Miss Dolphinia. "Who the fuck are you?"

"Lee. Lee Dolphinia. And you are the brilliantly narcissistic ass who raped those women," Miss Dolphinia said in a frighteningly cheerful way, and even dressed as Lee, her commanding presence demanded attention. Dilly had thought it was the blonde hair and shockingly revealing dresses that turned Miss Dolphinia into the queen, but it wasn't. Dilly could almost see how much space she took up, how much she bent reality to her will, even without the dresses. Even now, Gary had backed up a step, clearly not sure how to deal with the intruder.

"If you don't get lost, you're going to be in real trouble," Gary warned, but for the first time in his life, he sounded unsure. The king of the jungle had just met the queen of the fucking universe.

"Oh, there's trouble already. You're simply not bright enough to recognize the fact." A bit of the lilting drawl returned to Miss Dolphinia… to Lee's voice. Something in that tone made Dilly want to hide behind her until Gary and the court case and the rape victims all just went away.

"I'm not the one with a terminal case of stupid," Gary said. He had recovered from the shock of being challenged, and he strode forward, his arms held slightly out to the side and his body screaming aggression. Lee Dolphinia's eyebrow quirked, but he didn't move except to square off his stance, and every inch of him screamed masculine power now. As the distance between them narrowed, without warning, Gary swung a fist low. Dilly expected the hit to catch Miss Dolphinia in the gut. Instead, he sidestepped and brought his arm up, catching Gary just under the chin with his forearm.

Gary fell back, swearing and choking and grabbing at his throat with both hands, but in the next second, he launched himself at Miss Dolphinia—his shoulder in Miss Dolphinia's stomach as they both tumbled against the chain-link fence.

Dilly scrambled out of the car and looked around for anything to use as a weapon. He grabbed a piece of broken wood and held it up like a bat, but before he could do anything, the two of them dropped to the ground and then Miss Dolphinia came up, moving backward, his body almost vibrating with fury.

"You can't afford to be doing this, and I am old enough to no longer appreciate the joys of a good bruise, so I suggest you move on before I decide to call the police," Miss Dolphinia warned. He had a wide stance, his large hands held out defensively, and Dilly got the impression he could seriously kick Gary's ass if he decided to. The sight wasn't quite as amusing as it would have been had Miss Dolphinia worn four-inch heels and a corset to the fight. Still, Dilly had to hold back a grin.

"This is a family conflict, asshole." Gary still glared murder, but he didn't look likely to attack again.

"Do you spend all your time repeating yourself? Because I don't." Miss Dolphinia took a step closer to Gary. "I made my promise, and now you have to decide if you want me to call the police. And by the way, work on your insults. Trust me, your fists are not impressive, and you're going to need a good repertoire of quips and barbs if you want to avoid being utterly pedestrian or ending up as someone's prison bitch."

Confusion flashed across Gary's face, and his lips thinned to a tight line. If Dilly were alone, that expression would mean something he loved would end up cut into little tiny pieces and stuffed inside his pillow. Or maybe he'd get a little pile of ashes in the middle of his room with some unburned part set on the top like a cherry on an ash sundae.

"Dilly, you don't want to do this. Tell your *friend* to get lost." From the tone of Gary's voice on the word "friend," he'd figured out more than Dilly was comfortable with him figuring out. Now Gary had even more blackmail material.

Miss Dolphinia advanced, hand raised and one long finger aimed right at Gary. "You don't talk to him. You don't order him around, and you don't put your hands on him. You're just lucky he called me instead of one of his other friends, because I can promise you that plenty of people would love to have a good reason to beat the shit out of you. Me? Well, I'm a little old for fisticuffs, but you'd better believe I'm going to spend the next hour or two trying to convince Dilly to press charges against you. And if he has even one bruise—one scratch—one little red mark"—Miss Dolphinia held up two fingers to indicate just how small the red mark could be—"I'm going to photograph it and try to get Dylan to turn it over to the police as evidence of assault. Are we clear?"

"He wouldn't do that." Gary's eyes darted from Miss Dolphinia to Dilly and back again. In his entire life, Dilly had never seen Gary look unsure, but he did now. Dilly just wanted Gary to go away. He didn't want to deal with the anger or the guilt of having given Gary's defense strategy to the other side or the fear that Gary had figured out the whole gayness secret. He couldn't deal with any of it.

"There are a lot of things I don't want to do, like have to call a friend to protect me from my own brother," Dilly answered, bracing himself for the explosion. Gary blinked mutely.

Miss Dolphinia gave Dilly a wide grin. "I am just glad you called me instead of one of the others. Some people are so very unreasonable. Galvin, for example, would have insisted on calling the police and filling out all the correct paperwork in triplicate. That man lives in a world of black and white."

"Dilly, I'll see you back home," Gary said, his anger poorly hidden beneath the thinnest layer of polite. With one last sneer in Miss Dolphinia's direction, Gary gathered up his dignity and strolled off down the alley like nothing had happened.

Dilly felt his legs start to tremble. Dropping the board, he backed up until he could lean against the car, his whole body shaking as fear and relief and anger and helplessness washed through him in waves so fast he couldn't finish feeling one before the next hit him.

"Dylan, are you alright?" Miss Dolphinia moved to his side, resting a large hand on Dilly's shoulder, and a hard shiver took Dilly by surprise.

"Let's get you to sit down, sweetie."

"I'm fine," Dilly said, but he did let Miss Dolphinia help him down to the ground. "I'm not the one who got hit," he protested.

"Oh please. That was not a hit. I've ordered people to whip me far harder than that. Did he touch you?"

Dilly shook his head. He didn't want Miss Dolphinia making that call, and none of the bruises were serious.

"Good. I would feel bad about kicking your brother's ass. After all, I believe that a man shouldn't cause others pain without permission and a whole lot of pleasure on both sides, but for him I would make an exception."

"He...." Dilly stopped. He didn't know how to finish that statement.

"Trust me, I know." Miss Dolphinia sat next to Dilly right there in the weeds. "I haven't talked to my own brother in nearly thirty years, so don't you even worry about this."

"Is he a psychopath too?" Dilly froze, horrified to have used that word.

"No. Just narrow-minded. Trust me, I don't like either trait." Miss Dolphinia patted him on the knee.

Dilly let his head rest against the car as he tried to get his heart to slow. "He's going to make me pay for that." Dilly closed his eyes and fear rose up to push out the other emotions.

Miss Dolphinia harrumphed. "You have plenty of friends who will be delighted to teach him a few manners if he even tries."

"But I should be able to deal with my brother myself."

Miss Dolphinia was silent so long Dilly finally opened his eyes and rolled his head to the side to look at her. Miss Dolphinia studied him with this sad expression. "I remember when I was young and foolish and I thought I had to handle the world by myself. You'll get over the feeling, sweetie, trust me."

"But Miss Dolphinia...." Dilly stopped. It didn't feel right to call an older man with a military buzz cut "Miss" anything. And maybe he was right to stop, because he was getting the hairy eye.

"Do you see boobs?" Miss Dolphinia demanded in her grand voice, that one that simply dared anyone to disagree.

Dilly swallowed. "What answer am I supposed to give here?"

"The real one. I am not dressed as a woman, and you will not address me as one. When I am dressed as a man, I am either Lee or sir. Clear?"

Dilly nodded. He'd much rather know the rule rather than flail through the stupidity, so he appreciated the direct answer. "Yes, sir."

Lee shook his head with an amused smile transforming his face. "You would choose that option."

"What?"

Patting him on the leg, Lee said, "Nothing. I am simply remarking on the fact that you are still sweet enough to eat."

Dilly closed his eyes as his brain kept replaying the whole conflict in his head. "God. He knows. He knows I'm gay. Did you see his face?"

Lee sighed and used the car's bumper to push himself up. "There are worse things than being gay."

"Tell my mom that," Dilly muttered, but when Lee held out his hand, Dilly took it and let himself be pulled to his feet. "I'm really sorry I had to call for help."

"You have nothing to apologize for. You aren't responsible for that sack of human waste. I will admit that I am surprised you didn't call Vin. You two seemed so compatible last night." Lee's gaze turned sharp. More and more, Dilly was starting to think there was something between these two. Not sexual because something in his guts told him that Miss Dolphinia or even Lee did not match Vin's kinks, but there was something between them. Something that made Lee Dolphinia want Vin in a happy-ever-after sort of relationship. Too bad Vin wasn't looking for that.

Dilly shrugged. "He chained me to his bed, didn't touch me, and told me how dangerous he was before kicking me out this morning."

Lee's face executed a complicated set of grimaces and frowns. Yep, Lee definitely hadn't planned on that. "That man is an absolute idiot," Lee proclaimed in an utterly flat tone of voice.

"He told me all about Chase and then said I needed to stay away, that getting near him was stupid."

"Stupid is getting stoned and wandering the city streets. Getting involved with Vin is only mildly precarious, and some of us prefer a little peril in the bedroom. Of course, given that boy's penchant for overreaction, it's probably best you called me instead. You know, looking at you younger men, I do wonder how any of us survived our twenties. It's such a tumultuous and hormonally challenged decade."

"I'm not actually twenty yet," Dilly said.

For a second, Lee only stared at him. "Oh Lord," he finally said wearily. "Please tell me you're at least eighteen, because if not, I will have to apologize to Vincenzo for aiming him at a tasty bit of jailbait, and I do hate apologizing."

Dilly nodded. "Nineteen. And it's not like I'm some innocent virgin."

"Yes, it really is like that," Lee quickly answered. "Well, at least it's only a five or six year difference between you then. Trust me, by the time you reach your fifties and sixties, you will have lost more years than that through sheer forgetfulness. Look at me. The eighties are one giant blur. I can't remember a bit of them." Lee waved a hand and headed down the alley, leaving Dilly to follow.

"Funny thing, I don't remember them either," Dilly joked. He was sorry the moment the words were out. It was like he was trying so hard for normal, trying so hard to ignore the stones weighing down his stomach that he let the stupid slip right out his mouth.

Lee gave him a dirty look. "I feel ancient right now, and I am blaming you entirely."

Dilly sighed. That was him—putting everyone in awkward situations day after day. "Thank you for coming," he offered quietly.

Lee turned and put a hand on his shoulder. "You're welcome."

"I hope Gary didn't hurt you too much." The stones in his stomach ground against each other as he thought of Gary hitting his friend, whether his friend was Miss Dolphinia or Lee at the moment of hitting.

Lee rolled his eyes. "I was not kidding. I've been hit harder by men that I ordered to hit me."

"Really? You weren't, I don't know, exaggerating?" Dilly frowned in confusion, but Lee patted him on the shoulder before pulling him toward the street.

"Never mind. You definitely aren't old enough for that discussion." Lee pulled him toward a red Acura. "However, to answer your question, your brother hits like a ten-year-old child. Tackling me? Seriously? Unless he meant that as foreplay, as a fighting strategy, it left a lot to be desired. He doesn't get a good swing going, so he has no force behind his hits, and he goes for all the wrong targets. If you're in a fight, you go for the neck, the eyes, and the balls. Don't waste your time on any other body part unless you have a weapon ready, and I do not mean an old rotted board." Lee looked Dilly up and down with just a touch of disgust.

"I'm sorry. It's the only thing I could find. I didn't want him to hurt you."

Lee shook his head, but he smiled as he hit the remote to open the passenger side door. "Sweetie, I was a drag queen in the seventies.

Trust me, not only do I know how to fight, but I know how to fight dirty." Lee gave a little flip of his head, and drag or no, in that one second, he was Miss Dolphinia. "And you don't need to apologize for doing the right thing. There is, however, a cruel, bitchy part of me that wishes you had Vin's number. Your brother never would have recovered from that spat. Vin is... well, possessive is the kindest word you can put on it."

"He called himself obsessive," Dilly said as he got in the car. He wanted to convince his heart that possessive was bad, but listening to Vin describe what he'd done, Dilly had only felt more attracted.

Lee got in the car. "Oh honey, if you had called him in the middle of that little spat with your brother, you would have seen just how possessive and obsessive he can be, believe me. That boy falls in love too fast and too damn hard, so when he puts that love in the wrong place, it spurts out as obsession, which is why he won't let himself love anyone. Idiot." She added the last word in a soft, sad tone. After pulling away from the curb, Lee followed the bus route down Lexington toward the club.

"You know, dominants aren't perfect. We're aggressive and pushy, and each of us is pushy in our own sweet way. And there are as many reasons for being dominant as there are people who like that lifestyle. For some of us, it's about control. When I have a partner that I can lock into a chastity device, when I can control when he comes and lock that prick away like I own it...." Lee fanned himself with his hand. "Well, you know what I mean."

Dilly squirmed in his seat. He could imagine that a little too well.

"But there's also this need to protect, this need to be the knight in shining armor that rides in to the rescue. And that back there was the hottest, sexiest thing I've done in longer than I care to admit. If I didn't already know for a fact that Vincenzo had fallen for you, I'd push you over the hood of this car and nail your ass. Because you asked for me. You let me rescue you and protect you, and that is...." Lee seemed to think about that for a minute. "That is delicious. You watch. When Vin hears this story, he's going to be coiled so tight one of us is going to need to use a crowbar to get his ass to unclench. It's going to kill him that he wasn't here."

Dilly wished that was true. He really did, but Vin had been pretty determined that he wasn't going to get involved in Dilly's drama. Well, beyond calling Carmine, anyway. Dilly frowned. That had been him trying to fix things, but if Vin found fixing things hot, he was way better at ignoring sexual tension. "He doesn't want to fall for me," Dilly finally concluded.

Lee laughed. "He doesn't want to fall for anyone. Luckily life isn't giving him a choice."

Dilly shook his head. "I'm not going to push my way in."

Lee smiled. "Of course you're not. Any true submissive wouldn't, which is why I'm going to do the pushing for you."

"He thinks it will turn out like Chase. If you push, he's still going to think that," Dilly pointed out.

The light was red, and when Lee stopped the car, he took a second to reach up and rest his palm against Dilly's cheek. The heat soaked into Dilly's skin, warming the ice-cold fear that still settled in his guts. For long seconds they stayed like that with Lee scrutinizing him. The light turned green, and Lee put both hands on the wheel and drove in silence for a couple of blocks. "I'm trying to remind myself that I'm saving you for Vin, because pushing you over the hood is sounding better and better."

"You keep saying that, but I'm pretty average. Why would you want to?"

Lee didn't answer for a long time. He pulled into the narrow parking lot behind the club before he turned to Dilly with an answer. "The cliché of the pushy sub has permeated this whole culture, and a good old-fashioned sweet boy like you needs to be tied up and fucked often enough to keep him happy. But since you have your heart set on Vin as much as he is totally in lust with you, let me tell you a few secrets about dominants.

"We're all our own brand of delusional, and trust me, there are plenty of dominants who can't even figure out which end of a white horse to try and climb on. They're more like donkey asses than knights, but Vin… he's a good old-fashioned knight on his horse. And that does not mean he's safe, because knights have high expectations for themselves and everyone else, and they carry magnificently big swords."

"Is that a penis joke?"

From Lee's grin, Dilly was guessing it was. "You already know the size of that sword. No, I rather mean that he has a number of weapons at his disposal, some more legal than others. Like any good knight, he knows how to use them."

"And he doesn't want me," Dilly added.

"No, he didn't want Chase," Lee corrected him. "Oh, he thought he wanted that boy. Chase loved to look like the damsel in distress, but when push came to shove, that boy enjoyed being fucked up." Lee tapped his long fingers against the wheel. "That might be a little uncharitable. Maybe he didn't enjoy it, but that certainly was where he was most comfortable. If it weren't the drugs, it would have been something else, because Chase didn't want help out of the gutter—he wanted company in it. So Vin would ride in and try to save Chase and then wonder why that boy never appreciated what he did. I would call Vin an unmitigated disaster with relationships, except I have made far worse mistakes in my life, so I have very little room to talk." Lee laughed. "Oh, I talk anyway, but I have very little room."

Dilly frowned. That didn't sound right, because he had thanked Vin for helping with his sister. He didn't want to live in misery, although he'd seen guys working at the restaurant who did make an art out of despair. Guys and girls. They went out of their way to date the worst people and make the worst mistakes possible, and then they flailed loudly and publicly. It bothered Dilly to think Vin saw him that way. "He thinks I like being miserable?"

Lee reached over and squeezed Dilly's arm. "Vin thinks he can't tell the difference between someone who loves to submit and grows stronger in the shade of someone else's tree and someone who just likes to wallow in muck. Funny enough, he's right. He can't tell the difference. Luckily, I can. So when you're ready to talk about how to help that idiot we both adore, you come to me? Okay?"

Dilly chewed his lip. This made him intensely uncomfortable, but the idea of having a shot at Vin was worth discomfort. He'd almost made up his mind to agree when Lee got out of the car. "Come on. I still have my beauty regime, and I want you safely tucked away in the club before you manage to find some other trouble. Chop, chop."

Dilly scrambled to get out and follow. He'd have to figure the rest out later.

Chapter 12

DILLY hung up the phone, his stomach still uneasy. He hated lying to the guys at work, but "Hey, I can't get my uniform because my brother's busy being a psychopath" didn't have a good ring to it. He stared at the phone and considered calling his father, but he didn't know what to say. And he definitely wasn't calling his mom. Hell would freeze over first. How did you tell a woman that her firstborn son is a monster? But he had to talk to someone. Disappearing off the face of the planet would lead to badness. With a sigh, Dilly texted Carmine.

Im at friends. Gary avoiding

Y?

The answer came back immediately, so either Carmine had left class early or she was bored. Sometimes Carmine was smart enough to annoy people with her ability to be bored when everyone else was struggling to learn something really, really hard.

b/c he's ass-wipeish

LOL. Always. Why avoid now?

Long story. Small buttons. TTYL.

U better.

Dilly sighed as he stared at the phone. He'd rather avoid the whole mess, but with Carmine, that wasn't an option. At least she wasn't calling him. Sometimes she did that. He'd text her, mostly to avoid her tongue, and right in the middle of texting, she'd call his phone. It was hard to pretend you couldn't answer the phone when you'd just been texting.

Fingering the phone, he thought again about calling his parents, but he didn't have anything to say to them, which made him feel like a rotten son. His mother had held his hand through every major disaster in his entire life. She had always taken his side. Always. In ninth grade, he had Mr. Anderson, who was about nine hundred years old and always lost papers. Lots of students didn't turn in work, and then they'd complain because they wanted free points. But in Dilly's case, he had turned in work. He did every stupid worksheet, and Mr. Anderson would leave little piles of papers around the room like a giant hamster dropping poop piles everywhere, and then things would just vanish.

His mother had descended on that man like an avenging angel, a Michael driving Satan out of heaven kind of angel. After Mr. Anderson had basically called him a liar and refused to give him credit, he'd wanted to die, and his mother had fixed that. She'd damn near made Mr. Anderson cry, and for the rest of the year, whenever Mr. Anderson talked about rude parents, Dilly knew the man meant his mother—his mother, who had stood up for him.

And he wanted to trust her the way he had back then. But every time, she believed Gary and all his slick words. It made Dilly's chest ache when he thought about it, especially when so many other people could see behind Gary's façade.

But Gary had a special talent for inspiring avenger-Mom. If Dilly went home, he'd get the look and then the lecture about family and sticking together, and Gary would make it look like Dilly had done something unforgivable. On the other hand, not going home meant bills and couch surfing and trying to find some place to stay.

"Here." Miss Dolphinia appeared out of nowhere and put a rack of glasses in front of him. "That cretin from the warranty company cannot seem to fix the dishwasher, and I cannot abide spotted glasses. Polish these and I'm going to go get paperwork."

Dilly blinked. He'd almost certainly missed some part of the conversation, because that didn't make sense.

"Um, I can polish, no problem, but what paperwork?" Dilly's stomach grew heavy at the thought of restraining orders and police reports. If that was where Miss Dolphinia wanted to go, Dilly might just have to disagree.

"The employment paperwork. You're spending so much time here I either need to hire you or charge you rent. Since you can't afford me"—at this Miss Dolphinia gave her hips a twist, and her satin robe twirled around her body—"I'll have to hire you. The state says you can work in a bar at eighteen, so you are now officially the glass polisher and floor sweeper whose primary responsibility is staying out of the way if anyone who looks even mildly official walks in."

"Could I get you in trouble?"

Miss Dolphinia laughed. "Sweetie, you could get me in all sorts of trouble that I would enjoy the hell out of, but you're not going to jeopardize my legal standing in this state. That's why you're polishing glasses. And just because I'm paying you an absolutely deplorable hourly wage and regularly making you work off the clock, don't think I'll accept subpar work." She winked at him and then headed back toward the door that led to the upstairs apartment. Dilly pulled out the first glass and started polishing.

He worked his way through the first rack and headed into the kitchen to find more when a large woman with a very sharp butcher's knife pointed it right at him. "Do not come do any of your kinky shit in here. This is a kitchen, got it?" she demanded.

"Um. Yes, ma'am. Miss Dolphinia told me to polish glasses." Dilly held the rack up higher, and the woman eyed him. She was heavy, with a chef's apron on, and working in restaurants, Dilly knew just how mean chefs could get when you invaded their territory. They were the pit bulls of the restaurant world, only not quite so nice.

She snorted. "Put it over there and get another. If I find that you've done anything other than polish them, I'm going to wear your gonads as earrings, got it?"

"What would I do with glasses?"

The chef gave him an incredulous look, and Dilly suddenly remembered exactly where he was, and he had a feeling these people could do all sorts of things with glasses. Actually, the Internet had included one or two suggestions, including a thing with fireplay that looked entirely too dangerous for him.

"Um, scratch that. How about I promise I won't let anyone do anything to the glasses that the health department would call unauthorized use?"

For a second, she eyed him as though testing his veracity through the power of staring. "You'd better," she declared. Then, ignoring him, she went back to chopping potatoes for homemade fries. Miss Dolphinia definitely hired scary people. Well, except for him. Maybe he was the antiscary hired to balance everyone else out. Dilly grabbed the next rack of glasses before the chef could decide she didn't like him after all. Dilly claimed a corner near the kitchen and polished the glasses as men started showing up. Three giggling girls came through the door at one point and froze about three steps into the main room before clumping up and trading a few whispers. Then they turned and fled.

Dilly could understand why they didn't feel welcome. He liked the pictures on the walls, but he was guessing not everyone would be a fan of Glen Mitchell. Either that or the leather-wearing men leaning against the bar or playing pool scared them. The crowd was older and rougher looking tonight. But then again, Dilly thought Guard had the mustache of evil going for him, and Vin looked more normal. Clearly looks could deceive.

Around seven, Miss Dolphinia swept into the room in a full-length blue dress with sequins and a huge side-slit. She moved around the room, kissing one man on the cheek and teasing another. She flirted with Dilly some and then moved into the kitchen while Dilly kept polishing the glasses. Somehow Dilly wasn't exactly shocked when Vin walked in about thirty minutes later. He stood just inside the door and scanned the room, his dark eyes settling on Dilly. Swallowing, Dilly put the glass he was polishing into the rack and wiped his hands on his jeans because they suddenly felt sweaty. Yeah, Vin knew something. Dilly was starting to think if he wanted Vin to find out about something, he only had to tell Miss Dolphinia.

Vin let the door fall shut behind him as he walked across the bar, ignoring the few people who tried to greet him. He strode up to Dilly's table and looked down at him. Looking up at a very annoyed Vin was slightly terrifying in a way that made Dilly's cock sit up and take notice. His cock was definitely less conflicted than the rest of him.

"Hey." Dilly smiled weakly at Vin while his stomach did a nervous tango.

Vin eyed him. "So, is it true?"

"Um. What?" Dilly tried putting on a smile and ignoring the little voice in his head that told him to tell Vin, to sic Vin on Gary and enjoy the bloody and brutal aftermath. It was a nice fantasy, but considering that it would end with police and hospitals and his mother crying, he resisted the urge. It just wasn't easy.

Crossing his arms, Vin waited. Stoically. Silently. Showing every sign of getting pissed off. Dilly thought about the big plan, the plan where Dilly manipulated Vin into getting involved, only that was feeling so very wrong. Vin cared about him. Dilly could see that in every tense line. Even though Vin had only known him for a couple of days, Vin was barely holding on to his emotions because he suspected Dilly was hurt, and that warmed Dilly more than he could say.

"My brother tried to get me to lie for him," Dilly admitted, and Vin looked as tight as a violin string. "And he was a little physical, but that's why I hid in a car and called for help. I'm okay. You don't have to get upset. I mean, Miss Dolphinia told me to get you worked up about how my brother scared the snot out of me so that you would feel some sort of white knight syndrome or something, but you don't need to go white knight for me. It's okay." Dilly frowned. "Okay, it's less than okay, but that's a family sort of not-okay, not a slaying the dragon sort. So I really don't want to manipulate you into anything." Dilly stopped, not sure how to read Vin's dark expression.

"She wanted you to manipulate me?"

That wasn't where Dilly expected the conversation to go, but he pointed out, "I said 'no,' which funny enough didn't work, but I told her you're not interested, and I said I wouldn't manipulate you, so I'm just warning you up front."

Vin sighed and sank into the chair across from Dilly, shoving the rack of glasses to one side. "So she manipulates you instead. If you're trying to outsmart that old bitch, you took a water pistol to a gun fight."

"What?" Dilly thought he should be insulted, but actually, he was mostly confused.

"She manipulated me into taking you home, but she knew I would avoid any sort of commitment. Unfortunately, she also knew that if she could manipulate you into refusing to play mind games, I'd find that irresistible." Vin ran a hand over his face. "Hell, Dylan. You're not following the script here. You're supposed to be so angry that I talked to your sister and so embarrassed that you refuse to even talk to me."

"Why? Carmine kinda needed to get told off, and I'm not good at telling people off, which is why I'm a kick-ass waiter. Even when customers probably need to get told off, I just prefer to be polite. Conflict gives me hives. But when Carmine asked, I told her that I agree with you."

"You did?" Vin looked surprised.

"Well... yeah." Dilly felt really confused because he had no idea why they were having this conversation.

"Well your sister is not the one I want to deal with. I want ten minutes alone in a locked room with your brother. I hate those sadistic Doms who think that the lifestyle means they get to hurt people. I want to go over and kick your asshole brother's ass. What do you think of that?" Vin gave Dilly a hard look, almost daring him to argue.

"Can we stick with verbal ass-kicking? I think I already have enough legally messy messes in my life right now." Dilly frowned. "Hey. How do you think Miss Dolphinia knew about my brother? She called him a sadistic rapist, too."

"You're only thinking to ask that now?"

"It only occurred to me now," Dilly said, and now he felt a little stupid for having not realized it before.

Vin leaned back in his chair and shook his head. "The first night you came to the Stonewall, someone knew you. If someone hadn't told Miss Dolphinia who you were, no one would have touched you. That canny old queen won't risk having the city pull her liquor license for serving a minor much less letting someone tie him up in the back room and fuck him. After I showed a little interest, that manipulative old bitch called him up and asked for your background. Unfortunately, if you hang out with me, you're going to have her manicured nails sorting through your life on a regular basis."

"Someone… okay, that's a little creepy. How did someone know me?" Dilly had chosen the Stonewall because it was far enough away from home and work that he wouldn't run into anyone. There were definitely gay bars closer to home, but closer to home meant more likely to get caught going in or out of it.

"One of your old teachers spotted you—vouched for you that you weren't a cop."

"One of my teachers?" Dilly was officially creeped out. Teachers were like parents—sexless and definitely vanilla-flavored sexless.

"A lot of the more professional types come over here," Vin said. "We even have a cop that comes, although when he first showed up, that was awkward. Every time he came in the door, we all pretended to be good little vanilla citizens."

Dilly cringed as he thought of what he must have sounded like that first night with Vin. "Oh God! My teacher. My teacher heard me having sex." Dilly was fairly certain his balls were trying to climb back up into his body, never to be seen again. This was a nightmare.

"Is that worse than the cop hearing you?" Vin had the nerve to sound amused, and Dilly glared at him.

"Yes."

Vin laughed. "Okay, interesting set of ethics you have there, considering lots of people have a kink for teacher sex."

"Then I am not most people. Ew and ew. And double ew." Dilly struggled to remember that first night, but he'd had a couple of drinks to reinforce his courage, and he couldn't remember any familiar faces. Crap. What if it had been Mr. Anderson? That would rank pretty high on the totally and completely creeped out scale. "Please tell me you never had sex with my teacher," Dilly begged.

"Jealous?" Vin sounded surprised.

"Sometimes, but if you slept with my teacher, the ick factor would be way worse than the jealousy factor."

Vin leaned back and half closed his eyes. "Oh Dylan." His words sounded almost like a sigh.

"What?"

"Exactly. What are we doing?"

"Um, talking?" Dilly guessed.

"It sounds a lot like we're talking about hard limits."

"Whoa." Dilly frowned. It actually did sound kinda like that, only it wasn't as awkward as when Guard had started the same conversation. Being asked to rank individual sexual acts with some color code wasn't quite as creepy as a teacher hearing him have sex, but it was close. "Okay. But that was sort of accidental because I already told Miss Dolphinia that you weren't interested."

"Then you lied to her," Vin confessed.

"But...." Dilly leaned forward. "Chase and the whole lecture on how dangerous you were sounded like you saying that you didn't want to have anything to do with me."

"It was about making you realize you shouldn't have anything to do with me. Fuck." Vin sounded defeated, and Dilly's stomach flipped uneasily at the tone. "I could fuck us both up pretty bad, here. You may say you want someone who is dominant in and out of the bedroom, but the fantasy is not the same as putting up with me and all my issues twenty-four hours a day. I mean, the odds that I'll track your phone are pretty high because I'm going to start thinking about all the people in this city who get kidnapped or attacked for being gay. I'm going to call you out of nowhere, convinced that you've either decided to take up with some damn Jersey boy or that you're being attacked by your idiot brother and you need me. I'm going to get a sexual thrill out of pinning you to every wall in the house just because I know I can. I'm going to push and push and revel in every time you yield and worry about every time you don't."

Dilly tilted his head to the side and squirmed a bit to try and get more room in his jeans. "Is this you trying to scare me away?"

"This is me being as honest as I can."

"In order to scare me away," Dilly added. He thought about what Miss Dolphinia said... that Doms were their own brand of delusional. But most days, Dilly would rather live in a delusion than the real world, because as much as Vin's honesty should scare him, it didn't. It wasn't like Vin was trying to do stuff behind his back or hide who he was, but it was pretty clear Vin thought he should be scared.

Vin didn't answer.

"I'm not actually scared, you know. I mean, if you were willing to show me the ropes... or the whips or the floggers, I wouldn't say 'no'."

Vin's mouth twisted with some shadowy emotion. "Would you say no to anyone?"

Dilly thought about that. "Yeah. I mean, I like Miss Dolphinia, but she is a little too old and way too feminine for me. Women kinda don't do it for me, and she's a pretty convincing woman." Dilly left out that when Miss Dolphinia was Lee, he was tempted. "And Guard's made it clear he'd like to show me the ropes, but he had a bad habit of trying to have conversations in the middle of sex."

Vin gave a rough bark of laughter. "I dare you to say that to his face."

"And since I hate conflict, I'd say no."

Vin took a deep breath and seemed to think for a moment before he pointed out, "If I show you the ropes, I'm not going to be okay with sending you back to that house. I don't trust your brother as far as I can throw him."

Dilly leaned back in his chair and studied Vin, because this was feeling like more than just a discussion of sex. "Do you worry about where all your sexual partners live?"

"I don't let myself care," Vin said. The words were simple and devoid of any emotion, but they made Dilly's heart ache. Vin might say that, but Dilly knew better. He could read the strain in every inch of Vin's body.

"Why am I different, then?" Dilly asked softly.

"I don't know."

Dilly swallowed and thought about what Vin was saying. If he asked Vin for more—more sex, more relationship, more bondage or spankings—Vin wasn't going to get pushed to the side in his life, and that probably meant Dilly's parents were going to find out he was gay. Assuming they didn't already know, because Gary had definitely seen that cat out of the bag. Dilly chewed on his lower lip.

All emotion vanished from Vin's face. "Try Chris. He's the short man wearing the red shirt." Vin stood up, and Dilly realized he knew his answer.

"I want you."

Vin stood with his back to Dilly, and those tight lines were back. His whole body looked like an overstretched wire that almost sang with tension. "You don't know me."

"I know I want you. I know that you keep trying to scare me and I don't find it scary as much as I find it really amazing to think that someone worries about me and my psycho brother. I know that I liked the sex a lot better with you than with Guard, and I know that when you had me tied up in your house, I still trusted you a lot more than I've ever trusted anyone else because I never thought you'd hurt me, although I did suspect you might leave me to pee the bed if I annoyed you enough, which explains why I tried to not nag you. And I know that it makes me weird to want to get tied up even after knowing what my brother did, but I do, and I'm embracing my inner weirdo."

Vin turned around to face him, but his expression was still guarded. "You're not weird."

"Um, my brother likes to tie women up and rape them, and I've developed a taste for getting tied up. A psychotherapist would disagree with you."

Vin sat down and leaned forward to catch Dilly's wrist in strong fingers. The tightness made Dilly shiver. "I'm not surprised you like it. You know how much people lie. You know how they hide themselves. How can you ever trust someone when you haven't seen how they'll act when they hold the power?"

Dilly hadn't ever thought of it like that. "You make it sound almost sane."

"If you try calling kinksters insane, Miss Dolphinia is going to have a few words for you, and I doubt any of them will be kind."

"Well, there is that," Dilly admitted. "So, I don't always catch your signals. Is this saying you'll maybe give this a try?"

"And if it doesn't work?" Vin asked.

Dilly had the feeling this answer meant a lot to Vin. "I'd probably ask Miss Dolphinia for help if you scared me too much."

The tension seemed to drain from Vin as he leaned back in his chair. "And she's the one woman who could make me stop." He shook his head. "That old queen is about the most dominant, pushy son of a bitch I've ever known, but at least you have the common sense to look past those terrible dresses of hers."

"I like her dresses," Dilly said. "They're classy."

"Keep that up, and I'll start getting jealous of her."

"You two have a history, don't you?"

"Not the kind you're asking about, but yeah. We do. That's why she's being such a bitch about this."

"Because she doesn't want you alone."

Vin gave him a disgusted look. "I did warn you that I'm not the sort to do a lot of debating of limits right?"

"Uh-huh."

"Well then, be careful or I see a lot of gags in your future."

Dilly grinned.

"A whole lot of them," Vin warned, but the fact he was smiling took the sting out of the threat. "Come on. I don't want an audience this time, so let's head back to my place."

"Okay," Dilly said, standing up to follow.

"Oh no. I'm not getting chewed out because you didn't finish your chores. Put those glasses up before we go anywhere."

The order sent a shiver through Dilly. "Yes, sir," he agreed as he grabbed the rack to take into the back. Somehow, Dilly figured Miss Dolphinia already knew her glass polisher had other plans for tonight.

Chapter 13

DILLY'S stomach was in knots before they got to Vin's townhouse. Last time, he'd been stoned when he came and he'd been rushed out so fast he'd only seen closed doors and a stack of boxes near the front door. Other than Vin's bedroom closet, which he knew in some detail, he didn't know how Vin lived.

"Nice place."

"I inherited the house and the big fat tax bill from my father. Unfortunately, he didn't leave me any money to go with it, so I'm always trying to catch up, and the government is always threatening to confiscate it to pay the tax bill." Oddly, Vin didn't sound too upset about that.

"Really? That's not fair."

Vin glanced over as he turned the key in the lock. "In this world, you pay or you lose. I would have sold it, only I'd never get full price because the kitchen is stuck in the seventies, and I don't care enough to update it."

Dilly nodded. But Vin had paid to update the bedroom. At least he had his priorities straight. Unlocking the door, Vin stood to one side to let Dilly go in first, and a little shiver went through Dilly as the lock thunked closed and he felt Vin step up behind him. With a chuckle, Vin wrapped a hand around Dilly's waist and pulled him close. Leaning in, he whispered softly, "Go explore."

Dilly hadn't expected that, and it took a second for the big brain to process what Vin had said.

"I have to pick up messages and take care of some business first." With that, Vin let him go and headed for the pocket double doors that led to a living room or dining room. When Vin slid them open, it looked more like a computer store had vomited in the room. Dilly watched as Vin settled in behind an ugly old desk and powered up a fancy computer.

"What kind of business do you have?"

"Computer consulting," Vin said, and Dilly let out a relieved breath. He'd been half afraid that getting involved in Vin's business would be some sort of no-go zone and Vin would get offended. "Most companies don't know software, so for a considerable fee, you tell me what you need your computers to do. I come to your business and see how you use them. Then I bring out a bank of laptops with potential software packages and a list of recommendations."

"So you're like a sales guy?" That surprised Dilly. Most of the time, the salesmen he knew were more like his brother—which might explain why he had a general dislike for all people involved in sales.

"Most salesmen work for a company and push that company's software whether it works or not. I'm a consultant. I bring in different options and then call you a moron if you try to pick something totally inappropriate because a sales rep offered you a kickback."

"That happens?"

Vin stopped typing and took a second to consider him. "Dylan, that happens a lot. That's why I also do a little semilegal formal detective work. If a manager tries to screw me over by going behind my back, I have a bad habit of showing up in his boss's office with a recording of him and some slimy sales rep trying to screw the company out of money. I have a reputation for it in fact, which is why companies hire me."

Okay, that sounded a lot more like something Vin would do. Nodding, Dilly turned toward the narrow hall and considered what to explore. Behind him, Vin returned to typing. Deciding he didn't want to invade the upstairs without an explicit invitation, Dilly explored the first floor with its beautiful crown moldings and racks and racks of computers and boxes of software.

The place looked like either a really ghetto computer store or a seriously large fencing operation. The dining room had a whole bank of file cabinets, and the kitchen was as terrible as Vin had warned. Dilly was pretty sure his grandmother owned the same refrigerator somewhere in the midseventies. In contrast to the upstairs bedroom, the first floor looked kinda pathetic.

Dilly was exploring the questionable contents of the refrigerator when he heard a door shut. "Dylan?"

"Here." After closing the heavy door, Dilly headed back into the main hallway with its tall ceilings.

"Like what you see?" Vin asked. For some reason, Dilly had the feeling it wasn't a casual question. He kept his gaze on Vin as he said, "Yep."

Vin rolled his eyes as if Dilly had just made the corniest joke ever. "Come on," he said, amusement coloring his voice as he gestured toward the stairs.

"Sir, yes sir," Dilly agreed. Grinning, he trotted toward the stairs and offered a mock yelp when Vin gave him a swat on the ass. The sting and the heat made Dilly's whole body tingle, and Dilly wondered if he would get another spanking. He seriously hoped so, but he had the feeling Vin wasn't the sort of top who liked suggestions from the peanut gallery, so he just headed up the stairs and turned left into Vin's bedroom.

The burgundy bedspread was crumpled at the foot of the bed, but the dark four-poster frame with those heavy posts was exactly the same. It was set between two angled corners in the irregular ceiling, and Dilly stopped in the middle of the room to stare. He swallowed as Vin detoured around him and went into the closet where he'd chained Dilly to a much smaller bed.

"Are we... should I, in there?" Dilly recognized his own babble, but hopefully Vin got the gist of it. Chains clicked, but Vin's body blocked the view, so Dilly couldn't see what he was doing with that twin bed and all its restraints.

"Strip," Vin ordered.

Dilly pulled his shirt over his head without unbuttoning it and then spent a second looking around, trying to decide where to put it. He ended up draping it over the chair in the corner. Toeing his shoes off, he kicked them under the chair as he unzipped his jeans. His cock jutted out painfully and a little embarrassingly. Clearly Dilly had no control over the thing, but Vin had told him to strip, so Dilly did. After doing a sort of quick-fold that looked a lot like rolling his jeans and underwear into one bunch, he put them on the chair and turned around.

Vin stood there in his dark blue shirt and faded jeans, his dark eyes exploring every inch of Dilly. Trying hard to not squirm, Dilly forced himself to leave his hands at his sides even when he wanted to cover himself.

"Good." Vin moved closer, and Dilly's eyes moved down to the black cuffs in Vin's hand. They were the cuffs off the bed—the ones that had trapped Dilly and made him real when parts of him felt like they were going to fly off. He could feel his body tighten at the sight, but even more importantly, Vin was holding them. Vin would put them on him and hold him down until he was real again, and Dilly trembled at the thought of it. He wanted to grab his cock and jerk off until he came in a wave of pleasure, but at the same time, he wanted to be caught here forever, locked on the edge of coming, and he was already on an edge.

"Very good," Vin said as he closed the distance between them. He let his hand stroke Dilly's shoulder and down over his arm. "I'm going to fuck you, Dylan. I'm going to fuck your hot ass so hard that you'll feel me for a week."

"Um… okay." Dilly swallowed as he realized he didn't know what to say about that. Whoo-hoo came to mind, but it seemed a little inappropriate under the circumstances. Vin tightened his fingers around Dilly's forearm and squeezed just hard enough that Dilly could feel each finger pressing into his flesh.

Wordlessly, Vin guided him to the foot of the bed, where a low black bench with squat legs waited. Vin urged him forward, pressing until he forced Dilly to knee walk up onto the bench, but when Dilly tried to climb up onto the high bed, Vin stopped him with a hand on Dilly's chest.

Dilly looked at Vin, not sure what he should do. Vin stared at him with dark eyes, his pupils wide and the brown of them mere rings around those pools. Running his hands over Dilly's chest, Vin reached a peaked nipple and tugged at it. With a gasp, Dilly instinctively reached up to protect his sensitive flesh, but a long look from Vin made him drop his hands back down to his sides. Only then did Vin offer him a smile.

"Right hand," Vin said. He dropped four cuffs onto the bed and then chose one to carefully buckle around the wrist Dilly offered. After walking to the other side, Vin repeated the maneuver with Dilly's left hand. The leather warmed quickly, and Dilly shivered as the tightness around his wrists made his whole body seem to tense up. It was as if the cuffs rang some internal alarm that made everything sharper, brighter, more dangerous.

"What's the safe word?" Dilly asked, only now realizing he hadn't asked before. Vin used a hand in the middle of his back to push him down over the bed. With his knees still on the bench, the position put most of Dilly's weight on his chest and left his cock feeling rather neglected. Oh, Dilly could rub it against the edge of the bed rather easily, but if he did, first, all these bright, beautiful feelings would end, and second, Vin would not be a happy camper. Not at all.

"I don't use them," Vin commented as he ran his hands over the swell of Dilly's ass.

"But...." Dilly's words vanished as Vin squeezed, his thumbs pressing close enough to Dilly's opening that all the rest of Dilly's blood rushed south.

"Dylan, how much pressure are you feeling to make me happy? Right now... how much do you want to please me?" Vin let his hands migrate north over the plain of Dilly's back and then squeezed his shoulders hard enough that Dilly felt his body stiffen and then relax.

Dilly pressed his face to the bed and didn't answer. The truth was that he was almost embarrassed at the intensity of the feeling. He wanted Vin to want him, and he knew he didn't have nearly as much experience. The black man in the bar had stood under Vin's whip while marks appeared on him, but Dilly couldn't have taken that. He knew he couldn't.

Vin crawled onto the bench behind Dilly, pressing close so Dilly could feel the texture of Vin's jeans against this thighs and every button pressing into his spine as Vin pinned him to the bed before whispering in his ear. "If I count on you to use a safe word, I think we're both going to be in some trouble. So, how about you just tell me if something is too much, and meanwhile, I'll pay attention to your body language."

"Oh." Dilly wasn't sure how he felt about that—not because it sounded illogical, but more because it went against what everyone else said. But then if he listened to everyone else, he wouldn't be with Vin in the first place.

Vin ran his hands up and down Dilly's arms, urging him to move them up over his head, and Dilly complied. "Don't play poker, Dylan. You wear your emotions on your sleeve."

"I don't mean.... I trust you," Dilly rushed to say. Great, he was screwing up already.

Vin chuckled and let his fingers ghost over Dilly's shoulder. "No. It's okay. There are players I use safe words with. They're too good at controlling their bodies and their expressions, and I don't trust myself to spot if they're in trouble."

"And you think you can spot that with me?" Dilly thought he was good at hiding. He'd grown up in a home where he seemed to survive by making sure he always disappeared into the shadows before some disaster blew up.

"I think you don't hide much," Vin said. That was about the last thing Dilly expected, but before he could point that out, Vin pushed away and walked around to the right side of the bed to grab Dilly's cuff. "I do like the idea of you helpless and at my mercy." Vin threaded a rope through the D-ring on the cuff and tied the ends around the right-hand bed post. Dilly pulled at the restraint, but he didn't have the strength to make anything budge. Vin did the other on the opposite side, and now rope forced Dilly's torso flat onto the bed while he still kneeled on the bench. Dilly's face got warm as he thought about his ass up in the air, and his arms spread wide.

Vin wrapped leather cuffs around Dilly's ankles, forcing him to widen his legs as he knelt on the bench, and Dilly's breath came in little hungry gasps as Vin ran his large hands over Dilly's exposed body. The embarrassment of the moment faded into hot need. Vin pinched the soft curve of Dilly's ass, right where the thigh met the torso, and Dilly gave a short yelp. With a chuckle, Vin gave the spot a soft slap, spreading out the heat and the sting before he stepped away from the bed.

Trying to watch him, Dilly twisted his body around, but that earned him another slap. Following the tacit order, Dilly put his forehead to the bed and waited. He shivered, feeling a chill even though the room was warm.

He was Vin's now. Vin could do anything, and Dilly couldn't control it—didn't want to control it. A hand ran over Dilly's ass before kneading it, and Dilly wrapped his fist around the ropes that held him. He almost felt like if he didn't, he would fall off the bed… off the floor and off the earth. The first slap was light. Almost too light, and Dilly pushed his ass up into the air as much as he could. He was almost sorry when the second slap came, a sharp crack of flesh against flesh a split second before the sting and heat hit him. Dilly gasped, arching his back and silently fighting the ropes. The flash of pain faded into a heat that swallowed him whole until Dilly lived inside it.

A third hit came, and while the crack sounded as loud, the sting was muted. This time the pain passed faster into the warm tingling that made Dilly hold his breath as he struggled to find that one perfect second where he could get lost inside himself. Another hard swat forced the air out of him, and then Dilly sucked in more oxygen, his head feeling fuzzy as Vin started a pattern of hits.

A hard shiver took Dilly, making his muscles strain against the restraints; his bottom throbbed and all the heat of that soaked into his cock. If his cock got any harder, it was going to break, and that would be bad. But still. Dilly wanted more. He needed more, but Vin stopped. Mewling in distress, Dilly tried to wiggle his way back into that perfect moment.

Hands ran over his ass, sending new flares of heat through his body. Dilly sucked air through his teeth and arched his back. Vin leaned over him, pressed into his sore ass, and pinned him to the bed. "Are you ready for more?" Vin asked, each word a warm puff of air against Dilly's ear. Even though Dilly wanted to answer, the words darted away like silverfish.

Vin chuckled, and then his weight abandoned Dilly, leaving him feeling like he might float away. Something cool slithered over his ass, and Dilly sighed. When the hard snap came, Dilly jerked and clenched his ass. *Whip. That was a whip. Maybe.* Dilly expected a whip to hurt more, but pain wasn't the first word. It was the fourth or fifth, but not the first. Colors popped in front of Dilly's closed eyes, and every muscle strained; two more pops warned him right before new fire opened up on his ass.

"You turn red so nicely," Vin complimented him, his warm hand running over Dilly so lines of heat seemed to catch fire again. Dilly could feel every centimeter of his body, but Vin's words seemed to wash over him uselessly.

Dilly wanted to ask what Vin had used, but the words scrambled in his brain. Rather than babble, he just wrapped his fingers around the ropes holding him and sank into the all-consuming heat. Vin's words were nothing more than a distant rumble. Vin's hands vanished before something stung his butt again… it hit with hundreds of little stings that felt like sinking into an overheated hot tub. Dilly could feel his body yield as he sank into the moment, and the world began to evaporate into mist.

When his body started trembling, Dilly wasn't sure why. He could feel the heat verging on the edge of pain—the sharp, bright edge that turned the world into a distant whisper. The whip came down again, and then there was a bite, a vivid flash of pain that made Dilly cry out before the hands returned to smooth out the pain and rub it in until it became part of Dilly and the heat became bearable. Those hands moved down to Dilly's thighs, parting them, and Dilly drifted through reality as slick fingers opened him. The cold slick and the hot marks demanded every molecule of his attention, so Dilly felt like he—his personality, his being—had vanished. Only the cool slick against the hot skin was real.

But then Vin was pushing in, and Dilly's muscles, tight from the heat, struggled to yield. The pressure against his ring of muscle almost made Dilly feel like a virgin trying to figure out how anything cock-sized was supposed to fit up there, but Vin kept pressing. With a sigh, Dilly finally relaxed, allowing Vin to slam in. Vin took him hard, and the sound of flesh against flesh replaced the crack of the whip as Vin pounded into him.

Dilly's cock ached, the pain edging out the delicious heat before Vin took it in hand, and Dilly thrust into that fist, desperate to come. If he didn't come, his body would fly apart. The wave of orgasm hit him dangerously hard. Dilly heard his own heart drumming in his ears, and he lost the ability to breathe as every system seemed to shut down and then restart only sluggishly.

Lying limply on the bed, he felt Vin finish using him before pulling out. In some distant galaxy, Vin walked around the room, and a door closed, but Dilly couldn't bring himself to care. He sprawled boneless against the sheets. Eventually, Vin returned and used strong hands to urge Dilly up onto the bed, then crawled in next to Dilly. With a sigh, Dilly leaned into Vin, pulling against one wrist cuff.

"Shhh," Vin whispered, and hands worked at Dilly's wrist. Vin didn't take the cuff off, but he fixed something to provide slack in the rope, and that was all Dilly wanted. He didn't even open his eyes as Vin pulled him close and started stroking his shoulder. Vin petted him like an oversized cat, and nothing felt as right or as safe as letting the world slip away while he enjoyed the feel of warm fingers against his face. They lay there, half napping, as the tingles and the heat slowly faded from Dilly's body and his ass started aching from being overstretched.

"Are you coming back?" Vin asked softly, his fingers still skimming across Dilly's sweat-damp skin.

"Nope," Dilly muttered.

"Well, that's good to know." Vin chuckled. "You would spoil any Dom."

"You whipped me." Dilly could hear the surprise in his own voice.

"A light flogging, yes."

Dilly opened his eyes. "That was a light flogging?" His voice had a hint of squeak or squawk. Squawks were manlier, so Dilly was going with squawk.

Vin grinned, and where he normally looked way older than he was, in that second, he looked like a young guy in his twenties. "Yeah, that was light. You probably won't even have marks in the morning."

Chewing on his lip, Dilly squirmed around some. If he couldn't handle the kind of play Vin liked, he wasn't going to be able to keep him. The feeling was like rotting garlic in his stomach.

"What are you thinking?" Vin asked. When Dilly didn't answer right away, Vin caught one of the ropes still tied to his cuffs and gave it a hard yank so Dilly did look at him. "What are you thinking?" he repeated as he held Dilly's wrist tightly.

"I know you probably like more…." Dilly stopped.

Vin reached up and caught Dilly's chin in his hand before shifting to lie on top of Dilly, pinning him to the bed. The pressure against his ass made Dilly hiss in pain, but even now he could feel a deep itch that made him want more. "I like watching a submissive squirm and fight and finally settle under my whip," Vin said, his tone fierce. "That's what I like, and that's what you did. If you do something I don't like, I'll tell you. Are we clear?" Vin demanded.

Dilly swallowed as he looked up into those dark eyes that seemed to pin his soul as easily as Vin pinned his body.

"Um. Yeah?"

"Yeah? That's all you have to say?"

Dilly shrugged. "I would say 'sir, yes sir,' only the idea of being honest is… um." Dilly sighed. "It's a little foreign. In my family we sort of lie to avoid confrontation. Either that or we avoid each other to avoid confrontation. So… honesty. Can we settle for 'sir, I'll try to remember that, sir'?" Dilly looked up, and as much as he knew he sounded like a goober and as much as he didn't want to look Vin in the face, he forced himself to.

Vin rolled back to the side, leaving his thigh over Dilly's legs as he brought his hand up to trace the edge of Dilly's face. "Dylan, I only want you to try. If you can't try and trust me to tell you the truth, this is going to turn pretty bad, just like if I can't trust you to ask for help. So how about we both try to let a little trust in?"

"I can try. I've been told I'm very trying," Dilly joked.

Vin rolled his eyes and shifted around on the bed. One of the ropes got in the way, and muttering curses, Vin reached up and pulled the knot free. "Are your wrists okay?"

Dilly swiveled them and everything felt fine. "Yep."

With a nod, Vin pulled the second rope free and tossed both to the side, but he left the cuffs on Dilly's wrists before pulling him closer. In the club, Vin always seemed so much larger, but lying side by side, Dilly realized they were actually pretty close in size. Vin had an inch or two more in height, and he had more muscle, but they were similar. Weird. Vin definitely took up more space in the universe. Maybe there was just something about Doms that made them bigger and that made Dilly disappear into the background, he mused as he started drifting off to sleep. He shifted and the rasp of the sheets against his hot ass made him hiss. Vin chuckled, and Dilly didn't remember anything else as he fell asleep.

A SHAFT of light cut across Dilly's forehead, and when he brought his hand up to shade his eyes, he got a metal D-ring right between the eyes. "Ow. Fuck." Sitting up, Dilly rubbed his face and tried to take the sting out. While he had a taste for pain, he didn't like all forms of it. Getting hit in the face while half asleep rated a "no" in his world.

"Vin?" Dilly called. The bathroom door stood open, and there was a faint scent that suggested Vin had already showered. This was the awkward time of day—the morning after when the social rules weren't quite back in place. Dilly had lost one or two friends in that awkwardness before he'd learned friends do not let friends fuck friends. While on paper, the idea of friends with benefits worked, in reality, it led to bitching, throwing of video game controllers, and a general sense of badness.

Swinging his legs out of bed, Dilly took a second to finger the black leather cuffs around his wrist. They made his hands look larger, somehow. He held his legs out and looked at the black cuff that divided his leg. Clearly Dilly was a big old Pavlovian dog, because his cock started getting hard, which was going to make peeing awkward. Ignoring the feel of leather hot against his skin and the way the cuffs looked, Dilly hurried into the bathroom and took care of his morning business. He wanted a shower, but in all the Internet stories he'd read, the submissive partner wasn't allowed to take restraints off without permission, so he used a washcloth to clean up as best he could and then looked around for his clothes.

He searched the bedroom and bathroom with no luck, and had half decided Vin wanted to keep him naked before he spotted the heavy blue robe neatly draped over the side of the small twin bed in the bondage closet. Dilly grabbed it and then spent a little time exploring.

The rings in the walls were set into the studs with heavy bolts, and Dilly tested their height. They would keep his wrists at shoulder level, which wasn't particularly harsh bondage, but his arms would be sore after a while. On the wall at the foot of the bed, three rails ran the length of the short wall, and the tallest of them required Dilly to go up on his toes to even reach it. The first time Vin had spanked Dilly, he'd commented that he didn't fuck children or boys named Dilly. At the time… well, honestly, at the time Dilly hadn't cared about anything but sinking into the post-sex bliss.

But now, he could see where someone named Dilly didn't have a place in this world. Dilly was someone young enough that he still let people call him names he hated because standing up for himself was too much trouble. But he didn't know how to become Dylan.

He turned around and Vin was there, leaning against the wall as he watched silently.

"Vin."

"Dylan."

"Dylan. Yep, that's my name."

Vin looked at him oddly, but he didn't ask anything, and the silence stuffed into the room, filling all the nooks and crannies. When the room grew crowded with it, Vin finally moved forward, his rolling gait making Dylan's cock harden even as he backed up. He ended up with one of the horizontal bars in the small of his back, and Vin crowded still closer. Finally, Dylan was caught between Vin and the bar, pressed tightly against the wall until his cock was hard, and he gripped the bar, not sure what to do. Vin ran his hands up Dylan's arms and then leaned close to brush the softest of kisses against Dylan's lips even as his body kept Dylan hard-trapped.

"Good morning," he said, and Dylan could smell the coffee and the masculine soap. "So, is there something on your mind?"

"Sex?" Dylan guessed. With Vin this close, that was pretty much all he could think about, not that he was complaining. Vin smiled. He had a boyish smile, somehow. He was still scary as hell even with it, but he had a boyish smile.

"I guessed that." Vin shifted so he pressed his hip into Dylan's cock. "Anything else?"

"Um, I don't think I should be Dilly anymore because honestly, I always hated the name, and I spent most of junior high trying to get people to stop calling me that, only it didn't work, and somewhere along the way, I gave up."

"And something has changed now?" Vin sounded honestly curious.

"Lots of somethings. Dilly is the name of someone way too young to get tied to these bars and fucked hard."

"You haven't been tied to these bars," Vin pointed out.

Dylan gave him a hopeful look, and after a second, Vin laughed and shook his head. "If you're going to try to be manipulative, at least you have the good sense to be artless about it."

"So, yes?" Dylan guessed with a smile.

Vin leaned closer and gave him another featherlight kiss while pressing Dylan even harder against the bar. Moving his mouth to Dylan's ear, he whispered, "No." Then he stepped back and headed for the door. "I enjoy ignoring manipulation too much to pass up this opportunity."

Dylan sighed. Vin was leaving him hard and clinging to a restraint bar. He couldn't figure out whether he hated not having sex or if he loved how dominant Vin could be. Maybe both.

"Breakfast in fifteen minutes. Since scrambled eggs are the only thing I can fix without turning the eggs into rubber, I hope you like them."

"Love them," Dylan agreed. Discussing eggs while having an erection hard enough to tent the front of his robe… that was unique. "And I was wondering where my clothes were."

Vin stopped at the door and looked back. "You're only wondering? Not panicking or demanding?"

Dylan shrugged. "My panic button has been hit so many times in the last month that I think it broke."

Frowning, Vin turned to face Dylan. "I put them in the washer. They should be ready to go in the dryer now, or you can grab some of my stuff. The pants will be a little long, but they'll fit well enough."

"Unless you have a rule about dressing for breakfast, I'm fine with waiting," Dylan said. He got another long look from Vin before the man nodded and headed back out. Dylan was going to need another trip to the bathroom for a little self-loving, or he was going to have a miserable morning, so he headed that way, still rolling a dozen ideas around in his head.

Vin had washed his clothes, which was nice. But he'd taken them and put them somewhere Dylan couldn't find them, which was odd. Borderline not nice, even. And then he'd been less than direct when Dylan had first asked about them. Feeling a little like a Dilly who didn't understand the world, he headed into the bathroom and reached inside his robe for his still-hard cock. Yep, Vin might confuse him, but his prick definitely still liked the man.

Chapter 14

VIN'S breakfast didn't reach Mom-levels. The toast had one edge that approached black without achieving it, and even though they were scrambled, the eggs had a texture that reminded Dylan of Play-Doh with thin, crusty edges. Still, having a man cook breakfast was a special sort of hot and awkward all at once. Vin had his laptop open on the counter, and he kept getting distracted by whatever mail he had. So he'd stand there with the spatula or the butter knife in hand as he scrolled through the computer.

It gave Dylan a chance to study Vin. Without the leather, he looked smaller. Today he had on dark blue jeans with a jacket and tie, which made him look like a total computer geek. And he had the same classic Italian looks that Dylan had grown up seeing in the neighborhood. Dylan had a lot of that dark-haired dark-eyed thing going himself, but it was more pronounced in Vin. Vincenzo. His parents were either first generation, or they were those Italians who lived in Italian neighborhoods and shopped in Italian stores and who spoke Italian more than English. His mom's parents were like that. When his mom married the very not-Italian mechanic from down the street, apparently, fireworks and screaming had followed.

Dylan had almost finished before Vin got his own plate of food and sat down, abandoning the laptop.

"Busy?" Dylan guessed.

"The people who hire me are morons," Vin answered, which wasn't technically an answer, but Dylan was guessing something in the e-mail had made him unhappy. "So, did Gary give you more than that bruised stomach?" Vin asked. He then speared a forkful of eggs with a little more energy than strictly required, even for tough eggs.

"Um, if I say yes, are you going to get bent out of shape?"

"Yep," Vin agreed.

"Oh." Dylan ran his fingers over the fist-sized bruise, feeling very much like a Dilly in that moment.

"If you can tell me how you plan to avoid future problems, I could probably convince myself to sit on my hands, though." Vin didn't sound happy about that, but Dylan appreciated the offer. Vin was trying. He really was. And the fact that he clearly wanted to jump in and fix this was so very tempting. Unhealthy, but tempting.

"I figured I should probably avoid home. I had thought about doing some couch surfing. People usually don't mind me hanging out for a while. I'm pretty quiet."

"Couch surfing?" Vin carefully put his fork down. "You could stay in the basement. It smells like cat pee… or maybe that's the smell of the vagrants who were living in here before I inherited the house, but it has its own pathetic kitchen and entrance, so you'd have your space."

Dylan felt the relief like a stone dropping off his back. He'd much rather deal with cat pee than try to charm his way into different friends' houses or face going home. "That would be awesome."

"You haven't seen the place. Save your thanks because you may choose to couch surf."

"Nope. The basement is fine with me."

For some reason, that made Vin stare at Dylan for a long time. The old refrigerator motor whined to life, and the wind made something outside bang with a metallic rhythm, but Vin just stared at him. Dylan started to squirm in his seat. "What?" he finally came right out and asked.

As he leaned back in his chair, Vin's gaze just grew sharper. "You could stay upstairs with me, only I don't think you'd like the rules."

Whoa. Dylan had not seen that coming. That wasn't just out of left field—that was from the opposite side of the fence. That was from a hot dog vendor in the parking lot of left field. "Rules?" Dylan said, his voice squeaking a little.

Abandoning his breakfast, Vin got up, grabbed his laptop from the cracked kitchen counter, and snapped it shut before heading for the door. "Like I said, you wouldn't appreciate them much. I have about a hundred dollars set aside, so if you keep the receipts from any cleaning crap you buy for the basement, I'll pay you back."

"Hey! Wait." Dylan ended up chasing Vin out into the hall, but then Vin spun around, and Dylan froze, prey trapped in the middle of a narrow corridor. But even though he felt like a rabbit that had just poked a wolf, he didn't back up. "Maybe we could talk, because I'm oddly okay with rules, even ones that don't make sense like men not wearing white socks with black shoes because those black socks are not all that comfortable, not compared with a good pair of white athletic socks."

"Dylan," Vin warned. That was all he said, but the warning was laid out in big, flashing letters.

"What? Hey, we're just communicating here. Maybe a little clear communication could avoid some misunderstandings because I'm sort of out of patience for any more misunderstandings this week."

"The way you clearly told me you didn't want me to touch your brother?" Vin narrowed his eyes, and it took Dylan a second to get it. He never told Vin to leave Gary alone, he'd just sort of implied he didn't want Vin exploding. "I think we need a little space, and I shouldn't have made that suggestion. You shouldn't be considering it."

"But you got it," Dylan pointed out. "You understood me."

"And if I hadn't? If I got emotionally tangled up in your life and I found out your brother hit you, would you be okay if I was too irrational to notice that you wanted me to stay out of it?"

Dylan thought about that. Carmine did that all the time—rushing in to save him where he didn't need saving, usually from Gary. "I'd think you were pretty normal, actually."

Vin sucked in his breath. "You have a dangerous definition of normal." Vin turned and headed for the dining room/office area, but the confrontational tone and the hard lines of his spine were gone, replaced with something a little more approachable, so Dylan followed.

"I never claimed to be normal. Or I think I am pretty normal; it's just that most normal American families are kind of fucked-up, you know?"

Vin put the laptop on the desk. "I know."

"Do you want your breakfast? I could bring it in here." Dylan stood at the doorway to the room feeling intensely uncomfortable. This was Vin's lair—a part of Vin's life that Dylan didn't know, and that was true of most of Vin's life. Dylan didn't know about it or understand it. And Vin was right, he shouldn't be considering moving in, but he was.

Vin shook his head. "I overcooked the eggs. I'll get something later."

"I could throw together a fried egg," Dylan offered.

Sitting down in his big chair, Vin spent a long time looking at Dylan. "You keep pushing all the buttons, Dylan. I don't know if you're so good at manipulating that I can't see the craft behind all these offers or if you're just this ready to have a manipulative son of a bitch in your life."

Dylan shrugged. "I have a lot of manipulative bastards in my life already. Miss Dolphinia might even be one."

Vin laughed and shook his head like he couldn't quite believe Dylan. "She is."

Inching into the room, Dylan came right out and asked. "How did you two meet, anyway? I mean, you aren't exactly the sort that likes being manipulated, and she really likes to manipulate everyone, and that just doesn't seem like a good base for a friendship, but you two... you seem like good friends."

"We do, huh?" Vin scratched his neck and shifted in his chair. "I would have said that we seem like two junkyard dogs that have learned to share a space without ripping into each other."

"She wants you happy." Saying it out loud, Dylan could see how true that was. Miss Dolphinia had taken Dylan in from the first day, but from the first day, she'd been trying to get him into Vin's bed. He was starting to wonder if that had less to do with trying to help a newbie than it did trying to please Vin. And Dylan wasn't complaining. If sleeping with Vin made Vin happy, Dylan was perfectly willing to make that sacrifice again and again and again and twice on Sunday. Even now his ass ached deliciously, and Dylan wished he could get them off the awkward conversation and back to having hot sex.

"She feels obligated," Vin disagreed.

"Why?"

For a second, Vin looked around the room as though searching for something. Dylan waited, and it took some time before Vin finally settled his gaze on him. "When I first came on the scene, I was pretty lost."

"You slept with her?" Dylan had a very unpleasant image in his mind, and now that he thought about it, Vin always did wear a flag or he flagged right or whatever they called it when a man stuck a bandana in his pocket, but he wore a dark blue handkerchief in his right pocket to show he liked to bottom during anal sex. Oh that was a creepy image. Dylan liked to pretend anyone over fifty didn't have sex, and Miss Dolphinia reminded him way too much of an old aunt to think about her and sex. And the thought of Lee and Vin... that way led to more than a little jealousy and insecurity.

"No," Vin said firmly. "Even when I was confused, I had enough top in me that I couldn't see myself with her. That woman is all top, and so is Lee. Man or woman, Dolphinia is as dominant as they come."

"But she had a long-term partner. A switch. He subbed for Miss Dolphinia, but when he had the urge to be more dominant, he would play with the younger crowd. Rice." Vin said the name with such fondness that Dylan got a second jolt of jealousy. "He showed me the ropes," Vin finished quickly, and his face twisted with a sorrow Dylan didn't understand. Relationships usually ended with yelling or indifference, not with the sort of pain he saw on Vin's face.

"What happened?"

Vin shrugged. "Car accident." The emotion vanished behind his normal expression—a sort of cold disdain he showed the world most of the time.

"I'm sorry."

"It was years ago." Vin opened his laptop and turned his desktop computer on. When Vin turned his chair, Dylan had the feeling he was being dismissed.

His first instinct was to leave, but he knew if he did, he was going to come back to find the Vin who kept pushing him away, the one who chained him to a bed and tried to scare him into not having sex. And yeah, that Vin was exciting, but Dylan preferred having sex. He slipped farther into the room, staying along the wall, and Vin's back went a little straighter.

"I'm still sorry," Dylan offered. "So, that couldn't have been easy—sharing a lover with Miss Dolphinia." The truth was, Dylan couldn't see Vin sharing at all. He had a possessive vibe even when he wasn't running around telling everyone how possessive he was.

"It was harder losing him," Vin said dryly, and boy did Dylan feel about two inches tall. While he put a foot in his mouth on a semi-regular basis, he usually didn't get it jammed down there so far. Dylan wondered if he should just get the hell out of Dodge, only then Vin turned his chair toward Dylan. "Miss Dolphinia still thinks she owes me something for sticking with Rice when he got hurt. Either that or it's easier to try and micromanage my love life than it is to get out and have one of her own. Her and Rice were together almost thirty years."

Dylan blinked. "Wow." Gay people showed up all the time on television talking about their long-term relationships. They bought houses and redecorated their bedrooms on cable shows, and those gays always seemed to have been together forever, but not many of the gay people Dylan knew really stuck it out that long. Hell, most of the not-gay couples he knew had a major relationship blowout inside five years.

"Yeah. For an old queen from the free-love and wild-sex era, she settled down for a long time."

"And now she wants you settled," Dylan said softly.

Sighing, Vin leaned back in his chair and considered Dylan with a sort of weary caution.

Dylan put on his most charming smile. "So, you said something about rules for staying upstairs. Are we talking about being naked and having to bark like a dog rules or having to put the toilet seat down when I'm finished rules?"

"If I said the first?" Vin tilted his head up.

Dylan thought about it. He didn't want to give the easy answer because as much as being told to stay naked would be totally hot for about a week, come October, he would be ready for a peasant's revolution. "I would say that I would stay upstairs with you once or twice a week and spend the rest of my time getting used to cat pee," he finally answered.

Vin leaned back, and for a long time, he just stared. Dylan started to feel like he'd just totally fucked up. He had no idea how, but he couldn't escape that sinking feeling. "You surprise me, Dylan," Vin eventually offered.

"What?"

"You have your head on straight."

Dylan narrowed his eyes. "And that surprises you? I think I should take offense to that."

"Don't," Vin said in a tone of voice that made it pretty clear he expected Dylan to do just that. "I generally have a low opinion of everyone. But that doesn't mean this is a good idea. I told you I'm possessive, so if you're upstairs, I am not going to react rationally to you having sex with other men. I would expect that if you can't resist some top, you'd come to me, I'd consider your request, and nine times out of ten, I would tell you 'no'."

Dylan gave a little huff. "And here I thought it would be nine hundred and ninety-nine times out of a thousand."

"It may be easy to say that now, but when you're at the club, and someone catches your eye, I'm not going to handle it well if you decide to ignore that rule." Vin's voice had a deadly cold warning to it now. Dylan focused. Now was not the time for joking.

"There are only two guys at the club I've ever shown any interest in, and Guard kinda ruined the moment, even before I knew he was a lawyer."

Vin made a sour face. "I'm not even going to ask, because if you tell me about sex with that idiot, I'm going to hate him even worse, and he's not my favorite person in the world right now."

"He means well," Dylan pointed out. Guard was pretty much perfect if you believed what the Internet said about what Doms should be like. Then again, if you listened to the Internet, the universe was ruled by ceiling cat, so that might not be the most reliable source of information.

"If by well, you mean he thinks he has all the answers, sure," Vin agreed. "And I will never give you permission to sleep with him. Ever. Not if he grew a three foot dick and you were dying to try it on for size."

Dylan laughed. "Okay, that would not be my first reaction if someone had a dick that large. I think there would be panic and flailing and avoidance."

Vin rolled his eyes. "Not as much as you might think. But we talk to each other before we do anything outside, deal?"

"Deal." Dylan nodded, and he tried hard to ignore the hard little knot of fear in his stomach.

For a few long and awkward seconds, Vin just stared at him, and Dylan started edging toward the door. "If you ever take up poker, you're going to be either broke or naked inside an hour. Probably within fifteen minutes."

"What?"

"You have no poker face, which is good because at least then I know when you're not sharing everything. What is running through that head of yours?"

"I… what?"

Vin stood up. "Dylan, you have ten seconds to spit out whatever is on your mind." With slow, measured steps, Vin advanced, and Dylan was already backed up against the wall, so he had nowhere to retreat. Really, someone should tell his dick to stop getting hard at the sight of Vin stalking toward him, because from his expression, Vin did not have sex on his mind. Dylan, however, couldn't seem to think about anything else. Vin was fucking gorgeous when he got pissed.

"Now!" Vin barked, and Dylan's words escaped like air out of a popped balloon.

"I just don't know how long I'll be enough for you."

Vin froze. "Seriously?" In one second, Vin went from predator to confused geeky computer guy. The shift was so sudden and so complete that Dylan felt a little off-balance. "That's what's bothering you? You think I plan to what, get tired of you after two nights?"

"You are the one who told me you didn't do more than one night," Dylan defended himself, because when Vin said it, Dylan's fears sounded stupid.

"And I already broke that rule with you. I avoid spending time to avoid getting too attached to people. You, however, are an idiot, and you let me obsess over you, so I doubt you're going to have to worry about me getting bored. That's not one of my flaws, and trust me, I have many."

"But… I just know a lot of guys like variety…." Dylan let his words trail off. That wasn't what he meant, and from the look on Vin's face, he knew it too. Dylan didn't play as hard as Vin, and that was going to be an issue eventually.

"Do I seem like the kind of person who is comfortable trying to negotiate a lot of relationships?" Vin crossed his arms and his expression just dared Dylan to say yes.

"Um, can I claim the fifth on that?" The truth was Vin wasn't exactly a people person. He was a little gruff and kinda scary, not that Dylan had a problem with scary. But he wasn't the sort to cheerfully set up negotiations with a new player. Of course, as far as Dylan could see, Vin did just fine finding partners. Dylan felt a flash of jealousy when he remembered the man Vin had whipped and fucked right in the bar.

"Exactly. I don't like new relationships." Vin turned around and headed back to his computer.

"But you like whipping people and fucking them. I watched you. That night when I was a little…."

"Stoned off your fucking gourd?" Vin supplied when Dylan stopped.

"Yep." Dylan couldn't even argue the point.

"I do," Vin said. "I prefer to not talk to them afterward, but I love whipping someone, watching the strain and yield, and you strain and fight and lose yourself so completely that I am looking forward to fucking you night after night after night. I want to find out just how fast I can drop you into that subspace. I want to know every sensitive spot on your body, and I want to watch the muscles of your back stand out as you fight the cuffs." Vin twitched his body, and that dominant, larger-than-life Vin appeared, even if he still was wearing computer geek camouflage.

Dylan's cock started to make a valiant effort to rise even though he'd already come twice in the last twelve hours. "Somehow, I don't think I'm going to complain about that."

"Yeah, I can see." Vin made a point out of letting his eyes travel over Dylan's body and down to where his half-hard cock made a bulge in his robe.

"Want to try for another round?" Dylan suggested. With a little encouragement, he could get it up again.

"Nope," Vin gave him a devilish grin. "I want to think about you suffering."

Dylan groaned. Okay, that was hot. It shouldn't be, but it so fucking was.

"And I still hate your brother and would like to see him dead."

"Funny enough, so do I," Dylan agreed. Gary was a first-class asshole, no matter how you looked at it.

"I mean it. He hit you, and he'll do it again. Hell, how many times has he done it already, Dylan?"

Dylan shrugged. "Not all that many, actually. He's usually more creative in his terrorism."

Vin's eyes narrowed.

"Not that I want you to do anything, because he's also a master manipulator, and he'd somehow twist everything around, and Miss Dolphinia would be bailing you out of jail after he made everything look like your fault."

"I can take care of myself."

"Which oddly, I'm not questioning. Most people can't take care of themselves around Gary, but you can. That doesn't mean he wouldn't make one ungodly mess in the middle of your life."

Vin crossed his arms. "If you want this, then I need to know that you're not anywhere near him—not living in the same house or answering his calls or anything. I am not going to react well if I think he laid one finger on you."

"Deal," Dylan agreed. "I mean, that's not even a hard deal to make because Gary is not going to forgive me any time soon, and a pissed Gary is a dangerous Gary."

"Yeah, and an unpissed one is safe as houses," Vin said sarcastically. A few years ago, Dylan would have felt some sort of obligation to defend his brother. That was how he'd been raised. However, after seeing all his brother's tools laid out on the evening news—after hearing what his brother had done to women, yeah, Dylan really didn't feel like it.

"What did you do?" Vin had that calculating look again.

"What? Me? Nothing."

Vin narrowed his eyes again.

"Except maybe tell the victims all about the highly confidential legal strategy Gary's lawyers were going to use to make them all look like liars."

Vin visibly flinched. "I'm revising my earlier comment. I'm not just going to randomly call you, I'm going to put a fucking GPS and audio bug on you just to make sure your brother hasn't killed you."

"He won't kill me," Dylan said. "It's more fun to make me miserable. Besides, Gary doesn't actually believe he's going to jail. Even if everyone in the state signed a We-Hate-Gary-Carter petition, he would still assume he could talk his way out of trouble."

"Charming," Vin said, his voice flat.

"Not really."

Vin nodded. "So, I have to answer some e-mails, and then we need to go over and get your stuff."

"We?" Dylan could feel that bubble of panic again.

"I'm not letting you go there alone. I don't trust that asshole, and considering that I have one foot on the asshole scale myself, that's saying a lot. I usually have a lot of patience for antisocial behavior."

"But—" Dylan closed his mouth.

Vin turned away from the computer and refocused on Dylan. "But?"

"Um. Crap." Dylan ran a hand over his face as he came to a decision. "My parents don't know I'm gay, but a grown man shouldn't be hiding that, right?" Dylan looked to Vin for some sort of confirmation.

"A grown man can make his own choices about who he lets into his life."

Okay, that made it worse. That made it sound like Dylan was shutting his parents out of his life if he didn't tell them. He loved his parents, and as an added incentive, Gary was totally going to make hay with this little fact if Dylan didn't get ahead of the story. "Then this grown man says he should tell his parents. Only, maybe you should prepare yourself for some crying and some denial and some potentially embarrassing stories about ex-girlfriends."

Vin smiled at him. "It takes a strong man to face embarrassing ex-girlfriend stories."

"Yeah, save your encouragement for after I've actually gone through with this," Dylan said. At this point he wasn't sure he could. Imagining his father's stoic silence and his mother's crying was enough to make his stomach churn unhappily. But if he wanted to be a Dylan, he needed to do this. He needed to take this weapon away from Gary, and he needed to make sure his parents saw him. And here he thought today would be a good day. Yeah, not so much.

Chapter 15

"SO, ARE you ready for this?" Vin asked as he parked the old car across the street from the Carter garage.

"If I say no?"

Vin seemed to think about that for a second. "I could go over and get your stuff or tell your idiot sister to bring all your things to my house."

"Which sounds a little... cowardly," Dylan pointed out. That didn't mean he didn't want to do either of those. He did. He just figured he was getting too old to have other people clean up his mess. "How did you tell your parents?"

Vin's hands tightened around the wheel before he seemed to intentionally uncurl them so he could shift sideways in his seat. "I never knew my father. I inherited the house from him, and he seemed to think that putting my name in a will was fatherly enough to count. My mom...." Vin shrugged. "She thought I was going through a phase. She said that teenagers have so many hormones in them that table legs look attractive. She said we'd talk again when I was twenty-five and I didn't have enough hormones to pickle my brain."

"That didn't happen?" Dylan guessed.

"I turned twenty-five this year. She's been dead for eight years." Vin's emotions were shuttered, and Dylan reached out to rest his fingers against Vin's arm. Vin moved his gaze down to focus on Dylan's hand. "I honestly don't know how she would have taken it if I said I was still gay. I like to think she would have accepted me. It's not like she tried to change me."

Dylan figured getting dismissed as having a hormone-pickled brain would hurt about as much as open rejection. "I think my mom is more likely to go for the wailing and the self-blaming as she tries to figure out how she failed as a mother to make me turn out screwy in the head."

"So, she's fine with a rapist in the family, but a gay son would make her feel like a failure?" Vin's voice was thick with sarcasm, but Dylan couldn't exactly argue. Carmine had made the same argument about a million times. Vin shook his head. "Yeah, I shouldn't have gone there. Look, if you want to tell your father first, you can. If not, we can head straight to your house. So, what's on the agenda?" Vin turned to face forward.

"My father," Dylan said firmly. "Definitely my father." He looked at the garage. Only one of the bays was open, and the place looked oddly deserted. Usually his father had a half-dozen cars crammed into the place and there'd be a few men hanging around and drinking the coffee. It seemed like everyone was suffering except Gary. Well, Gary would claim he was suffering because he'd been forced to move back home, but that wasn't exactly punishment. "Probably my father," Dylan amended that.

"Do you want me to come in?"

"Part of me wants you to, but I really think I should be able to talk to my own father." Dylan took a deep breath before he opened the car door. He honestly didn't know how his father would react. His father wasn't a violent man, but he did have a habit of just avoiding anything that looked like conflict, and Dylan had a sudden image of his father avoiding him for the next thirty years or so. That wasn't what he wanted from life.

"Dylan," Vin called out, and Dylan bent down to look in the car. "I'll be keeping an eye out. If you need me, let me know."

"What should I do if I want you?"

Vin gave him a small smile. "Looking as panicked as you are right now would do it. This is your dad, Dylan. He raised you."

"Which is why I don't want him to hate me or hate himself or anything like that." Not waiting for an answer, Dylan slammed the door shut and trotted across the street, hurrying to avoid getting hit by passing cars.

"Hey, Dad," he called. His father stood under a Chevy that was on his lift.

"Dilly. You worried your mother not coming home last night."

"I e-mailed Carmine that I was at a friend's."

His father looked around the Chevy's tire at him. "Which doesn't mean much when your mother doesn't know which friend." He seemed ready to carry on with the lecture, but then he sighed and shook his head. "But a young man needs his space. So, what brings you down here?"

"Um, I thought we might talk."

Concern flashed across his father's face. "Did something happen?"

"Not really." Dylan took a deep breath and struggled to figure out how to start this conversation. Blurting seemed like a bad idea, but then so did everything else.

"Dylan?" His father put down his wrench and grabbed a red rag to wipe the grease off his hands. "What's going on?"

"Nothing, really. I mean, nothing that hasn't been going on for a long time."

"What's been going on?"

"Nothing. Well, something, but something that's pretty normal." His father frowned in confusion, and Dylan plowed ahead. "Because you know different people are different. And that's just how they're born, you know?" Dylan tripped over his own tongue.

His father took a step back as his face sort of cleared up, like when he put his glasses on after squinting at something for a long time. "Are you trying to tell me that you're gay?" he just asked.

Dylan stared at him, and he was pretty sure something was wrong with his face because he couldn't quite get his mouth to close. "But... I...."

"It's okay, Dilly," his father reassured him in that same tone he'd used when Dylan was ten or twelve and a movie had scared the pants off him. "It's okay to tell me that."

"You knew?" Dylan finally demanded. It was the only thing that made sense.

Shaking his head, his father laughed. "Dylan, I've known since you were nine."

"But... how?" Dylan took a step backward so he could lean against one of his father's benches. He needed to or his legs were going to go out from under him.

"Dilly, you've always cared more about how cute a baseball player was rather than his stats. When you traded sports cards, you always wanted Alex Rodriguez and Billy Ashley and Casey Candaele, for God's sake. I know you weren't collecting those for the stats."

Dylan felt the world spin around his head until he was almost dizzy. How the hell could he not have known that his father did know? "Why didn't you say anything?"

"I didn't want to push you." His father sounded defensive. "You hear all these stories about young people who can't handle knowing they're gay, and I didn't want to push you too fast—to lose you. Besides, this is not something I want to talk to my kids about. Sex, that is, not sexuality... exactly."

That was true. His father had stumbled through half of a "coming of age" speech before shoving a *Know Your Own Body* book in his general direction and then fleeing. Dylan opened his mouth, but he couldn't get any words out. Despite his best efforts, he couldn't get air into his lungs. He just couldn't.

He heard a car door slam, and Dylan knew he had a pretty small window before Vin appeared. He knew it. He just didn't know what he was supposed to say to his father. He'd practiced this speech. He'd agonized over it and had nightmares. He'd role-played conversations with one of the guys on a gay chat room. He'd... he'd been an idiot. His father knew. There was something so very wrong with this picture.

"Dylan?" Vin stopped at the edge of the work space, his feet bisecting the dark line where the garage door rested against concrete when the door was closed.

His father looked from Dylan to Vin a couple of times before he turned toward Vin and held his hand out. "Hi, I'm Ed Carter."

"Vincenzo Hauser," Vin responded almost automatically as he stepped into the garage and shook hands. After a brief glance toward Dylan's father, Vin focused on Dylan. "Hey, are you okay?" Vin took a step closer, and now his father and Vin were shoulder to shoulder.

"He knew I was gay. This whole time, he knew I was gay."

That seemed to surprise Vin, because he took a second to blink with this utterly blank expression. "Oh. I guess that's good. Right?" Vin glanced over toward Dylan's father. Dylan had never seen Vin this unsure. It bothered him a little.

"Are you two…." Dylan's father definitely looked pale at that thought, and Vin didn't offer any answer at all.

"Friends," Dylan offered quickly. There was having his father know, and there was shoving it in his father's face. Unless he wanted to change his name to Carmine and get some sexual reassignment surgery, he should definitely avoid that second thing.

His father didn't look all that convinced. He frowned for a second, and then turned to his bench and picked up a wrench. "Just don't tell me about it, and that is not because you're gay. I told Frank the same thing. I want to pretend he's marrying my little girl and then sleeping in a separate bed for the next sixty years, so let me have my illusions, okay?" His father delivered the speech to the bottom of a Chevy as he turned back to working on a long rod near a big curly thing between two of the tires.

Feeling was returning to Dylan's face along with a weird tingling like he'd been eating shellfish. Maybe he was allergic to conflict. "Does Mom know?"

His father froze for a half second, just long enough to set off Dylan's inner alarms. "If she doesn't know, it's because she doesn't want to know," his father finally offered as he went back to wrenching something on the car. "But you might not want to be real direct with her," he advised. "Or better yet, avoid the conversation."

All the relief that had washed through Dylan just seconds ago drained away as he realized he wasn't going to get off easy with his mom. She didn't want to know about his gayness; that was what his father was telling him. Maybe she was going to be like Vin's mother and tell him it was a phase, and he didn't know how he would handle that. Potentially not well.

"That's going to be difficult because we're going over to the house to pick up Dylan's stuff," Vin said when the silence drew out too long. Dylan's father had another of those awkward frozen moments. He let his wrench hang down at his side.

"Oh?" That was an unhappy tone. "Dilly—"

"Dylan, Dad. I mean, Dilly is kind of a kid's name, and it gets turned into Dill Weed a little too often, so I'm going back to Dylan." Dylan pushed away from the workbench and actually got his legs to hold his weight, and then set his jaw as firmly as he could. He was an adult man, and adult men didn't get called Dilly. Period.

His father's eyebrows flashed some sort of code. "Dylan," he said slowly. "Are you telling me you're moving out?"

"Um… maybe?" Dylan cringed. "Yes," he corrected himself. "I really do need to move out."

His father turned the hairy eyeball on Vin. However, unlike Dilly, who seemed to squirm the second his father gave him that particular look, Vin stood there looking comfortable in his own skin and slightly bored.

"So, will you be staying with Vin?" he asked Dylan even as he continued to pin Vin with his coldest look.

"Yep," Vin agreed for both of them. Dylan could feel his face getting warmer and warmer. At this rate, he was going to stroke out and avoid this whole emotional mess. Vin and his father both had stubborn expressions on their faces, and Dylan anticipated he'd have no success at getting either of them to change his mind.

Vin put a hand on Dylan's arm. "I'm not comfortable having Dylan in the same house with Gary."

His father narrowed his eyes in an expression that looked startlingly Vin-like. "Gary hasn't been convicted of anything yet."

"No," Vin agreed slowly. "But when someone I care about shows up with bruises, I get unreasonable."

"Bruises." Immediately, Dylan's father shifted his focus to Dylan. "What happened? Were you two fighting?"

"He, um, got mad at me." Dylan shrugged. He hated all this being an adult shit. If he was honest with himself, he would admit he wanted to go back to the car and let Vin handle this. In fact, Vin could chain him to the bed in the closet, and Dylan would be a happy little camper.

"And he hit you? Why? What the hell happened?"

Vin tightened his fingers around Dylan's forearm, and Dylan gave Vin a weak nod. "Gary accused me of helping the women he raped. He said I told them things and he was going to make me fix it."

"Did you?"

"Did I what?"

His father spoke each word cautiously. "Did you talk to those girls?"

Dylan froze. Okay, that was not the question he wanted his father to ask. After a few seconds of cold silence, his father rubbed a hand over his face. "Great. Your mother's going to end up in an early grave over all this."

"It's complicated and—"

"Dilly, no," his father said, stopping him. "You don't have to explain because we all have to do what we think is right." Again he rubbed a hand over his face, and Dylan felt guilt rise on a high tide because his father had never looked this old. Never.

"He can stay with me. The place is run-down and shitty, but it doesn't have rats, and the plumbing works. Mostly," Vin offered. "I'm only a couple of miles up, on the opposite side of Seventh from the restaurant."

"Shit." Dylan's father wasn't normally one for cursing, but he let out a soft string of "shits" as he turned his back and headed for the empty bench just inside the garage bay door. Sitting down, his father rested his elbows on his knees and let his head hang down. "You shouldn't have to leave your own home," his father said slowly. "That's not fair." The words were pretty clear, but Dylan could tell from the tone his father was struggling with them. If his father told Dylan to stay and kicked Gary out, the house would go to Defcon One as his parents squared off against each other.

"Dad, it's just time for me to get out. Hey, I should be off making my own way, not eating all you guys' food. I guess I was avoiding growing up because it looks a little messy from here."

His father laughed and sat up, but he still looked old. "It's a lot messy," he agreed. "But you shouldn't be forced out of your home."

Dylan looked over at Vin. "I'm pretty sure this is just speeding up something that might have happened anyway," he admitted softly. Maybe love at first sight was stupid, but after four or five sights and a chance to see how a guy handled a whip and getting to really peek into his soul... that didn't feel stupid. Dylan was comfortable with Vin.

"And I do have a basement apartment if he needs to get away from our relationship," Vin said. "It's not a nice one, but it's better than my second and third apartments."

"Not your first?" Dylan's father asked.

"No, sir. My first apartment was when I was seventeen. I had subsidized living because my parents died."

Sympathy flashed across his father's face, and Dylan could see Vin stiffen just the slightest bit. His father gave a curt nod and a quick, "I'm sorry about that."

Vin shrugged. "That was a few years ago. I'm over it, and the house I have now doubles as an office for my computer business. I'm not rich by any means, but I am very comfortable having Dylan come into the house."

"And I'm not freeloading. I can help with the bills," Dylan pointed out.

Vin gave him a cold look that made it clear he didn't like that idea.

"I will help with the bills," Dylan said mulishly. He'd already had this fight with his parents and lost, and he didn't feel like losing again.

Vin clenched his teeth, and for a half second, Dylan could see Vin's frustration rising, and then the tide turned and he turned more calculating. "You can put your money toward fixing up the apartment," Vin said firmly. "If things don't work out, you'll have a place to live. If they do, we can rent that space out, and we'll triple the money."

Dylan nodded. "Okay, that works." Now he just had to make sure things worked out. His father distracted him from those thoughts by standing up.

"If you two want to wait a few minutes, I'm going to finish up this car and then I can head over to the house with you."

"You don't have to, Dad."

His father looked at him with this fierce expression Dylan hadn't seen before. "Yeah, I do, Dilly. If Gary touched you, it's time for him and your mother to start facing a few facts. I'm not putting up with violence in my home." His father gave a curt nod as though he'd made up his mind and grabbed his wrench. "Maybe it's time for me to put my foot down. So just… go. I'll be there in about twenty minutes."

Dylan reached out and caught his dad's arm. "Thanks, Dad."

His father's eyes were suspiciously bright with moisture as he looked from Dylan to Vin before focusing on Dylan. "I'm just sorry that you went to someone else first, Dilly. You know I'm here for you. I always will be."

Dylan nodded. "I know."

"Good. And don't forget it. And just as soon as I stop worrying about how much I'm about to upset your mother, your gentleman friend is getting the same lecture and threat of bodily harm that Frank got when he proposed to your sister. Clear?"

Dylan smiled. "Clear, Dad."

"Good. Go away." Turning his back, Dylan's father attacked the nut-bolt-screw thingies on the car with the passion of the possessed. For a second, Dylan stared at his father's backside. Then Vin brushed his hand across Dylan's shoulder and moved down to settle over his right hip.

"Let's grab something to drink. I'll spot you for a soda," he offered.

Dylan nodded and let Vin guide him back out to the car. After today, nothing was going to be the same, and Dylan wasn't sure if that was good or bad.

Chapter 16

"SO, DO you want a soda?" Vin asked as they pulled away from his father's shop.

"If I put any more acid in my stomach, I'm going to have a hole in it," Dylan confessed. He stared out the window at the gray sky. He'd accuse the weather of reflecting his mood, only the city usually was gray and dreary, so it was nothing new.

"You okay?" Vin asked with a sidelong look.

"Peachy."

Vin's gaze flickered across Dylan's whole body. "Yeah, you look just great. If you look any better, I'm going to pull over so you can throw up on the side of the road."

Dylan glared at Vin. "I'm fine."

"No, you're not." Vin said that with this tone—this uncompromising tone that practically dared Dylan to contradict him or lie about this. "Don't say something that isn't true, not about something important."

Dylan sighed. "I'm as fine as I can be considering that an elephant is about to poop on my life."

"That's a little vivid."

Dylan gave a shrug. "Trust me, it's accurate. Me being gay—it's been this big pink elephant. Or maybe it's a big camouflage elephant because I've tried hard to keep it out of sight."

Vin nodded. "I remember. Before I told my mom, it felt like everything I said to her was some shade of a lie."

"Exactly." Dylan threw his hands up in the air. "I mean, my mom goes off on how Jennifer is the perfect girl for me, and what am I supposed to say? 'Gee Mom, I'm sorry, but I can't marry Jennifer because I'm into guys.' That's not going to go over well. So I just sort of let the words lay there all bloated and decomposing."

Vin frowned as he looked over.

"What?"

"I'm just starting to worry about you and your metaphors."

Dylan just made a face and stared out at the end of the block where his house waited for them. He really wished the shop was a lot farther away from home, like maybe a state or two. He loved his mom. He adored his mom. He just didn't think she always handled things well.

In ninth grade, they'd had a teacher give them this group project on Shakespeare, and she'd warned them over and over to choose partners carefully or do an independent project with a single scene instead. However, he'd picked his two best friends. Yeah, he'd been an idiot. He'd ended up having to try and create a diorama of all of act four by himself, soup to nuts, and no matter how many nights he'd stayed up until midnight or how many little dresses his mother helped him glue on pipe-cleaner ladies, he'd still gotten a C.

His mother had gone storming down to the school to rail about injustice and unequal work and how Dylan deserved so much more than the other boys. But Dylan didn't deserve more. He'd made the choice, and he knew he was being dumb when he made it. And he should have told Mrs. Ventali that Danny and Ronny had dumped all the work on him, but having friends had been so much more important than having a good grade. But his mother wouldn't listen to him. Dylan had stood there after school with his mother ripping into his teacher, and with every passing second, he wanted the ground to swallow him.

The next day, he'd tried apologizing to Mrs. Ventali, but she'd smiled at him and told him she understood. And that made him feel even worse because here was this really understanding teacher, and his mother had sort of lost her mind in front of her. It was weird, but most of his mother stories involved her torturing teachers on his behalf.

"What do you think is going to happen?" Vin asked, his voice softer as he pulled up next to the curb about a half a block down from Dylan's house. For a second, Dylan had to think about that. He felt like he was getting so tangled up in the cobwebs of his family's past that he didn't know what to think about the here and now.

With a sigh, Dylan shrugged. "I don't know. I don't know if she's going to be more upset about me being gay or me suggesting her firstborn is dangerous. I don't know what she's going to say, and if Gary is home, I'm pretty sure I'm the one who's going to end up looking like a psycho. He's good at twisting the truth until it's sort of a funhouse version of itself."

"If she doesn't see that your brother is dangerous, then she's living in denial."

"Yep. I can't argue that."

For long minutes, they sat in Vin's car, which smelled faintly of plastic and damp cardboard. "Do you want me to go in with you?" Vin finally asked.

"Oh no. There is bad and then there is world endingly, horrendously bad. I think I'll skip introducing my mother to my gay, kinky lover on day one."

"Your gay kinky lover?" Vin's eyebrow twitched. "I wasn't actually planning on telling her that part. I thought I might introduce myself as Vincenzo Hauser."

"Yeah, because that worked with my dad." Dylan rolled his eyes.

Vin nodded, but he had an odd look on his face. "From the sounds of it, your mother is very good at not seeing what she doesn't want to see, so I could probably pull it off with her."

Dylan looked out the front window at the neighbor's house for a long time before he shifted in his seat to look at Vin. "I don't want you to pull it off with her. I don't want you to be only Vin Hauser and not my gay, kinky lover. I never told my parents about the whole gay thing because I was okay with being...." Dylan searched for the right way to say what he was feeling without coming off totally in need of therapy.

"I'm good at fitting in the cracks, you know? I'm good at working around other people, and I don't need to be seen."

"And I'm not like that?" Vin asked. There wasn't even a second's pause before he continued. "Scratch that. I know I'm not. Fitting in is not in my skill set, so if you're more comfortable dealing with—"

Dylan cut him off. "I don't want you to work around her. I don't want you to avoid looking at me or touching my arm, because that would be you trying to fit yourself around my mother's delusions of having only heterosexual children. I don't want you to have to do that, and I really don't want to see it because I like that you don't fit yourself into others' lives. Watching you play nice with my mother would feel creepy because your charm is that you aren't someone who follows others' rules."

Vin huffed. "Most people don't like that very trait. Chase... he fucking hated...." Vin held up a hand as though trying to stop himself from talking. "Dylan, this is hard for me. Family... I never had it, not the way you do. Hell, it doesn't matter," he said firmly. "I'm not following this conversation very well, but I don't want you to feel ganged up on in there. I kinda like your father, but I'm not sure the man wants to go up against his wife."

"I know he doesn't," Dylan admitted. "But I don't want you going in and playing nice. I like that you do your own thing and don't change for anyone. I like that you're so unbending that maybe there's room for me to fit myself in the cracks of your life because I like your cracks a lot more than the cracks I have been living in." Dylan frowned as he tried to sort his thoughts. From the look Vin was giving him, he wasn't coming off as exactly sane.

"That doesn't sound healthy," Vin pointed out.

"For someone that's good at not fitting in, maybe not. Maybe it would be seriously bad for you to try and fit into someone's life. Hugely bad. Potentially homicidally bad. But honestly... that's what I do," Dylan pointed out. "And hey, I'm choosing your crack where I'm Dylan instead of trying to fit into the crack labeled 'Dilly' back here, so that would win me some points with a psychiatrist, right? I mean, I am making my own choices. It's like choosing to wear your chains. I like it when you chain me, but I wouldn't let just anyone tie me up. Guard was really clear that I could fit into his life, so it's not like I'm trapped and suffering through the only option I have."

"Guard?" Vin was definitely not happy at that name getting brought up.

"I don't think I'd like that crack, wearing his chains," Dylan admitted. "I mean, for a few days the cool apartment would be... well... cool. But if I was there too much, I'd start to wonder when he was going to trade me in the way he trades in televisions and computers because I don't think he had anything in there that was older than two years. And he had all these rules for how things were supposed to be, and I know I was going to be rougher around the edges than he wanted. And maybe I could fit in there, but I'd spend my whole life worrying about when one of my rough edges was going to rub him wrong. So see, I can make choices for myself. I'm not saying that I can't. I just like to pick a crack that I do like and then settle in, fit myself around someone else."

Vin blinked at him. "This is the oddest conversation I've ever had. Why exactly are we talking about this right now?"

Dylan watched his father's truck turn the corner to come down the street. "I'm explaining why I need to go leave a crack and why I don't want you in there trying to play nice and make yourself fit into a world that I don't really like. I have to cut these ties before I can wear your cuffs and fetters."

Vin reached out and rested a hand on Dylan's knee for a long time. "Okay," he said slowly. "I'll wait here unless you take so long that I start getting paranoid about whether they're picking out fucking Christian healing therapy to beat the gay out of you."

"*My* parents?" Shock seemed to make the words a little difficult to find. *Where the hell did that fear come from?* "My parents wouldn't do that. I mean, I expect freaking out, not total fucking insanity."

"I never said my paranoia was rational," Vin said with a shrug. "So, if I don't see you in an hour, who's knocking on the door: Vincenzo Hauser, random friend or Vincenzo Hauser, gay and kinky lover?"

Dylan smiled. "The second. Definitely the second." He stretched forward for a kiss. Vin caught him by the back of the neck and pulled him closer. Warm lips moved against Dylan's while Vin slid his hand down Dylan's arm before gripping his wrist tightly. Dylan gasped, the feel of the restraint tickling his need to life. He felt Vin's tongue invade, pressing in without waiting for permission. Vin still held the back of Dylan's neck in one hand, his wrist in the other, and the delicious feeling of being trapped made Dylan's cock harden.

Dylan was gasping for air before Vin let go. He settled back into the driver's seat with a cat that ate the canary expression.

"Oh fuck. I can't go in there now." Dylan might have lost the ability to walk, what with his jellified legs.

"I'm just reminding you why you like my crack," Vin smirked. The bastard honestly smirked.

"Sometimes I hate you. You're just lucky that I'm a masochist and I love being made to hate someone," Dylan groused as he pulled at his jeans to try and get a little more room in the crotch.

"You're lucky I'm a sadist and I like seeing you squirm," Vin countered.

Muttering curses, Dylan got out of the car and watched his father lock the truck and head into the house. He didn't look in their direction, so Dylan figured he'd seen the kiss. His father did the same thing when he caught Frank kissing Carmine. Usually those two went over to Frank's house, but when they did spend time here—back before Gary had moved home—sometimes his father would start to walk into a room only to wheel around and go the opposite direction. Dylan could always count on finding Frank and Carmine sitting scandalously close when that happened.

Looking back at the car, he toyed with a quick fantasy—running off and never facing his mother. She was going to wield guilt like a knife and gut him, even while believing she had to save the family— she had to save Dylan. Yep, that was Mom, rescues and avenging angels and parent conferences from hell, oh my. Even worse, he never stood up to her because he always felt so guilty when he hurt her feelings. Maybe they should all go in and get a group rate on therapy.

That thought seemed to settle his cock down, so with a final wave to Vin, he headed into the house.

The place was silent, no music drifting down from upstairs, no television blaring. That usually meant only his mother was home, and she would either be doing endless rounds of dusting or reading in the front room. Dylan carefully approached the archway. Sure enough, his mother had curled her feet under her in her favorite chair, a romance novel propped open on her knee while his father stood near the front window. Dylan wondered if his father was staring out at Vin's car or just staring into space, but he definitely hadn't started the conversation yet. His mother looked confused, not whatever negative emotion she'd flail through when she found out.

"Honey, you're home." His mother smiled at him. "Your father and I were about to have a conversation. Why don't you give us some space," she suggested gently.

"He should stay," his father disagreed, and Dylan could see the flash of surprise in his mother's face. Both his parents had a pretty strict rule about keeping kids out of adult discussions. As the youngest, Dylan was often invited to give the older people some "space" to have adult discussion, but now that Dylan thought about it, nineteen was a little old to have your mother dismiss you from the room.

"Okay," his mother said, her voice uncertain.

"I think Dad wanted to be here when I talked to you." Dylan stopped, not sure where to start. His mother looked from him to his father and back.

"Dilly, are you ill?"

"Christ, Alicia. He's a man. Do you have to call him Dilly?"

"Don't swear in this house."

"Fine." His father held both hands up in surrender. "I shouldn't have said that, but my point is that Dylan is too old for children's names. He's a man, Alicia."

His mother's hands came up to her mouth. Her book tumbled to the ground, her page lost. "You got a girl pregnant. Oh Dilly, how could you?"

Dylan could hear the edge of panic in his mom's voice. "No! Mom, no one's pregnant. Trust me, that's not an issue."

Her hands slowly lowered. "You didn't?" She looked at both of them, clearly more confused than ever.

"No, that is not ever going to happen," Dylan said with a laugh that threatened to bubble over into something darker and less controlled.

"What?"

Dylan's father sat on the wood chair shoved in the corner next to the window. "You know what he means, just like I did."

"What are you two talking about?" His mother crossed her arms, and Dylan braced himself for a Band-Aid ripping off fast sort of moment.

"I'm gay," he announced. It was a little like dropping verbal napalm. For a good minute, all life seemed to die in the room. His mother stared at him with eyes that grew larger millimeter by slow millimeter, and his father let out one long sigh.

His mother stood up, and he could hear her fast, panicked breaths, but before he could say anything, she'd fled the room. Her shoes clicked over the tile of the entrance, and the kitchen door opened and thumped closed.

"Well that went about the way I expected," his father said, "but you know she loves you. She just needs a little time. I'll give you a hand packing, Dylan." His father pushed himself up, like an old man.

If he walked out now, his mom would convince herself she'd misheard him or he'd meant it all as some elaborate practical joke. She'd bend reality to fit her needs, and when he talked to her, she'd try and make him go along with that party line. And maybe that would have been fine a few weeks ago, but Vin wasn't ever going to fit in whatever lie his mother made up. He lived so big that his reality would poke through his mother's stories, and it would get ugly. So if he wanted to keep his relationship with her, he had to deal with this. "I don't want to leave without talking to her," Dylan said firmly.

"Dylan, that's not a good idea."

"Maybe not," Dylan agreed, "but if I don't, that's a worse idea." His father looked at him without ever disagreeing, and Dylan turned toward the kitchen. When he slipped inside, his mother was at the stove watching the water in the pot, with a carton of eggs open next to the stove. "Mom?" he asked quietly.

For some time, she ignored him, and Dylan waited. The water started boiling, and she busied herself, running eggs under warm water in pairs to prep them for putting them in the water. "Dilly, you need to think about this," she said as she carefully placed her eggs on a towel.

"Um, Mom, I actually don't. I'm gay."

"You can have feelings for boys. Men do." She paused long enough to run a hand over her face. "But that doesn't mean you have to act on it, that you give up on having a family and kids. Think about what a lonely life that will be."

"Why can't I have kids?" Dylan asked.

His mother whirled around, an egg still in hand. "Because you won't have a woman involved. And you like girls. You adored Jennifer. I thought you were going to propose to her." The kitchen door opened, and his father appeared in the doorway, but Dylan focused on his mother. He didn't know how to make her see the world had changed and being gay wasn't something so alien he would have to give up any normal life.

"I adore her. I don't want to marry her, and I'm pretty sure she knew that, which is why we were the perfect couple. I'm pretty sure she's not ready for anything serious. And I can have kids with a surrogate or adopt them. It's not like there aren't needy kids out there. And can I just say that at nineteen, having kids really isn't my first or second priority."

"But... Dilly." She put the egg down and nearly whispered the next words in a horrified voice. "People aren't nice to gay men."

Dylan opened his mouth, but his mother cut him off.

"They aren't. There's gay bashing. They beat men just for being gay and being in a part of town where gay men go. And there are diseases and all these dangers. Just because you like men too, that doesn't mean you can't have a nice normal life. You'd make a good husband. You'd never be one to hit your wife or disrespect her, and as you get older and these girls get older and figure out what's important in a man, they'll be lining up to get your attention." His mom reached out and ran her fingers through his hair to sweep it back from his face. "You're just a lovely young man. You don't have to make this decision now. And just because you like men doesn't mean you have to be… gay." She gave him such a hopeful look that Dylan knew he would have folded like a house of cards if it weren't for the fact Vin was outside. He didn't want normal; he wanted Vin.

"Mom, it isn't a decision. I just am gay. I don't want to have sex with women. And I really, really don't want to talk about sex with you, but you need to know that part."

"But you'd… with a… man?" His mother was definitely struggling.

"Alicia," his father warned.

"But he's talking about…." She stopped.

His father stepped farther into the room. "Alicia, Dylan is who he is."

"I'm not saying he isn't." She turned around, picked up an egg, and put it on a slotted spoon before lowering it into the boiling water. She repeated that several times before she could find her words. "I just want… I want him happy."

"And I can be happy and gay," Dylan said firmly. "I can do that way easier than if I try and pretend I'm not gay. That's not going to work. Not well."

His mother dropped one of the eggs. It hit the edge of the pan and cracked, half the yellow yolk sliding down the side of the pan before hitting the hot burner with a scorched smell. "Damn!" His mother sounded like she might cry, and she jerked back as if she'd startled herself. His father stepped in to turn off the burner and move the eggs back away from the mess. They stood there, his mother and father. His father rested his large hand on the small of her back. "Alicia, don't make this hard for Dylan."

"I just want him happy," she said, her voice shaking with emotion, and Dylan's stomach soured. This was why he'd avoided the whole coming-out speech to begin with.

"Then trust him to find his own way. I don't like Frank, but I'm not about to tell Carmine that." His father's eyes went big, and he turned to Dylan. "And you won't tell your sister I ever said that." Dylan nodded. Shit. He had no idea his father didn't like the guy.

"Frank's a very nice man," his mother said, a little of her normal iron back in her voice.

"He's milquetoast. I have a daughter who is a vibrant, beautiful young woman, and she's marrying milquetoast," his father disagreed. "But if she likes the man, I'll bite my tongue."

"He's a kind man," his mother said softer, obviously not willing to concede the point. "And I do trust Dylan."

"Then trust that if he says this will make him happy, he's right."

His mother turned, and Dylan could see her chewing her lip. She loved him, and he knew she only wanted the best for him, but it still stung that she didn't want him gay. It was like she had decided she didn't want him to have brown eyes. He couldn't change it. And even if he tried hating his eye color as much as she wanted him to, it wouldn't change anything.

She gave him a weak smile. "I love you. You know that, right?" she asked.

Dylan nodded. "I know."

"As a bonus," his father added, "he's picked a good Italian boy. He's even named Vincenzo."

His mother's hands fluttered. "You... dating?" Clearly it was going to take a long time before his mother could form full sentences without hyperventilating—at least when it came to Dylan's love life.

"I don't think he would have talked to us about this if he didn't have someone special. That's why he's moving out." His father slipped his arm around his mother's waist and pulled her closer, but her hands still went from fluttering to flapping.

"But… we haven't even met the boy, and you're so young. You're not ready to move out. Your job… it's not the sort of long-term job a man has. You aren't ready."

"Alicia," his father said with a sigh. "He's safer being out of the house."

She frowned at him and pulled away. "What are you talking about?"

"I'm talking about Gary."

Dylan could see his mother's face harden at the mention of her firstborn. When the accusations had first come out and Carmine had tried talking to their mother, she'd worn this expression a lot. Gary was her son—her crown prince. He couldn't be a rapist. He couldn't be a bad man, because she'd raised him to be a strong, popular young man. He'd brought home medals for swimming and debate and lacrosse. He would always have this corner of her heart that her other children didn't.

His father sighed and backed away a step. For the first time ever, Dylan got the feeling his parents were repeating a fight they'd had before. Never in history had two people fought so quietly, but his mother's lips made a tight line, and his father grabbed the back of one of the kitchen chairs and held on so tight his knuckles turned white. "He got mad at Dylan and hit him. Dylan is a good forty pounds lighter. That boy had no right putting his hands on Dylan," his father said.

"They're brothers. They fight."

"I don't think Dylan was fighting. He was getting hit."

"Gary wouldn't—"

"He did, Alicia. Gary hit him hard enough that our son was bruised. He was so bruised that his Vincenzo came to my shop to say he wouldn't let Dylan get knocked around." His father's finger started poking the air, and he got uncharacteristically loud. Everyone else in the neighborhood had loud fathers, but not Dylan. "Vincenzo had to step in because of what's happening in my house, Alicia. Do you hear me?" his father demanded. "My house, Alicia."

His mother lost most of the color out of her face, and she started shaking her head like she could just deny reality and make it go away.

With a sigh, his father half turned away. "Dylan, go upstairs and get your stuff before Vincenzo gets tired of waiting," his father said with a practiced weariness in his voice, and Dylan took the opportunity to scramble out of the room and head upstairs. Maybe it was the coward's way out, but his father could take the heat for this one. Something was going on, and Dylan wanted out of the house before the powder keg of emotion he could feel under his feet exploded into something ugly.

Chapter 17

DYLAN carried a box down the stairs, balancing it on one hip in order to get the front door open. His parents were still going at it with voices that sounded urgent and strained, even if they weren't loud.

Sometimes Dylan wondered if they wouldn't all be healthier if they just sometimes yelled. Everyone else in the world yelled and got angry, but his mother called anger a sign of weakness, and his father pretty much refused to contradict his mother on anything.

He'd earned his only spanking, back when he was ten or eleven, when he got so frustrated he'd screamed that he'd hated his mother. At the time, he'd felt exactly that. He'd hated the fact she didn't see the world the way he did... that she wouldn't listen to him when he talked about Gary being mean. She'd listen to him if he said anyone else in the world had hurt his feelings. Let Danny next door make him cry, and his mother turned into Attila the Hun. But one word against Gary or Carmine or his father, and his mother pulled out the lectures on family and responsibility and never turning against your own. And considering she never talked to her own father after some big fight over who she planned to marry, that felt a little hypocritical, even when he'd been ten. But being that young, he hadn't had any other way to deal with the frustration. His mother had turned ghastly white, and his father had pulled him into the dining room for several swats on the butt and a very stern discussion about respect. The pain of the lecture and the guilt had lasted longer than the sting in his ass.

Dylan hadn't tried that again. But honestly, he wondered if Gary would have gotten to this point if he'd done something—if he'd forced his mother to face cold, hard reality. Maybe. Maybe not. He didn't have a lot of power to change the world, and Dylan had come to realize that pretty young. The best he could do was decide whose reality to support, and he couldn't stay in the home with Gary anymore. It felt too much like being okay with what he'd done.

Dylan shifted the box in his arms and smiled as he caught sight of Vin. He'd gotten up onto the trunk of his car, where he sat cross-legged with his laptop perched on his knees. With one hand shading the side of his computer, Vin stared at the screen. Even across the yard, Dylan could see the intensity on his face, but then everything Vin did was slightly intense. But Dylan liked that. He liked the fact that Vin's personality was so large Dylan never felt like he had to tiptoe around it.

Vin frowned and mouthed curses that Dylan could practically lip-read from across the yard. Shifting the box again, he headed across the lawn. Vin looked up when Dylan had covered about half the distance, and he snapped the laptop closed.

"Is everything okay?" Vin immediately asked.

Dylan turned to look at the house. "Okay might be too strong a word. More like it's an open and leaking sore instead of a festering one."

"That's progress." Vin slid off the back of the car and tucked the laptop under his arm.

"Trouble online?"

Vin shrugged. "Computers I like. People are idiots. Customers are complete morons."

Dylan laughed. "Well, yeah. But they're customers, so you pretend to not be annoyed when they get upset at finding spinach in their scallops Florentine."

"I'm not that good at acting," Vin said. He opened the back door and put the laptop on the floor before he reached for Dylan's box. "Tell me you own more than that."

"Of course I do, but I only grabbed what I need for a week or two. I don't have to take everything now."

Vin put the box in the car and closed the door before leaning against it. "Is this your way of hedging your bet, of only moving in partway?"

Shocked, Dylan couldn't come up with a response right away. "No," he finally blurted out. Vin raised one eyebrow, which was sexy, but unnecessary. "No, I am not. I just don't want to hang around long enough for Gary to come home. I have reached my limit for family confrontations."

Letting out a long breath, Vin nodded. "Okay. Give me even a hint that you're okay with it, and I would be happy to handle any confrontations with Gary for you."

"Are you going to wait for a hint?" Dylan asked with a laugh as he headed for the passenger side door. Personally he half expected Vin to go alpha dog on Gary the first chance he got.

"I'm starting to think you're giving me the hint now."

"I'm thinking that if Gary has me pinned in any abandoned cars or locked in any closets, I'm not going to stop you from getting involved," Dylan admitted. "I'm also going to tell you to steer clear before the lawyers drag you into this whole mess. I mean, I don't know how, but Gary would manage to make you look guilty of something."

"And I told you I can take care of myself. If your brother tries manipulating me, he's going to find he bit off more than he can chew," Vin said fiercely, his jaw muscle popping as he seemed to struggle with his own emotions for a second. Then he got into the car and slammed the door shut a little more aggressively than needed. Dylan got into the passenger side. "So," Vin said in an almost artificially calm voice, as if he hadn't been furious at the very thought of Gary two seconds ago. "When do you have work?"

"Shit." Dylan pulled out his phone to check the time. "At least I'm on late shift tonight, so I don't have to be there until five."

"So, we have a few hours to kill." Vin gave Dylan a truly wicked look.

"Um." Dylan closed his eyes. "If you keep giving me that look, my prick is going to break or something."

Vin laughed. "Oh, I can come up with much better things to do with it. I was hoping to parade you around at the Stonewall and make that asshole Guard suffer, but I don't want to make you late for work."

"We have time." The words slipped out before Dylan could edit them. He didn't want to be paraded around. He didn't. Only his cock seemed entirely too interested.

"If we want to catch the crowd, we'd have to be there much later than five. Miss Dolphinia doesn't even open until four, not unless you knock on the back door and ask nice."

"Somehow I can't see you asking nice."

Vin grinned. "Not usually, but then she thinks I'm cute."

"You are, in a dark and sometimes scary sort of way," Dylan pointed out. Vin gave him a very odd look. "But if we're not going to the club, we're going to have to find some other way to amuse ourselves." Dylan smiled at Vin, but the smile faded when something else occurred to him. "Unless you have to work. Hey, I know you keep business hours, not restaurant hours, so don't think you have to amuse me. You don't."

"And if I want to?"

"I'm good at amusing myself. I didn't bring my computer, but I'm guessing you have an extra, and I'm perfectly happy with an Internet connection and a little gay porn."

Vin had put the car in drive, but now he stopped and put it back into park. "If I'm busy, I'll tell you. And I won't lie about being busy to get rid of you. So if I tell you I have time to tie you up, I do. And if I tell you that I'm feeling an overwhelming urge to pin you against a wall and control your every move to reward myself for not going in that house and calling your mother a blind bitch, I mean that too."

Without another word, Vin put the car into drive again and pulled away from the curb. It took Dylan a few blocks to sort through all his feelings.

"She isn't a bitch," he said softly.

"Probably not," Vin agreed, which surprised Dylan. "But she's hurt you, and I get a little unreasonable. So I'm probably going to indulge in a little internal hatred until I can get past that."

"She didn't...." Dylan stopped and closed his eyes for a second as he tried to sort through nineteen years of reality to try and figure out what he really wanted to say. Vin's willingness to be honest here deserved an honest response. "She didn't mean to hurt me. Trust me, she didn't mean to. My mother obsesses over being the perfect mom and protecting her family, and you really should see her Xena, Warrior Princess impersonation when she thinks someone has hurt her kids because it's a little scary. And yeah, it has a little more Marie Barone in her than most—you know the overbearing mother next door from that old comedy show. My mom can do overbearing, but she never hurt me the way a lot of parents do. She never called me stupid or threatened to disown me. Even today, when she found out I was gay, her first worry was that I could get hurt. She wanted me to settle down with a girl, yeah, but she didn't call me sinful or evil or tell me that I was wrong."

Vin glanced over. "That's weak praise."

"Not really." Dylan shook his head. "I mean, Jennifer's mother never stopped her father from hitting her. I mean hitting her a lot. And Adam, at school, his mother is always calling him stupid. He's not. Okay, so he's a little shy of common sense, but I don't think I'm winning any awards on that front, either. But his mom...." Dylan cringed at the memory of that afternoon when he'd been over at Adam's place playing video games. It had not been pretty.

"Even Frank, Carmine's fiancé, has parental issues. His dad took off when he was about seven, and every time his mom gets angry, she tells him he's exactly like his father. Now I'm not a psychologist, but I'm thinking that's the stuff that permanently fucks you up."

Vin snorted. "Yeah, about as much as having your mother refuse to protect you from a sadistic brother."

"She doesn't see it that way."

"I think that was my point."

"Okay, this is officially the unsexiest conversation ever. I mean, if you plan to ravage me, shouldn't you be doing something to... I don't know... build up to it?"

Vin brought the car to a stop at a red light and looked over. Actually, he studied Dylan like a buyer considering a new purchase, and Dylan could feel himself blush. The heat rose to his face, and he turned to look out the window at gray skies and flat-bottomed clouds.

"So, you need build up? Should I tell you what I plan for you?" Vin asked with a teasing note in his voice. "Maybe I should tell you how I want to go get a chastity device. I could plug that beautiful ass of yours, lock that prick in plastic, and use leather and locks to put it all safely under my control. I can image you squirming with need, your cock filling up and pressing against that plastic as you mewl and twist in my hands. Is that the sort of conversation you're expecting?"

"Fuck." Dylan pressed his fingers into his own knees as he tried to avoid doing something humiliating, like jerking off in the car.

"I'm going to tie you down and run my fingers over your body. I'm going to pull at your nipples until they harden under my hands and then taste the salt-sweat as I kiss my way over your vulnerable chest. I'm going to explore every curve until I find that one spot that when I suck on it, you thrash and fight those cuffs until every muscle stands out. And then I'm going to keep sucking that spot. I'm going to mark you and listen to you beg as you squirm and strain."

Dylan only realized he'd stopped breathing when he started getting light-headed. "Oh fuck."

"I'm going to flip you over onto your stomach and chain your legs to the corners of the bed so that you're open to me, spread wide open. Then I'll run my fingernails over that beautiful ass, watch as the white lines pink up and get extra sensitive before I bring my hand down and smack you, and then I'll taste that heated skin, nip it until you mewl and beg me to pound into you."

"Okay. Stop. Seriously." Dylan panted between words, his cock throbbing as his imagination supplied the feeling of ghost fingers skimming across his skin already.

Vin smiled. "Is that what you're expecting from me?"

Dylan pressed his head back against the car seat. "Right now, I'm just hoping we can get to your place before I do something really embarrassing."

"Our place."

Rolling his head to one side, Dylan looked at Vin. He had a closed-off expression. "Our place," Dylan echoed him, and a slight smile pulled at the edge of Vin's mouth. Then another driver cut them off in traffic, and Vin cursed brilliantly as he made a few rude gestures out the window.

Chapter 18

"LET me put the laptop on the charger," Vin said as he headed for the office area. "You can claim some drawers upstairs."

"Okay," Dylan agreed, even though he felt weird pulling Vin's stuff out of a drawer just to claim it. He could work out of a box until Vin cleared out some space, but after that car ride, Dylan suspected Vin wouldn't be okay with it. Vin suspected Dylan planned to bolt, and Dylan had to disabuse him of that notion.

Maybe everyone thought Vin had too many sharp edges, but Dylan could handle dangerous. Vin with his larger than life personality and his wide shoulders and well-muscled body never made Dylan feel small, not like Gary did. Hell, even Guard had made Dylan feel smaller, as if Dylan had to be worthy of Guard's attention, and that definitely included a little bit of not feeling worthy. But he had the feeling that if he screwed up, Vin would just push closer, which felt good because Dylan knew he was going to screw up.

Even if he ignored the fact he was less than experienced with the whole bondage scene, he knew he had some serious failures on the interpersonal front. He let people get away with things, and he swallowed his own feelings until he felt like he would vomit out all the anger. And even then, he did most of his emotional vomiting in private. Yep, he wasn't a mentally healthy boy. But Vin had his own cracks in his psyche, and maybe that was what made it okay for Dylan to be less than perfect. Plus, the sex blew his mind. Dylan did not mind learning a few tricks under Vin's tutoring.

"Gathering wool?" Vin asked as he came in the room, and Dylan blinked as he realized he'd zoned for a little bit. Standing in the middle of Vin's bedroom, he was still trying to come to terms with the fact that he lived here now.

"A little. I'm not all that good with change," Dylan said.

That got a laugh out of Vin. "You're great with change. I'm the one who doesn't handle change well," he pointed out as he opened the lower drawers on the dresser and started pulling clothes out and shoving them in one of the higher drawers. He pulled open a second drawer, and Dylan spotted the toys. Black cuffs, dildos, plugs, and a few boxes that Dylan itched to open... they all ended up on the top of the dresser. "There you go."

"Thanks." Dylan swallowed, his cock aching as he watched Vin gather up the toys and head into the oversized closet with the bed. Dylan started unloading his clothes into the dresser. "Will I be sleeping in there?" he asked once Vin had disappeared into the room.

After a second, Vin came back out and leaned against the side of the doorway as he considered Dylan. Dylan fidgeted under the gaze and focused on rearranging his underwear in the drawer. "I like the idea of putting you in here like a well-loved toy, chaining you to the bed and knowing you're here, waiting. That you're helpless to do anything except wait for me," Vin said slowly. "If that's too much, the offer to let you stay downstairs is still open."

"Not too much, definitely not too much," Dylan admitted, swallowing as a shiver went through his body. Standing up, he tried to look Vin right in the eye, to force Vin to believe that Dylan wanted this. He might have a habit of not saying what he thought, but he wanted Vin controlling him. The way Vin looked at him made him want to squirm... or grab his dick and start pumping it as fast as he could.

"Don't move," Vin ordered, and Dylan was immediately aware of all the ways he wanted to move. His one hand hung at his side, and he'd buried the other deep in a pocket, and his fingers tingled like they were losing circulation. Worse, he felt almost off-balance. He definitely needed to lean against something, but Vin was stalking closer. Funny, earlier he had looked a little computer geekish, but now his dark looks and wide, toned shoulders made him look predatory... or maybe that was his rolling gait that made him look like an oversized cat.

Vin reached out and ran his hands up under the bottom of Dylan's shirt. Dylan wanted to grab at Vin's hands, to pull him closer or touch or do something, but Vin's words held him captive as Vin circled him. Then Vin pressed himself against Dylan's back. "Don't move an inch," he whispered, his breath stirring the hair around Dylan's ear.

"I can't control all the inches," Dylan pointed out as his cock hardened.

"Try," Vin said, his voice hard as he ran his hands up to Dylan's chest before catching the nipples. He pulled, and heat rushed to Dylan's chest. Hissing, Dylan twitched his body, but then he stilled himself.

"Good," Vin said as he released Dylan's nipples and then soothed the sensitive skin with his thumbs. Dylan let out a shaky breath as slowly as he could while he struggled to get his body back under control. "Very good," Vin muttered, each word a little puff of air against the back of Dylan's neck before Vin pressed his lips to that vulnerable spot. Dylan braced himself for the hard pressure of a hickey. Instead, Vin kissed the spot and then started pulling Dylan's shirt up.

Dylan let Vin move him, manipulate his arms and pull him this way and that as he pulled off Dylan's shirt and then unbuttoned his pants. Groaning with relief as his cock came free, Dylan rocked forward and then pushed himself back into place as Vin slid his hands over Dylan's hips and down to his thighs, bypassing Dylan's hard and aching cock. The touch glided over his skin, and little tingles followed everywhere Vin touched.

"I hope you know you're going to have to wait."

"I figured," Dylan admitted. He didn't know why, but knowing that Vin was going to use him however Vin wanted to... it was about the sexiest thing ever. Dylan let his eyes fall closed as Vin teased him. Vin lightly scratched fingernails down his shoulder, and again a hard shiver ripped through Dylan, making him rock forward and back.

"Stay still."

"I'm trying. You aren't making it easy."

"Oh, I'm going to make it a whole lot harder." Dylan tensed his muscles in preparation for whatever Vin had planned.

Dylan's erection felt strained, bordering on painful, but still he wanted more. He wanted so much more. Instead, Vin took him by the shoulders and guided him to the middle of the room, forcing Dylan to toe off his shoes and step out of his pants. Instead of throwing Dylan down and pounding into him, Vin started circling. He let a single finger trail across Dylan's stomach and over his hip before he reached Dylan's back and gave his ass a quick swat. Dylan gasped.

Dylan was naked, and Vin still wore all his clothes, which was odd. Dylan felt exposed and vulnerable and so horny he thought his cock might explode. He stood silent while Vin explored every part of him except his hard cock. Fingernails scritched over his back and soft fingertips trailed down his spine and tickled him right at the base of it. When those long fingers reached around him and brushed against the skin right above Dylan's curled pubic hair, Dylan's eyes came open, and he reached for Vin's hands.

"Someone needs to come," Vin teased, and Dylan forced his hands back down to his sides.

"You're killing me."

"Funny, you seem to be breathing."

"Yeah, but not easily." Dylan gasped as Vin brushed his fingers across the head of Dylan's cock.

"Fuck, fuck, fuck, fuck," Dylan muttered as he looked up at the ceiling. If he looked down at Vin's hand as it explored every inch of Dylan's cock—the hard shaft and the damp slit—if he looked at that, he was going to come all over Vin's hand before they got any further, and Dylan had high hopes for that whole getting tied spread-eagle on the bed scenario.

"Is that begging I hear?"

"It could be. I am more than willing to beg at this point."

Vin laughed. "If you have the brain cells to try and negotiate, clearly you are not distracted enough."

Dylan groaned. He started mentally reviewing every ingredient in the cod and mussels in tomato butter dish while Vin let his hands wander down to cup Dylan's balls. Dylan felt fever hot, but he mentally chanted and fisted his hands tightly while Vin played with him. A careful squeeze made Dylan jerk with surprise, and he lost his balance and fell back into Vin. Buttons pressed into Dylan's bare back, and Dylan dug his fingernails into the soft flesh of his own hands to keep from doing something—anything. His muscles trembled, and he felt like his whole body was developing pins and needles that made his skin tingle.

Vin stroked his balls with one hand and ran his other hand across Dylan's bare stomach, pulling Dylan closer. "Fucking perfect. You are fucking perfect," Vin said. His touches turned gentle, his fingers ghosting over Dylan's skin so Dylan twitched with a need to press into that touch. He was nearly there. He could feel his whole body stretch toward the orgasm just beyond his reach.

Without warning, Vin bit him right at the top of his shoulder. Dylan yelped and his hands came up, but then Vin tightened his grip around Dylan's cock, and the twin points caught Dylan. Those two sensations trapped him so when Vin started sucking at his shoulder, Dylan could only shudder as his whole body seemed to turn into one oversensitized nerve. He could hear himself pant, but he felt disconnected from silly things like breathing. Vin's hot mouth on his shoulder and Vin's strong hand around his cock—that was what mattered.

Tilting his head back, Dylan let it rest against Vin's shoulder. The lust surged almost unbearably, but Dylan could only gasp with his mouth open. His body had somehow become unmoored from his brain, and he didn't have any control over it. He was lost inside the moment as Vin ran hands over Dylan's hot skin. Dylan thrust into the air, his cock bobbing comically, but then Vin's hand vanished or maybe Vin's hands were the islands of heat that threatened to burn Dylan to a crisp as they glided over his sweat-slicked body.

"Fuck I want to pound into you so much. You're fucking perfect."

Dylan heard the tone, but the meaning of the words slipped past him. He stood at the center of a hurricane, and the winds howled around him while he stood in silence. His head spun and he arched his back as a hand tightened around his cock. The touch almost pushed Dylan over the edge, but he was caught, hanging over the edge without being able to fall into that moment of perfection.

Vin's touch gentled, fingers brushing across Dylan's balls, and darts of pleasure shot up Dylan's spine. Words wrapped around him, but it took a long time for Dylan to realize that Vin was whispering to him to breathe. Sucking in a loud breath, Dylan felt his orgasm rush at him. He thrust his hips forward, and this time his cock slid into Vin's hand. Moaning, Dylan sped up, thrusting into Vin's hand as his balls tightened. The pleasure and the pain of waiting spun around him until Dylan cried out.

Vin's arm came around his waist, holding him as Dylan came until he felt as though every bone in his body had dissolved, leaving behind his overheated flesh. Vin's buttons pressed into Dylan's back, and it took a moment for Dylan to realize that Vin was manhandling him toward the bed. When Vin dropped him onto the edge of the big bed, Dylan used the last of his strength to climb up onto the mattress.

"You are beautiful." Vin's voice gave Dylan an anchor to reality, but he let most of his brain wander the universe while only that one sound connected him to the real world. "I want to pound into that beautiful ass of yours. Now, some might take a little offense at getting used after they have clearly finished, but I get the feeling you might be the kind to be okay with the idea of me using you." Vin sounded amused. "Hell, I get the feeling you might like it… me using you to get what I want, especially when what I want is you."

Dylan felt his legs being opened and his body arranged. One hip was pushed an inch one way and an arm brought down to his side and a shoulder shoved farther up the bed. Eventually Dylan was facedown in the middle of Vin's big bed, his legs thrown wantonly open, and he couldn't find the energy to do more than breathe. Breathing took a lot of effort with all his brain cells offline for repairs.

Vin ran his hands up the back of Dylan's legs, and when they reached his ass, Dylan expected another smack. Instead, Vin squeezed the round of it, kneading it and pulling the two sides apart to expose Dylan's ass. Dylan moaned into his pillow, too exhausted to even twitch.

"Such a hedonist," Vin laughed. For a second, he just let his hands rest on Dylan's ass, and then he ran his fingernails lightly over the backs of Dylan's legs. Little warm tremors went up Dylan's spine, but even his nerves were too worn out to really react. The mattress tilted as Vin got up, and Dylan let himself drift into something that wasn't quite asleep, but that definitely wasn't awake. He felt his skin cooling, the air drifting past slowly. Every muscle was limp, and he could feel sleep tugging at the edges of his awareness even though he didn't want to fall asleep. He liked this place of utter quiet. He wanted to stay in the moment forever even though an itch on his shoulder kept nagging him to wake up.

Before Dylan could decide whether or not to scratch, the mattress tilted again. Dylan hummed as Vin ran his hands down over Dylan's shoulders and then pinned Dylan's wrists to the mattress. Then Vin pulled his hands up and over his head, and Dylan felt the leather going around his wrists. It was soft and warm against Dylan's slightly chilled skin. Only then did Vin go back to letting his hands run over Dylan's back and down to his ass.

A finger slipped inside Dylan, slicking him. Normally by the time they were to this point, Dylan was wild with lust, but now he drifted on the edge of some great, quiet chasm as Vin pushed a second finger in for a second before pulling out. Then Vin's large cock started pressing in. Dylan could feel his muscles stretch to accommodate, and his cock gave the tiniest little twitch. Then Vin pressed up against his ass.

"You are going to spend so much time chained to a bed, especially if you keep making this so damn easy."

"Sounds good," Dylan muttered, and then Vin was pounding him.

Vin set a hard pace that normally would have made Dylan cry out with a need to come, but his sated body yielded to every thrust, gathering up the heat as their bodies slapped together. Fingers pressed deep into his shoulders, and Dylan arched his back as Vin rammed into him over and over. With a cry, Vin came. His body trembled, and every place they touched, Dylan could feel that slight shiver—the inside of his thighs where his legs pressed up against Vin, his back where Vin's palms rested, his neck where Vin placed a small kiss.

"Fuck," Vin breathed, and then he slid off the bed, tending to the condom or cleanup or whatever he needed to tend. Dylan's job was to lie in the bed like a wanton slut—all spread out—and he planned to do that very well. Curling his hands around the chain that tethered him to the bed, Dylan sighed and let himself drift into the silence.

Chapter 19

"WAKE up, sleepyhead."

Dylan stirred as Vin kissed a line down his arm. "Don't wanna."

"Hey, I'm fine with you missing work." The kisses vanished and the mattress tilted.

"God, I wish *I* was." Dylan blinked his eyes open and groaned. "I think my muscles dissolved."

"I'm taking that as a compliment."

Dylan looked around and realized the second pillow didn't have an indent from a head, so he'd taken a solo nap. And the wrist chains had vanished. It would have been nice to think of Vin curling up around him, but Vin wore his slightly geekish gear—jeans with a white shirt and suit jacket. "You were working?"

"Yep. I had to go out and deal with a system that some idiots had fucked up. If people insist on changing the settings, they deserve what they get."

Dylan nodded and looked over the side of the bed to find the cuffs dangling there. He reached for one. "You didn't leave the chains on."

"While I'm out of the house? Hell no," Vin said. He came over and sat on the edge of the bed. "I'm a dangerous bastard who pushes too far, but I'm not going to risk you being helpless when I'm not around to watch out for you. And on that note, I'm driving you to work."

Rubbing a hand over his face, Dylan tried to wake up. He hated naps because they left him feeling so bleary, but lately he'd been so exhausted all the time. He probably needed the sleep. "You don't have to."

Vin caught his wrist, and Dylan looked at him in surprise. "Yes, I do. Do you think your brother will appreciate the changes in his home life?"

"Gary?" Dylan's brain definitely hadn't woken up yet.

"Unless you have another psychopathic brother out there, yeah. Do you think he's going to appreciate that conversation you had with your parents?"

Dylan frowned. "Probably not. But I figure my mom will obsess over the gay thing, so she won't have time to hassle him."

"And I think your father will obsess over the fact his oldest is a bully. I get the feeling your father is a man who just now figured out that he ignored an infection and let it spread to his family. And he did. Your brother will not like whatever he's about to do." Vin had this fierce expression that kinda scared Dylan.

Dylan opened his mouth to say that Vin was overreacting, but he remembered Gary's face when he'd trapped Dylan in that car. The fury had frightened Dylan into calling for help.

"Just consider it me being paranoid and wanting to take care of you, but I'm driving you to work and home until your brother is behind bars." Vin said the words firmly and sat up just a little straighter. Yep, that would be his resolve face making its first showing.

"And if he's not convicted?"

"Then I'm going to play chauffeur a lot. But I know bullies, and as long as he thinks he's stronger than you, he's going to go after you."

Dylan frowned as something occurred to him. "My parents. What if he gets upset with them?"

"They control the money right now. Trust me, an asshole like that is going to protect his own self-interest," Vin said with a snort. "But you're going to be open game until he figures out he's going to have to deal with me if he so much as looks at you twice. Well, that and he's going to have to figure out that fucking with me is hazardous for his health. But until he's locked up or I've convinced him that leaving you alone is in his best interest, I'll be driving you to and from work.

"And if you even think of taking off without telling me where, keep in mind that I'm going to go crazy with worry, and I'll be very unreasonable when I find you again." Vin had a defensive expression, but Dylan really could understand his concern. Gary tended to swim in the less sane end of the gene pool. At the same time, there was a limit to how much control Dylan wanted to hand over, and he did recognize the irony in that, considering that he was a little disappointed Vin had unchained him during his nap.

"But if I want to go somewhere with friends after work, I will."

Vin's mouth came open, but Dylan held up his hand. "I will tell you where I'm going, and I'll stay with a group, and I'll even call you to come and get me so I'm never alone somewhere that Gary might pin me in a car, and if he so much as shows up on the street, I will call you first. But I can go out with friends."

Nodding, Vin seemed to think about that for a second. "I don't mind you going out with friends," he said carefully as if thinking it through word by word. "I just worry about you coming home beat to a pulp because some shitty little bully needed to feel like some big shot. How about I add a program to your phone so I can track your location, even if it's off."

Dylan's mouth fell open. "Seriously? Do you really think Gary's that much of a threat?"

"Yes." Vin crossed his arms and stared at Dylan. "I've been in the scene for years, and I've seen my share of bullies. They come into the lifestyle because they think it's a kinky form of bullying—that they found themselves a nice pool of victims, and they're hard to disabuse of that assumption. Too fucking hard. And your brother sets off every damn internal alarm bell in my head."

"Okay," Dylan said slowly. He figured he was indulging Vin's insecurities more than defending himself against his brother, but that was fair. He wasn't a government agent who planned a top-secret mission to Istanbul he had to hide from his lover. And maybe he suffered just a teaspoon of Gary-fear in his heart along with that heaping cup of Vin-insecurity. "You can track me, but I think you're taking Gary a little too seriously. I mean, yeah, he's going to be a pain in my ass if he can get away with it, but you're acting like he's public enemy number one."

"He raped at least three women. He stalked them, raped them, and nearly convinced them to not press charges, which makes me wonder how many others are out there. I've been reading the news reports, and I am going to worry about you every single second until that psychopath is tucked away in some nice penitentiary with a man named Bubba."

"You're a worrywart."

"Hell yes," Vin agreed. "So what time are you off work?"

Dylan closed his eyes and groaned. "Fuck. I'm closing, so after we lock up at eleven, I have to do sidework and check out, so trust me, there will be no going out with friends tonight, not as tired as I am. Maybe eleven thirty if the gods love me and twelve thirty or so if they really don't." These days, he figured he had fifty-fifty odds on that. The gods of kink definitely had his back, but the family gods... not so much.

"I'll wait for a call then. Let me know about twenty minutes before you're ready to go so you don't have to wait for me."

"I'd rather stay here," Dylan said sadly. "I mean, this is our first night together living together, and I'm going to work. That sucks."

Vin reached out and caught Dylan by the back of the neck and pulled him close for a quick kiss on the lips. "So, you'd rather stay home and get tortured more?" Vin continued to hold him close so Dylan felt the heat of his breath.

"Hell yes."

Vin laughed. "I certainly have a few tricks up my sleeve if you're ready for them."

"Ready, willing, and able. And starting to get horny again," Dylan rushed to agree. He had no idea what Vin had in mind, but looking at the devilish expression on Vin's face, Dylan wanted to find out.

"We'll see. Stand in the middle of the room and spread your legs."

"Mmmm. Kinky," Dylan said as he hurried to obey.

"That is the point, yeah."

Dylan spread his feet until he felt a little off-balance and watched as Vin disappeared into the bondage closet. Oh yeah. Dylan's cock liked the thought of all the naughty toys Vin had put away in there. The man might not have spent money on a kitchen that worked, but he knew to invest in the things that mattered—good sheets, strong cuffs, and lots of toys. When Vin came out, he held up a black butt plug with a bulbous length and a flat bottom.

"You ever use these?"

Dylan swallowed. "Too afraid to order them. My mom has a bad habit of opening packages, and that was not something I wanted her to catch me buying."

"Well, let's see how it fits. After all, if you have to spend our first night living together being *not* tortured, the least I could do is provide a little torment."

Dylan swallowed, but he couldn't seem to find words to use as Vin went to the nightstand and took out lube. He rubbed the plug down, and Dylan could see it shine, little lines of lube caught in the ridges.

"Ready?" Vin asked as he stepped to Dylan's side and ran his free hand up Dylan's arm.

"Fuck yes."

Vin shook his head. "I can see I'm going to have to be careful with you, or you'd start topping from the bottom."

"Um, rather not," Dylan confessed. Lots of Internet porn had that whole stereotype of the pushy bottom, but Dylan usually didn't like those stories as much as the ones where the sub really did have to submit.

"Good," Vin said. "Because I'm not into getting pushed." On the last word, he pushed the plug in without warning or prep.

Dylan yelped in surprise and squirmed. "Cold, cold, damn that's cold," he complained.

"Oh well." Vin wrapped his arms around Dylan and pulled him close so Dylan could hardly move. The feeling of being held, of being controlled, was enough to make his cock start to sit up and beg.

"You can take this out if you need to, obviously."

"Yeah, fantasy porn does seem to assume no one ever has to use the bathroom."

"Yeah, it does. And sometimes the plug makes your skin too hot and you'll start to get inflamed. I don't want that. So, if it starts itching too much, take it out and stash it somewhere."

"Okay." Dylan tilted his head back to rest it against Vin's shoulder. But then Vin was moving, shifting to a point in front of Dylan so fast Dylan took a step back to regain his balance.

Vin's fingers caught him around the chin and forced him to look right at Vin. Dylan blinked, startled. "I don't want you ignoring pain because you think that you're proving something. I want you a little sensitive, a little hot and bothered. I don't want you so inflamed and irritated that I can't use this tight ass of yours. So, if it's bothering you, take it out. Clear?"

Dylan nodded, and Vin let go of his chin. There was a flash of guilt in his expression, and Dylan reached out and rested a hand on Vin's shoulder. "Sometimes it's hard to remember it isn't fantasy. Like you couldn't actually chain me to the bed all the time and keep me like some harem boy, which is only hot in stories. I think I'd get bored in reality."

Vin huffed. "As much as I want you, you wouldn't have time to get bored."

"We'll have to test that on Tuesday," Dylan said with a wiggle of his eyebrows. "I'm off Tuesday, Wednesday, and Thursday, so we can see how far the fantasy goes. But I do get what you're saying. I promise I won't do something stupid just to make the fantasy stuff real, even when it hurts."

Vin gave him a searching look. "You'd try. You'd try to endure serious pain for me."

"Where did that come from?"

Vin pulled him close, his hand going around the back of Dylan's head. "You let too many people hurt you, and I do not mean in any sort of way you enjoy. It makes me want to put you over my knee and spank you until you learn to cry 'enough'."

"That's an option," Dylan teased. When Vin pulled back to look Dylan in the eye, his expression was not amused. "Hey, I like spankings," Dylan defended himself. He especially liked them when Vin handed them out.

"Yep, but you need someone to say 'enough' for you." Dylan couldn't disagree. That really was one of his worst personality flaws. That and a bad habit of sabotaging other people's avatars when he was getting his pixelated ass kicked in online games.

"So, maybe I just need to keep you all full of the good sort of hurt so you don't go looking for trouble," Vin mused. He backed up, pulling Dylan with him. When Vin sat on the edge of the bed, Dylan happily went stomach down over Vin's lap, presenting his ass for whatever Vin wanted. Instead of spanking him, Vin pushed at the base of the plug, driving the plastic further into Dylan's body. With a grunt, Dylan struggled to not react when he wanted to grab his cock or grab Vin's cock or do something that would make him horribly late for work.

Then Vin started massaging his ass, working his fingers into the flesh until Dylan could feel the heat start to gather. Only then did Vin pull back and land a good slap on the round of Dylan's ass. Dylan yelped.

"Two more," Vin said, and Dylan breathed fast as the sharp heat settled down into something duller that spread through his body. The pain lasted a second, but the warmth and the tingling awareness of his body lasted so much longer. Eventually Dylan realized that Vin was waiting for him.

"Yeah, two is good," he agreed, squirming at the very thought.

"You'd say twenty were good."

"From you? Yep," Dylan agreed.

The second hit caught him so hard and fast he lost his breath for a second as that flash of pain caught him unprepared. But the sting quickly faded into the heat that made him mewl and squirm until Vin pinned him with a hand around his waist. He needed a word for pain that wasn't pain—for sting that sang across his nerves like the lowest string of a bass guitar being plucked over and over until his bones hummed with the ache of it.

Oh, it was a cousin of pain—a kissing cousin even—but Dylan didn't have a name for the sensation that made him want to live inside that ache. Maybe he'd just call it Bob. The last hit came lower down, jarring the plug, and Dylan fought Vin's grip, instinct driving him to try and get up. However, Vin was too strong and he had better leverage. He hung on until Dylan sagged back down, his hands braced on the ground as he rode waves of searing tingles that travelled up and down his body until he felt like he might catch fire.

"Are you okay?"

"Bob good," Dylan muttered.

"What?" Vin asked, his voice sharp.

"So very good," Dylan clarified. He'd explain the whole Bob thing, only his brains had leaked out.

"You are a beautiful shade of red back here," Vin commented.

"Yeah, yeah, fuck you," Dylan complained mildly.

"Eventually, I hope you will, yes. I can see you chained down so tight that you can't move, that thick cock of yours sticking up into the air waiting for me to ride you like a carousel horse."

Dylan groaned. "You're going to break me."

"I hope not. I like to keep my toys in good shape," Vin said, running his hands over Dylan's ass. When he ran a fingernail over the hottest part, a streak of cold made Dylan catch his breath. "Now for the real torture. You have to get ready for work." Vin used his hands around Dylan's waist to help him up so Dylan stood next to the bed with his red butt, his stuffed ass, and his hard cock.

"You're a sadist," Dylan complained softly.

"Yep," Vin agreed. "Feel free to tell me to back off."

Dylan grunted as he turned to head for the shower. He definitely wasn't telling Vin to do anything like that. He liked pushy, overbearing, sadistic partners. They were fun. The shifting plug felt weird, and for a second, Dylan balanced on his toes as he tried to figure out how to walk without making it feel like someone was fucking him right there on the spot. He hoped his ass didn't get too sore or his cock didn't do anything embarrassing, because this was shaping up to be one seriously good shift at work as long as he could keep everything in balance. And then when he got home, Vin got to do whatever he wanted to Dylan. Yep, life was good.

Chapter 20

DYLAN tried to roll, but the cuffs stopped him. Blinking, he squirmed around so he could find a comfortable spot without turning. Clearly he would have to get used to sleeping like this, not that he minded. There was something intimate and incredibly hot about coming home exhausted and having a lover run hands all over you, undress you, put you in bed with a kiss, and then leave you horny and frustrated. At least this time Vin had asked him if he wanted to sleep on his side or on his back, so Dylan lay on his side with both wrist chains going over the right side of the bed.

Closing his eyes, he tried to settle in, but he could hear something in the distance. Dylan focused, and it sounded almost like voices or a voice maybe. There were long pauses that didn't sound like television. "Vin?" he called. He expected the doors to come open immediately; however, he heard something thump and then more silence. The first wisps of panic settled over Dylan, and he pushed himself up on one elbow and started pulling at his cuffs, searching for a weakness. Unfortunately, Vin's equipment held. "Vin!" Dylan called louder.

The door slid open, and Vin stood there in low-hanging pajama bottoms with a phone in hand. "Your sister's in the hospital," Vin said, and Dylan froze. What the hell was Vin talking about?

Coming into the room, Vin shoved the phone into Dylan's hand before he bent down next to the bed. He pulled something and suddenly Dylan's chains all clattered free from the bed. Even though Dylan trailed the various lengths, he wasn't locked down.

"Hello?" he asked, sitting up and promptly cringing as the chain rattled across the bar on the side of the bed.

His father answered. "Dylan, your sister's been admitted to St. Clare's. You don't need to come down if—"

"Of course I'm coming. What happened? Was there an accident?"

"She's at St. Clare's," his father repeated.

"Dad, why?"

An uncomfortable pause followed. Finally his father said, "I'm not sure. Frank wasn't exactly clear." His father might be saying that, but the hard edge in his father's voice scared him. Fury. He heard controlled fury.

"Dad?"

"I don't know, Dilly, I really don't. Look, your mother and I are here, so don't feel like you have to come. I just didn't want you to feel left out. I should go find your mother." His father sounded oddly breathless, and then he disconnected the phone.

Dylan sat in bed with his mouth open, ready to ask a million questions, but there wasn't anyone on the other end of the phone to answer. He looked at Vin as he finished unlocking Dylan's second ankle. "He hung up on me."

"That's nothing. When I answered the phone, he thought I was you," Vin said, and cold fear started seeping into Dylan's bones. Vin didn't sound anything like him. Wherever Vin had grown up, he hadn't been in the Northeast, not the real Northeast. Maybe he'd grown up in Pennsylvania or that pointy tip of West Virginia where some people pretended to be from the Northeast, but he didn't have quite the accent. He sounded like some Midwesterner who had moved up here and never quite learned to say his vowels right. Besides, a father should know what his own son sounded like.

Pausing, Vin laid a hand on Dylan's knee. "He wasn't sounding all that rational. I assume we're going to the hospital."

"Hell yes," Dylan agreed. "I'll get dressed. Can you check the traffic sites to see if there were any big accidents?" Dylan's fears were slowly congealing into messy, greasy knots of terror. What if she was paralyzed? Maybe some terrible accident had mutilated her, and his father didn't want him to know.

"Deal," Vin said. He caught Dylan's last cuffed wrist and held it for a second. The contact forced Dylan to look at Vin. "Are you okay? You looked a little panicked."

"I am. My dad sounded a little panicked, and my dad does not do panic. Ever. Never." Now that Dylan had put a name to his emotion, he could feel it rise up like a tide swallowing entire continents into the ocean.

"You get dressed. I'll check the computer before we leave." Vin gave his hand a squeeze before he unlocked the last cuff, and then he left.

Dylan took a deep breath when he realized that his head was swimming from lack of oxygen. Then he shoved the chain off his lap and onto the bed before he headed for the corner where Vin had folded his clothes after undressing Dylan. They smelled of the restaurant—of salt and grease—but Dylan didn't care.

Heading out into the main bedroom, he detoured into the bathroom to take a quick piss before he headed downstairs. Vin perched on the bottom step with his laptop balanced on a knee. Vin's polished, dark look had a little tarnish. He had on a T-shirt with a faded and worn team logo, an old pair of jeans, and a cowlick that made him look like he'd just rolled out of bed. "I haven't found anything in the traffic reports," Vin said.

"Let's just head over," Dylan said. His mouth was dry enough he could feel his gummy lips trying to stick to each other. With a quick nod, Vin closed the laptop and headed for the door, opened it, and then held it open for Dylan to pass.

Dylan had to bite his tongue every time he glanced over and found Vin driving at the speed limit. He wanted to get there. He wanted to look his father in the eye and demand to know just how bad it was. And Frank. God, Frank had to be going insane. For all his faults, and Dylan thought he had many, Frank adored his sister. Stupidly, completely, and annoyingly adored her.

"Frank's got to be going insane," Dylan said softly as Vin pulled into the visitor's parking lot.

"I guess that depends on what's wrong. It may be that she broke a few bones or got a nasty concussion," Vin pointed out. "I get the feeling your father is the sort to not handle it well when his kids are hurt. He may be overreacting."

Dylan thought about how his father would sit at Carmine's basketball games, his whole body jerking every time Gianna DiVechi fouled Carmine. The two of them had a hate-hate relationship that led to full body slams and thrown elbows every time the refs' heads were turned. If they'd gone to the same school, Dylan was fairly sure one of them would have ended up on some police show about the school girl who'd been brutally murdered and messily dismembered. Dylan still didn't know what had set them against each other, but he suspected a boy was involved. Carmine could get a little intense with boys, despite the fact that their mother seemed to think she was a virgin. "Yeah, he worries," Dylan agreed. "But he sounded really wrong on the phone."

"Tell me about it. I was trying to convince him that I wasn't you, and I'm not sure he heard me until I'd said it about four times." Vin pulled into an open space so fast the front tires hit the concrete block and the whole car bounced back.

Without waiting, Dylan jumped out of the car and headed for the hospital. Behind him, he could hear Vin trotting to catch up, but Dylan couldn't seem to slow his footsteps. Vin caught up to him about twenty feet outside the main entrance. "He didn't say anything?" Dylan asked, and he could hear the edge of whining in his own voice.

"Nothing that made sense. We'll find out," Vin promised, and he slipped his arm around Dylan's waist as they went in. It took several minutes, two nurses, and an ID check before Dylan finally got the correct floor for Carmine's room, and even then, they wouldn't give him her room number. Dylan had visited the hospital a number of times. Ryan Rearick had broken his leg skating over Christmas break, and Gary had an appendix burst when he was sixteen. He'd walked in, given a name, and a nurse had waved him toward some room, clearly anxious to just get annoying visitors out of her way. This time, Dylan found himself the center of hard scrutiny from nurses in shockingly pink smocks.

The elevator doors were closing on them before Dylan leaned closer to Vin and whispered so the older couple on the elevator with them didn't hear. "Is it me or was that really a little odd?"

Vin shrugged. "Maybe they don't like gay couples," he said in a perfectly normal tone. The older couple both looked over while the elevator dinged away the floors, and Dylan felt himself blush. He kept quiet, but he didn't think so. When people didn't like gays, they had this expression of disgust or sometimes of hatred or even this weird envy—like they wanted to tell the world to fuck off and grab a hot guy to kiss, but they couldn't find the nerve. Or they had that slightly alarmed expression of the older couple right now—like gay men might strip naked and start fucking each other at any moment. The nurses had this guarded expression—a caution that set off all of Dylan's alarms. It wasn't the same.

The elevator stopped on the fifth floor and as the doors opened, Vin strode out, and Dylan hurried after. He noticed that the older couple got off on the same floor, but not before letting Vin and Dylan get some distance down the hall. Another day, Dylan might have been mildly annoyed, but he was too busy being totally terrified. Vin guided him to the nurses' station with a hand on Dylan's back.

"Carmine Carter, please," he asked with a small smile.

The nurse looked at him for a second before looking back down at her computer. "It will be a moment. You can wait over there." She gave a nod toward the hard plastic chairs in Popsicle colors. Dylan noticed his parents weren't there.

"We're looking for Dylan's sister, Carmine. If she's in surgery, we would be happy to wait with his parents," Vin said, this time with a little more steel in his voice. Now the nurse looked up, and Dylan knew he would have cringed away from that look. That was the sort of look teachers gave when you said something truly stupid.

"You'll have to wait over there," she said, raising her eyebrows.

"And why is that?" Vin asked, leaning forward so he could rest his hands on her desk. Her expression hardened even more.

"If you will wait over there, I'll call someone for you."

Vin sighed and stood back up. "I understand that the doctors need to focus on Carmine. However, Dylan can certainly go see his parents. Whatever waiting room they're in, that will be fine with us."

"You can wait there." The nurse picked up a phone, and Dylan felt a whole new reason for panic. Vin turned around, still calm.

"Dylan, try your father's phone. You two shouldn't have to panic alone, not when you can panic together." Vin took a step toward Dylan, his hand reaching for Dylan's pocket. Dylan reached for his phone before Vin could do something embarrassing like reach in there for it himself. Most of the time, Dylan was far more comfortable disappearing into the wall, but he did want to see his father. Really wanted to see him. With shaking hands, he started dialing, hoping his father would pick up. "You might want to try Frank's phone if your father doesn't pick up," Vin commented, and then he turned toward the nurse. Dylan saw him lift an eyebrow in her direction, but she was already on the phone. When Vin turned around, he looked smug about the whole thing.

"Vin," Dylan hissed, hitting the disconnect when his father didn't pick up after the fifth ring. He scrolled through his numbers in search of Frank's. "You don't have to make a fuss."

"The squeaky wheel gets the grease."

"But what if they kick us out?"

Vin frowned. "Why would they kick us out? We're just asking for access to your family. We aren't trying to break into the surgical suite." He sounded honestly confused.

"But she told us to sit down," Dylan said, punching connect when he found the right number in his phone.

"I don't take orders well," Vin said with a shrug. "And we're not impeding her ability to work or infringing on anyone else's rights. If she doesn't like that I won't play lapdog, then she'll have to either suck it up or find someone who can give us what we want."

Dylan bit back a response. He wasn't sure that was how it worked in the real world. However, Vin seemed fairly certain, and it wasn't like Dylan had any experience with how people reacted when you refused to go along. While he could refuse to do things, like when Adam Wiseman dared him to jump off the bridge out back of the school, he rarely did. Mostly if someone in authority told him to do something, he did it. Or he avoided doing it quietly—when the other person wasn't looking. Sometimes he got accused of being sneaky, but Dylan preferred to think of it as diplomatic.

Vin tightened his arm around Dylan's shoulders. "Hey, it's okay. We'll make someone tell us where Carmine is, even if your idiot family never picks up their phone."

Staring down at his phone, Dylan bit his lip. "What if she's hurt, like life-threateningly hurt?"

"Then your father would know you would want to be in there, and he'd answer his phone," Vin said with confidence. "If he has his phone off, I bet he's talking to the doctor. He'll turn it back on, and then you can get through to him."

Not sure whether that was true, Dylan shoved his phone in his pocket, feeling more and more uncomfortable. Something was wrong. A second nurse joined the first, but Vin didn't ask her for directions. He did glare. A lot. Unfortunately, both nurses just glared right back.

"Mr. Carter?" A strange voice called.

Dylan turned around to find a couple coming down the hall toward him. Both wore wrinkled suits, the man in a boring gray and the woman a pant suit that was at least three years out of date. The man pulled out a wallet to open to a badge, and the woman had a badge showing on her belt. Dylan blinked, confused by the appearance of the police. "Dylan Carter," he agreed. He didn't feel like a Mr. Carter. Hell, most of the time, he could barely manage to hold onto his Dylanness.

"Could we talk to you?" Both cops glanced toward Vin.

Vin took a step forward. "Is there a problem?" Both cops seemed startled. They exchanged a quick look, and Dylan's stomach lurched so badly that he could feel the acid burn his throat and the nausea crash into him.

"And you are?" The woman eyed Vin suspiciously.

"Vincenzo Hauser," Vin answered calmly, and that surprised Dylan given his history with police. "I'm Dylan's partner." He raised his chin, almost daring them to object.

The man nodded. "Mr. Hauser, we simply need a private word with Mr. Carter."

"No," Vin said firmly. "Not unless he wants to be alone. If his sister is…." Vin paused, but Dylan could hear the unsaid words echoing in his head. If she was dead. If they were investigating her death. The words seemed to play on a loop that Dylan couldn't stop.

"Ms. Carter is recovering," the woman quickly offered, and Dylan sucked in a breath, his legs going soft as he heard the words. She was recovering. She wasn't dead.

Vin caught him with an arm around the waist and urged him toward a chair, where Dylan practically collapsed. Vin stood next to the chair with his hand on Dylan's shoulder, and Dylan suspected it wasn't coincidence that he blocked the detectives with his body.

"Mr. Carter, I'm sorry. I didn't mean to imply she was in danger," the male detective said. "I'm Detective Gamble, and this is Detective Brinks." He gestured toward his partner.

"I know you," Dylan said. "Or I know your names. Why do I know your names?"

The two detectives exchanged another look, and Vin seemed to reach some tilting point. "Enough," he snapped. "We've been woken up in the middle of the night, frightened, glared at, ignored, and now questioned by two people who don't have the courtesy to tell us what's going on. So either you change how you're handling this, or I'm going to start making some calls to try and find out what the hell is going on for myself."

"Mr. Hauser, I assure you we don't want to make this more difficult." Detective Gamble almost sounded apologetic, which didn't match the whole cop stereotype. "Maybe we can talk privately." He gestured toward the hall, and Dylan looked up at Vin, more than happy to let him decide what they were doing, because he couldn't seem to think past the free-floating fears that kept bubbling up the base of his throat.

"Fine. But we want answers." Vin held his hand out for Dylan. Dylan wrapped his fingers around Vin's hand and held on tight. He needed some point of contact with the world because he felt like he was unraveling. Vin squeezed his hand back and then held on as they started down the hall in the direction the detective indicated.

"Were you at home tonight?" Detective Brinks asked as they walked.

Vin glared at her. "If we need an alibi, let me know right now, and I'll put an end to this whole discussion."

"Alibi? Why would we need an alibi? What happened?" Dylan asked.

"I suspect it wasn't a car accident." Vin stayed at Dylan's side as Detective Gamble invited them into a small room with a round table and four chairs. A coffeemaker had been left on too long, and the bitter scent of burnt coffee clung to the air. Dylan sank into a chair while Vin stood next to him, arms crossed and a full-on dominant expression on his face.

"Is that what you were told?" Detective Gamble sat at the round table while his partner took a position near a narrow window where she looked out.

Dylan looked around, feeling like the guppy in a room full of sharks, which was why he pressed closer to his own personal predator. "We weren't told anything. Dad just said that Carmine was here, that we didn't have to come if we didn't want to. What is going on?"

"Ms. Carter was attacked tonight."

"What? Is she okay?" Dylan started to get up, but Vin put a hand on his shoulder.

"And you're asking where *we* were?" Vin demanded. "I don't think we're the ones you need to worry about."

Detective Gamble leaned back in his chair. "And who should we worry about?"

Vin's fingers tightened against Dylan's shoulder, and Dylan looked up, surprised that Vin would hurt him when it definitely wasn't a good time for that. He opened his mouth to complain, but Vin's hard expression stopped him. Vin looked more than furious. He looked homicidal, and Dylan didn't understand his anger for about three seconds. That was how long it took him to realize who would hurt Carmine… who Vin knew well enough to get that angry with.

"No," Dylan whispered.

Vin looked down, his lips pressed into a tight line for a second before he answered. "He's an ass. He couldn't get to you, and I should have seen this. I should have fucking seen this fucking coming." Vin's voice rose with each word until he was shouting. Whirling away, he punched the wall so hard that Dylan could hear the crunch as hand and drywall met.

"Vin!" Dylan hurried to Vin's side. Standing at his back, he rested his hands on Vin's trembling shoulders.

"Has he made threats?" Detective Gamble asked.

For a second, Dylan waited for Vin to answer for him, but Vin was frighteningly silent. "Kinda," Dylan finally admitted. Vin gave him an over-the-shoulder glare. "Okay, he hit me and chased me into some stranger's car where I locked myself in and had to call for a rescue," Dylan blurted out. Detective Brinks turned toward them, taking out a notebook and starting to take some notes.

"When was this?" Detective Gamble asked.

"Two days ago."

Vin turned around, wrapped his arms around Dylan's waist, and pulled him close. "And today we came out to his parents because I said I wouldn't leave Dylan in that house with his ass of a brother. I knew Gary would be angry, but I thought he would come after Dylan. Better yet, I thought the ass would try to come after me, and I was ready for him."

Dylan leaned back into Vin's warmth. "You did the best you could. You were focused on keeping him from coming after me. And here I accused you of being paranoid."

Detective Brinks spoke up, her voice slow and measured. "Has he gone after you before?" She was an older woman with gray at her temples and pale blue eyes. She reminded him of a grandmother. Not his grandmother, who was loud and fat and dead, but someone's grandmother.

Dylan shrugged. "Brother stuff. Most of the time he's more about calling me names and trying to verbally eviscerate me."

"What made him turn physical?" Detective Gamble asked, and now Dylan felt a little like he was being tag-teamed. He leaned more of his weight back into Vin.

In return, Vin answered for him, his arms even tighter around Dylan. "He accused Dylan of helping the rape victims. He seems to think that not only is he innocent, but that every woman honestly wants to be stalked and beaten and that anyone who disagrees with him is personally trying to persecute him. He's an ass. I've never met him, and I can still say he's an ass."

Detective Brinks and her pale eyes turned to Dylan. "Is that right?"

Dylan nodded. "Is Carmine alright? Is she hurt bad?"

"She's hurt," Detective Brinks said. "But her fiancé is a good man, and I think she'll be just fine."

"Frank?" Dylan frowned, not sure when Frank came into the conversation. Why would it matter if Frank was a good man? Dylan's brain supplied a very unhappy answer to that question, and Dylan started to shake his head. Vin's paranoia had infected him, and he just needed someone to tell him he'd jumped to some totally irrational and disgusting conclusion. "Gary wouldn't. He wouldn't. That's his sister. Our sister. He couldn't." Dylan could feel his chest tighten. Both detectives stared at him with utterly blank expressions, and Dylan's world started to unravel around the edges. "No." Dylan could taste the bile.

"Hey, she'll get through it." Vin's arms tightened around his waist. "Whatever it is, she'll survive. She's a stubborn, annoying woman—she can do anything," Vin muttered into his ear, but Dylan could feel the bile rise so badly that his throat felt shredded. He started gagging, and before he could stop it, he coughed out bitter yellow slime.

"I'll get a nurse," Gamble said, hurrying out of the room, and Dylan felt Vin lifting him and settling him into a chair.

"That's our sister," Dylan protested again, every word raw in his throat.

"I'd offer to kill him for you, but there's a cop here. I'll offer later," Vin said, and even if Dylan could recognize the attempt at humor, he couldn't go there. He just couldn't.

Fisting Vin's shirt, Dylan struggled with unfamiliar emotions that rose up from his soul. Never before in all his life had Dylan felt such a black wave of overwhelming hatred. He hated Gary. He felt a hot, murderous loathing. And he couldn't do anything to undo history—that was the worst part.

Chapter 21

STILL feeling that lurching sense of wrongness and a simmering rage for their bastard brother, Dylan curled his hand around the handle of his sister's door. He needed more than one night to regain his balance, but he had to see her, even if the tsunami of emotions made it hard for him to focus. He feared he'd find her crying. He'd cry. He'd bawl like a newborn and refuse to see anyone if it had happened to him.

He braced himself for an onslaught of Carmine-emotion capable of crushing him into a crumpled ball of old paper. Taking a deep breath, Dylan eased his way into the room before Frank could get back from his shower. Between the doctors and Frank, who had turned into a mother hen with rabies, Dylan hadn't had a chance to see her in almost twenty hours.

He stopped just inside the door and looked at his beautiful sister. One eye had swollen shut, the skin purple and black like an overripe eggplant. That side of her face was mottled with blues and reds, with bruising that continued down the side of her face to merge with the fingermarks around her neck. "God, Carmine. You look…." Dylan stopped. It seemed unkind to finish that thought. He sucked at comforting.

Carmine was as weird as ever, because she grinned, her split lip opening a little to show its raw interior peeking out through the cut. "Hey, if I'm going to feel like shit, at least I can look the part so I get some sympathy. Get your ass in here."

Dylan came in carefully, not sure how to start this conversation or whether he should just ignore the big elephant. "You kinda do look like shit."

She shrugged and the false joviality fell away. "I should have said something. I'm a coward for not calling that asshole out, but after those women came forward, I went to the prosecutor, and he said that my case couldn't help. It was unsubstantiated."

"The prosecutor." Dylan echoed her words. The prosecutor knew. Which meant this had happened before. And she hadn't told a family member or, fucking forbid, her little brother, but a stranger with a tacky suit and a law degree.

"After those women had the balls to press charges... I had to tell someone." Carmine's voice sounded disturbingly normal... cheerful even. But her gaze kept skittering off to the side so she didn't actually look at him.

"You told the prosecutor." Dylan swallowed a hundred other things he wanted to scream out. Why hadn't she told him? Why didn't she shoot Gary in his sleep? Why was she in the house with him? Why hadn't she told their father, because Dylan had seen their father, and he looked even more homicidal than Vin. It was scary, but Dylan knew for a fact that their father would have stopped Gary. Possibly killed him.

Now their mother... Dylan didn't understand her. Carmine told the detectives to tell their parents everything; Dylan supposed that was easier than looking them in the eye when they found out that they'd raised a monster. But when the detective had talked about DNA evidence and vaginal swabs, their mother had gone from bewildered protests to silence. A day later, she still hadn't found her voice. She had sort of folded up into a tiny ball, whispering to herself and fluttering her hands until their father would move back to her side. And when the nurse had told them that Carmine didn't feel up to seeing her parents, Dylan had seen his father fold. If they found out this wasn't the first time... this was going to kill them. Both of them.

Carmine shrugged. "I had to tell the prosecutor. I mean, I never thought he'd.... Did you know that most rapists aren't serial rapists? They're serial criminals, and I thought he'd get arrested for stealing or conning people out of money or something, but then I found out that Gary had raped other women."

"I'm way more upset about the fact he raped you!" Dylan shouted. He took a deep breath and tried to get ahold of his raging emotions. Carmine was the victim, and he didn't have the right to make himself the center of all the emotions in the room, but damn it, she wasn't emotional enough. Dylan wanted her to scream and blame and possibly stab someone in the eye—preferably Gary.

Crossing her arms, Carmine glared at him. "So what makes me special? Do you realize that every two minutes someone is sexually assaulted? Seven percent of victims are raped by a family member. Seven fucking percent, so don't act like I'm some precious, special flower."

"But you are. You're my sister," Dylan pointed out.

Carmine stared at him like he'd grown a second head. "Do you really think that's more important than the fact he was a serial rapist and he wouldn't stop until someone stopped him? I wasn't going to let those women carry the whole burden of that, not when I could help."

"But...." Dylan stopped. He couldn't follow the logic. He couldn't. She couldn't tell anyone to protect herself, but she could tell to protect virtual strangers.

"One in six, Dylan. One in six women is assaulted. Don't look at me like I'm going to shatter. I'm not made of glass, and Gary can fuck himself for all I care, but I am not going to let that asshole ruin my life. I'm not." Her declarations might have been more effective if her face didn't look all eggplanty.

Dylan slowly sank into the visitor's chair, feeling so confused he couldn't even get his feet under him. He felt like he was swimming in emotions, only with less swimming and more drowning.

"They wouldn't even be keeping me here if I hadn't hit my head and got a concussion." Carmine sounded disgusted about that. "It's not the end of the fucking world."

"I should have stopped him," Dylan whispered.

"Oh fuck you, Dilly," Carmine snapped, and Dylan looked up at her, eyes wide. "I don't need you to play hero. I am your big sister. Don't give me any sexist crap about the little woman needing protection, especially since you're more of a 'little woman' than I am." The look she gave him was pure Carmine in her perfect, pure anger.

"How long?" Dylan demanded. No way had Carmine come to grips with this so quickly. No way. Carmine blew up and then she flailed and railed and did a little regrouping before she charged into whatever challenge life had thrown her way. He'd seen that same pattern over and over, and this was Carmine on step six of a disaster, not on step one.

She shrugged. "It stopped for a long time, Dilly. He hadn't come near me since… oh God… I must have been thirteen or fourteen. That's why the prosecutor called it a weak case, and it could only dilute the stronger case he had with the more recent victims."

"How could I not know?" Dylan felt physically ill. He could feel his head swim and his stomach churn.

"Because Gary was smart enough to avoid leaving marks." She reached up to touch her cheek with her fingers, and Dylan could see her torn manicure, one nail ripped down to the bed and a thin line of red where it'd bled. "He's getting dumber with age," she said as she probed the edges of the bruising.

Dylan flinched as he realized why Gary had blown. "I told Mom and Dad," he whispered.

"That you're gay? Good." Carmine grinned at him. "Because I think you exceeded even their ability to repress when you brought Vin to the hospital. Frank says that he growls at anyone who even looks at you wrong, which I'm thinking is a good thing."

Looking Carmine right in the eye, Dylan confessed, "I told them that Gary had gotten physical, that he hit me, and Vin told them he wouldn't let me live in that house because it wasn't safe. They must have talked to him. That's why he was angry."

Carmine reached out and caught Dylan's hand, squeezing hard. "Gary got angry because Gary has issues. Maybe had a loose screw at birth, maybe a nurse dropped him on his head, I don't know. But you didn't make him angry. He's pretty much angry all the time, and he just hides it under all that nauseating charm. If you even try to take any of the blame for this, I'm dragging you to my therapist."

"You have a therapist?"

She gave a quick nod. "A rape counselor through the university. I was getting tangled up in my own emotions and all this anger, and my relationship with Frank...." Her gaze skittered away, and Dylan glimpsed the pain she carried, even if she hid it. "I was afraid we were in trouble, so I started seeing someone through the university about two years ago." Her voice got soft. "Frank's been really good about hanging in there with me."

Dylan felt his own feelings for Frank get a little warmer. "Did he know?"

"About Gary? No. But he did know something was wrong." Carmine gave him a smile and patted him on the hand before smoothing out her bedding. "Don't worry. Frank had his chance to run for the hills, and he's stuck around this long."

Dylan leaned back in the chair and considered his battered sister. "I'm freaked out that you're handling this so well," he confessed.

"I've had a decade of practice and two years of therapy. I've worked through my demons. And if Gary thinks I'm going to stay quiet the way I did six or seven years ago, he's an idiot. Scratch that, I know he's an idiot anyway, but he's even more of one. He's going to prison, Dylan. He may not go for as long as I would like to see, but he's going."

"As soon as they find him," Dylan said softly. Four times the detectives had come back and had prodded and poked at Dylan's memory, trying to get one more friend's name—one more place—that they could search. So far, Gary had fallen off the face of the earth.

"They'll get him," Carmine said with confidence. "Now, you stink, like seriously stink. I've smelled three-day-dead fish on the beach that didn't smell as bad. Go home."

Dylan stood up to leave, but he paused next to the chair. "When we were kids, and Gary would lock me in the closet...." He stopped. His chest literally ached when he thought about how he'd cry and complain because Gary locked him in there. It was the big *trauma* of his life. He couldn't handle it if he'd been complaining all these years and that was when Gary had hurt her.

"You were a kid," Carmine said, pretty much confirming Dylan's worst fear.

Dylan swallowed down the scream that wanted to come out. He couldn't have been much older than five or six—right around kindergarten—when Gary started doing that. And he didn't do it often, but knowing why Gary wanted the privacy, it had happened too damn often for Dylan's peace of mind. "You must have been, what? Seven? Eight?" he asked her.

Carmine nodded. "Young enough to listen to him when he said Mom and Dad wouldn't believe me," she said sadly. "And by the time I got old enough to fight back and threaten to tell on him, he'd stopped."

"He must have been ten or eleven." Dylan frowned. He hadn't even found his genitals at that age.

"It didn't start with…." Carmine stopped, and Dylan saw the edges of that raw pain again. He felt like an ass for even bringing it up. "By the time he was sixteen or seventeen, he stopped. I thought he'd grown out of it. Now that I'm older and more cynical, I'm pretty sure he moved on to raping girlfriends. Or 'coercing' them." Carmine made finger quotes in the air and rolled her eyes. "Rape is rape. And that asshole is going to find out what that word really means when he goes to prison. Unlike those other girls, I have cold hard evidence. I have DNA evidence. Frank called the ambulance the second he found me at the house, so no way can Gary wiggle out of this. From now on, everyone is going to see him as a rapist, and trust me, that's almost going to hurt him worse than losing his freedom."

Dylan wanted to ask if Carmine had thought about all this, if she really wanted to put herself out there as a victim. Part of him wanted to protect her and make sure the neighbors never had a reason to gossip behind her back, but Carmine was still Carmine. She was a porcupine of a sister, and if he tried to wrap her up in a big hug, she was going to leave enough barbed quills in his skin to cause internal bleeding. Now that he knew the truth, he wondered how much of that prickliness came from what Gary had done.

"Go, get. Geez, you make the whole room smell like a locker room, and maybe your Vin likes that, but I don't. Go home," Carmine snapped at him when he hesitated too long.

"Fine, fine." Dylan held up his hands in surrender. "You'd think you'd never smelled body odor before. Did you catch a whiff of yourself sophomore year when you declared deodorant unnatural and ate wheat germ two meals a day? Trust me, you've smelled way worse than me." With that parting shot, Dylan darted out of the room,

Carmine's voice trailing after him, but at least she sounded normal. Mock-pissed, but normal.

"Frank." Dylan stopped the second he spotted Frank standing in the hall with Vin. As they stood next to each other, the contrast was remarkable. They were both dark-haired and dark-eyed, children of some Italian ancestor, and they both had red-rimmed eyes from lack of sleep and unshaven faces. However, Frank stood an inch shorter, wider in the waist and narrower in the shoulders with legs that didn't match his body. They definitely belonged on a much skinnier guy. On an uncharitable day, Dylan would compare him to a children's top that you could spin because of his shape.

"Dylan. Is she okay?" Frank glanced toward the door without showing any signs of going in.

"She kicked you out, didn't she? That's why you lied about going home."

"So is she okay?" Frank asked again without answering Dylan's question.

Because he didn't have an actual answer, Dylan shrugged. "She called me stinky, and I told her that after her year of the hippy when she refused to wear deodorant, she didn't have any room to talk. So, I think she's as normal as she can be."

Frank nodded, his Adam's apple bobbing as he swallowed over and over again. Dylan shifted from foot to foot, uncomfortable with this much emotion in such a small space, but not sure how to make any of this better. Vin reached over, caught his arm, and pulled him close.

"I should have killed the prick," Frank said softly. "I suspected. Oh, she never said anything in as many words, but I suspected, and I should have shot him in the head."

"You would have gone to prison," Vin pointed out, but when Frank looked at them with cold eyes, Dylan realized he didn't care. He really might have killed Gary had he known what Gary had planned. "You would have left Carmine alone to feel guilty about putting you in that position," Vin added. That earned a flash of guilt out of Frank.

"Look, no offence, but...." Frank let his words trail off.

"Dylan and I need to get going. Carmine's right. He stinks," Vin said, tugging Dylan back a step. "You might want to consider going home for a shower yourself."

Frank shook his head. "My sister's bringing me some things. I'll shave and try to clean up in the bathroom."

"I'll see you around then."

Vin urged Dylan down the hallway, and Dylan went, but under protest. "I'd rather stay here until they let her out."

"Nope, you're going home. You need a shower and some good food and a little distance."

"Frank's staying," Dylan pointed out.

"So would I if that were you in there. However, if that were you, I would want a little privacy to collect myself. I'd just be direct enough to tell Frank to back off, and Frank was trying to be nice."

"Frank isn't you. We're friends. Kinda. I should stay with him." They were at the elevator, and Dylan already knew he was losing the fight, but he felt like he had to go down swinging.

"His sister is coming. You need to get some rest because first thing in the morning, you're helping me find that piece of shit brother of yours."

Dylan's mouth came open, and he closed it with an audible click as Vin nudged him through the open elevator doors. "We're what?" Dylan's voice squeaked. He'd never voluntarily looked for his brother. Mostly, he just avoided him.

Vin poked the button for the ground floor with more force than strictly required. "Gary's friends will say things to you that they won't say to the police. And I know I will do things to get answers that the police couldn't do." Vin's jaw muscle bulged as he ground his teeth in anger.

"That sounds...." Dylan stopped. Part of him thought that sounded like justice, and another part thought it sounded like a recipe for Vin to go to prison. The elevator doors opened, and Vin strode out without even putting a hand on Dylan's back. Up until then, Dylan hadn't realized how often Vin touched him, but now he missed that contact. Running after Vin, he kept pace as they headed out into the parking lot. The sun was starting to go down, turning the blue sky a vivid shade of purple and casting long shadows. They'd spent all day waiting for Carmine to agree to visitors and waiting for Frank to wander away from her door long enough for Dylan to have a private conversation. No wonder he felt like roadkill. "Vin?"

Vin turned, and Dylan could see the raging emotions just under the surface of his skin. "The way I see this, you're my family. That makes Carmine the annoying sister I never wanted but I invite to Christmas anyway because I kinda like her when she isn't frustrating me. That means Gary attacked my family. Correct me if I'm making an illogical jump in there somewhere."

Dylan stood, looking at Vin and wishing he knew how to soothe some of that anger. Miss Dolphinia had warned him that when Vin fell, he fell hard and fast, and looking into Vin's eyes, Dylan didn't doubt the strength of his feelings.

Stepping forward, Vin cupped his hands around Dylan's face, his voice getting soft. "Dylan, tell me to back off if I'm in the wrong here. Tell me now."

"You're not wrong. I'm just afraid for you." Dylan rested his hands on Vin's waist.

Vin dropped his hands to Dylan's shoulders. "I can handle Gary," he said dryly.

"I don't want you in prison when you handle him to death."

For a second, Vin simply blinked at him, speechless. "You think I'd kill him?"

Dylan opened his mouth, but then he closed it without saying anything because from the expression on Vin's face, Dylan had clearly misjudged something. Vin looked shocked.

"I'm angry, yes, but I'm not out of control with rage. I'm less likely to kill him than Frank is… than your father is. Trust me, I'm not going to prison, but I'm not going to let Carmine go home and worry about whether Gary is going to show up on her doorstep. I want him behind bars." Vin's mouth twisted into a sadistic smile. "And maybe I'm going to give him a little taste of what it means to be powerless, but I'm not going to prison for that ass. Come on, let's go home. We both stink." Vin pulled Dylan into a quick hug and then shoved him toward the car. "I call first shower."

Another day Dylan might have made a salacious comment about sharing the shower, but right now, he was too worked up to want sex, too tired to do anything, and too stressed to sleep.

Chapter 22

DYLAN clawed his way toward consciousness, cursing Vin's east-facing windows and thin curtain. That lasted for about three seconds, which was exactly how long it took him to remember the events of the previous day. Rubbing a hand across his face, he tried to push all the emotions down, to quiet a million thoughts that clanged around in his head.

"You're up."

"No, I'm not," Dylan said as he crawled out of bed. He gave Vin the hairy eye as he dragged past the chair where Vin was sitting with a laptop balanced on his knee. For someone who had stayed up as late as Dylan, he was annoyingly awake and alert this morning. "Any word from the hospital?" he asked as he headed into the bathroom.

"I wouldn't know without hacking your e-mail or answering your phone," Vin called after him.

Dylan stuck his head out the bathroom and waited. For a half second, Vin tried to play innocent, but then he sighed and caved in. "Your sister e-mailed. She's heading over to Frank's sister's house, and your parents are quietly freaking out because she doesn't want to see them. But she's determined to not let them near until some of the bruises have healed."

"Idiot," Dylan breathed as he headed back into the bathroom to brush his teeth while the water warmed up for a shower. Last night he'd stood under the water more than actually washing, and this morning he felt scummy.

Vin appeared. "Your sister or me?"

Dylan squeezed toothpaste onto his brush. "My sister. My parents are going to be eaten alive by worry, and they're going to make up things in their heads that are way worse than reality. Why would I call you an idiot?" Dylan started brushing his teeth.

"For hacking your e-mail."

Dylan shrugged. As many times as a friend or one of his siblings hacked his e-mail, he didn't care. At least Vin couldn't blackmail him after finding porn sites in the cache. Thank God Dylan had learned to clear the cache before starting to surf the gay porn sites, or he didn't want to think what Gary would have done. Dylan froze. Fuck. How could he worry about Gary's blackmail knowing what Gary had done to Carmine? He seriously needed to rethink his entire life.

Vin came up behind him and wrapped strong arms around Dylan's waist. "Do you think she's trying to hurt your parents?"

Dylan scrubbed at his teeth as he thought about that. They'd both been frustrated with their mother more than once. Gary was her oldest, and he was handsome and smart, and he had some magical power over their mother that they both hated. Worse, he had a magical power over pretty much everyone, even most of the teachers, who thought he was the bestest boy in class. The few teachers who loathed him were definitely in the minority. Leaning down, Dylan spit and turned the water on to run his brush under it. "Maybe with Mom. We both… hell, she had good cause to get frustrated with Mom. I don't know how one woman can love her kids so much and make so many mistakes. But I don't think Carmine would hurt Dad." He grabbed the cup and rinsed, not wanting to think about it.

"When Chase went back on the drugs, I blamed myself because all the signs were there. Every single one. Money was missing. He would vanish for hours, he mentioned the names of friends I didn't know. And still, when he told me I was imagining things, I believed him." Vin clenched his teeth for a second. "But that doesn't mean that, looking back, I don't see all those signs like fucking neon blinking in the dark. Carmine has to know that Gary left his own signs. He was a kid back then. He didn't know how to cover his tracks."

Dylan frowned. "You can't think my parents knew...." He could feel his anger rise because there was no fucking way either of his parents would ever cover up for Gary, not like that. Even when his mother would try to get Gary off some detention, she would always give him the big lecture about responsibility and being the head of his own household someday and what it meant to be a man. True, it was wildly ironic that she would say that after getting him out of detention, but it wasn't like she wanted him to act bad.

"No," Vin quickly said. "No, I don't think they knew. Not at all. However, I do think that looking back, they're going to wonder why they didn't see it. I do think that part of Carmine is wondering why they never saw it. I'm just asking if maybe subconsciously she's...."

"Taking revenge?" Dylan thought about that. Carmine was prickly, but he'd never seen her intentionally hurt anyone. If she said she didn't want their parents to see the bruises, he believed her. "No, I don't think so. I think she's an idiot, but I don't think she'd be that cruel."

Vin nodded, but Dylan could see the shadow of doubt in his eyes.

"You don't believe me?"

"I don't know her all that well, and face it, people skills aren't my thing."

Dylan turned around and rested his hands on Vin's hips. "You seem to be doing better than I am lately."

"That's because I don't have my emotions tangled around my ankles."

Dylan cringed. "You have me there. I'm definitely still feeling a little hobbled here, and not in any sort of fun way."

Vin gave a huff-laugh. "I'll let you get a shower. I'm going to call and reschedule a few of my clients."

"You don't have to. The police—"

"Aren't going to fix this before Carmine gets out at noon. I told you—I'm not good at letting other people handle things. I fix my own problems. And if I make a bigger problem, at least it's my fault and I'm not left standing to the side waiting."

Dylan nodded. It wasn't how he would handle things, but that was why he liked Vin so much, because Vin wasn't anything like him. "I'll hurry," he promised.

Vin nodded and headed back out into the room. Dylan took the fastest shower in the history of the world, taking only enough time to actually scrub himself with soap and rinse before grabbing a towel and heading for the dresser.

"I can't make it." Vin had a full head of cranky going as he talked on the phone. "No," he snapped. Every line of his body was tight, and Dylan grabbed his jeans and hurried to get dressed. Naked around an angry Vin was a little uncomfortable. "Listen...." Clearly Vin had been cut off, because his expression turned almost murderous. He listened, his body getting more and more still in a dangerous sort of way. "Don't you—" Vin sighed. "Shit. She put me on hold." Vin took the phone away from his ear and glared at it for a second. "I hate people. Seriously hate."

"You don't hate me." Dylan went for cute, offering a quick ass-wiggle. Vin's blank stare made it obvious he wasn't in a mood to play.

"I'm going to strangle this woman with her own pantyhose. It's a manager's pitch. Three fucking people, that's it. I'm not training her whole department."

Dylan didn't say it, but he figured Vin wouldn't have the chance to train their department if Vin didn't play nice, and Vin wasn't exactly an expert in that. "Do you want...." Dylan stopped. He was sticking his nose in where it didn't belong, and he knew it. But he hated watching Vin trying to play nice. It was like trying to watch a tiger at the zoo get the meat out of one of those stupid pink balls as if the animal was some housecat to entertain the crowd. Some things were wrong.

"What?" Vin asked when Dylan didn't finish his thought.

"I could... I'm good at playing nice," Dylan offered, and he could feel the heat climb into his face. Vin looked shocked, and that made Dylan's face burn even hotter. "Never mind." Dylan turned around, opened a dresser drawer, and grabbed a shirt.

"I have my schedule here. I just need two hours to get a good idea of what they need their new system to do, and I'll schedule any open slot." Vin set the open laptop down on the top of the dresser. When

Dylan stood up, he could see two weeks' worth of work blocked out in neat lines on an electronic calendar. Tuesday and Wednesday were open, while most of the other days had work scheduled from six in the morning to six or seven at night. Dylan swallowed as he saw the evidence that Vin had tried to block out his schedule for Dylan's first days off. He had to clear his throat before focusing on the job.

"People always feel better if there's an asshole to blame. Are you okay with me implying you're a little impossible?" Dylan asked.

"I am impossible. And Sheila already thinks I'm an asshole," Vin said without any rancor. "I'm going to make us some egg sandwiches while you sort that. Bacon or no bacon?"

"Bacon," Dylan said. "And does she usually leave you on hold this long?"

"When she's pissed, yeah. I would love to shove the passive-aggressive right up that woman's ass. Give me your sister any day of the week," Vin muttered as he headed out the door.

Putting the phone down on the bed where he could hear the hold music, Dylan pulled on his shoes and socks and waited. By the time Dylan trotted downstairs to hand the phone back to Vin, he had rescheduled and discovered that Sheila wasn't nearly as hard to handle as Vin thought.

"You're rescheduled for Thursday afternoon," Dylan offered, trading the phone for an egg sandwich wrapped in a paper towel.

"How much of a discount did you have to give her?"

"Discount?" Dylan asked around a mouthful of egg. He didn't even know he could give a discount.

Vin's eyebrows came down into a frown. "Wait. She didn't even demand a discount?"

Dylan shook his head. "Nope. We agreed that you're nearly impossible, and she was so glad you hired an assistant because technicians with their bad manners should not be allowed near normal people, and she is horrified that your significant other's sister was attacked, and you may be an asshole, but you are such a good man for wanting to spend time with family. That's why she divorced her husband—he never put her first." Dylan took another bite of sandwich while Vin just stared. "She's right about you being a good man," Dylan added after a long silence.

Shaking his head, Vin grabbed his car keys off the table and caught Dylan's arm before guiding him toward the front door. "Feel free to handle my schedule any time. If you can get that old battleax to stop sharpening her knives on my paycheck, you're a miracle worker."

"She's fine. She wants to be right all the time, but she's fine."

"She's not right," Vin pointed out as he locked the front door behind them.

"Most customers aren't, but the trick is to tell them they are, while smiling."

Vin grunted. Dylan could pretty much guess what that meant. "Where are we going?" Vin asked.

"I give. Where?" Dylan asked.

Vin turned and looked at him, and Dylan looked right back. "Your brother," Vin finally said. "Where would your brother go?"

"Oh." Dylan frowned. "Um… crap. I don't know."

"He's a bully. He wants an audience, so we're looking for someone who always admired how much of an asshole he was."

"Then it's not anyone from the car dealership," Dylan said. He'd gone there with Gary once, and the others were all polite with a cold edge of hate. Gary had bragged about how they were all jealous of his sales numbers. And Gary could sell. Growing up, Dylan had always been annoyed at how everyone thought Gary was so damn awesome, at least until they got to know him.

"So, someone from high school?"

"He's twenty-four. He doesn't really hang out with them anymore."

"But he goes back to them when he wants to impress someone," Vin said firmly. "I know the type. I don't understand men like Gary, but I've met enough to know they need an audience. They need someone to tell them they're great."

"Do you know what really scares me?" Dylan asked. "Guard can't tell the difference between you and someone who likes to bully someone."

"Guard doesn't know a lot of things. So, who does Gary like to impress?"

Dylan thought for a second. "Alan Nickerson. He got in trouble with Gary all the time, and he's still living with his parents, in the basement. Gary could impress him."

Vin nodded. "Okay, Alan Nickerson it is. Where does he live?"

"Just two blocks west of my parents' house, but I already gave the police his name. They would have gone to him already."

"Yep, but I bet they didn't encourage him to talk," Vin said, and that scary smile returned. As much as Dylan loved Vin, sometimes the man terrified him.

"You aren't going to do anything that could lead to arrest records, right?" Dylan asked hopefully.

Vin opened the passenger side car door. "Nope," he said as he walked around to the driver's side. It wasn't the most reassuring comment in history.

"I don't want to visit you in prison. I don't think it would be nearly as fun as prison visits in porn always turn out," Dylan said when Vin got in the car. Vin reached over and caught his wrist and curled his fingers tightly around it until Dylan could feel his breathing slow and his world start to narrow down to that point of contact.

"Trust me, Dylan. I hear you. I hear your fears, but now you have to trust me, okay?" Vin tightened his hand a little more, and Dylan's cock started to warm to the idea of being pinned down. With his mouth dry, Dylan could only nod.

Vin gave him an open smile. "Good. Now let's go visit Alan." He started the car and headed toward Alan's place while Dylan tried hard to not panic. He hadn't succeeded by the time Vin pulled up in front of the Nickerson's place.

"Will the folks be home?" Vin asked.

Dylan shook his head. "His mom works as a secretary, and his dad is a trucker. He isn't usually home. When he is home, there's a big semi parked in the side alley. He gets in big fights with the city over parking it there."

Vin nodded. "Okay. He still may have friends in there, so we're going in quiet, and you're staying back. If it looks like things are going pear-shaped, call that detective from the hospital. If it goes wrong, call 911, but do not get involved for any reason."

"But—"

"Hey." Vin reached up to cup the side of Dylan's face. "If you get hurt, I'm going to hate myself and probably be insufferable with you. So duck any flying debris and call for help if you think I can't handle it. Clear?"

Dylan opened his mouth to argue, but he could tell from Vin's face that this wasn't open for negotiation, and Dylan didn't want to fight. He just felt it was his manly duty to offer to stand up for a friend.

"Good, that's agreed," Vin said without waiting for Dylan to actually agree. Sighing, Dylan followed Vin out of the car. Vin strode up to the front door and rang the bell, looking ready to pounce on whoever opened the door.

"Um, he lives around back in the basement," Dylan said, gesturing toward the side yard. Pausing long enough to give Dylan a weary look, Vin followed the worn trail around the side of the house to the concrete steps set into the ground that led down to the basement.

"So, here?" Vin asked.

"Yep," Dylan agreed.

Stretching his head from one side to another like a fighter about to go into the ring, Vin headed down the short set of stairs before knocking on the basement door. Dylan could hear the thumping of music from inside, so Alan's parents definitely weren't home. Vin knocked again, louder, and the music volume dropped. After a second, the door came open, and Alan stood there in an old T-shirt and dirty shorts. The smell of weed drifted out the open door.

"What?" he demanded, his red-rimmed eyes matching his red hair. Dylan remembered him as the basketball star who graduated a couple of years before Dylan got to high school, but now he looked smaller and shorter than he had back then. Realistically, Dylan knew

Alan hadn't shrunk as much as Dylan's own perspective had changed, but it was still a little disconcerting. Alan eyed Vin up and down, looking more and more confused. "Are you another cop?"

"Do I look like a cop, and think carefully before you answer," Vin warned.

"Man, what do you want?"

"An address." Vin shifted his weight, and Dylan started holding his breath as the sense of danger rose.

"Fuck you." Alan stepped back and tried to slam the door, but Vin rushed forward, hitting the door and sending Alan flailing back into the dark basement room. Dylan hurried to follow, his cellphone in hand as he watched Alan windmill his arms to catch his balance. The television flickered, but all the shades were drawn, giving the room an eerie vibe… or maybe the eerie came from Vin stalking after Alan. And he was stalking. For his part, Alan kept retreating. Eventually Alan ran out of room and stopped with this back up against the TV cabinet.

"Get the fuck out of my house," Alan snarled. It was actually a little amusing watching him growl while clearly terrified and backed into a corner.

Smiling slowly, Vin leaned in closer. "No."

Vin stood nose to nose with Alan, fury radiating off Vin in waves. Holding his breath, Dylan waited for the storm to break and prayed he wasn't about to become the primary witness in the DA's prosecution of Vin because right now, Vin looked ready to kill. "Give me a name and an address. And that name and address had better lead me to Gary."

Alan glanced over toward Dylan. "I'm not getting involved."

"I'm not giving you a choice."

"Who the fuck do you think you are?" Alan demanded. His fists curled, but surprisingly, the man hadn't thrown any punches yet. Maybe Alan recognized the danger and had the brain cells to know he should avoid poking the predator. If so, he was smarter than he looked.

"Last chance," Vin said, his voice so soft it almost qualified as a whisper.

"Fuck off."

Vin moved so fast Dylan wasn't exactly sure what he did. It looked like he just swiped his hand down Alan's chest, but Alan fell to the side, twisting to get out of Vin's way with his mouth open in shock. Vin followed him as he stumbled toward his couch, caught Alan's wrist, and twisted it out away from his body. Waving his free arm, Alan tried to get his balance back, but he toppled, hitting the couch before sliding to the floor, and Vin controlled the fall, guiding Alan to a spot in front of the couch and then kneeling with one knee in Alan's groin.

"Get off me, fag!" Alan cursed, but he couldn't do much else because Vin held his wrist out at an odd angle, and from the frequent cringes, Dylan figured that either Vin had weight on that knee braced against Alan's groin or he was squeezing the small bones of the wrist. Maybe both. Vin certainly looked angry enough to want to cause a whole lot of pain.

"Quiet down or this is going to get worse," Vin warned in an eerily cheerful voice. Alan opened his mouth—probably to call more names—but Vin put his free hand over Alan's sternum, knuckles down. Immediately, Alan's words vanished under a low, wavering cry like that of a wounded animal. Dylan got the feeling he was trying to scream, but he couldn't get the air to make his voice work.

"Are you ready to listen?" Vin opened his hand and rubbed Alan's chest. Alan panted, his eyes so wide Dylan could see the white of them all the way around, but he nodded enthusiastically.

"You *are* going to tell us where Gary is. And if I can't find him, that means you're back to being my only lead, and I'll be back here. So I want you to think carefully before you decide where to send me."

Alan sucked in a breath, but when Vin made a fist and rested it against his sternum, the words tumbled out. "The calligraphy studio on Fifteenth, the apartment on the second floor. He's got a piece of ass that always lets him crash. It's just north of Dewey Avenue. He's there. I know he's there. That bitch will take anything from him, so she'll hide him from the cops. I wouldn't. I told him I didn't need trouble. Honest."

"You know, I believe you." Vin patted Alan's cheek, and Dylan cringed at the condescension in that one gesture. Vin could be a bastard when he put his mind to it. "So you be a good boy and stop trying to cover up for sadistic raping bastards. Got it?"

Alan nodded.

"And don't fuck with my family again." Vin struck Alan's neck, and suddenly Alan was rolling to his stomach, gagging and throwing up on his own carpet. Standing, Vin looked down at him for a second. "Let's go," he said, offering his hand to Dylan. Dylan took it, but he kept looking at Alan. The man seemed to be breathing okay, but it was hard to tell with all the retching and spewing.

He waited until Vin had ushered him out of the basement before he asked, "Is he okay?"

Vin had been heading for the door, but he stopped to look back. "He's an entitled asshole, and life is going to eat him alive and turn him into its bitch, but I didn't do him any real harm. Those were pressure points. No real damage, pain and some autonomic responses, but no damage." Vin tugged at Dylan's hand, and Dylan followed. Rain drizzled down and grass smell rose from the narrow strip between the walk and the street.

"What if he calls the police?" Dylan demanded as soon as Alan's door closed. He didn't want to give the man any ideas, but if someone had done that to him, he totally would have been calling the police… just as soon as he could crawl out of his own vomit.

"He won't," Vin said with confidence.

"You assaulted him. And I'm actually fine with the assault, but not with you getting charged with an assault."

"I don't understand people. I don't know *why* they act the way they do, I don't, Dylan. However, over the years I've gotten pretty good at predicting *what* they're going to do. He's going to roll around on the floor and as soon as he gets up and washes the vomit off, he's going to realize he doesn't have a mark on him and his blood is full of drugs. Trust me, he's not calling anyone."

Dylan looked back at the door. That sounded logical, but he still worried. Vin brought his hand around Dylan's waist and pulled him close. "Trust me, okay? And if it all blows up, I promise you can say 'I told you so' until the cows come home. Deal?"

"I'll never let you forget it. And I do mean never. We'll be eighty, and I'll still be bringing up that time you got arrested because of stupid Alan Nickerson."

Vin laughed. "That's fair. I'm good with that as long as the story includes your asshole brother going to jail the same day. So let's go find him, okay?"

Dylan nodded. "Can we make a stop to buy Tums or Pepto or something first?"

"Yeah." Vin hugged Dylan closer. "Yeah, we can do that. Then we need to go find your brother before he takes off for good."

Chapter 23

DYLAN looked up at the graffiti-covered building. The shop on the first floor had been a calligraphy shop at some point in history, but squatters seemed to have claimed it. The wood boards used to block the main entrance hung from just one nail at the top. Sadly, other buildings on the block looked even worse.

"Do you think he's still here?"

"Do you think Alan wants another visit from me?" Vin asked in return. He headed for the stairs between the two halves of the building. A thriving tattoo shop in the other half of the building was doing a good business, and Dylan stuck close to Vin as they climbed past a number of men who sat on the steps drinking and talking loudly. "If he's here, call Detective Gamble."

"Before or after you kill him?" Dylan asked dryly.

Vin looked down at him. "I'm not killing him. I may want to, but trust me, I have a lot of experience controlling myself."

Dylan swallowed his fears and nodded. While Vin didn't look exactly happy, he did head for the second story apartment door. No one answered when Vin knocked on the second floor apartment, and Vin stood with his jaw muscle jumping as he looked up and down the dirty staircase.

"I'm wondering if pot-boy meant second floor above the shop or the second level of apartments." Vin looked up at the two floors above them, each with a small landing that led to another apartment. "Wait here. If your brother comes running out, let him. Do not stop him. Do not talk to him. Do not try to slow him down." Vin poked a finger at Dylan's chest.

Dylan snorted. "Clearly you've confused me with someone brave because none of those things even came to mind."

"You are brave. You walked into the Stonewall, and that took balls. However, if your brother did that to Carmine...."

"Yeah, yeah. He'll kill me. Trust me, I know. If he comes out that door, I plan to run up these stairs screaming for you at the top of my lungs."

Vin pressed his lips together, but after a minute of indecision, he headed up the stairs to the next apartment. Dylan's stomach churned so much he considered calling Detective Gamble on the spot. At worst, Gary wasn't here and the detective would be cranky about the wild-goose chase. That didn't sound so bad. Until the detective tried ordering Vin to stay out of it and Vin acted like Vin and then all hell broke loose. Yeah, maybe not.

Dylan inched his way up the stairs while keeping an eye on the second-floor apartment door. Standing at the halfway mark, he could see Vin knocking at the next door. "Who is it?" a woman called. Dylan took a few more steps closer.

"A man with handcuffs and a very well-used flogger," Vin answered. Dylan frowned, not sure where that came from, but the lock clicked, and the door edged open. A woman with impossibly blonde hair and dark eyes looked out. She had fading greenish bruises along the side of her face, and if she didn't work as a prostitute, then she'd gotten dressed up for Halloween a little early. Her shorts pulled tight against her crotch, and her top strained at the buttons. If Dylan had been pressed to describe Gary's "type," this woman would have been the exact opposite. Dylan had always assumed Gary would go for someone classy, someone who could charm the right people at company parties. But something in his gut told him that Vin had found the right place.

"Who?" She opened the door a little wider and twitched her body. Abandoning the second floor door, Dylan came up behind Vin, and he could see a flash of fear in her eyes. That was pretty stupid because Vin was way scarier than him. However, one look at Dylan and she stepped back and tried to slam the door.

Vin stuck his foot in the door. "I'm here to see Gary, so get out of the way."

Dylan could see her put her shoulder to the door. "He's not here."

"Yes, he is. And I don't blame you for protecting him because I bet he makes you feel good when he gives you all his attention, and lately he has given you every bit of the attention you've needed from him." Vin leaned closer. "But he's a rapist, and he raped someone I don't exactly like, but someone I can respect. So I'm here to talk to him, and you will get out of the way so you don't get hurt. Clear?"

The woman's eyes got big, and she seemed to shrink back from Vin. "He isn't here," she said so weakly that the lie dangled in the air.

"Okay," Vin said. He slowly applied all his strength to the door, forcing it open despite the way the woman kept pushing on the other side. "Dylan, wait out here and call Detective Gamble."

"What? Oh no. I'm not leaving you to deal with Gary alone." Dylan couldn't decide what exactly scared him, but he was so far out of his comfort zone he planned to stick to Vin's side until something pried him off. "But I am calling Detective Gamble," Dylan compromised as he fumbled for his phone.

Behind him, the woman headed out the door, her heels clattering against the concrete and metal stairs as she fled. From the look of the apartment, she wasn't leaving much behind. The couch sagged in the middle, and the cheap furniture leaned at drunken angles. The only nice thing was a flat-screen TV that took up one whole wall in the tiny apartment.

"Oh Gary!" Vin called in a sing-song voice as Dylan dialed the number he had for the detective. The only thing scarier than an angry Vin was a happy one. Dylan could feel the hairs on the back of his neck stand up. "Olly, olly, all in free," he called. It took a few seconds, but the curtain on the far side of the shitty little room started to stir, and Gary stepped out from behind it. His face had four hard lines down the right side, the scabs dark against his skin.

"Well, look who it is." Vin stepped forward, but Gary's eyes focused on Dylan.

"Who are you talking to, Dill Weed?" he demanded. Ignoring Vin was his big mistake.

"You don't talk to him, you walking piece of shit. You left your DNA on your sister, you idiot. You're going to prison, not just as a rapist, but as a pedophile, incestuous rapist. Welcome to the bottom of prison totem pole."

Gary finally focused on Vin, who still grinned like a madman. Dylan took a step back into the shadows and whispered out the world's fastest report for a very confused Detective Gamble.

"Who the fuck are you?" Gary demanded. He looked over to Dylan and then back. "Oh wait. You're Dylan's Vincenzo. You're the fucking hero on his white horse who stuck his nose into my business." Gary bridled his body like a stereotypical movie gangster or a sick weasel. Dylan had a friend who had weasels, and when they were sick, they tended to jerk their bodies that same way.

"Dylan's my business."

"My family isn't your business, fag," Gary snapped. "You turned him into a fag, and my parents may have given you a pass on that, but I won't. I'll be back for you. Watch." Gary poked a finger in Vin's direction and then tried to detour around him. Dylan sucked in a breath and retreated to the door, but Vin sidestepped to stop Gary.

"Dylan is my family, and that means I inherited this mess the same as he inherited a rusted water heater that breaks at least once a month." Vin shrugged. "It's a relationship thing, but seeing as how you can't have a real relationship because the second you let your mask slip, people see the monster below the skin, you wouldn't know about that. You won't ever know about that." Vin dropped his voice lower, and Dylan could see him shift his feet, one in front of the other. Oh yeah, fists were going to fly. "How did it feel, raping a child? Raping your sister? Going after Carmine again? Bad move. She is looking forward to eviscerating you in court. She pretty much loathes you and is looking forward to getting to tell the world how you touch little girls."

Gary had turned steadily redder, and Dylan opened his mouth to shout a warning, but before he could, Gary swung.

Dylan heard the slap of skin against skin as Gary's hit made contact. Vin's head jerked to the side, and Dylan flinched back. However, Vin just slowly straightened back up and looked at Gary. Being off to the side, Dylan couldn't see the full extent of the damage, but drops of blood splattered Vin's face. Vin ran his tongue along the inside of his lip, and the split opened. A thin line of blood sluggishly trailed down over his chin, but oddly, Vin smiled. "I'm so glad you did that," he said in a tone that actually sounded creepily grateful.

Dylan could see the confusion on his brother's face as he backed up a step. "Why?" That was a stupid question, and Vin didn't even try to answer. He just cocked his fist back and let it fly with so much force that when it hit Gary, Gary flew backward, crashed into the side of the couch, and sort of rebounded off to land on the cheap side table. Table and lamp shattered under his weight, and Gary ended up in a heap of broken wood and ceramic shards.

Before he could get up, Vin closed the distance and caught Gary's arm, wrenched it around to the small of his back, and held Gary's shoulder in his other hand.

"Get off me, you faggot!" Gary screamed.

"What? Don't you like being forced to the ground?" Vin pushed Gary's face closer to the green shag carpet, and Dylan sucked in a breath. Broken shards and splintered wood could do a lot of damage to Gary's face, and Dylan could almost taste Vin's fury. Vin stepped closer and used a toe to force Gary's legs apart enough for him to stand between his thighs. "Are you afraid I'm going to make you open your legs? That I'm going to fuck you while you scream? Maybe I'll tell the police how much you like it. What do you think of that?"

Gary started bucking wildly, but he didn't have any leverage. For the first time, Dylan could see how much sheer power Vin had in his hands. Yeah, Vin was muscled, but lots of muscled guys didn't actually have much strength in them. They'd pull muscles or complain about pain the second they had to help lift a refrigerator. Unlike them, Vin seemed perfectly comfortable and able to exert as much strength as he needed to get the job done. It took several minutes, but Gary finally gave up. He had one hand out, fingers sprawled against the carpet, and smudges of blood stained his tanned skin.

"Get off me."

"No." Vin was enjoying this a little too much.

"You fucking pervert." Gary arched his back and tried to get up again, for all the good it did him.

"Coming from a man who raped his sister, that's rich. You are the most disgusting piece of shit I have ever seen. The world would be better off if I just slit your throat right now. However, I have something better planned for you."

"Don't you fucking touch me! Dylan, do something. Get this fucking queer away from me."

"Me? You want me to save you?" Dylan's brain couldn't even process that. Clearly Gary was a moron.

Vin leaned in close and whispered in a frighteningly friendly voice, "Get used to being ignored, little man, because where you're going, you won't have any power ever again. You'll be one more monster locked in a cage with all the other monsters. Other people will control every second of your life for so long that you're going to forget what it even feels like to piss when you want."

Gary's face was red and swollen, and Dylan could hear the tears in his brother's voice even if he hadn't started crying. Yet. "I didn't fucking do anything wrong. They're playing games. They're all playing fucking games with my life. They hate me because I have what they want, and I won't let them control me."

"Well, that's not a problem now because you're going to be under control. Every guard is going to order you around, order you to strip, stick his dirty fingers up your ass and in your mouth in search of contraband. And whoever ends up owning you is going to rape you, and if you tell, the torture is going to be even worse."

"My lawyers—"

"Aren't going to work very hard when they figure out your parents won't foot the bills, not after Carmine's been added to the list of victims."

"She wouldn't… no fucking way. Maybe she told Dill Weed, but she'd never tell our parents." Shock. That was shock in Gary's voice. He was shocked that Carmine had told anyone, and Dylan's stomach turned as he thought about that. The delusional asshole really thought he controlled her. Up until this moment, Dylan had wanted to ask "why," but Gary didn't have any answers Dylan wanted to hear.

"Did you call the police?" Vin asked.

Dylan nodded. "Detective Gamble said to not do anything until he got here," Dylan said quietly.

"What the hell did you do, Dilly?" Gary screamed, the panic making his voice high. "They were games! Just games!" Gary tried to wiggle free of Vin's grasp, and he squealed as Vin did something painful.

"I stuck up for my sister," Dylan said. "Which I should have done a long time ago. You're just lucky Dad didn't find you first, Gary. He's going to kill you."

"He's weak," Gary snapped. "You know it. You know he is. This fucking country won't let men be strong."

Dylan opened his mouth, but he simply didn't have a response for that. None.

"Mr. Hauser, back away from the suspect. Police!" Dylan whirled around, and Detective Gamble stood there with a new partner, a man who didn't look old enough to legally drink much less be a detective. However, the fact that Gamble had his gun pointed at Vin was the real concern.

"Vin." Dylan breathed the name, too scared to even speak up.

Vin slowly let go, raising his hands and shifting to show the police his back. "I'm glad you're here, detective. Gary Carter just assaulted me, and I would like to press charges." Vin sounded impossibly calm for a man who had a gun pointed at him.

"You?" Gary demanded, and Dylan could almost see him gather that cloak of righteous indignation around him. "I didn't assault you; you assaulted me! I want him arrested!" The fact he had to crawl out of the remains of the side table somewhat muted Gary's fury. Gamble's gun followed him, steadily focusing on Gary, and Dylan quickly backed out of the way. "I'm the victim!" Gary defended himself when he turned to see the gun trained in his direction.

"Is that right, Mr. Hauser?" Gamble sounded pretty unconvinced.

Vin slowly turned, putting his hands down only once he saw that Gamble didn't have the gun pointed at him. "I have the split lip and bruised face to show he started it. He's just not very good at finishing what he starts." Vin gave Gary a nasty smile, and more fresh blood appeared on the edges of his cut lip, clinging to the edges of the crusty, dried stuff. "Then again, maybe if I was a woman, sixty pounds lighter, and not expecting a cowardly attack from a pencil-dicked asshole, he would have done better. Unfortunately for him, I know how to defend myself."

Gary breathed quickly and loudly, but he didn't comment as the young detective moved in from the side, caught Gary's arm, and shoved him into the wall while reading him his rights.

"Mr. Hauser, you and I need to talk about the fact that you involved yourself in my case," Detective Gamble snapped.

"You're welcome," Vin answered. Carefully walking around the back of Gamble to avoid getting in the line of fire, Vin circled around to Dylan and held his arm out. Dylan hurried to his side and wrapped his arms around Vin. "Can you keep him in a cell this time?" Vin asked.

Gamble glanced over. "You don't have to worry about that. No judge is going to offer bail after this. He attacked his sister because she had the bad luck to walk in her own front door when he was in a bad mood. It's not hard to argue he's a danger to the community."

"She pushed me into it. It was her fault," Gary complained.

"Mr. Carter, your lawyer would suggest you shut up. Gentlemen, I need your statements down at the station."

Vin nodded and pulled Dylan toward the door. As they went down the stairs, Dylan could hear the sirens, and by the time they got to the street, two more police cars had shown up. "Nice, now they show up. God forbid they find this place on their own," Vin complained.

"I don't think they get to question witnesses the way you do," Dylan pointed out.

Slipping his hand around Dylan's waist, Vin gave him a wide smile, which looked a little creepy with the blood splattered across his face.

"Gary really got in a good hit."

Vin shrugged. "I wanted some evidence that he started it. I got it."

Dylan stopped so quickly that Vin stumbled and had to catch his balance. "I'm buying you brake lights," he complained mildly as he had to turn around.

"She... what if she did the same thing?" Dylan asked. Turning, he looked at the stairs.

"Did what thing?"

Dylan turned back to Vin. "Carmine. She said she couldn't help because he raped her so long ago. She... what if she did what you did?"

Both Vin's eyebrows went up. "You think she did antagonize him? You think she put herself out there as bait?"

Dylan sat on the thin strip of yellowing grass between the street and sidewalk because his legs couldn't hold the weight of his newfound horror. Vin crouched in front of him, both hands braced on Dylan's knees. "She fixes things. She always fixes things."

"Fuck." Vin breathed the word. "And I thought I was crazy. If that's... your sister has balls bigger than anyone I've ever met if that's even a little bit true. She has huge fucking balls, and I'm never playing chess with her, because she plays to win and she fights dirty. Do you think...." Vin stopped.

Dylan could only shake his head. "I don't know. I can't...." Putting his face in his hands, Dylan felt himself start to shake. "He'd hurt her enough. He'd done enough to her already."

"Hey." Vin shook his shoulders, and Dylan's head came up in shock. Over Vin's shoulder, he could see the police bringing Gary down. Vin leaned close, his voice a rough whisper. "I don't know what she did. Maybe she used herself as bait and maybe she didn't. Maybe it was only subconscious—she felt guilty and things got out of hand. We don't know and you *can't* mention any of this to the police. None, Dylan. None of it."

Dylan watched as Detective Gamble came down the stairs.

"The defense, the police.... They'll use it to make excuses, Dylan." Vin tightened his fingers until they pressed into Dylan's arms.

Licking his lips, Dylan nodded. Vin was right. They couldn't tell anyone, but if she had... if she'd used herself as bait.... Dylan could feel the tears threaten to come, and he didn't want to cry in public. "Let's go home," he said weakly.

"Good idea," Vin said as he looked over to where Gamble watched them. "Come on." Vin helped him up and got an arm around his waist.

"I'm losing man points here," Dylan protested weakly. At the same time, he held onto Vin's shoulder to keep his wobbly legs from going out from under him.

"I think you have a legitimate reason for being knocked off-balance," Vin said. "Let's get home."

"Hold on. The police wanted us at the station."

"Tough shit," Vin said. "They'll wait."

Dylan would have argued, only he needed to sit down somewhere quiet, and a really big drink wouldn't be a bad idea, either.

Chapter 24

DYLAN looked at his house as Vin parallel parked at the curb. Two weeks. It'd been two weeks since he'd come home to announce he was moving out, and he hadn't seen the place since. He hadn't stayed away from the house for that long since eighth grade, when he'd gone to a baseball camp. Showering with boys had turned into pure torture as Dylan had tried to hide a half-hard cock, and he'd nearly wept with homesickness. When his father had picked him up and driven him home, the sight of this house had made all the knots in his thirteen-year-old stomach untangle.

Now, the house reminded Dylan of too many horrors. He remembered clinging to his brother's arm, crying as his brother shoved him in a closet. "It's good for you. You need to be a man, not a crybaby," Gary had said, shoving him back into the dark. But now the real horror was remembering Carmine with those big, dark eyes watching as she clung to her doll.

This house carried years of Christmases, and the memory of Carmine standing there waiting to be raped. Dylan had stood in the front room while his mother took a million pictures of him and Jennifer dressed up for senior prom, but now Dylan could only think about how Gary had attacked Carmine in that same spot.

Too many emotions traced back to this house, and Dylan was just glad he didn't live here anymore. He'd rather have their house, with the kitchen that smelled musky when they closed the windows during cold weather and the unfinished basement and the water heater that broke regularly. Working together, they were fixing all that, but Dylan didn't know how to fix all the emotional breakage in his parents' home. Dylan turned to say that to Vin.

The look on Vin's face stopped him. "You look terrified," Dylan said. Considering what he'd seen Vin do, that was ironic.

"It's a full meal... with your family. Interacting with people without either teaching or threatening them...." Vin made a face. "Not my strong suit."

Dylan snorted. "My dad likes you more than me. You'll survive."

"What are you talking about?"

"You are pretty much everything my father thinks of as being a real man. Trust me, he definitely sees you as the husband in this relationship."

"You're crazy." Vin opened his door and got out.

"Watch," Dylan said as he followed, locking the doors behind him. "He's going to try to get you to fix cars with him, which is fine because it saves me from the same fate. Me and tools are not friendly."

"Me and people are not friendly," Vin countered.

"You have met my father. Trust me, a lack of interpersonal skills is not going to bother him. Now me? I mean, I know he loves the crap out of me, but he totally does not know how to react to me."

"You're imagining things."

"Well, you kicked Gary's ass, avenged Carmine's honor, and protected the family as well as starting your own company. Trust me, as son-in-laws go, you have Frank beat." Dylan wasn't even kidding. He and his father rarely knew what to talk about, but when his father had found out that Vin had led the police to Gary, he had been more emotional than Dylan had ever seen him. For one horrified second, he thought his father might cry, but then his mother had started sobbing, and his father had focused on her. And no way did his father believe Vin's line about Dylan being just as responsible for the arrest. His father knew that Dylan would have avoided any and all conflict.

Vin leaned against the car and held out a hand toward Dylan. Dylan moved closer and let Vin pull him into his arms. "We'll see if that's true after tonight. And if he even suggests I avenged Carmine's honor, he's in for a feminist rant that would put Gloria Steinem to shame."

"No joke," Dylan said softly. He didn't know if his sister really had used herself as bait, but whether she did or didn't, she made it very clear that she intended to be the hero of her own story by testifying. And despite Dylan's fear that his sister would turn into the center of gossip, most of the neighbors had supported the family. They dropped by and tried to chat with his mother, and some of the men had started hanging out at his father's shop again.

Dylan figured they decided his parents had been punished enough. And they had. Neither had been able to talk about it, but his mother had taken to three-hour naps and general avoidance, and his father's hands would start shaking at the oddest times. Dylan was just happy that Carmine had moved in with Frank before the wedding, because he didn't think she needed to deal with their pain on top of her own. Part of him wished his parents would sell the house, move away from the memories, and try to heal. However, neither of his parents handled change well. So they gritted their teeth and bore the pain.

"Come on, let's get this over with," Vin said with all the enthusiasm of a death row inmate. They reached the door, and Vin hesitated. "This is where things started going south with Chase, you know," he said softly.

"What do you mean?"

"They didn't like that I was bossy, and I'm not good at pretending to be anything else."

Dylan leaned into Vin's side, pressing into the hand that always seemed to rest at the small of his back. "This is a family full of pushy. I think my father and I learned to be laid back because one more big personality in this house and something would have exploded."

"And here I come with a very big personality," Vin pointed out with a wry twist to his mouth.

Dylan shrugged. "There's more room in the family now." And it was true. Gary still filled the empty spaces when they weren't careful. His father or Carmine would mention something, and Dylan could almost feel his brother's ghost haunting the corners. However, with bail denied and a guilty verdict almost guaranteed, those moments were getting fewer and farther between. And his mother, who had always been the second-largest personality in the home, had shrunk considerably. Dylan actually worried about that, but Carmine was already nagging her to death about going into therapy, so Dylan didn't want to add more pressure to the cooker on that issue.

"Let's get this over with," Vin said.

Dylan reached out and rang the bell. It felt weird, ringing the bell on his parents' house, but after walking in on his father crying, he definitely needed to give them some warning before just breezing through.

"Vin, Dylan," his father said as he opened the door.

"Yep, you got first billing," Dylan whispered as he gave Vin a wink.

His father looked confused. "What?"

"Dylan's being annoying," Vin answered for him. Smiling, Dylan gave his father a quick hug before heading for the kitchen. That was where everyone else would be.

"There are days I don't understand him," his father was saying behind him, but Dylan left his dad and Vin to talk stereotypical men stuff.

"Hey!" he said as he came through the kitchen door. He'd expected to find his mother at the stove, and he hesitated when he found Frank and his mother sitting while Carmine stirred a pot of something tomatoey. And clearly dinner wasn't anywhere near on time, because a box of dry spaghetti sat on the counter by the sink. Dylan was surprised his mother had even allowed that in her house. Her Italian heart should have stopped at the sight of fake pasta.

"Dylan!" His mom got up, came over, and hugged him tightly before kissing both his cheeks. "You look so good. Your father says you're working with Vincenzo on his business on top of working at the restaurant, so I was afraid you'd be run-down. But you look good. You should eat more." His mother gave him a smile. Her enthusiasm was a little over-the-top, and she clung a little too tight as he hugged her back.

"Helping Vin is only an hour or two a day. It's not hard. So, what's up with you guys?" Dylan looked at Carmine and Frank, hoping for some normalcy. Talking to his mom was still so strained. His mom backed off and sat back in her chair and started watching Carmine.

"She got a scholarship to get her full RN degree," Frank said proudly.

"Whoa. Carmine! Hey, that's awesome!" Dylan went over and gave Carmine a big hug. "And here I thought you were destined for a life of cleaning bedpans."

"Watch it! I'll bring out the baby pictures and show Vin," she threatened.

Dylan held up his hands in surrender. "No need to bring out the big guns." Dylan took his dad's chair at the small kitchen table between his mother and Frank. "You must be so proud," he said to both of them.

His mother's smile didn't quite reach her eyes.

"With the salary she'll bring in with an RN degree, I was thinking of quitting my job and writing the great American novel while she supports me in the manner to which I've become accustomed," Frank joked. Carmine turned around to poke a finger at him.

"Oh no you won't, mister. If you start acting like a fifties housewife, I reserve the right to treat you like one."

"Oh no, Ricky," Frank mimed in a fairly good Lucille Ball imitation. Carmine put her hands on his shoulders and leaned in for a kiss.

"Idiot," she said fondly. Dylan watched their mother, her eyes softening when she watched Carmine and Frank kiss.

Carmine pulled back, and the second her eyes met their mother's gaze, Dylan could feel the temperature of the room drop a little. Yeah, this wasn't a wound that was going to heal quickly.

"So, you're doing dinner?"

Carmine looked at the stove. "Sorta. Mom had a migraine, but I'm starting to think that the dinner has me beat."

"You need more salt," his mom said quietly.

Carmine rolled her eyes. "God, Mom, you're going to give us all high blood pressure."

"It'll taste bland until you add more salt."

Dylan grabbed a piece of buttered bread off Frank's plate and let the familiar fight wash over him.

Carmine's meal ended up being an hour late and not nearly as good as their mother's cooking, but he could almost feel them all stretching for something normal. Frank kept telling them about the scholarship and how hard Carmine had worked until her ears turned red. Dylan explained how Vin had managed to build his business from one computer. The normalcy lulled Dylan into an almost giddy sense of relief, so much so that he wasn't prepared when his father stood up from the dinner table and made his announcement.

"I want to show Dylan a car. He should have a car now that he's working more hours," his father said.

"Dad, I'm good, really. I mean, it's nice for you to offer, but...." As far as Dylan was concerned, a car drained your money. He could use his bike or a bus on those days when Vin wasn't around to drive. Weirdly, his father looked at Vin. Dylan felt a little flutter of worry in his stomach.

"You should go," Vin said. "Go see if your father has anything that you like."

Dylan frowned at Vin for half a second, but then he shrugged. "Um, okay. We can see what you have," Dylan agreed. Unless his father had something pretty awesome, Dylan didn't plan to spend his money on a car, but he could look. And while he looked, he could ask his father what the hell was going on.

Carmine rolled her eyes. "Way to get ordered around, Dylan."

"Bite me," Dylan suggested as he grabbed his sweater. His father was already going for the front door. The first cold of fall had hit, and the brisk night air rushed through the open door.

"Now that's original. You should go to school to learn some new insults," Carmine called after him as Dylan followed his father.

"Vin, are you coming?" Dylan asked, stopping when he realized Vin still sat at the dining room table. For some reason, he didn't mind leaving Vin with his father, but the idea of leaving Vin alone with Carmine and his mother terrified him.

"You go," Vin said, using his fork to spear another bite of store-bought chocolate cake. Dylan paused, but after a second of doubt he turned to follow his father out into the night.

"Wow, he really is whipped," Carmine said as Dylan reached the door.

"Don't talk about your brother that way," his mom scolded, and for one second, he could hear their real mother in her exasperation. Then Dylan closed the door, leaving Vin to handle the nuttier side of his family. He trotted to catch up with his father before he headed across the street.

"I've got a couple of nice cars," his father said. The streetlights created pools of yellow in the gray twilight created by the city.

"So, you're back to fixing up cars?"

His father nodded. "Business isn't up to usual, but a couple of the guys on the street are looking for solid work cars, so I'm fixing a couple up. I bought a car with the money you gave me, so I should have a check for you in a few weeks. She's a solid little Toyota. She'll sell easy once I get her running again."

"That's good." Dylan stopped, not sure what to say. "Dad, are we doing something other than car shopping here?"

His father passed three houses with their narrow, cracked driveways before he answered. "It's ironic. Your grandfather is probably laughing in his grave."

"Grandpa Carter?"

"No. Your Grandfather Ristagno. He never approved of me. He wanted your mother to marry a good Italian man. He even had a couple picked out—strong men who would be the head of the household."

"Why is that ironic?"

His father's mouth twisted into a wry smile. "It seems you've chosen the man your mother refused to marry."

"What?" Dylan did some mental flailing because none of this made sense. Mostly, he focused on walking on the edge of the curb. That seemed so much less dangerous than fully engaging in this conversation.

"We all make our own choices, Dylan. You never knew your Grandfather Ristagno, but he was a hard man. An unforgiving one, and his mistakes cost him a relationship with his grandchildren and his grown daughter."

"Uh. Really?" Dylan had no idea where this conversation was going, other than somewhere uncomfortable.

"I'm not ever going to make that mistake. So you chose an old-fashioned Italian man who your Grandfather Ristagno would have loved, Carmine is marrying a man who will follow her lead, and both of you are just fine as far as I'm concerned." His father kept his eyes focused firmly forward, and Dylan realized his father hoped, in his own awkward way, to give his seal of approval. Dylan only had to hope his father never figured out how much Vin liked running the house—and Dylan.

"Thanks, Dad."

"Vin told me what you suspect about Carmine."

Dylan slipped on the edge of the curb where he'd been walking and stumbled into a parked car before he could right himself. "He what?"

"Now don't be angry with him."

"Oh, he can defend himself just fine, Dad. Trust me. So he can handle a little bit of me being annoyed."

His father nodded. "Well, he thought he should say something to me. As much as it's his job to take care of you, it's mine to take care of your mother. If she ever heard you saying anything like that, it'd kill her. It'd just kill her, Dylan. Do you have any idea how much she hates herself for never noticing that her firstborn son had turned into a monster? I tell her that's more forgivable than seeing and doing nothing, but...." His father stopped and then gestured as though pushing the rest of the words away.

Dylan ran a hand over his face. What had happened to his family's ability to repress, because right now he missed it. Badly. "Is she getting any help, Dad? I mean, Carmine's being a little obnoxious about it, but I think she's probably right about the whole therapy thing."

"I'm working on it," his father said. From the way he said it, Dylan didn't plan to hold his breath. "But you can't mention this to your mom," his father finished, his voice fierce.

"Trust me, I don't plan on mentioning it to anyone. Ever. I'm starting to wish I hadn't mentioned it to Vin." Most of the time, Dylan loved that Vin made decisions without torturing Dylan with round after round of questions about his preferences, but just this one time, he would have liked a little discussion first. However, that wasn't Vin's style.

"I told him that your mother felt guilty. We told Gary to get his things out of the house, and when he refused to leave, we went to the Ferguson's place. We told him he had to be gone before we got back."

"Ouch." Dylan cringed for his father. He didn't really do conflict, and that must have been one hell of a fight. Leaving was smart, though. It'd be hard for Gary to argue with them if they weren't there, and Will Ferguson wouldn't have allowed Gary in the front gate.

There'd been this whole explosion when Gary'd been in eleventh grade and Jack Ferguson had gotten caught with Gary as they pulled some prank on the school. Dylan's mom had argued that the boys had simply had a joke get out of hand. The Fergusons had banned Gary from their home, grounded Jack for pretty much life, and a twenty-year friendship between the parents had been kinda shaky there for a while. Dylan wondered if his mother ever thought about the fact that Jack Ferguson had a wife, two kids, and a stable job as an accountant now. Not that a little discipline would have fixed Gary—Dylan figured Gary had something wrong that no grounding would have fixed, but it might have slowed the evil down some.

His father looked intensely uncomfortable with the whole conversation, but he kept plowing through. "I asked your mother to call Carmine. I stayed behind to make sure Gary didn't follow, and I asked her to call your sister and warn her to not come home. I thought she called Carmine's cell. I never asked, though. I knew she was upset. I knew it, and I knew she would never want the Fergusons to hear her talking bad about Gary, and she had no cell phone so she would have needed their phone. Why didn't I just ask if she'd made that call?" His father's voice shook with either anger or frustration.

Dylan felt his eyes get warm as he imagined the scene. His mother was upset because she didn't want to believe Gary had gotten physical. Maybe she was angry, still trying to explain it away. His father wanted to avoid creating more conflict. He would have rushed past the conflict, uncomfortable with the heavy emotions. And through all that, the call never went through. That was why Carmine had come home in the middle of Gary's temper tantrum.

"Carmine didn't put herself in that spot on purpose," his father said quietly. "Now, your sister is your sister. I don't know what she did once she found herself in the house with Gary, but she didn't track him down. She walked into the middle of that mess, and your mother and I carry enough guilt for that. If your mother thought Carmine had endured that to try and make a point, to get her own mother to see Gary's true colors, to get me to do something about it…." His father's voice cracked. Dylan hated the pain he could feel radiating from his father. Part of him wanted to track Gary down in his jail cell and stick a knife in his guts and twist until the bastard hurt as much as the rest of them.

"Dad, I wouldn't hurt Mom like that," Dylan promised. Right now he hated that Vin had even brought it up.

His father gave him a thin smile. "I know you wouldn't, not on purpose. You're a good son. But you have to be careful, okay? I know you don't plan—" His father stopped midsentence and took a deep breath.

"You talked to Vin about me?" Dylan asked softly.

His father kept looking out into the night. "We talked around a lot of things." He sighed and finally looked over to Dylan. "He's a little overprotective of you, isn't he?"

Dylan narrowed his eyes. "Why? What did he say?"

His father wiped his face as though wiping off the emotion. "Enough to make me think he cares."

Dylan snorted. "You two are not allowed to talk anymore."

"Good. It's awkward. Neither one of us talks much, so mostly we stared at the walls."

"Yeah, well it sounds like you found plenty to talk about."

Moving closer, his father rested a hand on Dylan's shoulder. "We love the same people. We figured it out."

Dylan ducked his head. If he looked at his father right now, way more emotion was going to spill out than either of them wanted. "Dad, are we really looking at cars?" he eventually asked.

"Nope."

"Okay, good to know."

"Did you want a car? I've got some good options." His father sounded confused now.

"I don't want a car, Dad, so thanks but no thanks."

His father nodded. "Okay. So, we head back?"

Dylan thought about what would happen if they walked in the door right now. "Only if you want to come up with a story for Carmine," he said.

His father seemed to think about that for a second. "Let's go look at the Toyota I bought with your money."

"Sounds like a deal," Dylan agreed.

Chapter 25

DYLAN waited until Vin pulled up in front of the house before starting a conversation. "So, you had a nice talk with my dad."

"Yep," Vin agreed, not even a little apology in his voice. Dylan sighed. Okay, guilt wouldn't work.

"You could have warned me," he came right out and said.

"About what?" Vin looked over as he pulled the keys out of the ignition. From his expression, he had no idea what Dylan meant.

"That you were going to tell him about the whole Carmine theory."

Vin reached out, caught the back of Dylan's neck, and pulled him in for a kiss. Dylan was starting to think Vin had a neck fetish as often as he did that. Vin pressed his lips against Dylan's in a hard kiss, but just as Dylan opened his mouth for more, Vin pulled back. "I didn't know I was going to tell him anything until your father started asking about whether or not Carmine had talked about the fact they hadn't called. He suspected she left them off the visitors log in the hospital because she hated them," he said softly. "He's a good man. I'm not going to keep important secrets when it comes to his family."

They got out of the car and headed up to the house as the sky started to spit rain. Dylan could understand the logic. He didn't want his parents to suffer, and if they suspected Carmine blamed them half as much as they blamed themselves, the guilt would eat them alive. That said, Dylan squirmed at the thought of Vin telling either of his parents too much. "Just as long as you don't tell him everything," Dylan said firmly.

Vin glanced over his shoulder and gave Dylan one of those wicked grins that seemed able to kick-start Dylan's cock into overdrive every single time. "Oh trust me. I plan to do things to you that neither of us will ever mention to the man. Besides, I don't think he wants to know."

"He doesn't," Dylan agreed. He could feel his skin start to warm already. "So, would these things have anything to do with a certain delivery today?"

"Someone's been snooping." Vin held the door open, and Dylan went inside, jumping when Vin smacked his ass in passing.

"Snooping, paying attention—it's such a fine line." Dylan gave Vin a grin.

"Really? Because I think I have a good idea of where that line is. Now, you didn't open that package, did you? Maybe sneak a little peek?" Vin moved forward, using his body to crowd Dylan up against the wall, and Dylan could feel his heart start to race.

"If I say yes, will I get spanked?" Dylan asked hopefully.

"You're getting spanked either way. If you say yes, you're getting punished, and if you lie, you're getting punished in a way you're not going to like."

"I didn't look," Dylan said. "Not that I didn't want to, because there was a whole lot of wanting going on."

"Honestly?"

"Yep." Dylan hadn't, either. As much as the curiosity was killing him, he trusted Vin to make the wait more than worth it.

Leaning close, Vin gave him a small kiss, nothing more than a brush of lips against lips. "Good. Because I want you surprised."

"That actually sounds a little ominous."

Vin's evil smile returned. "Get upstairs, strip, and get back down here in five minutes."

"That sounds even more ominous."

Making a show out of looking at his watch, Vin announced grandly, "Four minutes, fifty-three seconds."

Dylan turned and darted upstairs. He shed most of his clothes by the time he hit the bedroom door and shoved them mostly into the dirty clothes hamper, although one pant leg hung out the side. Dylan threw his shoes at his bed in the closet and then headed for the bathroom to take a quick piss. By the time he finished and then shoved the last pant leg the rest of the way into the hamper, Dylan knew he was cutting it close. He dashed downstairs, his cock already hard and bouncing merrily. Vin stood at the bottom of the steps, leaning against the arch that led into his work space. God he looked hot. With his black shirt and five o'clock shadow, he had a dangerous vibe, like some thug from a mobster show.

"I make it?" he asked.

Vin looked at him with such intensity that Dylan started to blush. "Turn around. Let me see you."

Standing naked in front of his dressed lover was more of a turn-on than Dylan had expected. Slowly, he turned as the heat came to his face, and his cock got harder. "Stop," Vin ordered, and Dylan stopped with his back to Vin. When Vin leaned close, the buttons of his shirt pressed against Dylan's back, and every nerve in his body blazed to life. Dylan had to fist his hands just to avoid grabbing his cock and masturbating right there.

Vin ran his hands down Dylan's sides and then rested them against Dylan's hip bones, teasingly close to his cock. "You are beautiful," Vin whispered, his breath sending shivers down Dylan's neck.

"And horny," Dylan added.

Vin laughed and gave him a slap on the hip. "I think I can help with that." Vin used his hands on Dylan's hips to guide him into the office, where he'd pulled the blinds and made a few changes to the equipment. "On your knees, Dylan."

Dylan sank down, offering a quick "Kinky."

"I'm starting to wonder if I should invest in a gag."

Dylan didn't comment, but he wouldn't exactly protest. He loved it once he fell into that quiet where everything Vin did sent him flying, but sometimes he hated the stupid shit that fell out of his mouth unedited right before the brain turned off for good.

"So, let me explain the game." Vin patted Dylan's bare ass. "I seem to have lost the Sunrise Cleaning Service file."

Dylan frowned. No way had Vin lost a file. He was so anal he probably knew to the inch how much dental floss he had left. But Vin kept right on talking.

"So you know I have copies of all timesheets and receipts scanned or saved." Vin walked over to the computer set up on the floor. Then he walked over to a box of receipts mixed together in a shoebox and toed it. "But I might have some paperwork I need lost in here. Or maybe I left them in here." He gestured toward a white plastic bin like the post office used, but it was packed with file folders.

"So you want me to…."

"Put the file back together with all the required paperwork for me to get my paycheck." Vin crossed his arms and looked down at Dylan.

"And if I can't? Is there a spanking at the end of this if I fail?" he asked hopefully. Dylan would never turn down a good spanking. Vin came over and went to one knee beside him. After putting a hand under Dylan's chin, he lifted it so he could look in Dylan's eyes.

"There's a spanking waiting for you either way this goes. But if you fail, I will be very disappointed in you."

Dylan swallowed, surprised by how much that bothered him.

"You have one hour."

"That actually seems a little…." Dylan hesitated to say *easy* because something warned him that the other shoe was about to fall. Right on cue, Vin got a wicked grin on his face.

"We can make this more of a challenge. Spread your legs and thrust your ass back," Vin ordered. After a second's hesitation, more out of confusion than anything else, Dylan followed orders. Vin rattled around in some boxes, and Dylan twisted around to try and see what he was doing.

"Eyes forward."

With a heavy sigh, Dylan shifted to face forward. Just because he loved it when Vin took control didn't mean he couldn't make his frustration clear. It earned him a loud slap on the ass that brought the heat to his skin. The heat sunk down into Dylan's cock, and Dylan had to fight an urge to press back into Vin or wiggle in anticipation. When Vin pulled at his ball sac, Dylan settled down. There was pain and then there was pain. Dylan really didn't want to have Vin punish him there.

However, Vin seemed to be taking his time with Dylan's balls, squeezing them and poking them oddly. Despite the lack of sensuality, being handled so intimately and so impersonally made Dylan's cock harden. Dylan sucked in a breath when something cold pressed up against his balls. Dylan struggled to keep his eyes forward as he gave a little experimental wiggle as he tried to figure it out. He earned another slap.

"Fuck," Dylan breathed as he put his forehead down on his arms. It made his ass stick out more, and Vin caressed it for a second before squeezing Dylan's ball sac again. Something brushed against the back of his thighs, and then Dylan felt the hard, rounded edge of something pressing against his balls. With very little pressure, that would be pain, but for right now it was simply uncomfortable. Something clicked, and a half second later, Dylan identified the sound of a lock.

"That looks stunning on you."

"What does?" Dylan pushed himself up to all fours, but when he started to twist around, the thing holding his balls pinched and pulled hard enough for Dylan to suck in a pained breath.

"Easy. Don't pull at those too much. I like your balls where they are." Vin sounded amused, and as Dylan eased his butt back onto his heels, he realized what Vin had bought.

"It's a humbler," Dylan said as he felt for the toy. Cool plastic met his fingers when he found it. The plastic had a hole to capture his balls, and then the two side pieces rested just under Dylan's ass. If he tried to stand up, he would pull his own balls backward through a very tiny hole. Since he had no intention of doing that, it meant that Dylan couldn't straighten out his legs. Dylan had looked at them online more than once, but honestly, they'd scared the shit out of him. Now that he wore one, he realized it forced him to follow the rules and keep his thighs tucked up close to his chest without causing more than discomfort.

"Yep," Vin agreed. "So, let's start the game. You have one hour to fix that file, or I will have to be disappointed with you."

Dylan sighed. He had been waiting for the other shoe to drop, and this would be it. Wearing the humbler, he would have to crawl on the ground at Vin's feet, and his cock was already starting to darken as all the blood in his body tried to rush into it all at once. "You're a sadist," Dylan complained softly.

"It's a good thing you like sadists. Go on, get to work."

With one more dramatic sigh, Dylan eyed his task. He'd helped Vin with enough files to know exactly what went in one, but Vin had set up the computer on the floor of one corner of the room and the boxes with the receipts were on the other end. Tilting his head so he could give Vin a dirty look, Dylan started crawling over to the boxes.

Dylan reached for the box of receipts, fighting an urge to press himself against Vin's legs as he crawled past. He opened the first file and hadn't read so much as one line when he felt Vin's fingers tickle up his spine and then scratch lightly over his hot back. "Shit," Dylan breathed, all concentration gone as his dick got harder than ever.

Vin chuckled and moved behind Dylan so his jeans pressed into the back of Dylan's thighs. "You'd better hurry up, or you're going to lose the challenge," he pointed out, but his palm came to rest on Dylan's ass, squeezing gently.

Putting his forehead to the floor, Dylan groaned. "You're cheating."

Vin's finger brushed against his hole before a sharp smack on his ass made Dylan's head come up. "Yep," Vin agreed cheerfully.

With a growl, Dylan pulled at the plastic box, but nothing moved. "What the hell?" Dylan gave it a harder tug. He wanted it next to the computer, but the damn thing acted like it was nailed to the ground. *Hell.* Dylan realized what Vin had done. This room wasn't renovated, and the old wood floors had stains and some of the corners had rot, so obviously Vin had decided a few nail holes wouldn't hurt anything.

Vin laughed and then forced Dylan's knees apart so he could kneel between them. Running his hands up and down Dylan's naked body, he lingered when he reached the spot just under Dylan's underarm. Dylan had to swallow his laughter as Vin's clever fingers ghosted over his ticklish skin. After a few seconds, Vin moved back down to explore the back of Dylan's thighs. The lust rose until Dylan was panting with need. Vin skimmed his hands up Dylan's back and then down his sides, and Dylan could feel the trails of heat made by each individual finger.

"I am so thinking not nice thoughts about you right now," Dylan complained from between clenched teeth. He tried to focus on the page in front of him, but it took a full minute for him to realize he had ahold of the file for Home Health Providers. Clearly the English language was beyond him at this point. Throwing the page aside, he shook his head and tried to focus on his work. Meanwhile Vin massaged Dylan's ass cheeks, and every once in a while, the motion would just happen to pull his cheeks apart and expose Dylan's hole to the air.

Grunting, Dylan tried to ignore the way his skin felt overly sensitive, but then Vin blew across his exposed hole, and Dylan swore wildly, dropping the file he was trying to search.

"Someone sounds like he can't control his mouth," Vin said. Dylan knew he should prove Vin wrong. He knew it. One more piece of bondage, and he would come all over himself, but common sense had fled at some point.

"I could if you were fucking playing by the fucking rules," Dylan cursed. Vin paused, and Dylan put his forehead down on his arms. "My cock is going to explode," he complained softly. "I can't be expected to control my mouth with body parts threatening to explode."

"Well then, I'll have to help you. By the way, the only rule is that you have one hour and I make all the rules." Vin slapped his butt before standing up, and Dylan panted, desperate to get some control back. His whole body fought him. He wanted to disappear into that quiet that loomed just at the edge of his awareness. He wanted to check out and let Vin control his body, but Vin had said he would be disappointed if Dylan couldn't get the Sunrise Cleaning Service file together. The twin forces caught Dylan in the middle of a storm that left him almost shaking.

Vin came back and rested a hand on Dylan's shoulder as he knelt down beside him. Pushing himself back up onto his hands and knees, Dylan opened his mouth and waited. Sure enough, Vin pushed a mouth stuffer between Dylan's teeth, and the pliable bag filled his mouth before Vin strapped it around his head. The good part was that now Dylan could curse up a storm, and he did. The gag transformed his complaints into grunts, which was good because too much complaining might mean that Vin stopped playing, and for all the frustration Dylan was enduring, he didn't want that.

Vin stood above him, brushing his fingers over the top of Dylan's hair. Dylan found the first missing paper—an invoice for software. Looking over to the computer, Dylan knew he should find all the papers before trying to crawl the length of the floor. That would be the smart way to play. But he couldn't resist. He wanted to crawl at Vin's feet. Pushing the paper ahead of him, Dylan crawled the length of the floor. Vin paced him, walking beside him, and Dylan took a second to lean into Vin's leg, brushing up against him like a cat before he reached the computer.

He used the receipt scanner to enter the page, and let the computer search for the rest of the Sunrise Cleaning Service. After all, the software categorized receipts automatically. The computer correctly recognized the receipt Dylan entered as Sunrise Cleaning Service, but it flashed a warning, asking what file Dylan wanted to put it in because no other papers matched.

Leaning back on his heels, Dylan cursed loudly and viciously, grateful for the gag. Vin had cleared all the tags and fields, so Dylan would have to go through all the unfiled receipts to find them. Well, if that was the game, Dylan could play, and he'd play to fucking win. Shifting forward on knees that were already getting sore, Dylan settled in to work. Then Vin ran a hand down his back, tracing the line of his spine, and every thought in Dylan's head scattered as the quiet pushed against him. Dylan had to shake his head just to clear it of all the cobwebs that tried to trap him in that silence.

Every time he shifted, he jostled the humbler and it gave his balls another little pull. Sweating from the effort of crawling and from the assault on his senses, Dylan found it more and more difficult to work as time ticked away. Vin's hands seemed to find him at his most vulnerable moments. When Dylan crawled across the room, Vin would step just a little too close so Dylan would either have to detour around him or slide his body along Vin's leg. When he reached for a file, Vin would tickle down his side or massage his shoulders. When Dylan settled on his heels to work on the computer, Vin would crouch behind him, knees trapping Dylan while he would stroke down Dylan's chest and pull at his nipples.

Dylan was sucking air through his nose as fast as he could by the forty-five minute mark. Always before, Vin's hands on him had sent him into a white-out. His brain got soaked with so many happy juices that he could only lie limp as Vin used him. But now he had to focus, and that focus kept him poised on the knife's edge, unable to fall into the quiet. However, the humbler and the gag and Vin's presence hovering over him… they all made that white quiet press in against him until Dylan wanted to surrender.

Trapped between, Dylan crossed the room over and over, putting the pieces of the file into place as the sweat rolled down his shoulders. His teeth ached from biting the gag so hard, and every inch of him throbbed, particularly his low swinging cock. It actually hurt worse than his balls, and it had turned a rather alarming shade as it swung like a pendulum under him as he crawled.

Dylan even felt like he could feel his heart beat in the back of his neck. Every heavy thump stuffed his head as much as the gag stuffed his mouth. Dylan was hyperaware of every brush of Vin's hands against his bare skin, but he had to focus on work. He had to finish the file. The reason for that had slipped out of Dylan's brain at some point, but he had to finish. He turned toward the file box again, but two legs stepped in his way.

Dylan tried to detour, but Vin crouched down in front of him, hands on Dylan's shoulders. "Hey, you finished. You finished, Dylan."

Dylan blinked, his brain not up to processing that thought. He could only crawl between his two goals… that was all he could remember because the rest of his brain was too busy feeling everything that touched his body. The thin carpet covering the old wood floors had a knobby texture that Dylan pressed his fingers to. If he didn't, he would grab his hard cock, and there was a reason for not doing that. What the reason might be, he didn't know.

Vin reached up for the gag, but Dylan weakly swept his hand away while jerking his head back.

"Okay. Okay, Dylan. Shhhhh." Vin reached out again, this time moving too fast for Dylan to intercept, but he didn't unlock the gag. He caught Dylan by the back of the neck and pulled him closer. "Good boy. On your back. Come on, let's get you on your back." Vin urged him to the side before coaxing him to roll to his back, and Dylan went with a relieved whine through his nose. He tried to put his legs down, but Vin caught him behind the knees.

"You do not want to do that, babe. Oh man. You went deep. Come on, hold your knees for me. Be a good boy and hold your knees."

Dylan wrapped his hands around his knees and held on, pressing his knees tight against his chest. Opening his legs wider, he looked down his body at his hard cock lying against his stomach. The end was white with precome, and it looked alien... dark... like one of the pictures off Internet porn. Dylan started laughing, the sound vanishing into the gag, but his body shook with it. Vin returned, resting a hand on Dylan's chest for a second, but Dylan was starting to get light-headed. He leaned his head back against the floor and just waited. All he had to do was wait now, and the white crashed in on him.

Vin touched his balls, and Dylan arched his back, convinced for a second he might come, but the weight of the white and the sound of his own heart beating weren't quite enough, and Dylan was left squirming as he tried to find that perfect edge where he could come.

"Up you go." Dylan sucked air through his nose as he flew up into the air; he still had his hands on his knees, but he dropped one leg, and it flopped down as Vin carried him up the stairs.

"Fuck, you are not light. Next time I send you this deep, we're doing it upstairs," Vin said between grunts, but Dylan just let his head rest against Vin's shoulder as he got bounced up the stairs. "Live and learn," Vin groaned as they reached the top. For a second, Vin leaned against the wall, and then he slowly sank down until Dylan's ass touched the ground. Dylan lay with his back arched over Vin's legs, their bodies tangled at the head of the stairs.

Dylan could hear Vin's heavy breathing, but like most things, it faded to background. When Vin reached down and pulled at a nipple, Dylan screamed into the gag and reached for his own cock, only to have his hand intercepted by Vin's strong hold on his wrists.

"Almost. We just need to get to the bedroom. Come on, hands and knees." Vin pushed him so he rolled, and Dylan went with it, going to his hands and knees and then crawling down the hall to the bedroom. Vin lifted him up to the bed, and Dylan reached for his cock again.

"Someone is determined. Lucky for you, so am I," Vin said, and this time when he caught Dylan's wrists, he brought them up over Dylan's head. Dylan wiggled as he felt the cuffs going around his wrists. Now he could lose himself. Arching his back, he dug his heels into the mattress and grunted into his gag. He felt Vin lift his knees, and the cool of slick against his hole. Breathing fast, Dylan let himself drift as his ass stretched to let Vin's fingers in. Then fingers were gone, and after a second, Vin pressed his cock up against Dylan's entrance, pushing in slowly.

Hooking his ankles around Vin's body, Dylan tried to pull him close, but he didn't have the leverage. One of his feet slipped against the sweat of Vin's body, but then Vin grabbed his hips and thrust in so hard and fast that their bodies slapped together.

Dylan bit his gag as hard as he could as Vin filled him, pushing into him and becoming part of him. The pressure built until Dylan mewled with need. Only then did Vin grab Dylan's cock, and Dylan's orgasm tore through him. Every muscle spasmed and he felt his own warm come splatter against his chest. Dylan cried out as Vin kept up a hard fucking for several minutes. Then finally, Vin came with a shout and collapsed onto him. His weight pinned Dylan to the bed, and Dylan sank into the white, utterly helpless.

This, this was the moment of perfect that he wanted to live inside forever. He could feel the heat pouring off both their bodies, and his heart pounded in his chest, but with Vin's weight and the cuffs and the gag, there was utterly nothing Dylan needed to do but lie helpless and boneless under Vin's body.

Time slipped past, but eventually their bodies started to cool, and Vin started shifting to the side. With a grunt, he dropped onto the bed next to Dylan. Still feeling disconnected from his body, Dylan blinked owlishly at his lover.

"You okay being ungagged now?" Vin asked, reaching up. Dylan held still as Vin unfastened the straps and pulled the gag loose. "Sometimes you surprise me," Vin commented as he studied the black stuffer bag. After a second, he tossed it toward the nightstand. It hit and slithered off the other side and fell to the ground.

"Good surprise or bad surprise?" Dylan asked, already half asleep.

"Always good." Vin punctuated that with a kiss on Dylan's shoulder. "I guess someone's sleeping in the big bed tonight."

"I'll sleep in the other bed, but you'll have to carry me because I lost all my bones somewhere."

"That's not happening," Vin said as he pushed himself up. "I'm going to be sore tomorrow." He rubbed at his thighs before heading for the bathroom. "But that was very worth it."

Dylan smiled. The edges of his mouth felt stiff, and he used the tip of his tongue to soften the spit that had dried and crusted there. "I like your surprises." Shifting to his side, he used the cuffs' chains to pull himself closer to the top of the bed so he could claim a pillow. "Do you have any more?"

After a second, Vin came out of the bathroom in just pajama bottoms. "I have all kinds of surprises," he promised as he sat on his side of the bed.

"Could you wipe off my chest?" Dylan asked when he noticed that Vin had cleaned up. The come streaked across his chest itched, and with his hands cuffed, he couldn't scratch.

Vin leaned his weight against Dylan's shoulder, pinning him to the bed before leaning in for a quick peck of a kiss. "Nope," he whispered. Giving Dylan a devilish grin, he reached for the lamp on the bedside table and clicked it off.

"Sadist," Dylan complained in the dark.

"Yep," Vin agreed as he pressed up against Dylan's back, spooning him. His hand came around to rest on top of one of the cuffs, squeezing Dylan's wrist for a second before he settled in to sleep.

Dylan smiled and closed his eyes.

Chapter 26

DYLAN squirmed to try and move the edge of one of the straps that managed to hit him in the wrong place. The armbinder was new and the leather still needed some breaking in. After all the ways they'd found to have dirty, kinky sex in every corner of the house, Vin still managed to surprise him.

"Keep doing that and the coat is going to slip," Vin said, but from his amused tone, he wouldn't be sorry if it did. Without the coat draped over his shoulders, Dylan would be a man in a set of leather straps and not much else, buckled into the front seat of a car where everyone they passed could see him. He settled back against the seat and watched the city pass. The first buds had appeared on the trees, and somehow that made Dylan aware of how much time had passed. The legal system dragged slowly through the gears of justice, but Gary was less and less important in their lives and everything else had started moving forward, including the first signs of spring.

"Hey, you okay?" Vin asked when Dylan was quiet too long.

"Are you sure this isn't going to make me the center of attention?" Dylan asked again. While he'd found that he had a much bigger side of kink than he'd known, Dylan still didn't think humiliation would be his thing.

"If someone is looking at you, it's because you're gorgeous," Vin said. "On a Monday night at the Stonewall, that outfit is going to be conservative."

Dylan wasn't sure about that. His leather underwear had a crisscross lattice over the cup where his cock lay, and he had a plug held in with a gold padlock hanging from the belt that locked all that in place. A harness over his chest and an armbinder that locked his hands behind his back and cuffs on his bare ankles finished the outfit, and Dylan pretty much looked like a model for kink-wear. When Miss Dolphinia needed help, Dylan still went in and swept floors or washed dishes, so he spent enough time at the Stonewall to know that no one dressed like this.

"It's Monday, Dylan," Vin said again. Sometimes Vin's form of reassurance was repeating something louder, but Dylan took the volume in the spirit that Vin intended it.

"I've been there on Monday. Before we were dating, even."

"You were stoned," Vin pointed out.

"But I was there."

Vin glanced over before focusing on the road again. "Do you remember the pain play, the human puppies or the naked boys crawling on the floor?"

Dylan blinked. "Really?"

"On a Monday?" Vin snorted. "Hell, yes. Miss Dolphinia is one of the few old-school leather folk around here. Most of the people on the scene spend more time writing contracts and talking about safe sex than they do having sex. Every serious pervert in the state shows up to the Stonewall on a Monday when they want to cut loose."

"Let's avoid the word pervert," Dylan suggested dryly. It reminded him too much of people he was not going to name when he planned on having a very good time getting very well fucked.

"What should I call someone who likes to tie up his partners, shove a vibrator up their ass, and then drive them around town while they're utterly helpless?"

"Kinkster?" Dylan guessed. He'd seen the term floating around the Internet a lot.

Vin took a brief second to glare at him. "I hate kinkster. A kinkster is someone who writes out contracts and lectures people on the Internet while drinking a vegetarian algae shake."

Okay, he had a point there. Dylan offered, "Kinky people, then. Non-vanillay. Unconventional. But pervert? Yeah, not the right word, Vin."

"Oh, I'll get you to agree to anything, just as soon as I tie you down and offer to fuck you brainless." Vin's smile grew into a smirk.

Dylan tried to shrug because he knew it was true, but all the leather around his body tightened and pinched in uncomfortable ways. Vin pulled in behind the Stonewall, knocking over two orange cones that clearly warned people away from one parking spot.

"It doesn't look like anyone's here."

"Because they parked far enough away that the cops won't realize Miss Dolphinia is open for business," Vin said, ignoring that he'd just parked right next to the back door, but that was Vin. He didn't follow anyone's rules. "So, let's get you ready for your big entrance."

Vin got out of the car and walked around to the passenger side, where Dylan waited helplessly. The more they played, the more Dylan realized that Vin loved to keep him helpless, and Dylan loved the feeling of Vin taking control. "Open up," Vin said as he stood at the passenger side door. Dylan opened his mouth, and Vin slipped Dylan's favorite gag in place and buckled it around his face. Dylan expected Vin to take him out of the car, but he didn't. He stood up and rested his forearms against the top of his car.

"You are a beautiful man," Vin said. Dylan settled back into the seat. Sometimes Vin got verbal when he had Dylan tied up and gagged, and Dylan enjoyed having a lover who would sweet-talk him.

Before Vin, he'd had quick fucks and one very awkward night with Guard. None of them ever sweet-talked him. "One of these times when I have a break from the business, we're going to have you take a week off work, and I'm going to keep you chained up the whole week. I'll make you eat out of my hand and crawl on the ground the whole time, and you will look so beautiful with that ass of yours wiggling. And if you don't wiggle it enough, I'm going to shove the biggest vibrator I can find up there and tease you until you shake with need."

Dylan moaned into the gag and shifted as his cock hardened. The leather cage had some room, but not enough for Dylan to get hard. Vin reached up under the coat and kneaded Dylan's vulnerable thigh, high enough for Dylan's cock to get the wrong idea. Suddenly the plug in his ass started vibrating, and Dylan bucked up, glaring at Vin for triggering the remote in his pocket.

"I would apologize and claim that was a mistake, but we both know that'd be a lie, don't we?" Vin asked. Dylan nodded and Vin leaned forward to give him a chaste kiss on the forehead.

Finally, Vin hit the release on the car's seatbelt and pulled Dylan out into the cold air. Winter still had a tenuous hold on the city, and Dylan was very grateful for the thick slippers on his feet as he headed for the back door. Vin rang the bell next to the service door and then stood right in front of the peephole until the deadbolt slid back and someone Dylan didn't know opened the door. He was a bear of a man with a leather vest that set off a full chest of white hair.

"Vin! Long time no see, you old bastard," the man greeted Vin, and Dylan felt a flash of jealousy as the man reached out to give Vin a hug. Vin sidestepped so the gesture turned into more of a one-armed half hug. At the same time, Vin pulled Dylan close.

"Jerry, this is Dylan."

"Well, it looks like you've started already. Get your boy on in here." Jerry stepped back, and Vin urged Dylan inside. The back room was still a little chilly, but as soon as they stepped into the kitchen, Dylan could feel the heat. He was grateful when Vin unbuttoned the long coat covering him.

"Kick the slippers off," Vin ordered, and Dylan did, feeling the cold tile under his feet. As warm as the club was, it felt good.

"You really did get started," Jerry said as he leaned on the metal prep table. "You have him tied up but good."

"And with a few bonuses," Vin agreed, taking the remote for the plug out of his pocket and showing it to him.

Jerry laughed. "Oh my. You have a streak of evil. I'm surprised the boy isn't decked out with nipple clamps and a ball stretcher."

"Give us time," Vin said with one of those patented smiles of his. Then he pulled Dylan closer to the prep table and pushed him stomach down before triggering the vibrator. He left Dylan squirming and mewling into his gag as he hung up the coat on the far side of the room and stuck the slippers into the deep pockets.

"Are you looking for a third to play tonight?" Jerry asked, eying Dylan. Normally Dylan would have been nervous about a stranger giving him that look, but he was too focused on the huge plug up his ass that was vibrating right into his prostate. No matter how he squirmed, he couldn't get enough pressure to make it feel perfect, and he couldn't escape the not-quite-enough sensation.

Vin came back and pulled him upright, locking a hand around Dylan's chest. "We're good tonight."

"You always were a jealous bastard," Jerry said, but with a shrug, he headed into the club.

Vin waited a second, leaving Dylan to hump the air before he turned the vibrator off. Dylan leaned back into Vin's chest. "Are you okay to walk?" Vin asked after letting him rest for a bit. Dylan nodded.

Vin pushed him up onto his feet, but he kept both hands on Dylan's shoulders as he marched them out to the main club. Dylan appreciated it because he was a little shaky on his feet.

Normally the club throbbed with music and people crowded around the bar. A few guys would dance, and groups would gather around the tables. Tonight it was a lot quieter. No music played, and several of the men were gagged, which reduced the amount of talking. Men sat with their boys kneeling on the floor next to them or lying on the ground while the masters rested their feet on the smalls of their boys' backs. Dylan looked again.

And Vin hadn't been kidding. Dylan's outfit was conservative compared to some of these others. He couldn't stop staring at the man on the floor who wore nothing but a butt plug with an upturned tail, a dog mask, and mitts on his hands. The boy leaned against his master's leg, clearly enjoying it when the man would pet him with a few thumps on his shoulder. And Dylan did think of that man on the ground as a boy, even though his body looked about forty. Something in that worshipful gaze focused on his master made it clear he was a boy... a slave... but not a sub with all the careful trappings of that world.

Dylan was starting to think it was a good thing he was gagged because he totally would have said something stupid. Totally. If this was what he'd missed when he'd stumbled in here stoned and in search of Vin, he needed to never get stoned again. Oblivious didn't even describe him. *How did he miss this?*

"Come on, let's give our regards to the queen," Vin said, aiming Dylan toward the corner. When he spotted Miss Dolphinia, Dylan started toward her. She was looking through a notebook, but something made her look up, and when she did, she gave them a huge smile.

"Well look what the dog dragged home," she teased as she looked Dylan up and down. Dylan could feel the heat come to his face as she gave him all her attention.

Vin stepped between them, and Miss Dolphinia laughed. "Now Vin, there's no rule in here about looking."

"And there's no rule that says I can't get unreasonably cranky, either," he countered.

She laughed again and waved a manicured hand toward the three empty chairs. "Go on, sit yourself down so I can gloat about how well this has all turned out."

Vin did sit—in the chair farthest from her. He reached out, caught one of the straps of Dylan's harness, and pulled him close before urging him down toward the floor. Moving awkwardly because of the stiffness of the new leather, Dylan managed to get himself down to his knees without doing too much damage. Leaning against Vin's leg, he let the real world start to drift. Kneeling was so viscerally connected to his cock that it got harder, pressing against the straps that trapped it. Worse, that dull and aching pain just made him hornier.

"You have him wrapped up like a Christmas present, and I do love opening a present," Miss Dolphinia teased.

"You know better than to touch him without permission, so you can drop the act," Vin suggested.

"Some people." Miss Dolphinia sniffed. "The lack of manners is quite shocking. After all, sharing is caring, sweetie."

"I've shared enough already," Vin said dryly. Dylan rubbed his cheek against Vin's knee to try and distract him. After a sigh, Vin did start carding his fingers through Dylan's hair. "Maybe we can get everything out in the open now before something gets said in front of...." Vin hesitated, and Dylan looked up, confused by what Vin wasn't saying.

"Oh please. Darling, there is no way I would say anything around those sanitized, Friday-night Doms. So I take it that I was right about you two fitting together quite nicely."

"Don't push your luck."

"Your manners with a lady are quite shockingly bad. I remember when you quailed in fear of my displeasure," Miss Dolphinia said archly.

"Yeah, well I was young and stupid."

"I would certainly agree with one of those."

"I'm not thanking you," Vin said firmly.

"Have I even asked?"

There was a long silence, and Dylan looked up to see Vin glaring over the table. Considering that these two had shared their lover, that Rice had subbed for Miss Dolphinia and had taught Vin the ropes, Dylan was pretty sure that Rice must have been a superhero to keep these two agreeable enough to share. Dylan wasn't that good, and he didn't want to be. Vin was enough for him.

"Don't meddle in my life again," Vin ended up saying.

"Then don't fuck up again, darling," Miss Dolphinia answered in the sweetest tone of voice Dylan had ever heard. Vin's glare turned sharper. "Sweetie, my goal was to get you back on the horse. I did it. So you can do whatever you want, and I promise to not bail your sorry ass out again. Deal?"

"Deal," Vin said firmly.

"And if you don't treat Dylan right, I am so going to try and steal that adorable piece of candy," she added after Vin's tense body started to relax. That wound him up all over again, but then Dylan was fairly sure that was the point. Dylan truly did not understand dominant people. They were crazy—all of them.

"Try it and you'll have more of a fight than you can handle," Vin warned as he urged Dylan to stand up. Dylan had to wiggle a little, but he finally got his feet under him, and Vin stood up with him.

Miss Dolphinia gave them a smile and one of those finger-wiggling waves. "You have fun now."

Vin didn't answer. Urging Dylan toward the opposite side of the room, Vin grumbled about pushy, overbearing men, and with his mouth full of gag, Dylan couldn't even point out the irony. They headed toward the pool tables, but as they got closer, Dylan realized the tables were covered in heavy cloth of some sort. And that was good, because one man was tied with his stomach down on the edge of the table, his legs spread wide and tied to the thick legs. White cum was splattered across the back of his legs and his asshole was stuffed full with a black plug. Okay, that explained why everyone was so careful to keep the police in the dark. That definitely wasn't legal in public.

"Hey, Hauser, long time no see."

"Jason," Vin said, and he sounded more polite than when he'd talked to Miss Dolphinia.

"Well, what do you know. Is that the little bit of cute that I found wandering the streets a couple of months back?" Jason stood up and came closer, peering at Dylan's face. He looked vaguely familiar. "I guess he found you." Laughing, Jason turned his back and headed for a bench against the wall.

"He did," Vin agreed.

"Did you kill whoever gave him those drugs?" Jason asked. Dylan's memory finally clicked, and Dylan remembered Jason finding him on the street after Amy had given him some magical mystery tour pills. Embarrassment made his face heat up as he thought about being stoned and practically mauling Jason in the street, although at the time he had been more concerned about falling off the planet.

Jason turned to one of the other men on the bench, a huge bear with a heavy mustache who had his boots resting on one man while he played with the ass of a second man who was draped over his lap. "I found this one wandering the streets, high as a fucking kite and looking for Miss Dolphinia. He was squirmy as a puppy until he spotted Vin."

"He needed a strong hand, but not yours," Vin said with an edge of warning. "Now if you two wouldn't mind, I wanted to put that bench to use."

Jason exchanged a look with his friend, and Dylan got the feeling that Vin wasn't looking for a place to sit. "Knock yourself out," the second man said. He gave the sub over his lap one hard slap across the ass, and Dylan could practically see the handprint forming. "Over to the bar, boy," he ordered the man with the bright red handprint forming on his ass, but when the sub got up, he was grinning.

"Yes, sir," he agreed. He paused only long enough to help the man on the floor up. That sub had his feet chained together so closely that he could only shuffle inch by inch across the floor.

"Nice to see you back, Vin," Jason's friend said with a tilt of his head.

"You too, Bill."

"Have fun now." Jason slapped Vin on the shoulder as he passed.

"Oh, I plan to," Vin agreed in an evil voice. Jason laughed again, and Dylan could feel his cock getting harder in its cage. Maybe he was okay with a little public humiliation, because if Vin planned to fuck him in front of all these people, Dylan was totally okay with that. He was ecstatic about that. He was ready to fucking pay for that because the lust was an itch that was starting to drive him mad.

"This is going to be fun," Vin said in that tone of voice that usually meant Dylan was about to get tied to something. The last time he'd sounded that excited, Dylan had spent the day doing paperwork while sitting on an exercise ball with a big old dildo attached to it and his legs chained to the desk at an angle that made it impossible for him to bounce himself to orgasm and a cock cage that kept him from jacking off. Vin did know how to make secretarial work fun. And talking to clients while attempting to not groan with lust... it was a challenge that Dylan enjoyed.

Vin turned him around and started doing something with the armbinder. At first it got tighter, and Dylan grunted as his shoulders practically creaked from the pressure. However, then the pressure eased off, and Dylan realized Vin was taking it off. That was unexpected.

After dropping the armbinder to the floor, Vin took a second to hold Dylan with his bare hands. Vin's fingers pressed tightly against Dylan's wrists, reminding Dylan again of the sheer power in his lover's body. However, after a second, Vin let go and maneuvered Dylan around to the bench. Dylan felt weirdly uncomfortable with his hands free, and he crossed and uncrossed his arms as Vin pulled the bench away from the wall with a screech of wood against concrete.

"Down you go," Vin said with a frightening cheerfulness in his voice. Dylan moved to lay stomach down, but Vin turned him around so his back was on the bench. It was narrow enough that Dylan's body barely fit, but when he wiggled around, he found that the wide legs were more than stable.

"Hands over your head," Vin ordered, and Dylan complied. He wasn't exactly surprised when Vin quickly buckled and locked cuffs around his wrists, then attached them to the bench over Dylan's head. It left Dylan's chest vulnerable to tickling or nipple play or anything else Vin might want to do, and Dylan groaned with need as his lust began to white out large portions of his brain.

Instead of doing any of that, Vin moved down to his feet, attached a clip, and then pulled hard so Dylan scooted down the bench and the chain holding his arms grew taut. Vin tied off the chain to Dylan's ankles, and now he was laid out, unable to move much at all as Vin looked down at him on the low bench. Worse, the way his legs were pressed together made the plug up his ass feel huge. He was going to die of frustration if Vin didn't get to the main event soon.

"This is going to be fun. Now, don't go anywhere," Vin teased, patting Dylan on the cheek before he headed to a nearby door. Dylan followed with his eyes, but when Vin vanished, he looked around the room. Jason sat on the edge of the pool table where the sub was tied, watching without even trying to hide his interest. In fact, he rubbed his crotch, and Dylan looked away. Most of the room was involved in their own games, but on the far side, Miss Dolphinia was watching, one fist curled under her chin as she leaned forward.

Vin came back, and Dylan blinked up at him as Vin rolled some sort of rack over Dylan's body before locking the wheels down. Sometimes Vin's creativity worried Dylan just a little, but this time he couldn't even fathom what Vin was up to.

"Comfortable?" Vin asked.

Dylan gave a quick nod. He wasn't totally comfortable, but he was tied tightly enough that he didn't care about much else.

"This is the part that may hurt," Vin said as he held up a small bit of leather that Dylan didn't recognize. He reached for the lock on Dylan's belt, unclipped it, and slipped the cage off Dylan's cock. Dylan couldn't see what Vin was doing, but it wasn't comfortable. Dylan groaned into the gag as Vin pinched the base of his cock, making him soften somewhat. A sharp stab made Dylan cry out, tears gathering at the corners of his eyes, but then Vin was soothing him, stroking those talented fingers along Dylan's thighs.

"It's okay. It's on now. It's okay now," Vin muttered, and Dylan squirmed as his cock felt odd. Something was wrapped around his cock and balls, and Dylan tried to thrust up a little. Shit. As the pain faded, that lovely ache settled in place, and Dylan could feel himself getting hard again.

"Now it's time for my fun," Vin said happily. Unfastening the crotch from the rest of his chaps, Vin set it to the side, and now Dylan could see Vin's thick cock standing up against his olive skin. Dylan sucked at his gag, wishing he could taste it, but that wasn't the game Vin wanted to play. Vin straddled him before Dylan finally figured out the game, and his eyes went wide. Holding the rack with one hand, with the other, Vin reached back for Dylan's cock and lined it up with his own slicked hole.

Dylan shouted in surprise as the head of his cock popped through the ring of muscle and into Vin's ass. With a smile, Vin lowered himself. "I do love the feel of a nice big cock up my ass," Vin said. "But I don't think you're squirming enough."

Vin tightened his ass muscles around Dylan's cock, and Dylan arched his back and pressed his head back as much as he could as his whole body fought to thrust. He couldn't, but the instinct drove him to try anyway. When Dylan started to pull in a breath through his nose, the vibrator in his ass went off, and Dylan lost all his air as he tried to scream in pleasure.

He strained against the chains, desperate to thrust up into Vin, but he couldn't. He could only lie on the bench as Vin watched him squirm and writhe. For some time, Vin just sat on him, turning the vibrator off and on, increasing the intensity and then turning it down until it was little more than a buzz in Dylan's ass. Every time Dylan tried to calm himself, Vin would change something until Dylan was almost wild with lust. He could feel the sweat sliding off his body, and every breath through his nose wheezed heavily.

Dylan fisted and opened his hands, the only part of himself that he could control. "Suffering?" Vin asked with amusement, but Dylan knew that was part of the game too. If he was truly suffering, Vin would stop… he had stopped in the past. But Vin wanted to see him fighting the lust, losing himself to the need to let Vin control every twitch. Dylan looked up at Vin, not hiding any of his distress. He needed to come, he needed Vin to come, he needed to move or the urge to thrust was going to tear him in half.

Slowly, Vin pulled himself up, using the rack to steady himself. The move was so incredibly slow that Dylan stopped breathing, the feel of Vin's heat sliding slickly across his shaft more than he could take. His whole body shivered, and he felt a dozen new trails of sweat start to roll down his sides.

Reversing direction, Vin started lowering himself just as slowly. The muscles stood out on his arms, and Dylan's whole world narrowed to his cock, to Vin's weight resting against his hips as he lowered himself, to the sight of Vin's muscles straining as he slowly lifted and lowered himself. Crying into the gag, Dylan tried to beg for more, but still Vin moved in slow motion, his body a sculpture in muscle. That was Dylan's only hint at the effort it took Vin to do this. Reaching down, Vin triggered the vibrator and then marginally increased his movements.

"You do make for a nice ride," Vin grunted out. Every time he came to rest against Dylan, he grunted, and Dylan almost felt that grunt echoing in his skin. His arms ached from fighting the chains, but then Vin sped up again, really starting to ride Dylan hard, and Dylan couldn't keep himself from fighting the chains even more. He wasn't designed to lie still as his cock slid in and out of a hot, slicked hole, but that was what Vin was forcing him to do. The vibrator turned up a notch, and Dylan screamed, coming hard. He thought Vin would have to stop, but the contraption around the base of Dylan's cock kept him hard as Vin rode him harder and harder.

Dylan's entire body was one exposed nerve now. The whisper of heated air against his skin made his hairs stand on end, and every time Vin's body slapped down against his, Dylan felt the sting of their combined body heat. Finally, Vin came, splattering his come across Dylan's chest and the bottom of his chin. Dylan mewled, desperate to move, but Vin settled down on Dylan's still hard cock, wiggling just a little. Dylan opened his mouth and cried out, the gag muffling most of it.

Panting through his nose, Dylan watched Vin to see what he might do, but Vin only trailed fingers over Dylan's slick skin, mixing pools of sweat and come between the leather straps that crossed Dylan's body.

"You didn't sink as far, but somehow, I do think you liked that."

Dylan would agree, but he would also say that his cock was aching now. He could feel each heartbeat echoed in the throb of his dick.

"I love the feel of you up me. One of these days, I think I'm going to set up a bench at home or maybe bring a television here," Vin commented, still exploring Dylan's exposed stomach and chest. "I'll ride you hard and then plant myself on top of you so I can feel your cock twitching in me all day. I could put in a movie," Vin said in a conversational tone. Dylan closed his eyes and moaned because that sounded too entirely good, and his cock ached and the damn thing was already thinking about round two when it hadn't entirely finished round one. He'd come, but with the cock ring or cock harness or whatever the hell Vin had put on him, he couldn't go soft.

"Would you protest?" Vin asked.

After a second, Dylan shook his head. As much as he was almost trembling, he wanted more.

"I didn't think so," Vin said. Resting both his palms on Dylan's chest, he smiled down on him. Vin pulled out the remote and fingered it for a second, giving Dylan a wink before he flicked the power off.

Dylan sighed through his nose.

"I can't break my favorite toy now, can I?" Vin asked as he slowly stood. Dylan suspected Vin wasn't talking about the vibrator. With a quick flick of his wrist, Vin took off whatever was around Dylan's cock. Relief washed through Dylan as his cock finally started softening, and now the familiar lethargy started pulling at Dylan's limbs. He was ready to curl up and sleep, preferably at Vin's feet. Unfortunately, he didn't have the chance.

Vin was unbuckling his wrists when Jason came up. "So, are you offering free rides?"

"Nope," Vin said as he pushed Dylan to sit up. Dylan could feel sweat sliding under the leather as he did, but Vin picked up the armbinder, and Dylan leaned as far forward as he could, putting his hands behind his back.

"Is he ever going to be available for play?" Jason asked. Dylan tried to glance back, but Vin was pulling the binder up, and Dylan couldn't turn far enough to see his face.

"Nope," Vin answered. "And if too many people ask, I'm likely to get unreasonable," Vin warned.

Jason took a step back and held up his hands. "Just a question. If he's yours, he's yours."

"He's mine," Vin said as he pulled the armbinder tight. Dylan grunted as Vin worked the buckles.

Jason shook his head. "Young love," he said in an indulgent voice before wandering back to his friend. A third sub had joined them, and Jason pulled the man over his lap and started playing with the end of the plug sticking out his ass.

Vin grabbed the crotchpiece for his chaps off the ground, hooked it to his chaps, and took the time to smooth everything out before turning to Dylan. "Lie back," he ordered, holding Dylan's arm steady as Dylan did. The armbinder was uncomfortable as hell under the weight of his body, but Vin quickly hooked the cockcage back to the harness and then locked the whole thing back into place before unhooking Dylan's feet from the bench.

Dylan sighed happily when Vin helped him to his feet, and he leaned into Vin to let him know how much he had enjoyed the game… that and to let Vin know he was a little unsteady. Vin started walking them over to a table, and Dylan saw Miss Dolphinia get up and pull something off a chair before coming to intercept them. Beside him, Vin stiffened, but he kept heading for the same table. Whatever history they shared, Vin wasn't going to back down. Dylan shouldn't be surprised, because Vin didn't back down to anyone.

Miss Dolphinia came over and held out a gray cushion of some sort. "His knees would probably appreciate this."

Vin hesitated, and Dylan wondered what the cushion meant because from the way Vin stared, it was more than just a cushion. Slowly, he reached out and took it. "Thank you," he said, sounding honestly grateful.

"Go get some water before both of you are dehydrated. I'll keep the little one safe enough." Miss Dolphinia sat down in one of the chairs and then gave Vin a shooing motion. "Go on, get some water. No one's going to serve you except Dylan, and he doesn't have a brain cell that hasn't leaked out his cock. So go."

Vin nodded and put the cushion on the ground next to Miss Dolphinia's chair. "Stay here, Dylan," he said, and Dylan sank gratefully to his knees. His legs were feeling a little shaky and the ground kept tilting dangerously. Vin looked at him for a second and then turned his back and headed for the kitchen.

Miss Dolphinia waited until he was gone to pet Dylan's sweaty hair, separating strands with her long, red nails. "Aren't you a pretty boy? I don't think I'll get to play with you, though. It was hard enough for Vin, sharing Rice. He always hated me for being there first. Rice loved that boy, though. I told him it was unfair to train Vin up to these old ways. I told him to walk away before he dragged that little lost boy into our world, but Rice wanted him so much, and I never could say 'no' when that man turned his big blue eyes on me." Miss Dolphinia stopped and pulled a handkerchief out of her sleeve, then dabbed at the corners of her eyes as she looked out over the club.

Dylan looked out, and there were more older men than young. A couple of younger guys knelt on the floor, one licking his master's boots. Someone had chained another man in his early twenties up against the wall, but for the most part, gray hair dominated. Dylan hadn't noticed before. Then again, he had good cause to be distracted.

"Some days I think the whole culture is dying, and here we brought a nestling into the nest and taught him to want all the things that society tells us we shouldn't want. The world belongs to Guard and his world of safe limits and play and parades. But for us, it's not really play, is it?" Miss Dolphinia pulled at his ear. Dylan looked up and shook his head. She nodded and patted his cheek fondly. "Well, you just take care of your Vin, you hear?" Dylan nodded seriously. He planned to do exactly that. He had the feeling that Miss Dolphinia had more to say, but Vin was already hurrying back toward them.

Miss Dolphinia stood up and gave him a quick smile before stepping up to block Vin. "Be good now," she said, leaning in to give Vin a kiss on the cheek. Then she sashayed away, leaving the scent of her perfume and a smudge of red on Vin's cheek.

Shaking his head, Vin put two glasses of water on the table and sat. "I don't get that old queen, I really don't," he said as he reached over to unbuckle Dylan's gag. One of the glasses had a straw and Vin held that glass down for Dylan to drink. Grateful, Dylan leaned against Vin's leg and sucked on the straw as he watched the various men playing in ways that Dylan hadn't dreamed existed outside of Internet porn.

"Are you okay?" Vin asked.

"Perfect," Dylan admitted as he put his head down on Vin's knee. Vin ran fingers through his hair, and Dylan let himself drift away to the sounds of men getting fucked and the feel of Vin's hands gently running over his skin.

LYN GALA started writing in the back of her science notebook in third grade and hasn't stopped since. Westerns starring men with shady pasts gave way to science fiction with questionable protagonists, which eventually became any story with a morally ambiguous character. Even the purest heroes have pain and loss and darkness in their hearts, and that's where she likes to find her stories. Her characters seek to better themselves and find the happy (or happier) ending.

When she isn't writing, Lyn Gala teaches history in a small town in New Mexico. Her favorite spot to write is a flat rock under a wide tree on the edge of the open desert where her dog can terrorize local wildlife. Writing in a wide range of genres, she often gravitates back to adventure and BDSM, stories about men in search of true love and a way to bring some criminal to justice… unless they happen to be the criminal.

Also from LYN GALA

URBAN SHAMAN

LYN GALA

Also from LYN GALA

http://www.dreamspinnerpress.com

Also from LYN GALA

LINES IN THE SAND

Lyn Gala

http://www.dreamspinnerpress.com

Also from LYN GALA

http://www.dreamspinnerpress.com